To I

ETHAN 👁 MOON

Remembering Obscura

by

Krystem W. Jones

[signature]

DORRANCE
PUBLISHING CO
EST. 1920
PITTSBURGH, PENNSYLVANIA 15238

This is a work of fiction. Names, characters, places, and incidents are either the product of the author's imagination or are used fictitiously, and any resemblance to actual persons, living or dead; events; or locales is entirely coincidental.

All Rights Reserved
Copyright © 2024 by Krystem W. Jones

No part of this book may be reproduced or transmitted, downloaded, distributed, reverse engineered, or stored in or introduced into any information storage and retrieval system, in any form or by any means, including photocopying and recording, whether electronic or mechanical, now known or hereinafter invented without permission in writing from the publisher.

Dorrance Publishing Co
585 Alpha Drive
Pittsburgh, PA 15238
Visit our website at www.dorrancebookstore.com

ISBN: 979-8-89211-287-1
eISBN: 979-8-89211-785-2

ETHAN MOON

Remembering Obscura

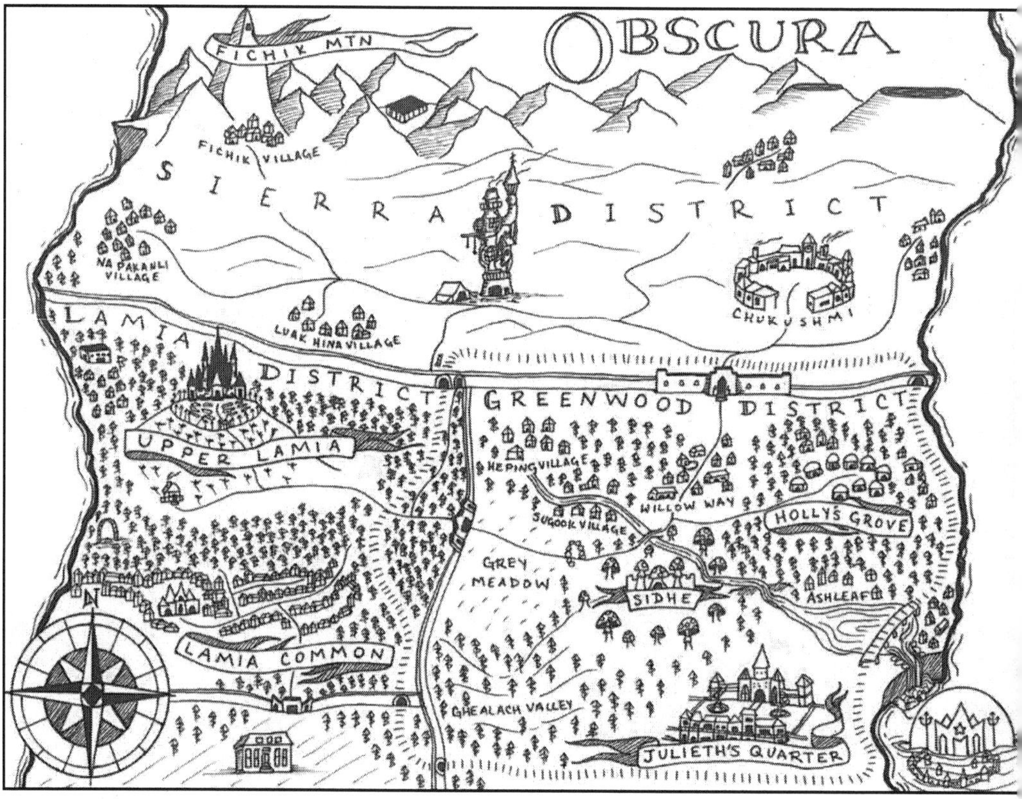
OBSCURA
FICHIK MTN
FICHIK VILLAGE
SIERRA DISTRICT
NA PAKANLI VILLAGE
LUAK HINA VILLAGE
CHUKUSHMI
LAMIA DISTRICT
UPPER LAMIA
LAMIA COMMON
GREENWOOD DISTRICT
HEPING VILLAGE
SUGOOK VILLAGE
WILLOW WAY
HOLLY'S GROVE
GREY MEADOW
SIDHE
ASHLEAF
GHEALACH VALLEY
JULIETH'S QUARTER
N

1

Inception

Something is wrong.

Every inch of my skin feels as though it's engulfed in flames. I can somehow tell that my eyes were no longer brown, but an abnormal shade of green, and are smoking—no, glowing, so unnaturally bright, I don't know what to make of it. There's the scent of cinnamon and vanilla in the air that is painfully familiar.

There's screaming, chaos, and suddenly, hot tears streaming down my face.

"Ethan! Run!"

But I can't run. In fact, I can't move at all. Someone has me by the arms, and although I open my mouth to cry out, not a sound can be heard. There's a sharp pain in the left side of my neck and then the blurry scene of shadows, oranges and reds is reduced to darkness.

I feel nauseated, and I'm painfully aware of my shirt clinging to my back and my hair stuck to my forehead. My chest heaves as I suffer a breathing fit.

"Ethan," I hear my name called again but it wasn't quite the same voice. "Ethan! Ethan, please!"

There are cold hands on my forearm, shaking hard to wake me up.

To wake me—to wake…

"Ethan, wake up!"

The sound of my grandmother's voice suddenly pierces my ears, and my eyes fly open. I sit up way too fast, causing the old woman to jump backwards with a start, and to give myself a sense of vertigo.

"Goodness, boy," she begins, "you nearly scared me half to death."

She watches me as I grab my now aching head.

"Are you alright?" she asks.

My eyes move slowly to look at her, but the churning in my stomach keeps me from answering. Instead, I involuntarily dry heave, bending over the old wooden floors of my room.

"Ethan! If you have to vomit, get to the bathroom." My grandmother takes an exasperated breath. "Breakfast is almost ready. Hurry up and collect yourself."

Without another word, the old woman turns and leaves my room.

I frown slightly as I sit there in my bed a little longer, trying to settle my stomach, rid myself of a sudden headache, and collect my thoughts. But of course, I'm only human and there's only so much I can will myself to do.

After a short time, I swing my feet onto the floor and sluggishly make my way to the bathroom. My reflection is ghastly. I'm covered in sweat, and my cheeks are stained with tears.

This is the fifth time I've had to be forced awake by my grandmother in the last month. My dreams are becoming more vivid, each more life-like than the last. It's becoming hard to focus, hard to live outside of my head, and my emotions are all over the place. But I'm not sure why. Headaches, voices, strange thoughts. I think I must be losing my mind.

I want to tell my grandmother. But I know if I do, she'll only reassure me that everything is fine.

Once I wash and dress for the day in my staple as of late: my white hoodie and gray sweatpants (because I'm too lazy to wear anything else), I go downstairs to find my grandmother in front of the stove. She wears the same beige apron she wore yesterday. Her silver hair is in its usual tightly pulled knot.

"I'm sorry I scared you," I murmur. I know that recently I've been having a hard time while sleeping but, never to the point where I've been sick because of it; which I'm sure might be something to worry about. At least now I don't feel ill anymore, except for the faintest pang of a headache that still remains.

As I take my seat at the table, I hear a clack—the window is rattling. As a matter of fact, all the windows are rattling. Both Gramma and I look out to see a busted, white convertible rolling down the street. The radio must be turned all the way up, the way its music is shaking the house. Both Gramma and I know exactly who it was.

"Last thing we need is this boy," my grandmother grumbles and turns away. The car slows to a stop in front of our house, and finally the ear-splitting music shuts off. Out of the car climbs a strawberry blonde, fauxhawk-wearing boy the same age as me. He's thin and wears a sleeveless band tee (even though it was the middle of autumn), titled "Nothing Interesting". This, I know, is his own band that he had started himself. I once asked him what his motivation was for the name, and he said, "There is nothing interesting that happens in this town, so now I've nominated myself to bring excitement to the kids of Whitechapel."

Soon he's at our doorstep, and instead of knocking, he leans over toward the window and waves to my grandmother and me.

"Wanna let me in?" he asks, his voice muffled through the glass. I roll my eyes at him, but I can't help the smile creeping onto my face. Carson's my best friend.

I go to the door and let him in. He doesn't great me the way he normally would—immediately rambling on about his latest band activity or the most recent girl he thinks is hot. Instead, he crosses his arms and glares at me.

"What?" I grumble as I shut the door and walk back into the kitchen.

"Don't 'what' me, *Ethan Jae Moon!*" he mocks a little too loudly.

I roll my eyes at him. Jae is short for Jaehyun, which is my second name. Though everyone uses the shortened bit as if it were a middle name—which I don't have; but, just about everyone does this when they're upset with me, or just pretending to be, like Carson.

"Hi Gramma!" Carson says with a huge pearly grin when he sees her. He then takes a seat at the kitchen table.

My grandmother rolls her eyes as well and turns her head away. I never understood why she doesn't like him, although I've never asked.

"I'm not your grandmother, Carson," she murmurs and sets my plate on the table.

I sit down and begin to eat.

"Now please explain to me why you haven't returned any of my texts, any of my calls, any of my tweets—"

"I don't have Twitter," I reply without looking at Carson.

He pauses for a moment, as if confused by my answer.

"Oh," he murmurs, "well still, you've been avoiding me. Are you mad at me? Was it something I said? Did you find out about the volunteer work I signed me and you up for?"

I look quickly up at him.

"You did what?" I ask.

Carson only smiles at me, rounding his bright blue eyes in hopes of me taking pity on him.

"I did it because my band wants to perform up at the café, but Bobby won't let us play unless we work without pay."

"Why can't you and your band buddies work then? Why am I involved?"

He smiles at me again and then steals a piece of bacon from my plate.

"Because I love you," he tells me.

I glare at him.

"I really think you need to spend some time around other people. Setting aside all bull, Ethan, I honestly think that you've been unhealthily distancing yourself. So, as your friend I'm asking you to do this with me... Actually, I'm telling you to."

With a small sigh I look back down at my plate. Carson is that kind of person who would set aside his usual childish antics to take care of someone he was close to. That I can respect. I knew that whether or not his decisions made sense, everything he does is out of love. So instead of being upset with him, I just agree.

"What time?" I ask, and push around my eggs. His grin returns once again, and he reaches out to take my plate from me.

"After school today," he replies and then takes the fork from my hand. He knows I won't continue eating, so he will dispose of it for me.

I turn my head to see if Gramma was still there, but she has abandoned the kitchen and has gone to the living room to catch up on some reading.

"Alright, let's get out of here," I tell him after checking the time. I wasn't trying to be late for school that morning. Again. I stand up and go into the living room to tell my grandmother that I was leaving for the day, then I grab my worn-out backpack and wait for Carson to finish inhaling my breakfast. After he clears my plate, he puts it in the sink and then goes before me out of the door.

I forgot how rundown his car is. The white Mustang convertible is rusted near the edges; its paint is chipped and scratched up, probably from trying to squeeze into tight parking spaces. The right back light is smashed somehow, and the right side-view mirror looks one tap away from falling off. Cautiously, I step inside the disaster on wheels.

"So, are you planning on getting a new car?" I ask nonchalantly as I throw my backpack in the backseat.

"Why, what's wrong with this one?" he asks me, pure curiosity in his voice. I only look at him and then turn my gaze forward. I shake my head, deciding it best to leave it.

"Nothing," I murmur. Carson shrugs and pulls out his car keys which had a My Chemical Romance keychain attached to it. He starts his car, knowing that I was sensitive when it came to his driving (which could be quite reckless) he remains the legal speed limit through the neighborhood and all the way to Whitechapel High without him daring to blast his radio as loud as he does when he's alone or with other people. The last time I rode with him and he decided to "grace the city with his music", I had ringing in my ears for nearly a week.

It wasn't long before we pull up to the white bricked building. It's quite an old school, founded in the 1910s. Thick green vine-like weeds creep up the walls of the building at every corner. Coming from each window are stains of rust, discoloring the white paint. Frowning at my next destination, I could hear the bell from inside ringing; hopefully only the second bell.

"Well, what are we waiting for, we're gonna miss first hour," Carson beams as he unbuckles his seat belt and opens his door to step out. I internally roll my eyes as I too unbuckle my belt.

"The only reason why you're so worried about making it to first hour is because of Mrs. Taylor. You could care less about any other class." I step out of the car after grabbing my backpack and shut the door behind me.

"She's a beautiful woman," Carson replies whimsically as he slings his bag over his shoulder. I can't help but to scoff. He is always like this. It never really bothers me because it is usually lighthearted, but it does get annoying.

"She's too old for you, kid. And married," I tell him matter-of-factly.

"A boy can only dream."

We walk into the building, making it just in time before the late bell. Our teacher, Mrs. Taylor, stands at the front of the class. Her blonde hair is pulled into a donut bun at the top of her head, tied with a bright red ribbon. Her ocean-colored eyes glared lightly as for yet another morning, Carson stops in front of her as I pass him and take my seat in the second row from the back.

"Teachers like apples," he says and pulls from his bag a shiny red apple and holds it up to her. "I'm sure that you'll find that I picked the most exquisite apple just for you." With an inward groan, the woman accepts the apple and places it down on the corner of her desk.

"He actually didn't," I chime from my desk.

"Please take your seat, Mr. Foxx," she says to him. He grins, becoming excited that today she used 'Mister' with his name, then he turns to take his assigned seat in front of me. As class begins, I find it quite hard to focus. I had gained a headache the moment she began explaining the next few week's assignments. She has a stack of books on her desk which she begins to pass out to each of us. *Vlad the Impaler*, it is titled. I study the narrow-faced man on the cover of the book with a slight twinge of repugnance. I knew he was the so called 'real life Dracula', but the last thing I felt like discussing was vampires. Although fiction, something about the thought of them gave me an unsettling feeling. I wondered if I could get away with not reading the book if I told Mrs. Taylor I have Sanguivoriphobia.

After the books were handed out, Mrs. Taylor returns to the front of the class and clasps her hands together.

"Now, by just looking at the cover of the book, can anyone predict what will happen during the story?" she questions the class. Most are quiet except for one girl who sat closest to the window. Patty Wright who's probably the smartest person in the classroom has her hand stretched high. She looks as though she can barely keep her mouth closed before Taylor calls on her. "Yes Patty, what do you think?"

"Well, Vlad was a Romanian king," she begins to explain, "I'm guessing that this is just a biography about his life and how he became known as Vlad the Impaler or Vlad Dracula."

Patty knows everything. Many people looks at her as a know-at-all, and I am guilty of that crowd. However, I am also a bit envious as to how smart she was. I once even tried to study with her, but it was like she spoke at a hundred miles per second so that ended very quickly.

"Yes, that's correct." Taylor nods and leans back against her desk. "Have you read this before, Patty?"

"As a matter-of-fact, I did," she replies proudly.

"Has anyone else read this book before?"

Looking around the classroom to see that everybody else was looking down and fiddling their thumbs I take that as a no, and so does our teacher. It isn't much of a surprise; this is usually how class goes.

Mrs. Taylor explains some of the themes in the book and lectures about the author before she begins to read the first chapter during the last fifteen minutes of class. This, of course, becomes nap time for most of the sleep deprived kids in the room, including myself; and here I am nodding off while hearing something about steaking people's heads to giant wooden poles before my face reaches my folded arms on my desk.

I sleep for a good ten minutes, probably a bit too comfortably. My mind doesn't race, and I don't dream; I just sleep, and it feels good. But just a few minutes before the bell was about to ring, all these thoughts began to flood my mind. I saw flashing lights like in the dream I had just this morning, whispering and humming. That same scent of cinnamon and vanilla washes over me and there is a flash of a young girl crying. I can't make out her face but her large coily hair tied messily behind her is unmistakable.

All of a sudden, a shrilly voice pierces my right ear as if someone was standing just right there.

Ethan, don't leave me!

I flinch and spring out of my desk and onto my feet, now wide awake. The room falls silent and all eyes are on me. I haven't realized how much I was hyperventilating yet.

"You…" I start and spin around to look behind me where a girl sat. She looks more frightened than I do.

"Did you say something?" I question her, immediately demanding an answer, but she only shakes her head at me and shrinks down in her seat.

"Ethan," Mrs. Taylor snaps as she began walking slowly toward me, "I hope you feel accomplished for interrupting my class, please take your seat or I will have to—"

She is cut off by the ringing of the bell which causes me to jump. Carson stands up and slings his bag over his shoulder before he takes mine in his hand. By the look on his face, I can tell he is concerned by my sudden outburst.

"You might not want to sleep through any more classes today, man," he murmurs to me and hands me my backpack. I frown lightly and drop my arm that now carries my heavy bag. My mind is still reeling from how real the voice sounded only moments ago, but only now could I write it off as just a dream. Right?

I sigh to myself and began toward my next class, which I am nowhere near mentally ready for. Could math be any more spiritually draining than it already was? My day continues on this way and I have barely said any words and focused on nothing other than what I heard that morning. I still couldn't decipher whether or not it had been a dream or if it was something real that I heard. But where could it have come from? I am bothered by this even after school had ended, and before I know it, I am back in Carson's car again.

"Let's drop by my house first. I gotta get this janky old clock this dude I know from woodshop fixed up for my mom to her. I asked her why she didn't just throw it out, it's wicked hideous. But she went on about how it was 'a family heirloom' and it 'couldn't be replaced', blah blah—hey, did you hear me?" He looks at me through his black sunglasses as he has already begun to drive us toward his home.

I squint through the sunlight and frown lightly. I barely understood a word he said.

"You what?" My brows knit together, slightly annoyed that I have to speak up at all. "My head hurts, alright? I just wanna get this over with and go home," I mumble to my friend. But he only shakes his head.

"I'm not your friend just to hang around some mopey loser," he responds and shoves my shoulder. "I want the old Ethan back. Remember him? That guy who didn't go around whining and sulking everywhere he went. Did we just wake up someday and he disappeared or what?" Through his sunglasses I can see him squinting at me. He is annoyed, I know it, but he wouldn't say so. It did seem that way that I had just woken up one day and I wasn't myself. So, I can't blame him for being upset with me, especially because I had no reason at all for the way I've been acting in the last month or so.

Sighing softly, I shut my eyes and shrug a shoulder. I will at least try to be somewhat interested in what Carson wants to do.

Carson grins suddenly and steps on the gas petal. The car jerks before it speeds down the street, fast enough for my back to be stuck against the seat behind me. Having shouted several swears and gripping on to the ceiling's handle for my life, we arrive at his house in no time at all. The small bungalow house is no bigger than mine. Most of all the houses in Whitechapel were small and kind of ugly. Or at least outdated; we are a poor old town.

In the window of the faded yellow paneled home, Carson's mother can be seen inside. Her age was obvious in the wrinkles around her eyes and forehead. Despite the age difference, she looks exactly like Carson. The same bright blue eyes and strawberry blonde hair, although she is a bit more faded and a lot more stressed. Carson's father passed away when he had just turned seven years old. He was diploid in the Navy Seals, and while on the job was involved in a missile accident. Ever since then Mrs. Foxx was left to provide by herself. Pay the bills, pay for groceries, and saving for Carson's tuition. She had aged tremendously from then till now.

"What are you doing?"

Carson was turned completely sideways in his seat and looking at me. I hadn't realized that he had already pulled up into the driveway and parked. Too deep in thought about when my friend needed me most…but I wasn't around much then either. I had been sick with something…

"Nothing…" I blurt and shake my head. I get out of the car and step up to the door with Carson following behind me and I knock. After being given an awkward look, Carson simply pushes me aside and opens the door, stepping inside and tossing his bag to the floor.

"You act like a stranger sometimes, dude," he remarks before going to the kitchen where his mother sat. I frown lightly. I had been coming to their house for years and stopped knocking a long time ago. I even had an emergency key that I didn't think about till now.

"Mom, I'm home! And I've got that ugly clock of yours!" Carson almost shouts. He hasn't realized that the woman is sitting at their round wooden kitchen table with a pile of bills in front of her. She has the landline up to her ear and is currently trying to pay their electric bills. She says nothing to the boy but instead scowls angrily at him and motions for him to be quiet before politely answering a question into the phone.

Once noticing what the woman was doing, he winces in apology and gestured for where he should place the clock under his arm. The thing was ceramic, vomit green with pink and yellow flowers stuck all over it. It really is quite hideous, and I was sure deep-down Mrs. Foxx thought so too. It was the emotional attachment to it I suppose mattered most.

She points toward the living room where Carson promptly turns on his heels and makes his way to place it somewhere in that area. Moments later he returns, phone in hand, vigorously thumbing the screen until he was earshot of his mother again. He taps her on the shoulder and smiles almost sweetly at her. If I didn't know Carson to overall be honest and respectful to the woman, I'd think he was about to tell her some made up lie.

"We have to go; I'll be back home later," he whispers. The woman looks up, and just a second later she hangs up the phone.

"Wait just a second," she says and stands up. She looks over at me and places her hands on her hips. "Ethan Jae Moon," she calls with a light frown. I raise my eyebrows curiously and looked down at the woman.

"Yes ma'am?"

"I haven't heard from you in God knows when," she exclaims. "I don't get a 'hi' or anything. You just waltz in here and then waltz your way back out? I know you're better than that." She looks sternly at me and I can't help but to feel embarrassed. It was quite rude of me to do so, having just walked in without a word or even a gesture to the woman.

"I'm sorry, Mrs. Foxx," I murmur, "I guess I've just lost my head." I step up to her and gave her a meaningful hug. Next to Gramma she, too, is like a mother to me, and I was grateful for that.

"Alright, alright." Carson tugs at my collar and pulls me away from his mother. "We have to go; I think if we're late this time Bobby won't let us work or anything," he tells me.

I furrow my brow at him curiously. "This time?" I question.

"Yes, this time. I've done this before, remember?"

I roll my eyes and turned around to face the door. That was right; he had done a series of begging just to play somewhere. Anywhere. But not many people let his band hang around, especially since their music was way too loud and…annoying.

"I'll come around more often Mrs. Foxx; I'll see you later." I wave goodbye to the tall slender woman and open the door to leave with Carson right behind me. Then soon I returned to his lesser car.

2

She

The smell of fresh roasted coffee beans immediately fill my nose the moment I step through the café doors. There isn't many people in today, it seems, but there is still a live set up and a girl named Yuri Hwang who has a smooth house voice. She performs often at the café and often at the Whitechapel Theater. Unlike "Nothing Interesting", she is praised for her comforting voice and was constantly asked to perform anywhere that needed live music.

"Moon!" a voice calls from the other end of the room. Mine and Carson's heads turn toward the bar where Bobby, the owner, is drying a few freshly washed glasses. He waves the both of us over and we soon stand before the bearded man. His thick marble brimmed glasses always seemed to be foggy and he, as did the rest of the building, smelled strongly of fresh coffee.

"You proved me wrong, Foxx, you must be serious about this," Bobby says as he puts away the final glass in his hand and then drapes the drying towel over his shoulder.

"Of course, I am. And maybe at some point you'll pay me, right?" Carson nods his head vigorously, in hopes of hearing a positive answer, but Bobby only laughs in response and mutters a sarcastic, "You wish."

"Anyway, you two can get started. I want one of you in the back doing the dishes. And the other can be out here manning the bar." He pauses for a moment before adjusting his glasses and looking up at me. "Actually, I'd prefer if Moon stayed out to run the bar. I don't need any…issues." He glares at Carson as he is reminded of the many explosive mistakes he has made in the past. He is very clumsy at times, and once I specifically remember him causing the espresso machine to go out of control and spray espresso everywhere.

Carson pouts lightly at the man before turning to go through the "Employees Only" door.

"Fine," he grumbles, "just call me out if you see any cute ladies go by who might be interested in ol' Carson, alright? And why don't you chat one up yourself?" He turns his head to flash a playful grin before disappearing into the back to get the dishes done.

I roll my eyes and scoff to myself quietly. I don't even bother replying, there was no use. Bobby shakes his head at me and tosses me a white, slightly warn apron; then he ruffles his curly dark hair. "You've done this once. Recipes are in the bottom cabinet if you need them," he tells me before leaving me in charge to man the station. I have only worked here once before during a time where I was trying to earn enough money to buy a really nice gift for Gramma during Mother's Day. The job did pay off, but working in general at the café was not fun at all.

Having served multiple people, overall, the café has been running slow all day. No one was around. Although, the regulars were indeed present, sitting in their usual places. One bald man who always sat in the corner of the building to read the daily news and sip on a cappuccino. There is one other girl who always seemed to be wearing large sunhats and what looks like short cowboy boots. She always sat near the stage where she has out her Mac and works whilst listening to whomever is performing that day, which was usually Yuri and her accompanists Michael Smith.

There were a few other familiar faces, but one person in particular caught my attention. The jingling of the bell that is strung up at the top of the door jingles and a very unfamiliar face appears. The strangely familiar scent of cinnamon and vanilla filled the air and a young girl around my age wanders in curiously as if she has never been in a coffee shop before. She's wearing a sheer white shawl over her head, and underneath were stunning raven black coils billowing out past her shoulders. She wore something that looked like a sort of laid-back Edwardian/Victorian type gown that was shades of faded purples and grays draping delicately over her small frame. Although I don't catch a clear glimpse of her face, something seems so familiar about her. From the coils resting gently around her shoulders, to the glowing shade of brown of her skin. She certainly looks nothing like any other Whitechapel girl.

I couldn't take my eyes off her. I watch as she glides from the door towards an empty seat near the back of the room, just out of my view to get even the slightest look at her face. But even as far away as she was, that scent was still unmistakable and the more I could smell it—even through the distinct scent of ground coffee beans, the more I feet as though I were intoxicated; dizzy even.

The small dessert menu she held covers her face now and I find myself rising on my toes to see just a little more. I was all too intrigued, but I definitely didn't have it in me to just go over there and talk to her. Especially if I end up just creeping her out.

I could just see her peeking up in my direction. And her eyes…maybe I just wasn't seeing them right. They pierced into mine with some light color I can't quite make out. They looked almost gray or even lavender, but I wasn't sure. What I was sure of was that headache I've had since this morning gradually became more persistent, however. And something in my stomach twists and knots up. Actually, I felt as though I'd be sick.

"Ethan?"

My eyes dart in front of me and I nearly fell forward onto the counter I was leaning on.

"Hey, are you okay? You look a little pale, like you've seen a ghost…"

In front of me there stood one of my classmates Hailey, and beside her the girl I embarrassed myself in front of this morning, Julia.

"Are you sick or something? You've been acting weird all day, actually," Julia says this time, "particularly when you lost your mind this morning."

"Hey don't mention that, I'm sure he's already beating himself up about it. It *was* pretty embarrassing."

"Yeah, sorry about that…" I mutter. I can feel the heat rising in my cheeks. Honestly, I hadn't really thought about the fact that I sort of lashed out at Julia this morning. I can only think about the voice that I heard. Even now it still bothers me. But thinking about embarrassing myself in the middle of class was a bigger punch in the face.

"But seriously, Ethan, how are you feeling? You really haven't been yourself lately." Hailey tilts her head and measures me with her large black eyes. She was twisting a long rope of hair around her finger, waiting to see if I'd really tell her the truth.

Hailey was always sweet, never ever had she been problematic. For as long as I've known her, she was always popular with everyone; popular with the popular kids, and generously kind with everyone outside of that particular circle. Actually, if I were being completely honest, I had the hardest crush on her more than once. One time when we were in elementary school together after she shared her Go-Gurt stick with me after another kid had thrown half my lunch on the floor. And then freshman year of high school after she defended the lunch Gramma had packed for me from this kid who had never seen kimbap before. Once Hailey heard every blinkered thing he had to say, she shut him up immediately by telling him that he ought to step outside of his bubble and learn there's more to life than "gross, crusty sandwiches and grocery store brownies that give you high cholesterol". Strangely both encounters had to do with food, but regardless, I liked her a lot for her generosity and courageousness. That is until she started dating that football player, Eric Fuller. So, I made those feelings go away...

"You're right, Hailey, I haven't. I've just been having these crazy migraines recently. It's also been affecting my sleep so, Julia...I feel so bad for freaking you out earlier."

Julia shakes her head to say it's nothing, and Hailey wears an apologetic expression.

"That really sucks, Ethan. If there's anything I can do to help—Oh, my mom has pretty bad migraines too from time to time, I could probably let you borrow this stuff she takes for it. Maybe it can—"

She's interrupted by a wet-armed, sweaty Carson who kicks his way through the kitchen door and leans against the counter at my side.

"LADIES!" His lips curve up into a grin reminiscent of the Grinch, and he does Hailey a once over and Julia a wink. "Hailey, your braids are extra cute today. You always got somethin' new. Don't she, Ethan?" He nudges my side and I'm reminded of the knotting in the stomach I had just before the girls had distracted me from it.

"They're not braids, stupid, they're passion twists." Hailey rolls her eyes, tossing the rope she had in her hands behind her shoulder.

"Ah right, twists. How could I be so naïve? Do forgive me." He pouts his lips, leaning in towards her face where she takes a significant step back.

"You're such a creep, Carson, back off!"

"Oh, stop it, it's not like that. I'm just hopeful that you'll finally spill your true feelings for Ethan already!"

"Stop talking!" I demand through grit teeth. The second-hand embarrassment adds to the rest of the stress shooting through my temples. I look at Hailey apologetically, but she waves me off as she can understand that I am definitely not the same as my half-wit friend.

"Fine. That was my wingman attempt that clearly failed. Anyway, are you guys gonna order or what?"

Julia eyes Carson irritably and then shares a look with Hailey.

"I mean, as long as you're not making it, sure. A white mocha frap for me and a chai tea latte for Hails."

"Not too much sugar, m'kay?" Hailey smiles my way while Carson is looking for a new way to get the girls' attention.

"By the way, Ethan, if you're not busy Saturday night, Eric is throwing a party at the forest for Halloween. I think you should come if you aren't feeling too bad. Maybe you just need a little time out with others."

Carson gawks and starts nudging me excitedly. Parties weren't quite my thing, but they certainly were his. Though when it came to the school jocks, Carson wasn't exactly ever invited to those because of…well I think anyone could guess.

Hailey and Julia watch Carson eye me for an equally excited expression, and they both shake their head.

"Carson, don't come."

"I. will. be there," he replied, pointing his finger vigorously.

"FOXX!" Bobby's voice booms from behind us, causing all of us to jump and a sharp pain to shoot across my skull. The man's huge beefy hand claps down on Carson's shoulder, making him wince. "Shouldn't you be at those dishes instead of bothering these guests?"

"W-well I just thought I'd come out for a little fresh air, boss."

"A little 'fresh air' won't get those dishes done! When all of them are gone *then* you can get your fresh air. That is unless you don't want a chance up on that stage."

In a second Carson had disappeared behind the kitchen door again after being reminded of his goal to perform with his band here. Bobby gives me a lighter handed pat on the back but didn't say anything more before he disappears to his office.

After that the girls smile at me and go to find their seats until I finish their drinks.

"I hope you can be there," Hailey says before moving out of ear shot.

My shoulders tense after I finish a few more orders. I'm in my head again. And right; after the spicy smell of chai cleared from my nose and I became numb to the coffee beans again, I kept picking up cinnamon and vanilla.

My head whips around to where that peculiar looking girl was sitting before but I don't see her anymore. But the scent was suddenly so strong, it was like she was right next to me. But I didn't see any sign of her. I was sure she had gone when the girls came up to talk.

But…why did something about her seem so familiar?

Yes, our town was small, and everybody knew everybody. But I was sure I have never seen that person before.

I am putting together what I remember about her in my head again. Her hair, her dress, her scarf. And…the strange hue of her eyes.

I wince.

Thinking about her was making my head hurt worse. At this point my brain was throbbing and my eyes were watering because of it. I had to lean against the wall behind me to steady myself. I can't understand why it won't stop, so that I could get just a moment's peace. The doctor's always said it was due to head trauma I suffered as a kid.

I close my eyes, hoping that if I rest them for just a second, the pain will subside. But when I do there is a flash of light and suddenly, I can see my grandmother's face, clear as day. But her eyes were strange, they weren't brown, they were blue. She is holding me by the face and distantly I could hear my younger self crying.

You must forget, my Hyunnie. Don't fight it. Let yourself forget and the pain will wash all away.

She's shushing me, and somewhere in my chest I feel something heavy. Like some deep suppressed sadness. But I really don't know why.

Don't let them lie to you. You belong here!

There was a different voice that I couldn't place. It spooks me, though; sending chills all across my body. It sounded distinctly like the one I heard that morning at school. But hearing it that time made my stomach churn, and a more severe pain ripped through my head, making my knees buckle and waver.

My eyes flood with tears now, but I wasn't sure if it was from the pain or the unexplainable emotion that washed over me. I try to open them to at least figure out where I was in the room and get my bearings again. But with another flash of light, and the throbbing that wrap at my head like a whip, I knew that this episode wouldn't end well this time.

I am blinded by the involuntary watering of my eyes, and I am overcome by dizziness.

"*I'm so sorry, Ethan. Just endure it a little longer…*"

That voice. It didn't come from my head, but it was directly into my ear. My head whips around to see who it could have been, but the tears and the pain is too much. That damn scent of cinnamon and vanilla, that scent I've been smelling all day was so strong just then, as if someone had been holding the two things directly under my nose. It am so overwhelming that I can't stand it any longer. I stumble backwards into the wall behind me, holding my head in agony. My senses were overloaded and in the next second, I find myself sitting on the floor, hot tears streaming down my face. I need to get out of here. I had to, but I can't move. I can't see. And when I tried to open my mouth to call out to somebody, anybody, I find I havn't the strength.

I am nearly hit by the outward swinging door which Carson was exiting. He has a slightly confused expression on his face as he doesn't see me right away on the floor and wonders where I had gone. Finally, he looks downcast to see me and he immediately bent down in front of me.

"Dude, are you alright?" he questions and grips my arm.

"No," I gurgle and pull away from him, feeling immensely uncomfortable with him touching me at that moment.

The moment I pull away, he pulls his arms back and shuffles backward a little. This has happened only once before when we were just ten years old. And he knew immediately the moment I pulled away.

"It's not that thing again, is it? You know when you had your accident?" He suddenly gasps and covers his mouth with his hand. "Is that why you've been so distant lately? You're sick?"

I don't know how to answer that question. I don't know if I am exactly sick, but I have been having a lot of familiar symptoms I had when I was younger lately. Symptoms I've been told had been from a brain injury. It used to happen so much when I was young that Carson had been told by my grandmother that the moment something like this occurs that he needed to step away and call her immediately. And that was what he does.

"Just stay there, man, I don't like this."

Carson calls my grandmother while I fall over onto my side and now lay in the fetal position. I can't open my eyes at all. The throbbing in my head has radiated down my jaw and through my neck to my spine. I can't move. It all is happening so suddenly.

I can hear my grandmother on the other end of the phone. The volume was up way too loud on his device making it almost clear to understand her from afar.

"Whatever you do, Carson, don't you let him lose consciousness," she orders to him. "Keep him awake, I'm on my way."

I winced from the sound of the guitar again. The strum of his instrument worsened the pain in my head every time. I was sure my skull was splitting open.

"Ethan?" Carson calls and bends down beside me. He taps my shoulder and waits for me to respond, but I don't.

"Dude, don't go to sleep. I don't know if it'll kill you but that grandmother of yours will surely kill me if you do."

I can't move. One shifting motion and I could swear I was dying. Carson remains quiet for a moment, as for once he was using his head to think the situation through. I feel him sit down beside me. He kept his hand on my arm and would lightly pinch me every few seconds to make sure I was still awake. This is a tactic he often uses to make sure I had his attention. And it surely worked. Even though I was barely aware of my surroundings anymore, I would jump every time he gave my arm a pinch.

It seemed like years before Gramma finally arrives. And by the time she had, Bobby is now at my side as well, continuously questioning if he needs to call an ambulance, but Carson would refuse every time like he was asked to.

Gramma is rushing through the door, the bell rang hard enough to make me squirm and groan out in pain. The woman is still in her house slippers and the apron she was wearing this morning. She carried a bag around her wrist as she came in. No one else in the store had really noticed that anything was going on at all. But by this time most people were heading home anyway and the café itself was emptying.

Gramma crosses the room, her eyes scanning and analyzing every inch of the place. In a second, she reaches the counter, but she's sucking in a quiet gasp, not by the state of myself, but her eyes catch something at the far corner of the room. Even Carson notices her shocked expression and turns his head to see what she was looking at, but he doesn't see a thing, causing a puzzled look to cross his face.

"Gramma, is Ethan gonna be alright? What's wrong with him?" he asks nervously.

She ignores him as she corners the back of the bar. Her expression darkens now as she looks to me, squats down and shakes her head.

"Ethan, are you awake?" she questioned as she began digging through her bag. I grunt as a sort of reply to her, but I was only just barely comprehensible.

"This isn't like what happened before, is it Gramma?" Carson asks and looks up at the woman who seemed immediately bothered that he continues to call her his grandmother. But she holds it in her to continue ignoring this.

"It might be," she responds quietly, "but you need to keep quiet and we need to get him out of here right now, it's too loud in here," she tells him.

Bobby looks up at the woman, having no idea what exactly was going on, but he wants to at least help get me out of the room. Both he and Carson lifts me to my feet and helps me out the back door to sit on the patio at the back of the building. Other than the whooshing of the cars that went by every so often, it is overall quiet here which allows my migraine to calm down enough for me to be able to open my eyes again.

Gramma pulled a tiny bottle from her bag and opened the bottle. She poured out two tiny pink colored tablets into her hand, then she looked up at me.

"Take this, dear," she whispers softly to me and rests her other hand at the back of my head. "I'm going to get you to Dr. Valhera. He'll know just what to do."

This particular migraine took a lot out of me. I am exhausted and barely had the strength to lift my arm and accept the medicine which I thought were just some pain killers.

Bobby had gone off to bring me back a glass of water, and no longer had he gone he is back by my side again. I am able to take the tablets at once, and the moment I had I feel dizzy and unsteady even as I am sitting.

"Help him to the car, won't you? I can take care of the rest," I hear Gramma say as everything became a blur again. Slowly and then all at once I was out of it. Everyone's voices had become muddled as if I were under water. Then my vision began to go and I knew I was out just like that.

I had been helped to the car with little to no dialogue between the three. Carson questioned what I had been given but he received no answer. He had also questioned if he should come along to help, but he had been refused. The moment he and Bobby finished getting me into the car, they were shooed away to go back to their work, wondering what happened to me so suddenly.

"This won't do at all…" my grandmother said aloud to seemingly no one. "Does this have to happen so soon?"

• • •

By the time I finally came to, I am lying in a hospital bed with my doctor and my grandmother standing over me. They were having a conversation that of which I couldn't comprehend. My vision is still blurry but is slowly clearing up.

"Ah, here's our boy," Dr. Valhera says with his stunningly white smile. He is a handsome man about in his forties who looked as though he should have been a model rather than a doctor. I had been going to this doctor all my life and he was always around when I had my medical issues. Grandma swears up and down that he should be the only doctor I should ever see. Even for just a checkup. Which is why she tells everyone not to call an ambulance should something happen to me. Which when I think about it seems…a little much…

I blink, trying hard to focus on the room I was in and to gather my bearings. It didn't take me long to realize that I was in the hospital. My eyes look upon the brunette in front of me. His hair was gray by the roots, but his style was cool and tasteful. He adjusts the black-rimmed glasses on his face as he studies me more than I had been studying him.

"Does your head still hurt?" he asks me.

I only nod in response. It wasn't nearly as bad as it had been when I left the café, but I still had a headache.

"Right, that's normal." He looks up to my grandmother who looks frustrated to say the least.

"Excuse me, but…" I begin as I try to sit up, "what is this?" I ask him. "This has happened before, I remember, but you never told me what it actually was. Is it really a brain injury or what? Can't something be done about it? I think I'm old enough to handle it." I'm slightly annoyed, having lived with these headaches for such a long time without any sort of solution to get rid of them. It almost felt like no one really cared.

Scott purses his lips at me and then looks down at the clipboard in his hands. He looks quite hesitant, and so does my grandmother which makes me suspicious.

"Hello?" I call impatiently. I have a sudden feeling of involuntary anger that washes over me. I don't know what it was and why I had become so hotheaded all of a sudden which was almost immediately recognized by my grandmother.

"Listen Ethan," Scott starts and crosses his arms across his chest, "there's not much I can say, unfortunately." His eyes flick over to my grandmother before he looks back down at his clipboard. "I know what you're experiencing is concerning but these are all normal symptoms for a brain injury. The brain can be very mysterious. If injured, you can be okay some days and other days you're just not. Hallucinations, wild dreams, migraines, mood swings and so on, they all can come from a brain injury. The only thing I can do is give you medication to take to deal with these symptoms."

I couldn't believe it. Did this mean I was just stuck with these problems for forever because of a car crash I was involved in as a child? I looked to Gramma to see what she thought and if she was just okay with this. Surely, she couldn't be. But to my surprise...she is.

"Hyunnie, today is just a bad day," she says. "It's difficult but a brain injury is irreversible. I'm sure you'll be fine again after some medication and some rest, right doctor?" She turned to Scott and raises an eyebrow at him almost expectantly.

Scott nods and pulls off his glasses. "Yes, you may be overexerting yourself lately so you're having more problems than normal."

I press my lips tightly together and frown at the both of them. They don't understand what it's like going through each day like this. To feel like your head could burst into a million pieces from one little shake, or to feel so unfocused you could do nothing but sit there and hope someone guides you through whatever is going on.

I pull the blankets off of me and stand out of bed. I wavered only a little but was able to swipe up my shoes and storm out of the room on my own without another word. It would just be a waste of breath.

After slamming the door shut behind me, I turn to find an elevator to leave the hospital, but I barely take a step once I left that room. I only stop, and gaze down the all-white hallway, when I hear my name mentioned by my doctor. Slowly, I press my back against the wall and slide down by the doorway to sit on the floor. There I wait and listen in on what the two have to say.

"When are you going tell him, Cath? I hate to see him so lost and out of place like that. Don't you think this has gone on long enough?" His voice is muffled through the shut door, but I can decipher each word.

"He's not ready," Gramma said in a solemn tone.

"What do you mean he's not ready? The boy is nearly an adult, and I'm quite sure that he's so out of it because that damn potion is wearing off." He sounds frustrated. Scott was known for being soft-spoken and level-headed, so the fact that he sounded even a little upset is something new.

"Someone let her out, Scott, she's here. I saw her…"

There was a pause of silence in the room and then the sound of his clipboard falling.

"Who let her out?" he whispers harshly. "You don't think it was Aero, do you? He should know that it's still too dangerous…they could use her to get to him."

"I don't think it was him. I have a feeling she's done it on her own."

"Well, either way, it's not safe for her to be out yet. Annika is—"

"I know," Gramma interrupts, "but someone needs to tell that girl that if she wants to see Ethan again, she should stay at home."

There's another pause before Scott's voice could be heard again.

"It's going to be hard, Catherine, but you need to tell him soon. Imagine how he must be feeling. When that injection wears off completely, he'll need a bit of a kick start, but what he possesses will be all the more dangerous should he stay here unlearned. I fear you've lost sight of why we're here in the first place, Cath. He can't be away from home forever. Both of you. Remember the dangers of what could happen when it all starts coming back to him. There's only a matter of time and… he's outside the door."

I jump instantly. Did he know I was listening in? The door opens and Gramma steps out as I scramble to my feet. She looks more upset than she had when she arrived to get me to the hospital.

Neither of them say a word to me and only Scott looks at me with an awkward smile. I look at him, but then away when I saw Gramma leaving. As she got further away, I was preparing to follow when Scott stops me.

"Ethan," he whispers to get my attention, "I bet you're curious about a lot of things recently, huh? There's an old friend of your grandmother's coming into town tomorrow. I think you should go to her. She'd be happy to see you." He smiles and before I can question him, he's pushing me away to catch up with Gramma. "She'll be at the library. Don't mention it to

Catherine...or she'll have both our heads. Go on, now." He's shooing me away, but even with how confused I am I dare not say a word and hurry to catch up with my grandmother.

Not a word through the halls, not a word in the elevator, no words through the lobby, and nothing at all in the car. I continuously glance at my grandmother, hoping she will look at me or say something. I am curious, and probably just as upset as she is at the same time.

Finally, I had enough of the silence, and I decide to speak up.

"Who is she?" I dare to ask and turn my head to watch the woman's expression. But it is blank as she drives us home.

"She's not from here? Do I know her?" The more I ask questions the more she remains quiet. Although I wasn't exactly sure who the "she" was in question, I had a hunch that it had been that girl I saw earlier at Bobby's that they were talking about at the hospital, never mind whoever Doc V. was talking about as we were leaving.

"Won't you say anything? Tell me what going on!" I snap, nearly stomping my feet in frustration.

Gramma suddenly slams on the breaks, causing me to lurch forward. If it weren't for the hitching in my seatbelt pulling me back against my seat I would have gone flying through the windshield.

Gramma pulls to the side of the road that had become dim in the last bit of light from the setting sun. She shoves the gearstick forward into park and then sits still. For all of a minute, she is silent, and I remain that way as well, realizing that this has to be something serious if she was acting this way.

"Do not put any more weight on my shoulders as there is already enough," she says between clenched teeth.

I swallow and relax myself. I haven't seen her this bothered since the time I had asked where my parents were when I was a kid.

The woman inhales and then turns to finally look at me. Her hand reaches out and she brushes my bangs back lightly.

"I know it's hard, Hyunnie," she begins with a frown, "but there are just things that aren't easy to understand."

"Then help me understand," I retort frustratedly.

She leans her head against the window beside her and she looks up toward the darkening sky. I wasn't quite sure what she was thinking but I was hoping she would clarify.

"I can't."

"What do you mean you *can't*? There is absolutely nothing stopping you."

I can see her getting frustrated and her expression twists with a flash of her fierce personality.

"Ethan," she began sharply, "you just have to trust me! The more questions you ask the more complicated things become. Just stop. You're worried about all these things and doing nothing but stressing yourself out. You have a brain injury, so of course your memory is a little strange. I'm sure it'll all clear up in its own time."

I don't like this response. It's so dismissive, so unhelpful. It was pointless to have even said anything at all. I cross my arms across my chest and slouch down in my seat.

"You don't understand. You'll never understand. I can't even remember my own parents all because of a stupid car crash when I was a baby."

"Ethan, you weren't a baby when she died. You were going on nine."

Her words came out so fast I wasn't sure if she even knew what she said. I look at her quickly, totally misunderstanding what she was saying. It was my understanding that I was baby all this time when my parents died. What was she saying all of a sudden? Was she telling me that she lied about my parents' death?

"I'm not following," I said to her. "How could I have been going on nine?"

Her eyes are shocked, as if she couldn't believe herself. She turns away, avoiding my gaze as best as she could in the car.

"No, I didn't mean to say that. I'm just…confusing some memories myself."

"Memories like what?"

"Do you remember her? That girl? Did she seem familiar?"

I'm confused again, and I was almost sure my grandmother was losing it.

"Does Nari ring a bell to you?" Gramma asked. "Namu? Your aunt and uncle?"

I don't answer. Even when I tried to think about it, nothing she was saying sounded even the slightest bit familiar. She turns her head again, and when her eyes meet mine to see how perplexed I was, her hands move back to the wheel of her car and she starts up the engine again.

"That's what I thought…" she mumbles. "Don't ask me any more questions tonight, Ethan. It's just—it's way too soon, okay?" She lets out a breath, and for me my mind is so boggled I can't even argue or fight for myself anymore.

It was raining now, and I hadn't even noticed until she turned the headlights on. It was dark and there were no streetlights to light the narrow road. She pulls off, and we go home that night without another word between us.

3

An Old Friend

"Why didn't you call me, or at least let me know you were alright?" Carson sits at the foot of my bed, his head hanging low and reluctant to look me in the eye.

I sit at my desk tugging at a loose string at the hem of my sweater while mulling over what I could possibly say to Carson that could justify why I wasn't capable of picking up the phone to let him know I was fine after the fiasco that happened at Bobby's. It was already two days later, and I know that Carson is probably already fed up with my odd behavior.

"What even happened? Like, what was wrong with you?"

I watch him pick at his nails and then I'm finally met with his sharp gaze. The tension in the room was like loud static in the ears.

"I'm sorry, Carson," I say first, my eyes pleading for forgiveness, but he only shakes his head and rocks to his feet. His back is to me now as he gazes at the doorway, as if contemplating whether he should just go.

"...You really scared us back there," he mutters, "and not just that. But it reminded me of..." he trails off and turns on his heels to catch my eye once again. "...It reminded me of when we were kids. That time when you were really sick. Even to this day, ten years later, I still don't know what happened to you then. What you were sick with. But it was so scary. It was like you were gonna die. I didn't think I could deal with that since my father—the year before—"

He cuts off with a waver in his voice and I'm afraid he might cry. But as I read the look in his eyes expecting to see sadness or even mourning, he looks almost angry instead. Which was probably more terrifying since Carson only ever seemed to be hyper and happy *all* the time.

"You're my friend, Ethan." His voice is quieter now and his eyes meet the floor.

"You were the only one there for me and my mom when we hit…a rough patch. And you're the only one who not only puts up with my crap, but you also care about how I really feel too. You're the only one I can open up to. … But why is it that you won't open up to me? Like, if there's something wrong, or if you're terminally ill or somethin', you can just tell me. It won't make you any less of a friend."

He quiets and soon the room is full of silence. I take my time to absorb everything Carson is saying, and he's right. I know full well that I have always been the friend Carson goes to for anything and everything. Even if he just needed to come cry about something without saying a single word, I was always there for him. But for me, I have always, *always*, kept my emotions to myself. Though I have never been as…*brooding* as I may be now, I never like feeling sad or angry and talking about it. I'd rather those emotions don't exist. But then again that's not possible, is it?

"Carson…I'm sorry," I say again, "I didn't mean to scare you, even ignore you as much as I've been doing lately. It's just been a lot on my mind."

"Like what?" He scans my face skeptically for what I assume to be any trace of a lie.

I sigh and swivel around in my chair, trying to figure out how to even begin.

"I'll tell you everything…But you'll probably be just as confused as I am."

Carson moves away from the doorway and finds a seat back on my bed as he waits for me to go on.

"I don't think I ever had any kind of brain injury." I look up at him and he cocks an eyebrow.

"What do you mean?"

"I mean, I think something happened to me when I was young. Some kind of accident. But I don't think I was sick when I had to go to the hospital when we were kids. What I do think is that a side effect of whatever happened to me was what caused me to go to the hospital. I'm not entirely sure yet, but I heard Gramma and my doctor whispering about something and it didn't sound like they were talking about some car accident."

"But what kind of accident? And why would they be lying to you about it?"

I shake my head.

"I don't know, that's what I need to figure out. But when Gramma was leaving, Dr. Valhera said something about a friend of my grandmother's coming into town. He sounded like he wanted me to go meet her without Gramma knowing."

Carson raises his eyebrows at me and I could see his mind working.

"Didn't know she had any friends…" he grumbles. I want to scold him but honestly, I had the same reaction. Then suddenly I hear him chuckling and he's stretching his lanky body across on my bed. "Is this it, though," he asks, "your grandma's bein' all secretive as usual and that's bothering you? You could've told me about this forever ago."

I frown and shake my head stiffly.

"No," I hiss, "that's not it." I hesitate before deciding to continue. I had already said that I'd tell him everything. He deserved to know anyway. I go on to explain everything from the dreams I've been having, to the voices I've been hearing. And the headaches…that are the worst of them all. I can't quite tell if Carson is following, and by the way his expression twists and turns with every new profession of distress and confusion I'm almost certain by the end of it he just might laugh in my face… but he doesn't.

"I know it all sounds really weird," I mutter, trying to feel less embarrassed about explaining what's been going on, "but something just isn't adding up and I need to figure out what it is. Gramma let slip something about my aunt and uncle yesterday. I didn't even know I had an aunt and uncle… I tried to think if I just couldn't remember them because I was so young the last time they came around but I have absolutely no recollection. Actually…come to think of it, I can barely remember anything passed the time I was in the hospital at eight…" I trail off a bit as I think about it again. But it's all static.

"You mean you can't remember, like, your fifth birthday or something like that?" Carson wears a baffled look and watches me in disbelief. But I only shake my head no. "What? How can you not…well if you can't remember that then that means that," his back straightens but he leans forward, his neck craning downward as if he were trying to find a better angle to gawk at me from, "you don't remember when we first met."

His eyes are searching mine, but they had glazed over the moment his final words left his mouth. I lean back in my chair and I'm suddenly racking my brain for answers. Any memory of how Carson and I had met. I was stunned that I had never even thought of it until now. And even though I was scraping every corner, every crevice in my head, just like I told him just moments before, my memory would not go past eight-year-old me in a hospital bed. Oxygen mask over my nose and mouth. My arms hooked up to machines and monitors. My wrists and feet bandaged up tight… I was in so much pain. That I remember vividly. The pain all over my body. Like acid was coursing through my veins. Every nerve was on fire, and not to mention the extreme migraine that I was sure I would die from. I couldn't even open my eyes. The smallest bit of light was excruciating to endure.

But to think that I hadn't the slightest idea how Carson and I came to be such close friends bothered me beyond words. How could I not know how I met my best and *only* friend? This bothered me so much that I hadn't realized I had begun to panic. Fear injected itself inside of me and illuminated through my eyes like a New York billboard sign. To think that not only did I not remember something as important as when, where, and how I met my best friend, but I couldn't remember my mother, when, how and why she passed. I didn't remember my mother had two other siblings. And the fact that I couldn't remember something common like a 5th birthday.

My breathing is picking up, and the familiar throb in the back of my skull has appeared.

"E-Ethan. Are you alright?" Carson is now on his feet as he watches me gradually lose control of my senses.

"I-I don't r-remember," I stammer. "I c-can't remember."

I'm hyperventilating now, and tears gather in my eyes. My hand reaches up and presses against the side of my head as the pain forming there spreads, while I continue searching for the smallest fragment of a memory.

There I am, with Carson, nine years old riding our bike down the middle of the street on a particularly sweltering summer's day. Laughing like idiots after we had just come from somehow knocking over an entire basketball hoop in the courtyard at Whitechapel House of Faith and Praise church. A fond memory. But not what I'm looking for.

"Ethan."

Carson calls my name again but my eyes squeeze shut and I see another flash of light and then a twelve-year-old Carson storming off after a girl he had sincerely liked all through elementary school called him a freak to his face and shattered all of his hopes and dreams of ever being with her. His cheeks flushed tomato red. He refuses to look at me no matter what I do to try and calm him down. I remember next to being reminded of his father's death, it's the most upset I'd ever seen him be.

But…it's not what I'm looking for.

There's a sharp throb in my temples and I wince. I try to open my eyes, and when I do a number of tears escape and hit the floor. And there I see Carson's worn, gray socks in front of me. He bends down, worry all over his face.

"Please don't have another episode like what happened at Bobby's," he says under his breath. "I can get your grandma if you want. Don't stress yourself out, okay?" His hands are on my wrists and are actively prying my hands away from clutching my pounding head. "Ethan, please," he pleads again, "just calm down! Breathe!"

My face is red, and I finally become aware of how heavy I am breathing. Carson is trying to catch my eye, and although I was now actively trying to avoid it with the growing amount of embarrassment that was now washing over me, I meet his gaze and see the silent pleads he's sending me.

Seeing how much I was affecting Carson almost bothered me more than my initial panic attack. My breathing slowed to a calmer rhythm, and when my shoulders relaxed, Carson released my wrists, allowing me to wipe the tears from my face.

"I'm sorry," I mutter hoarsely, "I-I didn't mean to react like that."

Carson straightens up, his lips pursed worriedly. There is a long pause of silence between the two of us before he slowly backs up and finds his seat once more on my bed. I watch his expression carefully, but even though he continues to look worried, he's suddenly chuckling.

"Hey," he began, "you know, I should be the one panicking and crying like you just did. My best friend doesn't remember how we met. What's up with that?" He shakes his head, pretending now to be upset with me. "And that fifth birthday, man. What a party that was. There was a DJ and everything."

I sniff.

"...there was?"

"Well...if you count my mom's old stereo she brought over, then yes." He smiles sheepishly at me before flopping backwards onto the comforter and staring up at the ceiling as he falls quiet once more.

I wipe my face once again, wanting to be sure it was free of any moisture and then I spin around in my chair to look out of the window.

"Something is really not right," I say weakly. "And I want to get to the bottom of it. But I can't do it alone."

"Listen, I have always told you, if you ever need somethin' just let ol' Foxxy know and I'm right by ya. But I can't ever be there if you don't speak up. Look at you, you've been keeping all this stuff to yourself this whole time. Come to find out it's really somethin' serious..."

I frown lightly and nod my head.

"Yeah...you're right."

I'm thinking for a moment, and then my head turns to look at the blonde who seems surprised by the look on my face. My eyes widen a little, I spin around in my chair and I'm already standing up to my feet.

"Carson, we have to go to the library right now."

"What? Why?" Carson sits up, brows knit together while surprised by my sudden burst of energy.

"Obviously if we're gonna get any kind of answers about what's going on we have to start somewhere. Doctor Valhera said I could find Gramma's friend at the library. We should go talk to her now while she's still in town and see what she knows!"

"What...? Right now?"

Carson's tone drops in pitch as he flops back down against the bed, becoming lazy at the worst possible time.

"Yes, right now. Get up!"

I am already at my closet, pulling on my hoody and then quickly making my way to the door. Carson is still trying to wrap his head around everything that was just said, but he reluctantly stands up and follows after me.

After a short drive, we're running up the cement stairs of the library. After a quick scan of the inside, it seems like all the regulars and then some were there. And it only now occurs to me that I really didn't know who I was looking for.

"Mrs. C! Long time no see, honey!" Carson is cheerfully distracted and approaching the front desk where Mrs. Crawford seemed to be rubbing in what I assumed to be honey water on her arms as the old women attests that honey water keeps the skin "young and healthy".

The woman looks up at the loud sound of Carson's voice, and although she points a finger to scold him, she couldn't help but smile at the boy.

"Oh Carson, you never fail to share that young energy of yours," she reveres.

"You know me, the life of the party. This place could use a little bit of that."

They engage themselves in conversation, Carson clearly forgetting why we were there. They begin talking about why Carson hadn't visited the library in so long, and how Mrs. Crawford ran into Mrs. Foxx at the market and had asked the old woman if she'd bake a pie for some event Mrs. Foxx would be attending. But I didn't stick around to listen as I began analyzing every person I came across.

I had absolutely no information about her. No name, no physical description. How could I know if she was even here to begin with? I could only assume she was old like my grandmother. But of course, the city being so small gives me a little bit of an advantage. I'd be looking for someone I don't recognize.

I wander around aimlessly, leaving Carson behind as I weave through every aisle, nook, and corner of the library. The longer I wander around the more I gradually become hopeless. Not a single person in the whole building was unrecognizable.

It's becoming frustrating, particularly because I don't know what else to do. And without any real help it all seemed pointless. I round another corner of the library, nearing the back of the building, and not a single person was around. I'm preparing to completely give up when my ears perk at the sound of someone's voice.

"*Ethan*"

I feel as though a jolt of electricity ripped through my temples and I'm jarred to a stop. I didn't know if I was beginning to hear things again as the voice almost didn't seem real. But no one was around that I could see. I shake my head to rid myself of the sudden fogginess that began to cloud it and looked behind me to see if Carson had finally decided to join me. But he wasn't there.

"Okay, Ethan, don't start losing it again…" I mutter to myself. The last thing I needed was another episode.

"*Ethan. Ethan, focus.*"

There it was again, the whisper of a voice. My head starts to throb almost immediately, but before I could react to the awful pain wracking my skull, I hear my name a third time but from behind me. The sound echoes unnaturally and I'm spinning blindly on my heels hoping to find a face. I strain hard at anyone walking by or sitting in the distance, but no one seemed to be the owner of the voice.

I begin to feel dizzy and everything around me is buzzing. I blink once hoping to clear my blurring vision. I blink a second time and then there was nothing.

Everything had gone black and at that moment I thought I had fainted. But I hadn't, I was too self-aware to have passed out. I could no longer hear low talking, the sound of people walking, or pages turning. All I could hear was an aggressive buzzing and it was all I could feel. I look left and right and I blink my eyes but still it was black as if I wasn't in the library at all anymore.

"*Ethaaan.*"

It was the voice again and it was softer this time. I turn my head to where I heard it coming from and I move my feet to follow after it.

There is humming now. A gentle, sweet hum of an older woman's voice. I'm wandering aimlessly after it in the haze that I was in. But little had I known that Carson had finally caught up to me. He called my name, he tapped on my shoulder and tried to get my attention, but I didn't hear or feel him. I continued walking, following my ears and my feet carrying me out of the aisle and toward the back of the large building.

I wondered who the voice belonged to and wanted to open my mouth and call out, but I could not find the strength to speak. I felt almost like my body wasn't my own and the only thing that I could do was let my legs carry me. Step after step my body heating and the buzzing around me intensified. I'm rounding another corner and my feet find the back stairwell to the basement where many old and unused books that could not fit on the main floor shelves languished. Where the maintenance offices and control rooms were. I find myself crossing the basement floor and approaching the old office Mr. Crawford used to use for sanding and polishing the miniature wooden figures that were strewn in random places throughout the library before he passed away. It was there that the humming that had been growing louder the closer I came had then silenced. And with another jolt of electricity through my temples that caused me to involuntarily lurch forward, my eyes squeeze shut and then snap open.

"Ethan!"

I jump in place and then spin around to see Carson gaping at me. I study him, registering that that time it was his voice that called me, and then realizing where we stood.

"Didn't you hear anything I said?" Carson takes one step back as he eyeballs me, analyzing my eyes, my face and the rest of me. "Ethan your eyes…"

I blink stupidly before I find my voice.

"M-my eyes?" I stammer, still assessing my lightheadedness. I turn around once again to look at my reflection in the window of the office door. Albeit a little pale, I looked fine. Eyes brown, face…stupid.

"I know I'm not on anything, dude…your eyes were really freakin' me out."

"What are you talking about?" I grumble.

"Dude, they were *green*. You looked like you were possessed by a ghost! Are you okay? Why did we come down here?!" He looks between me and the office door, his body tensing as apprehension washes over him.

I frown lightly at my reflection. Why would my eyes be green? Of all the silly things Carson could think or say, that one was surely unique. Before I could answer him, I grimace after an abrupt shot of pain rips at the top of my head, causing me to reel backwards. There's a flash of light in front of my eyes and I see an image of an old woman with a long-beaded chain around her neck that was attached to a pair of half-moon glasses. She is running her aged fingers along the page of a book and talking to someone else just out of my view. The words are muffled and distorted and I'm not able to make them out.

"What's wrong, Ethan?!" My friend has his hand around my arm, shaking me a little until I'm standing up right again. "Come on, we should probably go before someone catches us down here."

My eyes open once more and I turn to face him.

"No," I say firmly, "let's look in here for a minute and then we can go back." I turn and put my hand on the door handle.

"Why?! It's hella creepy down here. What makes you think you're gonna find that woman in old man C's office?"

"Just a feeling…" I mumble before turning the handle and pushing the door open.

With a spine-chilling creak, the door swings open and I stand there in the doorway eyeing the darkness of the room, hesitating to walk right in. I reach my arm out and feel around for a light switch. With Carson standing behind me, he impatiently pulls out his phone and switches on the flashlight to help me see. He does a once over the room with the light, but it wasn't until he was moving to wave the light in the opposite direction did we both freeze at what our eyes caught sitting in the darkness.

"Y-You saw that too, right?" Carson whispers to me and swallows hard.

I nod my head, my eyes blown wide as my fingers finally locate a switch. Flipping it up, our eyes adjust to the new found light. And in the room full of unfinished wooden figurines sitting there in the corner was an old woman I had to believe was who we'd been looking for.

Hands folded in her lap and collar still hiked up high, the woman sits in a chair unmoving which almost leads me to believe she wasn't real. But when she draws in a deep breath, I remind myself why we are there.

"Who are you?" I ask without wasting any time.

There's a pause of silence and everyone stood still. The room seemed to buzz; the feeling almost similar to how I felt upstairs. It rang in my ears and it made everything seem tense.

Her eyes open and the color pierces through the dull green she wears. She raises her head slowly and turns to face me. And there around her neck I catch the same red colored beads I saw in the vision I had just moments ago.

"A friend," she answers finally, her voice calm and assuring. Her voice… like what I heard that led me down here to begin with.

"This is really creepin' me out, man," Carson whispers at me, his hands wringing as he attempts to coax me backward and out of the room.

"Hush," I snap at him, swatting his hand away from my sleeve and I then step farther into the musty room. "You know me?" I ask the woman and crane my neck to try and get a better look at her face.

She smirks and stifles what might have been a scoff. Her eyes never leave mine, and even when I'm expecting to read something distrusting from them, all I can pick up is a sense of shame.

"Know you," she repeats, "of course I do. I've spent all this time watching over you, dear."

"What do you mean you watch over me? I mean…I just came because someone told me you were a friend of my grandmother's…and you were visiting town. Why and how could you be watching over me?"

"It's a favor your grandmother asked of me," she responds, her tone unwavering. I was almost surprised that she was answering anything at all. If she were anything like my grandmother, she would have just kept quiet. But I didn't know what to make of this at all. A favor for my grandmother to watch me? I knew Gramma could be quite strict and often coddled me, but even this seemed to be a little much, even for her.

"So, you *do* know my grandmother then," I respond quietly. "Do you know Dr. Scott Valhera? He's the one that mentioned you in the first place. Though…I'm not exactly sure why. If you are friends with my grandmother, then you must know something about my family right? Would you tell me?"

I am hopeful now. I'd do anything to hear someone tell me about my family's past. Especially when my grandmother makes it seem like it is somehow

39

forbidden to even think about it. But that is also the problem. Thinking about it. I can't even attempt to without my head wanting to split in two.

I see the woman pulling down her collar and smoothing it flat against her shoulders. There I could see her face, and with a sharp pain to the side of the head I knew for a fact I've seen her face somewhere else before, in a dream or distant memory.

I watch her as she looks back up at me, and there I can see her eyes welling up with tears. She smiles kindly to me, and my shoulders drop, no longer tense with uncertainty. Instead, defeat takes hold before I can understand why.

"It's starting," she whispered. "Maybe you haven't seen it before today, but your friend sounds like he has."

I frown.

"What do you mean?"

"Just what she said!" Carson retorts. "D'ya think I made it up, or what? Your eyes were **green** and you looked like a zombie up there, dude! It's not a lie, it was crazy and I wouldn't have believed it if I didn't see it for myself. You better hope no one else did!"

"I don't understand," I grumble, "why would something like that even be—"

"Because you are special, Ethan. I'm sure you've heard Catherine say that to you recently." She stands up slowly and I see now that she was a short pudgy woman who perhaps outside of this moment was warm and bright. She reaches back behind her head and she gathers her hair into her fist and begins to pull for what seemed like an eternity. Her white hair comes out from inside her jacket and finally when she let the strands loose, they fall in a wavy pattern around her. The length ending just at the middle of her calves. She smiles up at me and is still choking back tears.

"Look at me," she says softly, "I loved you like you were my own."

I take another small step back when she took one forward. Though on second thought I felt embarrassed that I had. It probably hurt her as I knew then that she was trying to remind me of something indirectly. I frown deeply, wishing I had whatever memories she had. The more I tried to think back in time, the more my head ached.

I see in her expression that she picks up that I can't recognize her, causing her to shake her head. She holds her hands up and clasps them together over her heart before taking another step forward. This time I don't move.

"Catherine, your grandmother, she is the strongest woman I know. My best friend, I've known her since we were very young," she explains. "And your mother, what a *bright* girl she was. My most brilliant student."

"You knew my mother?" My eyes widen as I am now more than eager to hear what she had to say. The buzzing in the room grew as the woman took another step closer. It seemed like it was coming from her, and the closer she came, the more intense it felt.

"Of course, I did. She grew up in our guild, Ethan. She never stopped learning, was always in my books, reading and studying. She wouldn't quit even when she couldn't—" She cuts herself off, covering her mouth with her fingers.

"When she couldn't what?" I step closer this time, urging her to continue but she wouldn't.

"I shouldn't say…" Her eyes are pleading with mine, looking as though she dreaded the fact that she couldn't continue. "Your mother was a part of our family," she says instead, "and she'll always be. When you find your way back home, I promise to tell you all about her. But for now, listen to me. Scott believes what has been done to you is finally beginning to wear off. Because of this, you will begin to experience things that you might think are impossible. You need to come home, as quickly as possible. I understand your grandmother may be opposed to it but… it's imperative for your safety and everyone else's. I've also caught wind of certain… *individuals* who may want to prevent that. Watch your back, dear, and keep your friends close. Your grandmother asked me to watch over you and I will continue to do my part. Someone will soon come for you to bring you back where you belong."

"But I don't—"

"Just trust me," she says, "soon that awful injection will wear off and you'll be just like you used to. We're all waiting for you, Ethan."

I feel sick to my stomach and turn my head to look at my friend who looked just as confused as I was. Glad to not be the only one, I look back to the woman who I find to be wiping an escaped tear away.

"I'm sorry..." she murmurs, "I told myself I wouldn't cry but...look at you." She gestures in my general direction and sniffs. "You grew up so fast, I can't believe it. I can't wait for you to see what you've missed."

I frown again as I watch her wipe furiously at more tears. It hurt me knowing that she viewed me as family and was close with someone like Catherine Grey, my grandmother who made no deep connections with anyone. And who had my own mother as a student of some kind which meant she must have watched her grow up. I wanted to know her more, I wanted to understand what she knew and our exact relation. But moreover, I wanted to know what the actual hell was going on that someone was watching over me because there are "individuals" who don't want me to...come home? What did she mean by that, anyhow?

The woman is sobbing now, turning away to hide her shame.

"Wait..." I say after taking a moment to think, "an injection? I overheard Gramma and my doctor talking about something like that the other day. Do you know something about it too?"

She sniffs again and nods her head without looking at me.

"I-I was the one who made it," she confesses weakly. "There was nothing I could do. They forced me and threaten not just yours but Nari and Namu's lives."

"Namu? You knew my aunt and uncle as well!" I exclaim, not exactly asking as it was clear that she did.

"Yes, I know them."

"Well, where are they?! They're alive right? Why haven't they ever come to see me or even just Gramma? I want to talk to them!" I'm almost jumping up and down, wanting nothing more than to meet others from my family. But the woman waves her hand at me to calm my excitement.

"They're alive," she confirms, "and they long to see you again. But they can't come here. They cannot leave Obscura. If you want to see them, you have to go to them yourself."

"How?! What is Obscura? Is that where the rest of my family is? Where is it? *You* could take me there!" I step closer to her, now standing directly in front of her.

"I can't." She takes a step back and turns again to avoid my gaze.

"Why not?! You must know how to get there!"

"I told you!" Her voice raises this time and she covers her face with her hands. "You have to wait. Just a little longer…"

Defeated once again, my shoulders drop and I straighten up. There's a pain in my chest, not like what goes on in my head, but more like an emotional pain that gnawed at my heart.

"…I just…wanna remember…" I say quietly, "I'm *sick* of not knowing what I don't know…"

The woman meets my eyes this time, looking apologetic for raising her voice, even when it wasn't that loud to begin with. Her hands move from her face and presses at her chest again, while she raises one of them up to cup my cheek. The moment her skin came in contact with mine I feel a shock of electricity course through my body, and for all of a minute all I could see was white, and through the brightness was that short pudgy woman laughing brightly next to a figure that faintly resembled my mother. The old woman carried a toddler in her arms whose hands tangled in her long white hair. The boys' eyes were unnaturally green and he babbled passionately to both women. That boy was me.

I gasp, not realizing I had been holding my breath the entire time, and the old woman in front of me smiled faintly.

"You remembered something," she whispered knowingly.

It was my turn to have tears welling up, but I refused to cry over something I couldn't wrap my head around.

"I don't even know your name," I say to her.

The woman drops her hand and steps back.

"I'm River," she replies quietly, "River Dallas. It's nice to meet you again, dear." She offers another kind smile and I watch her sadly. River, what a unique name.

"And I'm Carson!" Carson chimes in and raises his hand, causing me to flinch from forgetting he was even there, "Carson Foxx, yes nice to meet you. Ethan's best friend by the way. Glad we're all chummy and you're not some weiro. Oh! You're friends with Mrs. Grey, maybe you'll let me call you Gramma since she won't. She hates me or something." He showcases his huge grin after speaking a mile a minute, opens his arms up wide and approaches to pull her in for a hug.

"Oh, I seriously doubt she hates you." River giggles and accepts his forward gesture.

"You should see the way she looks at me! I ignore it 'cause I think she's really cool, but it hurts ya know?"

"No," River pats his back and pulls away from his long embrace, "it would take an awful lot for Cathy to hate anyone," she assures, "the fact that you're Ethan's best friend—why, I'm sure she cares deeply for you than you'd ever know."

"Well, she has a funny way of showing it," he grumbles.

"You'll see in due time, friend. Just you wait." River turns her head now and pulls something from her coat. "Before I forget…take this, Ethan."

She pulls out an old looking book and hands it to me. I hesitate but I take it from her as she says. It looked old and it seemed to be a journal of some kind.

"This belonged to your uncle," River explains. "Maybe you'd like to return it to him."

I look down it for a moment longer, almost in awe of it, like it were some old precious relic. I wanted to say something, or just thank her for giving it to me, but I can't find the words at all. I simply turn the book around in my hands as I try to make sense of everything.

The old woman is smiling and looks to her wrist to a funny looking watch. Its needles spun wildly and there were strange symbols in place of where numbers usually are.

"Oh my," she sighed, "it seems like this will have to be goodbye for now."

"What? Wait, I still have questions! Tell me more about Obscura. Who's coming to take me there? And if I go there, how could I even *begin* to look for my aunt and uncle? What about the—"

She cuts me off with her hand again and she begins to walk backwards toward the corner of the room where we found her.

"Ethan, you amazing boy, you will meet them all soon, I swear it," she says. "Just remember everything I said. Do you hear me?"

While wearing a puzzled expression I nod my head anyway. She continues walking backward and I wondered what it was she was doing. I turn to my friend who was back at my side and he simply shrugs his shoulders.

"I'm just kinda hoping I passed out at some point and this is all a crazy fever dream," he states, "take good care of me, won't you, Ethan?"

I roll my eyes at him and look back over to where River was. She was gone.

"What? She was just there!" I step forward ogling over the dimmed corner. But there was no trace of her as if she had never even been there.

I sigh heavily and turn away from where River once was. I was at the very least glad to have heard something new. Namu and Nari are still alive, and I've met a woman who seemed to know my family well. I prayed that meant that once I saw her again, she'd tell me more about my past and about my mother. Maybe she knew who my father was. Gramma sure kept her mouth shut on that.

I decide to have a positive attitude toward this. That woman told me so much more than my grandmother ever had, and I was thankful. I turn again toward my friend and I slapped my hand against his back, causing him to rock forward on his feet.

"Carson," I smile, "let's go to that party."

"What? You mean it?!" He perks up and is already turning on his heels to make a beeline for the door.

"I guess I can tolerate a little social gathering for one night."

Nope, parties weren't really my thing, but Carson stood by me through… whatever any of that was. So, I thought it was only fair to do something he was more interested in doing.

4

The Hunt

"What in God's name are you wearing?"

Carson squeezes more jelly-like fake blood onto his face, smearing it all over his chin while I peer into his bathroom. He wore a cheaply made black cape that was red on the inside. High-waisted trousers, a red velvety vest and a shirt complete with frilly, lacey sleeves and collar.

"Uhm, a vampire costume!" He makes a face at me through the mirror as he continued with the poorly done theatrical makeup.

"You look like Great Aunt Tessie."

His mouth drops open at my comparison of his costume to those rather awful dress robes from the one movie.

"How could you say that," he responds in a northern English accent, face twisted with offense.

"It's hideous." I cringe, quietly hoping he'd change his mind so I didn't have to show up to a party with him looking like *that*.

"F you, I'm beautiful." He puts down the tube of blood in his hand and then tousles his hair a few times. "And anyway, it *is* a Halloween party. People are gonna be dressed up. Are you that much of a sour-puss to not even try?"

I press my lips together in response and stared at his reflection. I guessed he was right. At least he was dressed up, no matter how ugly his choice was, he probably wouldn't stick out as much as someone who wasn't.

With a defeated sigh, I join him in the bathroom and pick up a black makeup crayon and draw dark circles around my eyes. Carson watches me closely, more concerned with whether or not I'd misuse the soft crayon and snap it in half with the way I rubbed it against my skin.

After my eyes were completely black, I lazily draw lines on each corner of my mouth, and run my fingers through my hair to close the middle part in my bangs. I faced Carson and threw my arms up to ask what he thought.

"Skeleton..." he shrugs with a less than impressed expression, "I guess that'll work."

I shrug as well and then leave the room without another word. I was wearing a black sweatshirt and my black three striped adidas pants. If anything, because I was wearing all black, with a touch of "spooky" makeup I was the least bit worried about what anyone else might say about how I looked.

"Let's go, princess, you've been in that mirror long enough, don't you think?" I taunt as I make my way to the door of his bedroom.

"Beauty takes time, Ethan, I don't expect you to understand!"

"Keep on and take your beautiful time and miss the entire party."

I leave the room and make my way down the stairs and toward the kitchen but was stopped by Mrs. Foxx who waved at me from the couch in the living room, where she was shelling nuts as she watched an old sitcom.

"Ethan, come here a sec," she calls.

"Yes ma'am?" I say as I find a seat in a chair beside the couch.

"Ohh that's a cool zombie makeup you got going on!" she laughs.

I smile sheepishly.

"How are you feeling? You're really okay to go to a party? I know Carson is dragging you into it." The woman smiles softly at me. She must have heard that I took a trip to the hospital just two days before and had been monitoring me the second I walked through the door that afternoon.

"Don't worry, I'll be just fine," I reassure her.

"Well alright..." She pauses to scan over me, looking for any sign that I might not be feeling well or hurt somewhere. "You know that I care about you, Ethan, if something is wrong you know you can tell me."

"I know."

She nods her head as she takes the time to focus on a particularly difficult shell to crack. After a bit of struggling and continuous repositioning of her hands, the shell snaps into pieces, and she recovers the nut from inside. Then all of a sudden, she begins to chuckle.

"It's funny," she began, "I asked Mrs. Crawford if she'd bake me a pie to take up to that old golf club my father practically lives at. He's having some kind of get together, probably to do nothing more than gamble with those old fuddy-duddies up there. He asked me if I'd make something for him, and sure I said I would. But actually, I didn't want to."

I raise my eyebrows, not sure exactly why she was telling me this or where she was going with it, but then again maybe she was just speaking her mind to pass the time.

"So, I just asked Mrs. Crawford if she'd do it for me, and I'd pretend I was the one who made it. But then I ran into some man I'd never seen before. He was tall, well groomed, salt and pepper hair kind of guy. I met him at the golf club and he told me he was in town visiting his mother for a few months. But now that I think of it, I don't think I caught where he was from. Orlando? Oklahoma? Well, I think it started with an O…"

My eyes widen and I start to listen carefully. I knew I had a knack for getting ahead of myself, but someone from "out of town" from a place that started with the letter "O"? That was a little too coincidental for me. She continues.

"Anyway, we were talking about deserts and I mentioned something about my *killer* walnut butter cake and I invited him to try some sometime. It's funny because my own father asked me if I'd bake him a pie and I had no intention of actually doing it, but here I am deshelling some walnuts to bake an entire cake for a stranger. Absolutely ridiculous." She's shaking her head, and when she didn't hear me respond she looked up to see my perplexed expression.

"Ah…but you probably don't care about any of that," she says. "It's just that we ended up on the topic of children and he told me he had a little girl named Layla, I think it was. He told me all these beautiful things about her and you could tell he just adored her. He even showed me a picture he kept in his wallet. Very pretty. She really was. But of course, as a mom myself I had to bring up Carson and tell him all the great things about my son too." Her lips set in a line and she catches my gaze again.

"…I told him he was musical."

There was a pause and then we both shatter into a guffaw. It was probably the funniest thing I heard all week.

"I guess if you count arbitrary strumming and beatless drumming music then yes, the most musical of them all!" I almost had to wipe a tear just thinking about every time he nearly made my ears bleed until I had to threaten him to never make me listen to his music again. And it's not an exaggeration. He once caused me a trip to the audiologist.

"Yes! He asked me what instrument he played because I mentioned that he was in a band. And I told him he plays the bass. But I think he misunderstood and thought I meant that oversized cello." She's shaking her head again and shoving a walnut she finished cracking into her mouth. "But anyway," she continues, "I say aaalll of that to say, and maybe there was a *much* shorter way to say it, that guy said that he knew you."

"Huh?" I tilt my head to the side. I didn't know a single person outside of Whitechapel. So, anyone from out of town claiming to know an Ethan Moon was probably a liar—or from Obscura.

"Yeah, after I mentioned that Carson was doing some volunteer work up at Bobby's and had brought you along with him, he told me that he was an old friend of your grandmothers and knew who you were."

"Did he say his name?" I ask. Could it have been my uncle? I knew that River told me earlier that day, Namu couldn't leave that place, Obscura. But maybe she just meant it like it would be breaking a rule and not that he physically couldn't leave. I was hopeful that it would be him, and that I could finally meet him and learn about my family's history.

"Julian," Mrs. Foxx answered, eyeing my dimming expression. "He said his name was Julian."

I frown. That name didn't ring any bells. My mind goes back to when River told me to watch my back. I still didn't understand why, but this couldn't have been a coincidence. Someone from out of town knew me somehow and it's not like I'm internet famous. This Julian guy had to have been the sort of person River warned me about.

"Is everything alright?" Mrs. Foxx watches me closely as my face darkens, my mind quickly overflowing with new questions, and new thoughts.

"Oh..." I mutter after registering her voice, "yeah, I just—"

"LADIES!"

Carson's voice booms and enters the room before he did. His arms were out stretched wide as he did a little spin and dramatically flipped his cape back.

"I can see you all were waiting for me patiently, well done! What do you think, I can REALLY pull off this frilly stuff right?!"

He's grinning from ear to ear as he strikes...I guess you could call it a pose. He certainly had no interest in what Mrs. Foxx and I were discussing before he arrived.

"Yeaaahh..." She makes an awkward face. "You look...well, you look..." Her eyes widen as she does a once over his...*unique* vampire costume and then darts her eyes at me, pleading for me to help her out.

"Dashing," I jump in to rescue the poor woman. "Really, really...*jjang* man." I give him two thumbs up and nod my head to assure him but he only makes a puzzled expression in return.

"*Jjang?*" he questions, tilting his head way over.

"Really cool," I clarify with a sigh. I've used the word around him many a time, I'd think he'd understand it by now.

"Ah Korean!"

"Mhmm..." I roll my eyes and push myself to my feet, hinting that I was ready to get this party over with.

Carson laughs a little and goes to pat his mom on the head as I guess was his way of kissing her goodbye. She punches him lightly in the side and pushes him away.

"Quit before you make me spill my nuts!"

"Maybe you should keep them where they belong." Carson gestures to his pants and then bursts into laughter, moving to push his mother playfully in the shoulder while she swats at him to leave her alone.

"Don't tick me off or you can stay your butt right here!"

"Okay, okay, I'm sorry! Ethan, how do you say we're peacing out now in Korean?" He slaps his hands hard onto my shoulders, causing me to grimace, and pushes me toward the hall.

I look back at him and offer my most endearing smile before answering: "*Nal dashi ddaeri-myeon kal-lo majeul-geoya~.*"

Which roughly translates to: If you hit me again, I'll strike you with a knife.

Carson repeats with basically gibberish, waving his mother goodbye as we walk out of the house.

It was dark now and after a little over a ten-minute drive, we pull up to Whitechapel Forest's nature trail entrance and we walk it for a short time. Hailey had sent a text earlier that morning with the details of when and exactly where the party was. But because it was set up off the trail, it wasn't exactly that easy to find. "*A little-ways left of the blue and orange trail intersection,*" her text had said. That wasn't really that descriptive but we just followed our ears anyway to where the party was.

The music was loud and the bass was certainly reverberating off of every tree. Soon bright lights became visible and the sound of laughing and mingling was very distinct. There, just a few feet away was a clearing with yellow fairy lights strung up on trees around the surrounding perimeter. A group of people much larger than what I would have expected gathered in various places dressed up in all sorts of costumes. Many of which entirely nicer and more unique than Carson's ruffly suit.

There were smoke machines hidden in corners under foliage. A generator draped in a tarp that powered those machines, the lights and the "DJ setup" which was actually just a folding table with some kid's laptop connected to two stereo speakers. There were also some rather impressive animatronics triggered by hidden foot-pads placed randomly around the area. Jumping spiders, a dead girl on a swing that hung from a low bearing tree branch, creepy clowns, zombies, etcetera. But the one I thought was particularly cool was this *massive* creepy pumpkin man that sat on top of a wooden crate; and every time someone approached it, it rose to its feet rapidly, lunging at the trespassers with a more excellent pose than I've seen similar animatronics do. There were screams every so often in response to the pop-up decorations, but that one in particular got the most. I wanted to get a good look at it for myself.

"Ethan, I—" Carson had drawn in a deep breath as he took in the scene. I would give them props for creativity, but I could see Carson overflowing with excitement.

"Go play," I tell him before he could finish. Usually if he succeeded in dragging me with him to a party, he'd try for only a minute to hook me up with someone before going off to act cool and fail at women. I suppose he's in his element.

"You don't have to tell me twice!" he exclaims before running off to join a group of girls he must have recognized from our science class.

I shake my head as I watched him do so. Quietly I hoped that one day he'd just find a girlfriend that would take the free time off his hands so he could stop looking for so much attention. I know it's really all he wants.

I stare at my feet, watching my Fila's cake with the damp forest floor as I cross the clearing toward the animatronics I had my eyes on earlier. Only I never make it after I collide with another who was running almost full speed across where I was walking.

"Ouch!"

The person had fallen over onto the ground and I had only stumbled backward a little. I look down and realized I'd knocked over a girl whose face had been covered by the cap she wore that fell when she did. I pull my hands from my pockets and reach out to give her a hand.

"Sorry," I say quickly while I watched her rub her hip. Then I realize exactly who I'd knocked over the moment she pulled her cap off, smoothed out her long, thick hair and looked up at me with huge round eyes. Of all the people to run into first, Ruha Kapoor, who was just a year below me, extremely popular, extremely pretty, and super into me. The only problem was I wasn't into her. Although it was strange to me that someone so popular paid any attention to a wall flower like myself, I supposed the reason was more so because I was neither a "nerd" nor "lame". And there was nothing people could really say to me that really affected me so typically no one tried unless it was to comment on something that always made them look like an ignorant jerk. I had a neutral character that was either cool enough or just completely ignored, and I don't think I'd want it any other way. But Ruha was persistent. No matter the plain and obvious hints I'd drop, she simply didn't care, and it was every bit of annoying.

Her mouth opens once she too recognized who I was from underneath the black scribbling I had done to my face earlier that night. And I guess, maybe it was supposed to be discreet, she made a quick move to adjust her breasts and tugged the top of her costume down some.

"Ethan," she starts, pretending to be more upset than she was that she had been knocked over, "didn't you see me?!"

"Well not exactly," I answer with a sigh while still waving my hand around for her to take and stand up.

"Then you should pay more attention. I don't know if you've noticed but you're a really..." She swallows as she looked me up and down, not that I would think there was much to see in all black in the dark. She reaches up and takes my hand finally and I pull her up. Once on her feet and taking advantage of the skin contact, her hand lets go of mine and she grips my forearm instead, running it up the length to feel the firmness of my arm. "...tall...and broad... shouldered..."

Her eyes meet mine again and I gently pull my arm out of her grasp without a word.

"Maybe I wasn't watching where I was going but you should be looking out for girls like me. I could've really got hurt! See?!"

She rocks quickly to the balls of her feet, pressing her body into my chest while she pretends to be distraught about the barely noticeable spot of dirt on her skin tight shorts. She tugs at the handcuffs hanging from them, and then is where I realize she's dressed up as a sexy female cop. ...That's all I'll say about that.

"That's what I fell on, dummy; made me hurt my hip."

She eyes me again, gauging what I might say, and when I stayed silent, she stepped to the side and gripped me around the arm and began to pull me to where she was originally going in the first place.

"Ugh," she huffs, "just come with me to get a drink and then I'll forgive you."

She drags me along toward the food and drink table and I sob on the inside. I turn my head and watch where I was trying to go move further and further away.

Goodbye super awesome pumpkin man…

"Look who I found, guys!"

Ruha shouts toward her clique of snobs and jocks as she pulls me in close to the group. Kyle, probably the biggest Chad of them all, scanned me over before shoving a sucker into his mouth. His arm was wrapped tight around his girlfriend's…basically her neck rather than her shoulders, which looked awfully uncomfortable for her, but she stood there just as judgmentally as he did with her hand in his back pocket.

"And what are you supposed to be?" he sneers.

"Obviously Ru's Ken doll," Olivia, his girlfriend, replies with a laugh.

"That would have been a *cute* idea!" Ruha exclaims while tugging at my limp arm. "If *someone* didn't act all standoff-ish then maybe we could have collaborated!"

"Ethan doesn't strike me as the Barbie, Ken type," another girl in the clique chimes in. "I'd say he's more like a lost puppy, or Leo DiCaprio as Romeo. Particularly when he's around you-know-who." She where's a smug look as she darts her eyes to the right a few times. Only a few feet away with that *jerk*, Eric wrapped around her was Hailey. She laughed with some other football players and even I couldn't help the puppy dog look that invaded the expression I tried to keep uninterested. She was right, I couldn't help the way that I looked at her, even with how hard I swallow my feelings in respect to her.

"Well don't point her out to him," Ruha chides, "he just has to start looking in the right direction."

She finally lets me go but to my dismay she jumps in front of me, flips her hair back off of her shoulders and then places her hands on her hips while pushing her chest out further than necessary.

"Ethan, how do I look? What do you think of my costume, it's hot right?" She smiles up at me trying to distract me from gazing over at Hailey. I hadn't even thought about trying to meet her when she was the one to invite me here in the first place. I wanted to talk to her. But as there was Ruha nearly about to break her spine trying to look as appealing as possible, I just look at her worriedly.

"You look cold," I answer. I was dead serious but the others took it as a joke and burst into laughter.

"For real," Olivia cackles, "put on some pants and act like it's not a sun state!"

"Oh, shut up, it's not even that cold out. But Ethan being Ethan is clearly worried about me. Unlike Kyle who could care less about whether or not he snaps your neck, Olivia."

"Please, won't you two grow up." Kaitlyn, the other girl, rolled her eyes before taking a sip of what I assumed to be alcohol in a Solo cup. She then turned to me once the two others stopped bickering over nothing. "But real talk, E, if you'd just move on from *her* then you could seriously get some girls on your arm. ...Or dudes. I mean you're cute, and definitely a better catch than anyone around here."

"Excuse me?" Kyle enters the conversation again. He wasn't really listening the entire time, though I wouldn't blame him with the way it was going right about now. With his arm still locked around Olivia's neck he had been scrolling through his phone and taking selfies, but I suppose he caught the tail end of what was said since he was now ripping the sucker out of his mouth and shooting daggers into Kaitlyn who only shrugged back at him. "You're trying to tell me bean poll over here is better than *me*? Don't make me laugh!" The brunette sizes me up as if he were going to do something.

"Duh," Ruha sneers at him and then adjusts her shorts that were riding up. "All you are is a—"

"Excuse me," another voice interrupts and I already feel the heat rising in my cheeks, "I think that Ethan never asked for relationship advice."

My face is burning and I'm urgently wringing my arm from Ruha's grasp before I am met by another group of people joining where the five of us stood.

Hailey steps in between Ruha and I, and lightly pushed me backward in the chest to put space between me and the unwanted company.

"I think I could have said that..." I mutter, eyeing the other girls who were analyzing Hailey.

"You could have," she says, "but we all know you wouldn't. You're too nice." She smiles up at me and I find myself pouting back at her.

"What do you want Hailey, can't you see we're busy!" Ruha crosses her arms, jealousy immediately rearing its ugly head.

"I mean…you're standing directly in front of the punch so, I don't know what you expected," she said.

"Yo, E!"

There's a powerful slap on my back and I rock forward a little before turning to see who's booming voice it was. Of course, not to any of my surprise there now stepping in between Hailey and I was football star Eric, who grinned crookedly at me.

"Long time no see man; glad you could make it to my party."

"Really?" I look at him blankly. There was always tension between me and him, and there were days he would ignore it, and days where he had something slick to say to me. He was full of jealousy, even when I did not actively pursue his girlfriend, he hated the way we interacted with each other. But it wasn't just me he acted that way to, it was anybody with an extra leg that he felt intimidated by, and it was painfully obvious that it suffocated outgoing Hailey. Her kindness to anyone was a threat to his ego.

"Sure," he throws his arm around Hailey who was now measuring the situation and eyeing me apologetically, "the entire school was invited, plus some of my buddies from out of town. It's good to see you come and enjoy yourself. Except I would've thought you'd be here with that loser you hang around all the time. Where is he anyway?"

He stops to look around the area for the rambunctious blonde, but he was off somewhere out of clear sight in the mass of people dancing, talking, and drinking.

"He's here somewhere," I tell him. "Why? Do you miss him?"

"What? What are you—"

"Eric! Babe, I think I lost one of my web shooters over by the DJ table!" Hailey exclaims suddenly. I look at her and watch her pull her hand behind her back and pull off one of the toy devices around her wrists and dropped it behind her before pretending to be frantic and showing off her arms to him.

"Can you go find it for me? Please, please? I'll make a plate for you for when you come back!" She rounds her dark eyes at him and he's already forgotten our little exchange before he agrees.

"Okay, baby, calm down. I'll go look and be right back." And then he's off on the goose chase.

Once he was quite a ways away, she picks up the slyly dropped toy and slides it back on her wrist, and that's when I got a good look at what she was wearing. A complete replica of the Miles Morales Spiderman costume. Complete with red and white sneakers, and a red and black hoodie. Her long twists had been pulled back into a high ponytail and only two of the twists in front were left out to frame her face. What was that Ruha asked me just before? Was her costume hot while she nearly broke her back to show it off?

No.

But Spiderman?

Yes. Spiderman is hot.

"Oh, that's where you ran off to!" Again, there's a new voice yelling over the music. There in a creepy clown costume was Julia who ran up to Hailey and hugged her around the arm.

"Ugh, it's getting lame over here," Olivia speaks up with a roll of the eyes once Julia joined in. She pushed her boyfriend in the direction of all the dancers and naturally, Kaitlyn and Ruha follow; though Ruha did hesitantly, looking between me and Hailey before catching up to the others without a word.

"Hey, Ethan." Julia waves after watching the others leave, but I had yet to take my eyes from Hailey's *awesome* costume.

"Huh?" I shake my head before tearing my eyes away to look at the other girl, "oh, hi Julie…"

"I didn't think you'd actually show up, considering…you know, your trip to the hospital."

"What?!" My eyes widen at her and Hailey is punching her in the arm.

"Ouch, what was that for?!" she cried.

"Because you always bring up stuff people clearly wont wanna talk about!"

"You mean...you guys were there when I..." I frown lightly, thinking back to my episode at Bobby's. I couldn't help but to feel embarrassed, even if it wasn't something I could have controlled.

"Yeah, we were still there. We saw you when you went down and we went over there to see if you were good but then Carson came out and...well it looked serious."

"I'd never seen him look the way that he did, he was really worried. I mean we all were, but Carson especially," Hailey adds. "We wanted to help but he told us not to do anything."

I didn't know that. After I went down, I wasn't aware of much anything else other than Carson continuously making sure I was still conscious. And when Gramma had come to take care of the rest.

"So, what happened to you?" Julia bounces on her toes, anticipating my answer but I only look at her.

"Don't ask him that, it's clearly personal," Hailey retorts, pulling at her arm to still her, "besides, what matters most is that he's alright now. ...right?" She looks at me, her eyes full of worry until I nod my head.

"I'm fine," I say to them, "I don't really want to talk about it, but I'm completely fine now." I wasn't sure if that was exactly the truth, but other than whatever it was that happened to me earlier that morning, I hadn't had any kind of headaches or heard any weird voices the entire day. I hoped it would stay that way.

"That's fair," Hailey began slowly, "but you know if you need anything... or want to talk about it, we're here."

"Yeah, don't forget you have friends outside of that crazy dork you hang out with!"

My brow furrows a little. I wasn't sure if Julia and I were quite *friends*. She rarely ever talked to me until recently, but I suppose if she likes it, I love it.

"Where is he by the way? Hope he's not harassing any—"

"YOOOOO! I feel high as a freakin' KITE right now!"

Carson's voice bellows from behind the girls and he's stumbling his way over, one Solo cup in each hand sloshing mysterious liquids around. The fake blood he smeared around his lips before was somehow smudged across the bottom half of his face. Although he wasn't that put together in the first place, he was even more disheveled than the last time I saw him. Shirt untucked, seams starting to split, buttons undone, and incredibly sweaty. As he approached, he wrapped his long arms around the girls and rocked forward on his toes, and then backward again.

"You look high as a kite too," Julia grumbled.

"And smell like a brewery," Hailey adds while covering her nose.

He frowns a little and drops his arms from them, more liquid pouring from his cups as he did.

"Where have you been?" I asked him.

"Oh, you know," he runs three fingers through his short hair and the remaining contents of the left-hand cup being held between his thumb and pointer finger is dumped onto the ground behind him, "just showing everybody how hot I make the dance floor." He smirks.

"You mean with your body heat?" Julia asks tauntingly.

"No, not with my body heat, *Rebecca*—with my awesome dance moves, obviously." We all wore perplexed expressions, not sure who 'Rebecca' was. "Everyone loved it, of course, I even danced with some pretty girls. Scored a number too! ...My stomach hurts a little though, probably from my *awesome* dancing... or this tiny cookie someone gave me..." Our eyes widen at this and we look between each other before looking at Carson who would most likely be green if it weren't for the white makeup. "Yeap, I'm seein' colors."

His body sways a little as he holds his stomach, but he shakes his head as if to shake off the sick feeling he had.

"That's why you shouldn't be taking stuff from strangers; your decision-making skills really suck. Also, what's your costume, by the way?" Julia turns to completely face him as she looks him up and down trying to figure out his costume choice.

"What?" Carson exclaims with exasperation. "I'm a vampire! Isn't that obvious? What does that have to do with anything, though?"

"It's not that obvious. You sorta look like a cross between an edgy Ronald McDonald and a Spanish pirate. Your decision-making skills."

He looks dumbfounded at this and crosses his arms across his chest. They continue to go back and forth for a good minute, and not just I, but Hailey as well began to check out of the conversation. As normal with me my gaze is downcast and I'm drifting off into space. Thinking back to my encounter earlier with that River woman.

My thoughts are interrupted by my name being called and a push of my arm.

I look up and I see Hailey looking up at me with her head tilted to the side. Her eyebrows are furrowed and she seems not exactly worried like I would have expected, but puzzled.

"It must've been a trick of the light," she suddenly said while analyzing my eyes.

"What do you mean?" I asked

"Just…I thought your eyes were green or something. But that's silly of course." She smiles innocently while the other two continued their bickering. "Anyway, there's something I wanted to ask you…"

I measure her, eager to hear what she had to say. But my mind was louder than ever now. Did she just say she thought my eyes were green just now? That can't be right. But Carson said it before, River said so too. Why is everyone seeing it but me?

I watch Hailey as it seems she can pick up on whenever my thoughts are running wild. She reached out and gripped my wrist gently and tilted her head the other way.

My heart skips.

"You have to stop letting your mind engulf you like that," she says instead of asking any question. She lets my wrist go and it drops to my side. "That wasn't what I was going to say, but you make it too obvious when you do that."

My hand moves to press under my nose as if I were going to sneeze, but really, I was moving to hide the pathetic look that I knew I would have. And to hopefully push the heat in my face away.

"Well, what were you gonna say besides that?" I say muffled against my hand.

She laughs a little at me and crosses her arms.

"It's not that important now. I don't want to add anything else to that cluttered head of yours until you've filed some of it away. Besides. You should be having fun; it looks like you've only been existing next to people that only bicker all night so far." She turns her head to the left of her where Carson and Julia were still toe to toe. They were much more animated now. I was sure with the way Carson's arms were swinging in the air the contents of the two cups he had in his clutches were completely empty now. And none of it actually made it to his mouth. They were now passionately shouting something about popular horror movies and what monster/killer/creature thing is more important to the Halloween industry. ...Or something like that.

"That's all I have to my name, I think. The skill to exist."

"Nonsense, skeleton man!" she laughs. "You just might have the skill of fashion. Here." She pulls something from her jacket pocket, reaches way up for my head and I bend down a little bit for her. I feel her parting my hair at the top and tying them up with rubber bands. "There. This'll pull the whole look together."

I squint at her and stand up straight. I feel the two stalks on top of my head that she has fashioned and then I place my hands on my waist.

"I don't know of any skeletons with antenna," I tell her.

"Not human skeletons, obviously. But alien ones!" She's laughing again and I shake my head at her.

"I see, you've upgraded my costume to alien skeleton man." I pretend to pull a space gun from behind me, miming it with my fingers. "I do not come in peace!" I say in an alien voice.

She's pulled me out of my shell and we're laughing and playing until…

"*Hailey!*"

We both whip around to see Eric stalking over, looking exasperated and almost irate.

"Uh oh…" she grumbles and holds her hands behind her back sheepishly.

"I looked everywhere for your toy but I didn't see a single thing. What are you still doing over here with *him*?" He glares at me and I shove my hands deep into my pockets. Even though the heavy feeling I had been having the entire time I was there was just starting to lift up off of me, it was coming straight back down again.

"I don't know if you've noticed Julia currently in a heated debate right now. So, who else am I supposed to talk to while I wait for you?" Hailey replies as she too shoves fists into her jacket pockets.

Eric scoffs and stands across from the two of us.

"As much of a social butterfly you are, you could have chosen anyone else if you wanted to."

"Eric, don't start," Hailey sighs, "you act like he's not standing *right* here."

He gawks when he realized on both of her wrists were the web-shooters she claimed to have lost.

"So, you had it the whole time? You thought you should send me on a wild goose chase so you could spend time alone with him, right?" His hands ball into fists as he lets unnecessary jealousy churn into rage.

"It wasn't really that wild," Hailey responds, "though you were gone for an awful long time just to check by the dance floor."

"It *is* my party, Hailey, I was obviously stopped by other people!"

I feel my face heat while I listen to them. There's an incredibly annoying buzzing sound in my ear, similar to what I heard and felt earlier at the library. It was giving me a headache just in between my brows… Unless it was one of *those* headaches in which wouldn't be very ideal.

"Shut up, Hailey, I'm not gonna listen to that! I'm so sick of seeing you around this joke, maybe I should mess up his face so you'd lose interest in it!"

"Stop it, Eric!" she shouts in protest while he moves forward in my direction.

I take a step forward and gently pushed Hailey aside. She looked up at me confused but her face was also riddled with exasperation. Carson cocked his head to the side while he rushed over to wrestle with Eric to keep his arms down, while his non-existent temper flew out of control. "A-are we 'bout to do this?" Carson asked with a playful grin spreading across his face. "I didn't know you had it in you!"

People start to gather, seeing the commotion and spotting that the people getting in to it where two dorks and the host of the party himself. Eric rips out of Carson's grasp but he doesn't make a move to attack me. Instead, he adjusts the varsity jacket he wore over a blue Michael Myers jumpsuit.

"You've got a lot of nerve," he huffs, dusting himself off and then cracking the knuckles of his fists.

"Me?" My brow lifts and I almost laugh. "From minding my own business? I think you got a serious problem."

"I have a problem, and it's you!"

There's a ringing in my ear piercing through the buzz that was already there. I wince and shake my head a little, tuning out of the situation for a moment once more.

Ethan.

At first, I thought someone was calling me. Hailey? Or Carson?

Ethan, be careful, Ethan.

My brow furrows at the whispers I suddenly hear and I begin to feel a little light-headed.

They're coming, Ethan!

I flinch, noticeably so, and people on the outside might have thought it was a reaction from Eric who was still fussing about how big of a nuisance I am to him. He moved closer with every word, and eventually he was toe to toe to me, screaming in my face and others were egging him on to fight me for real. But I couldn't focus on him. The world was fading in and out and I felt as though I was leaving my own body.

"What's the problem, Ethan! You can't handle what's coming to you?! That innocent act you keep up pisses me off! Why don't you drop it and show everyone you're just like everybody else!"

He pushes me in the chest with all of his strength and I go flying backward having been caught off guard. Once I hit the ground everything in my vision shifts uncomfortably and goes gray and fuzzy. I feel nauseous almost immediately, struggling to hold in a retch. If I were going to do something I would have, but the timing of my "episodes" really sucked, and I felt unable to control myself enough to fight back.

"Leave him alone, Eric!" I hear Ruha's voice muffled through my ears as if I were under water. "Ethan's never done anything to anybody! You're the only one being a huge jerk right now!"

Eric shouts something back to her but I don't hear it. As I stare at my own feet, hoping to get my composure back, there is the sound of police sirens blaring from afar and whoever was DJ-ing cut the music almost immediately.

"SCATTER!" someone screamed, and all at once, kids were making a beeline in every which direction to avoid getting caught by the police officers crashing the party…that already crashed when Eric lost whatever braincell he had left.

"Ethan, get up! We gotta go, man!" Carson was shouting now, suddenly sobered up and yanking at my arm to pull me up.

"Is he gonna be okay?!" I look up and I see Hailey being jostled around by people running past her; Julia ran to her side and gripped her around her arm before stopping to watch me gain my composure. With another tug, I was up on my feet. I shake my head once more and my vision cleared and I didn't feel like I would spew chunks everywhere. But I still felt incredibly hot, and that buzzing just wouldn't let up. "Ethan…I'm so sorry about—"

I cut her off with my hand.

"I'm okay," I say to her. "Just get out of here." I felt in my stomach that I was a little upset with her. Not because of what Eric chose to do on his own, but just the fact that she chose to stay with such a…*gae-saekki*. Or perhaps it wasn't quite her choice and it wasn't right to assume like that. But the bottom line was I was sick of watching her be with him. It was too obvious that she was miserable whenever he came around. And maybe he wouldn't be so outwardly idiotic if he didn't have Hailey as an excuse to be so. "Just go!" I raise my voice at her this time, watching as she just stood there staring at me with tears in her dark eyes. Julia measured me and her before tugging at her arm to leave.

"Oof…" Carson muttered beside me, watching Hailey and Julia run off, Hailey continuously looking over her shoulder at me before disappearing behind a crowd. "That sucked. Are you okay?" He looks at me now, checking to see if I was hurt anywhere.

"I'm fine, just a headache," I say. "Let's go before we get caught and your mother rip both our heads off."

"Right."

Carson and I move to run the other direction, into the many trees outside of the clearing the party was held in. It was rather dark without the fairy lights used for the party. We could hear radios in the distance of police officers who were catching some kids, but most who fled fast enough got away in time. But Carson and I continued, catching up with some others who were running in the same direction to where the exit of the forest was.

Be careful.

Something whispered to me. A voice sharp and urgent. It sounded familiar…

Something black, darker than any shadow, rushed overhead. Carson shrieks and reels backward. It crosses again, swift and nimble. And like a bolder it tumbles down the length of a tree and crashes to the ground below. Carson had tripped after his initial shock. I reached down to help him up but wince at a piercing sound it seemed only I could hear. The black mass seemed to have doubled, no tripled and suddenly it was only Carson and I alone in those woods. I pull at his arm, and he moves to stand but never makes it to his feet as he starts kicking at something, scurrying backward in response to something I hadn't quite captured yet.

"What's wrong?!" I ask him, tripping over myself while still trying to hold onto him and hoist him up.

He's making sounds that I guess were supposed to be words, and points over at something in the distance. It's quiet…and those masses from before are nowhere to be found. I turn my head this way and that but I didn't see whatever Carson did. And after a while, it seemed whatever it was had gone because Carson had calmed down and pushed himself up to his feet.

Carson dusts himself off and looks up at me sheepishly.

"If I *ever* take random deserts from strangers at a party again, open hand slap me," he said. "I'm still trippin' or something because I could've sworn I saw—"

He cuts off at the sight of something whipping by again. This time it's directly in front of us and the three I saw before turned into four, and then five. All five masses hit the ground just yards away and billow out like smoke until it forms the silhouette of a person. Five persons.

Both of us are staring, more so because we weren't sure exactly what we just saw, but for me I am squinting to make out the person in front of us. Their hands were behind their back and they slowly began to walk forward. As the black shadow casted over them began to dissipate the easier it was to see the person who was closer to us than the rest. I watch their feet, and I see that they are wearing some sort of brown dress shoe. Lilac colored slacks, and a baby blue dress shirt with the sleeves rolled up over the elbows. I trace the person up to see their face, that of which I could finally see clearly. It was a man grinning almost wickedly. His salt and pepper hair was raked backward and his eyes…

His eyes were unnaturally golden and they pierced directly into mine.

Carson and I took steps back as the strange man stepped forward. The others behind him sneering, chittering and growling. All of them ugly and threatening.

"So, the rumors are true!" the man suddenly bellows, throwing his arms up and laughing jovially. But nothing about him seemed inviting. He looked demented, like one too many screws were knocked loose. "Of course, we all had our suspicions that you were still alive. But I wanted to come see for myself just how alive you are."

"Who are you?" I calculate the odds of Carson and I making it past whoever this guy was, but it seemed our chances were quite slim and that we were better off stalling somehow. My mind drifts back to what River and Gramma told me… *"there are certain individuals who are after you."*

"Me? I'm someone who knows you," the man laughs. "Isn't that something you'd like to hear? I could tell you about anything you want, Ethan; I know you must be curious."

I watch him, unsure what to make of any of it. I turn my head to look at Carson who was shaking his head vigorously at me. I knew he was right and that I definitely shouldn't trust this guy, but finding out what he knows seemed all the more tempting.

"Like what…?" I ask. "What could you possibly know about me? I've never seen you a day in my life."

"Sure, you haven't. But isn't that all the more fun?" He grins, mischief twinkling in his abnormal eyes. "You're just like her, old Cathy. But of course, you'd have to be since she raised you. Took you off to this drab place, fed you *lies* and brought you up believing *garbage*."

"W-what?" My brow knits together in disbelief. How could he say any of that, I've been in Whitechapel my entire life; so, what would he know?

"W-w-what?" The man tilts his head, taunting and mimicking my stutter. He grins again, the smile stretching from ear to ear and then he crosses his long arms across his chest. "How long are you going to play so impossibly dumb, kid? You don't belong here, mingling with nohabs." He gestures in Carson's direction who looked immediately offended as if he knew exactly what that meant. "If you're interested in hearing the truth, just say the word. You can come with me and I can show you. BUT…" he waves his arms in the air before pointing a finger in my direction, "you'll have to give me something in return. What d'you say?"

I frown at him. A bargain? What kind of game did he think this was? He couldn't even tell me his name but he wants me to do him a favor in return for telling me whatever truth I was missing? Well…that was rather tempting as well…

"How do I know I can trust you? You come out of nowhere in the middle of the night with goons behind you…what does that make you look like?"

"Yeah!" Carson chimes in. "You look like a real freak if ya ask me!"

"*Nobody* asked you!" the man snaps at the blonde, eyes suddenly blazing as if they were made of real fire. Carson flinches backward, cowering slightly behind me. "Ethan, no one will tell you the truth like I will. People want to protect you, shield you from reality. Eventually they won't be able to shield you anymore, and you'll face a rude awakening. I can help you; I just need your help in return. No strings attached. We're both looking for something, so let's help each other. You must know by now that there are people who want to get their hands on you. I'm not one of those people." He's taking steps toward me again and I take more backward. "You'd be lucky to have me by your side. All you have to do is—"

"JULIAN!"

A female voice cuts him off, and seemingly out of nowhere a figure is falling from the sky and landing directly in front of Carson and I, facing the strange man who seemed to be called Julian.

"You know you shouldn't be here; I could turn you in and you'd be severely punished!"

Carson and I exchange looks after watching the person in front of us, wrapped in a woven grey cloak, hood pulled up over the head, tell off the man three times their size. It was the first time we saw him frowning save for snapping at Carson earlier, and he looked all the more menacing. But he also seemed as though who ever this person was could actually have some influence over him.

"And what about you," his eyes narrow, "certainly our little princess would face severities from simply leaving Lamia grounds."

"That's something I can deal with. You on the other hand…have no more chances. I would leave now and speak of this to *no one* unless you're looking for Lamia to have real reason to seize you and your undeserving freedom."

The more I listened to this person talk the more I felt heavy in the chest. The sound of their voice made my brain ache and wrack with all kinds of confusing signals. The familiarity of it was excruciating, but having no face to connect it to was complete torture.

But it wasn't until I caught a whiff of a scent that had been bugging me that entire week.

Vanilla and cinnamon.

My eyes widen and I'm suddenly having visions of running through fields, chasing after a small, coily-haired girl, and, strangely, the taste of roses and goguma (sweet potato) flooding my mouth.

I stare into the back of the hooded persons head, and as their scent floods my nostrils, I'm reminded of that evening at Bobby's with the strange girl I had never seen before triggering one of the worst migraines I'd ever had.

"Let's go, boys!" the sound of that Julian person's voice startled me out of my train of thought. I look past the figure in front of us to the man in colorful clothes and unnatural eyes. He's smiling again, that same wicked smile from before as he turns and rallies his goons to depart in the opposite direction. "Think over what I said, kid," he calls to me, "if you want to find me just remember the Grey Meadow. Trust me, I know *everything* about *everyone*." And with those final words he completely disappears behind a tree in the distance, as if he were never there to begin with.

"I know you," I speak up after the silence settles. "I mean…I know you but—I just…" My shoulders drop feeling defeated. "Could you just be plain, no suspenseful, dramatic theatrics and tell me… I mean, *remind* me who you are?"

The person seems rigid as they continued to stand there, back to Carson and me. The energy around them felt intense in a way I can't quite describe.

But not just that, there was a sense of hesitation and uncertainty coming from them. Slowly I watch their hands move up, grasp their hood, and pull it down off of their head to reveal a tangle of black coils tied loosely in a black scrunchy, creating the biggest, curliest knot I'd ever seen. Their hands drop to their sides and they spin slowly on their heels to finally face us.

One pang.

Two pangs.

My head is aching again and I was afraid something like what happened at Bobby's might happen again. Through my squinted eyes I look over the girl's delicate face. Her cheeks were full and round giving her a cute youthful charm. Her nose was flat and small, and her cheek bones were high and pronounced. Her lips were full, tinted with browns and pinks. Her skin was a flawless deep chocolate color; and her eyes were round, innocent and … unnaturally grey with hints of lavender swirling around in them.

She looked almost saddened as her eyes met mine, and a sense of shame and guilt washed over my entire being. I felt as though I did something terrible to her, as if I'd broken her trust, or let her down somehow. And honestly, I felt more upset at myself, just as much as, or even more than how I felt meeting River. My mouth goes dry, and I feel a terrible churning in my stomach. The pounding in my head was trying to best me, but I wouldn't let it this time as I had to remember who this girl was completely. Another flash of light flickers before my eyes, and I see children's dress shoes, billowing white lace, and an old dark wooden floor. There are children dancing but the image is skewed and chopped up. The longer I stare at her, the more her face seemed to morph and fade into something more familiar to me. A younger version of her.

"I wasn't sure what I would do when this moment finally comes," she admits, breaking the silence between us. She flashes a smile that looked more painful than comforting. I notice the tears welling in her eyes and it was just like meeting River all over again. I was sure now that when I finally met my aunt and my uncle it would also go just like this.

I wince at a pounding in my head.

"Are you Rose?" I ask her. I watch her eyes widen a little, surprised that I would know her name. But it probably wasn't exactly how she thought it was.

Perhaps she believed I could recognize her completely and could name her myself. But in actuality, I was only remembering what Gramma told me.

"Y-yes," she stammers, "Ethan, you have no idea how long it's been."

"I think I have some idea," I mutter, remembering the fact this seemed to have all started from eight years old.

A tear slips down her cheek and she bitterly wipes it away, then readjusts her cloak over her shoulders.

"I could hug you," she sniffs, "and all the things I must tell you—"

"What things?!" I interrupt her, by mistake of course, coming across a little too strong. But to be told *anything*, I was desperate for it. And obviously this girl with her funky eyes and all knew everything. She seemed to be the same age as I was. She knew me, so she must have known me while we were young. But shouldn't that be clear by now? I was slowly piecing together the fact that this person—this girl is the same little girl that comes out in my dreams the most. It's her voice that I hear calling my name through those fields, and it's her that I see running away in the distance. This I know now, but I still don't understand the dream itself at all. "Sorry," I say, "I mean, I'd like to hear whatever it is you have to tell me."

She shakes her head, wiping away another tear that had escaped and then straightens up, putting on a more solid expression.

"You won't like to hear me say 'not now'."

"You're right," I grumble.

"You won't like it, but you have to endure for just a little longer. I don't have enough time now, but I want you to come with me soon."

"Come with you where?"

"Back home, of course." She's smiling faintly now and I notice there was something a little unusual about her teeth as they were very sharp. Although it piqued my interest, the way she wraps her arms around herself drew in my attention more as I could sense her trying to guard herself. "Where you belong. If you would just go back there, perhaps your memory can heal much faster."

"Wait we're going somewhere?!"

We're both startled by Carson's booming voice. Neither of us had realized he had stepped away. He was walking up from behind, shoving his cracked phone into his back pocket as he joined us again.

"Had a call from Mom; let's just say I'm on strike two point eight," he told me after reading my puzzled expression, "but anyway, who are you exactly, pretty lady who made scary guy go away?"

Rose eyes Carson cautiously, her nose wrinkling just slightly.

"You may call me Rose," she answered. "I am a very dear friend of Ethan's."

Carson just about squawked from stifling a scoff.

"I'm sorry," he began slowly, "but I do believe that is who *I* am. Ethan's 'dearest' friend."

I measure Rose's reaction and she seemed to also be mulling over her next words carefully. She swallowed dryly and gave the end of her cape an idle tug.

"Yes…" she said with an unsure nod, "it does appear to be true. However, I am not specifically talking about in this instance. I meant quite far in the past. But enough of that now; I am Rose, and I will be your friend from now on." She nods once more as if she were assuring herself more than Carson. She then turns her gaze toward me and lets out a heavy breath. "Anyway, Ethan, jumpstarting your memory is what's most important now. There's little time left to wait on it. And…speaking of time," she looks down at her arm and uncovers her wrist from her sleeve where I spot a very similar watch to what River had earlier with the many needles spinning wildly across unknown symbols, "I haven't got any left…" she grumbled mostly to herself. "There's no time," she says again a lot firmer. "You will come back home with me tomorrow." She's walking now and Carson and I turn as she passed the both of us.

"Wait," I call, "are you taking me to Obscura?" River said before that she couldn't take me there herself, but someone else would. I watch her turn to catch my gaze again and a shadow of a smile appears on her face.

"Yes," she answered simply. "That is your home. It's *our* home." Her foggy eyes glisten in what was now only the moon lighting our surroundings. They were captivating, and so painfully familiar that I didn't want to look away. Actually, I didn't want her to go at all. But her back was to me again and she was moving further away. That scent moving with her. "Meet me here in this spot no later than three pm. You *must* not be late, Ethan, I mean it. Otherwise, I can't take you." She turns again as she stood yards away now, spinning sharply on her heels. "I mean it. There's only a short window and we simply can't miss it."

"Okay but...what do I say to my family if I go with you? I can't just leave," I say, thinking about what terrible emotional explosion Gramma could have next.

"Yes, you can," Rose says firmly. Her words full of blatant disdain. "You can and you will." She looks hurt all of a sudden and I felt like I had wounded her somehow. Guilt washes over me faster than I could even understand why. Which I didn't by the way. "You will tell Madam Grey...that time has run out. And that she cannot shield you any longer. Th-that...you deserve to know the truth, and the only way you can do that is to...is to..." Her eyes meet the ground and she seems heart broken. I only wished I could know why and somehow make it better for her. Although I've never met her before—I mean, to my knowledge in this moment, seeing her like this made everything ache inside. As if I had watched her fall to her lowest point and she was struggling to get back up again. Rose drew in a sharp breath and throws on a brave face now as if I hadn't seen what she looked like just seconds before. "The only way you can do that is to come back home. And see your family...and friends."

Well, she wasn't wrong. That made sense to me for what I could make of it anyway. I didn't know what I would be getting myself into in the slightest bit, but from what I could tell, I had to do this eventually. And now there seems to be "little time"... for whatever it may be.

"Okay," I agree and this makes her face soften a bit, her shoulders relaxing. "I'll go with you."

"Good. Because really you have no choice. But you might as well find out this way." She's leaning on a tree now, kicking around its roots as if she were looking for something. "I must leave you now. We'll meet again tomorrow." She looks up for a second but her eyes are now on Carson who looked more perplexed than when we were at the library. "What are you wearing by the way?" she asks him. His mouth falls open, and any trace of perplexity is immediately erased and instead replaced by all the offence in the world.

"I'm a vampire!" he retorts, gesturing at his own outfit as if it really was that obvious.

"Oh..." I watch her eyes widen with pure shock, then she's hiding a laugh. "If you say so. And..." she's pushing at the trunk of the tree but takes a moment to gesture at me, "nice hair. Very modern."

I think she was teasing, and I myself had forgotten about the stalks of hair that Hailey had put on my head. I turn to look at Carson who was fuming and turning away to leave, and when I turn my head back, Rose was gone. Question marks are flying out of my skull but I wasn't sure if I should question it anymore. It's the third time today I have seen this happen. And if I think about it too hard, all the times Gramma suddenly disappears becomes extremely suspect to me.

"Ethan!" Carson snaps at me as he's storming away. "That two point eight is long gone!"

Right. Mrs. Foxx definitely will have our heads now.

5

Origins

"How could she say things like that? Like…I'm your best friend! Since when? Since forever!" Carson is fussing through the phone and I barely have it against my ear as his voice was loud enough that even speaker wasn't necessary. "I'm just not understanding this 'past' thing. She's not the first one to say it, you know that. And you and I both know I am *ass* at math, but even I can see a conflict between this 'home' thing and your life here right now."

He had a point. Even though I can't quite pin point when exactly Carson and I first met, according to him we were both quite young. Babies even. And the last time I checked; I've been in Whitechapel my entire life. I was born here, raised here, lived here with Gramma for almost eighteen years now. So, he was right, things weren't quite adding up. At all. When exactly did this *past* happen?

"I dunno," I mutter into the phone. I was in the living room, leaning against the front window and idly opening and closing the blinds. I felt a little numb to everything at this point, aside from worrying about how I'm going to tell Gramma that I'm going to run off with some stranger to some mysterious unknown place later today. I didn't have to keep saying that things didn't make sense and that I basically understood nothing about this *unusual* situation, so I felt I would just have to wait and see what happens after today. Perhaps everything could change. I wasn't sure if I was really going to meet long lost relatives of mine, and I wasn't sure if my memory was as jacked up as everyone kept saying (though it did seriously seem like it). I've just decided that I have to wait. I will have answers after today.

"What d'you mean you don't know?" Carson gripes. "You have to know *something*. Are you really gonna go with that Rose girl today?"

"Yeap." My eyes fix on the string that connects the blinds together and I twist the stick thing that controls them. I watch them move up, and then down, and then up again.

"…Can I get more than one-word answers? Maybe I should come with you. Cuz like if she turns out to be a loon, you shouldn't be stuck with her alone. …Except I've never seen such a pretty loon before…"

I roll my eyes.

"You think everyone is pretty," I mutter. It was true, but Rose really was pretty.

"That's not true, and you know it! Anyway, lemme come with you."

"Whatever, Carson, do what you want but, I thought you got grounded last night."

"No. After you left the moms yelled at me for about five minutes and then told me I didn't have car privileges for a week. She was also gonna make me spend the weekend inside, but then I told her how I thought she was the most wonderful mother of all. Because I'm that good at smooth talkin'. So that's the only punishment. But it's cool, I can use my legs."

Gramma's gray Focus was pulling into the driveway. The time. What time was it? My neck nearly snapped as I whipped my head around to the little clock on the mantle. It was already noon which meant I only had three hours before I had to be there in that spot Rose told me to meet her. Which meant there was even less time to tell Gramma I was leaving. But obviously it wouldn't be for that long. I'll just go and see what this Obscura is all about, and come back. No big deal.

"Helloooo?" Carson must have said something else, but I didn't hear it at all this time.

"I'll call you back," I said as I was already hanging up the phone. I shove the device into my pocket and I dash out of the living room and up the stairs. I needed more time. Aside from having to make up some lame excuse about why I came home so late last night, I had been avoiding my grandmother since then. That was because the more I kept thinking about her and what she could know, and having counted the amount of people that has said she is purposely keeping information from me (which is already four by the way), I didn't think I could face her without becoming angry. I think there is nothing I hate more than being lied to.

I slip into my room and shut the door. Just as I had, I heard the front door being keyed open. Gramma was coming from church, and usually when she came home from there, she would go to wash her feet then go to the kitchen to cook Sujebi which was her favorite thing to eat on Sundays. She would want me to come eat it with her. I was thinking I should tell her I was leaving then. It would be hard on both of us, but the more I thought about it, lying to her would not better our relationship, and wouldn't bring us any closer to her opening up honestly to me. I would eat and go.

I pull out my phone again and I send Carson a text.

Me: 2:30 be at the forest.
Me: don't be late if you're srsly coming

In the meantime, while I wait for Gramma to go through her motions I go to my closet and pull out a medium sized cross body bag. I didn't know how long it would take to get to this Obscura place, so at least I could bring a few things just in case. I shove extra clothes, my phone cord, portable charger, Airpods, wallet, and a few other things inside. I go to grab my portable toothbrush case from a different bag. Vitamins because…who doesn't carry vitamins in their bag? Lip balm 'cause I can't be crusty, and then of course *hyangsoo* (perfume)…because, I smell good for a reason, just sayin'.

This has been What's in My Bag with Ethan Jae Moon.

I stand up after adjusting my things and my eyes land on my uncle's journal still atop my desk. I didn't need to think hard to decide whether or not to take it. If I were meeting him today, perhaps he'd like it back. I cross the room and reach out to grab it. But the moment my fingers touch the cover I am hit by the worst sort of vertigo, that sent me lurching forward. My vision went blurry and grey, and then I wasn't seeing at all.

I felt like I was outside of my body and everything felt both cold and warm. I blink my eyes a few times and once I finally open them all the way again, I realize I am standing in a bedroom. Except…it wasn't *my* bedroom. I twist around, confused and slightly panicked as the room was unfamiliar and I couldn't put together how exactly I was in the comfort of my own room one second and somewhere else the next. I look down at myself, still unable to feel my own body. I turn my hands over and notice the bag I was holding was nowhere to be found. And for some reason my skin was a ghostly faded shade of green. I touch my face but realize I can't feel it at all.

"What the actual fu—" My astonishment is cut off by a sudden voice that had me jumping to the moon. I spin around, expecting to be caught trespassing by someone (even though I didn't know how I got there in the first place), but no one was standing behind me.

Instead, it was much more curious.

I face a single bed and two individuals were sitting together on the edge. They were both facing me but it seemed like they hadn't noticed me yet somehow.

"*I know how you feel,*" one said to the other, "*but even if you feel like you've let others down, you can't let it take over you.*"

"…Excuse me?" I speak up, unsure if I should have at all. But I was obviously intruding on something personal. "I'm sorry, I don't know how I got here but…can you just help me get back?" I step forward, but the more I stare at the two, the more an unsettling feeling builds in my belly. "Excuse me?" I say again a little quieter.

They don't hear me. They don't see me either, even while I'm standing directly in front of them. I take a more focused look around the room and notice how unusual it looked. It was pretty normal at first glance like any other bedroom, but when looking at the things inside specifically it wasn't quite right. On the wall was a clock that resembled the watches I saw on River and Rose's wrists. I look around the ceiling and the floor and there were plants everywhere. Hanging plants, drying flowers, and potted ones of all shapes and sizes lining the walls. There was a small case with a few strange vials and jars on them, but I couldn't quite tell their contents. There were melted white candles on the window sill and a few on top of a tall dark wood dresser. There was a fragrant scent that I hadn't noticed before that smelled of lemon balm and chamomile. It was actually rather relaxing. I had almost forgotten I was somehow transported to another place less I had fainted and was having the most terrifyingly realistic lucid dream of all. I'd almost forgotten…until voices reminded me of the two people in the room with me.

"*Aigo! Cheer up, or else I'll have to take drastic measures.*"

I notice a crack of a smile on the boy's face. Yes, I realize it's a small boy sitting there staring glumly at his own hands. And a woman with short dark hair cut under her ear with frizzy permed bangs sat beside him with her arm wrapped around his shoulders. I stare for a long time, and when I hear his voice, my heart sinks to the floor with my jaw following close behind it.

"*I want to cheer up,*" he says, "*but I keep wondering if I'm bad…*"

"*Bad? Oh no, no, no, you are far from it. Exactly the opposite.*"

He lifts his face to look at the woman and there are tears in his eyes.

There are tears in *my* eyes.

His face. His voice. I was somehow looking at myself but definitely about a decade younger.

I look down at my own hands again and observe the strange ghostly hue, then I look back up at the scene in front of me. This is…a memory.

"*Listen, Joka, you have so much good in you. Anyone who knows you knows that. You're sooo smart and intuitive for your age, Ethan. And you already study so hard. You aren't bad. You are full to the brim with good, and don't you doubt it for a second. Some days can be very hard, and sometimes things just don't turn out the way we want it to. Sometimes we make mistakes and sometimes we hurt others unintentionally. But what makes a person good is the way that they react to that mistake or wrong-doing. Ethan, I think you've done that a hundred times over already and you're still pained by what happened.*"

The younger version of me looks to be carefully processing and digesting the woman's words. The woman who I now understand must be Nari, my long-lost aunt. A deep frown crosses my face and I feel emotionally overwhelmed by all the praises given to me, except I don't know what prompted the conversation in the first place. I take a few steps closer to the two who clearly weren't aware at all of my presence. I could reach out and touch them if I wanted. Here is my aunt in front of me, so life like and so real. I wished she was. She was pretty. Her eyes were big and round except, they weren't a normal color, instead they were a peculiar shade of yellow. You wouldn't have noticed at first glance because her messy curly permed bangs stretched passed the bridge of her slim delicate nose. Her demeanor was very strong like she had a tough personality, but she was also clearly very caring. At least when it came to me anyway.

"*Ethan?*" she calls my name suddenly and I flinch, feeling as if she were talking directly to me. Well technically she was, but not *me*, me. But past me. I watch little Ethan raise his head curiously, his eyes huge, round, and innocent. His thick black hair looked fluffy and soft; bangs cut shorter than mine are now above the eyebrows in the same mushroom shape. "*Let's try something,*" Nari says. "*I'll say a name and you tell me the first things that come to mind the second I say it. You can't think longer than a second, okay?*"

"*Okay,*" little Ethan answers with a nod.

"*Uncle Namu?*"

"*Strong silent type,*" I answered immediately with a quite giggle. Nari laughs at this as it must have been an inside joke of some kind.

"*I won't tell him you think that way about him too,*" she laughed. "*Okay, how about Gramma?*"

My eyes widen a little, curious to hear my younger self's perspective of Gramma. If I were to answer now, I'd say something like: secretive rock.

"*Warm and sweet! Like goguma with butter.*" I watch my younger self forget whatever was eating at him earlier. I watch his face brighten and his smile grow. I felt a little jealous as I wanted to feel the same way. I wanted to know what he knew and to recall Gramma being anything less than rigid and strict.

"*She is like that isn't she, Gramma's always looking out for us.*"

"*Yeah,*" I'm nodding energetically and I'm leaning over into my aunt, "*especially when she makes yummy foods and desserts. I want to hear her tell more stories about Grandpa. That's always really fun.*"

"*Yeah, he was a great old goof, wasn't he? I hope there can be more books written about the adventures he went on.*"

I'm looking down. The real me. I didn't think very much about who my grandfather was and what he was like. There were times that I could remember where I asked Gramma about him, but she always reacted as if I had shot her through the heart, like the very memory of him was too painful to bare. So, I just stopped asking all together; lost interested and never thought about him. But it's strange to hear now that there was a time that Gramma told stories about him with no problems at all. Again, I feel jealous of my younger self having the luxury of knowing all these things and having these positive experiences.

"*Me too,*" little Ethan responds while embracing Nari in a warm hug.

"*Now how about me?*" The woman smiles down at the boy and smooths his bangs backward to expose his forehead. He smiles brightly in response and he reaches up to poke the tip of her nose.

"*You're always so cool, Auntie. And I think you're brave, like a warrior.*"

"*Really?*"

"*Yes! You promised you would teach me how to use knives like you. When will you?*"

Nari's face is full of endearment as she combs her fingers through the boy's hair. He ends up laying in her lap now, having twisted his small body in every direction that he was now sideways on the bed.

"*One day soon,*" she answers, "*when you're a little bigger.*" He pouts a little and Nari laughs. "*Okay, now how about Eomma?*"

My ears perk up and I anticipate any and every word that would come next. *Eomma*, my mother. Oh, how I wished to know her, or to at least remember her. I watch the pout and the glisten in my younger self's eyes lessen, and instead something more solemn appears in his expression. Was my mother already dead? I would've hated to hear it.

"*Eomma is…*" little Ethan began carefully, "*so bright. Like the sky on Samhain night.*" His gaze lowers and he's fiddling with his fingers much like I do now when I'm unsure if I should say anything else, fearing saying the wrong thing. "*I feel so sorry to her,*" he said suddenly and looked up at the woman who also seemed a little saddened by something. "*She's looked so sad ever since what I did. It's my fault she keeps being called to Lamia. It's all my fault…*" He sits up with a start and covers his face with his little hands.

Nari shifts a little and wraps both arms around him, resting her cheek on the top of his head. They sit in silence for all of a minute before the woman draws in a new breath.

"*You know,*" she began, "*even though I might be brave, your mother is so much braver than I think I ever could be. She loves you more than anyone, Ethan. That's why she's been working so hard the last few weeks. She's doing what she must to make sure you get a chance to prove how good you are. And no matter what happens in the end…*" her voice breaks a little and it seemed like little me didn't quite notice it, especially since he wasn't looking up at her. But from here opposite of her she seemed like she was using every fiber of her being to keep her composure, "*you deserve a fair life and to be able to be happy like every other kid your age.*" She pulls away and sits the boy up straight and finally he meets her eyes again. "*Don't forget that. Don't forget anything I've said here tonight. You are good, Ethan, and your mother will love you beyond her last days.*" She reached into her pocket and she pulls out a locket that I didn't recognize, but young Ethan seemed to have. She took his hand, opened it, and placed the locket into his palm. It was an iridescent color, made from some sort of crystal. I had no idea what was inside of it, but I was more curious to know what it was given to me for. "*She asked me to give this to you. To cheer you up.*"

"*But she never takes this off,*" little Ethan said quietly as he rolled the necklace around in his hand.

"*I know. I guess you can ask her the next time you see her.*"

Something about that sounded untrue and quite strained. And something told me that perhaps in this very moment, my mother was alive…but it was her last days. I wondered where the necklace could be now, because I had never seen it before until this moment.

I look back up at the two after mulling this over, but then I noticed that the image has frozen. The both of them have stilled as if paused like that of a movie or video. My head tilts to the side, and I'm unsure what to do now. I wave my hand around at them, but they don't move. I reach out to touch my younger self, but as my hand would have connected with a shoulder, it passes through and the image skews all together like a hologram. I brace as I stumbled forward, but when I catch my footing, I spin around to see the room but the surrounding area is morphing and blurring together. I didn't have time to react as I began to feel that terrible sense of vertigo like before, and then everything goes black once more.

. . .

"Jesus, Ethan, it's like I can't leave you alone anymore!"

I'm startled and I'm jumping to my feet after the sound of Gramma's voice pierced through my ear.

"What?! Where—I don't understand!" I look around the room frantically and realize I'm back in *my* bedroom. The one in little boring Whitechapel.

"You don't understand what? I came up here to get you for lunch but you're on the floor. How long you've been like this?"

I blink stupidly at her and then hold my head. I was struggling a little to get my bearings, and what I just saw that I deeply remember really struck me. I look suddenly down at my hands again and flip them this way and that. But they aren't faded or greenish anymore. They're normal and solid. I touch my face and realize I can feel it unlike before and I even look at Gramma skeptically and reach my finger out to touch her, just to check.

She slaps my hand a little, her lip turned up as she was confused by my strange behavior.

"What has gotten into you," she huffs. "Maybe next time I should take you with me to church."

"B-but," I stammer, "I was just—"

"Come on if you don't want to eat cold food." She cuts me off and turns to leave my room without a second glance, but I reluctantly follow after her, not sure if I should try to get her to understand or not.

Once we're in the kitchen she's transferring the pot of Sujebi onto a portable eye on the table. I shuffle my feet around the surface and I stand there, watching her grab a container of kimchi, and another of fish cake. She places them on the table along with two plates and silverware. She pauses after doing this, eyeing the table setting until her eyes trailed up to meet mine. I stare at her awkwardly, still shaken up by what I had seen, but equally put off by having to confront Gramma about everything. My eyes dart from hers to the nearest clock before returning to hers again.

1:30 pm. One hour left before I have to meet Carson at the forest.

"Why are you acting so strange?"

"Sorry."

Gramma sighs heavily as she too sits down. She murmured a quick prayer over her food before she picked up a ladle and spooned the hot soup into her bowl. I watch her, analyzing her blank expression, and her walled off body language. I was starting to feel the irritability returning, and I've noticed that it mostly occurred while being around her.

"Gramma," I call out abruptly.

She looks up, her dark eyes somehow full of fire. "Is there something you'd like to say?" I swallow thickly as I reach over to take the ladle.

"Well…kinda—I mean, yes. I just…"

Just let it out! was all I was screaming to myself from the inside. If I could just lay out all of my thoughts, stop bottling it all up like Hailey would point out, then maybe I could see things a little clearer. But Gramma just had a way about her that made it so difficult to say anything.

"My mother's locket," I start again, "you know the one, don't you, Gramma?"

I'm avoiding her eyes but I could feel the vibrations lower in the room, and tensions rising even more than normal.

"Now, what suddenly brought this about?" she asked slowly in a level tone. She didn't look at me, as she kept her gaze fixed on her beloved Sujebi. "It's a little random, isn't it?"

"Not exactly," I say. "Actually, I *know* that…it was given to me, wasn't it? But it seems to be misplaced. Where is it?"

She sets her spoon down and it hits the edge of her bowl with an echoing clink. She finally looks at me again and I know for certain I wasn't mistaken that her deep brown eyes had flashed a watery blue color.

"How do you know," she asks almost as tightly as her lips were being pulled. "You remember someone giving it to you?"

"Yes. Aunt Nari gave it to me and told me not to ask her why." I look down. "But I think I do."

Clearly it had been a parting gift. Something to remember her by, especially if it was something she always had on her from what I could gather. And if I thought about it, in any picture that I could readily remember of her (like the one on the mantle in the living room) she was in fact wearing the very same locket from my dream/memory/vision…thing. Perhaps she couldn't bring herself to give it to me herself and instead had my aunt do it. I frown lightly at this thought and push around the contents of my soup.

Silence falls between us once again, and it lasted much longer this time. It was as if Gramma was going back and forth between just telling me and just dropping it all together and shutting me down like always. But she surprises me this time.

"Namu has it," she replied just as plain and level as before. "You dropped it on your last day in Obscura, and he's been holding it for you ever since."

"And when exactly was my 'last day in Obscura'?"

She eyes me carefully.

"June 21st of 2009. The day your mother died."

It's my turn to set my spoon down. If I was even the slightest bit hungry, I sure wasn't anymore. I fold my hands in my lap as I think about what Carson had said again. The timeline just doesn't make sense.

"I was in Obscura the day my mother passed away, but I don't remember it at all. It doesn't make any sense."

"How far does your memory go back to, Ethan? Honestly."

I pause to think, and just like before, everything goes blank should I try to remember passed the day I'd been hospitalized when I was eight.

"When I was in the hospital before," I say, "but even so, I know for a fact that we've been here all this time. Together, just you and I. Except, River mentioned something about an injection—" I grimace at my own words and realize I may have said a little too much now. Gramma had no idea I had met that woman, and she certainly told me a lot. Not exactly *much* but a lot more compared to my grandmother. There was no telling how she'd react knowing I'd met such a woman, and I didn't plan on telling her this way. But there was no taking it back now. I clear my throat uncomfortably and stare into my bowl, waiting to hear the old woman lose her composure, but her voice never came. I raise my gaze cautiously to meet hers and she is boring into me with an expression I rarely ever saw—if not never. Her eyes were round, shocked, but also sad in a way. It seemed like she too must have lost her appetite as she no longer hovered over her bowl.

She sits back against her chair and that strange blue color crosses her pupils again. I wasn't sure what it was but it reminded me a lot of River and the way that her eyes were so pigmented and so blue like a clear deep ocean. Gramma is drawing in the slowest breath, and finally she speaks again but seems unsure of her own voice.

"S-so," she started. "You've met her, then."

"Yes."

"What did she tell you?"

I hesitate.

"She...told me that I needed to go home. Back to that Obscura place. And...and I've decided that's what I'm gonna do."

Her eyes widen as expected and I was half certain she would blow up at me and half guilty for saying anything like that at all.

"You have no memory because your memory was wiped, Ethan. Your memory had been wiped in order to *protect* you. If we hadn't you wouldn't have been able to live normally like you do. There are people who would rather you be erased from the picture. By means of...anything necessary." She looks at me now and she's becoming angry. I could see it in her eyes as I watch them closely. I watch as they gradually begin to shift in color, from brown to blue. It does not flash by, and again I am sure I am not mistaken. But instead of shifting back, they remain that color. "I shouldn't be saying any of this anyway. You're making a mistake, Ethan, and you'll find out the hard way if you keep digging your nose in places you don't belong!"

Her anger is rising, but this time I do not waver. I've come this far and I feel I am so close to figuring out what's going on. I can't let my grandmother's insecurities stop me.

"I think the secrecy has gone too far," I tell her first as I glance at the clock to check the time. "I met Rose last night. She will be taking me to Obscura later and I'm leaving in less than an hour." I watched her suck in a panicked breath but I stop her before she could interrupt. "Do *not* try to stop me, Gramma, I have to go and see it for myself. Since you like keeping secrets so much, I think I'll be taking it into my own hands now. I want to know what happed to my mother. I want to understand my dreams, and I want to know why I have a target on my back for some reason. Who is my father? Why am I 'special'? They're far too many unanswered questions and I could go on and on; I'm sure you can see that. I'll be eighteen in two days, so when will I stop being treated like a child by you?"

She blinks and closes her mouth. Whatever she was going to say she looked like she changed her mind. She shifts uncomfortably in her seat and then wipes her face free of any moisture.

"So, there's nothing I can say to change your mind?" she asks without looking at me.

"No," I answer firmly. Firm like Rose told me to be. I watch her sigh but my eyes couldn't leave hers. I still couldn't wrap my head around how they were one color one moment and a new one the next. I know I wasn't seeing things, but I also wondered if I should be all that surprised anymore. "What is with your eyes by the way?" I just blurt it out. It's not the first time I saw them change color but this has definitely been the longest they've been abnormal.

She scoffs all of a sudden as if I asked her something stupid. But she still wouldn't look at me.

"It runs in the family," she answered simply and didn't go on to explain. I figure I ought to leave it there and prepare to leave. I certainly ruined her lunch, which I felt bad about, but the conversation needed to be had. I push my chair back and stand up to leave.

"I'll text you or something when I'm on my way back," I say before leaving her there by herself in the kitchen.

. . .

"Bro, where are you?"

I'm idly kicking my foot against the tire of my mountain bike as I look around me desperately trying to spot my semi-unreliable friend. This is exactly why I gave him a thirty-minute window. It was already fifteen minutes passed our meeting time.

"I'm sorry!" Carson wheezes into the phone. "It's been a while since I rode my bike. I'm almost there!"

"Hurry up."

A brisk wind blows by, reminding me that it really was fall. I tucked my phone between my ear and shoulder and moved to zip up my heavy dark gray fleece.

"Do you see me? I can see you! Look at you, like a little old man." Carson is laughing and I look up to see him in the distance, peddling his old green bike that had been abandoned since he got his car two years ago.

"Sure. While you look like you're being introduced to cardio for the first time."

I shake my head, and as Carson was scoffing and prepared to tell me to shut up, I end the call and drop my phone into the bag across my chest.

With a few more pedals and heavy breathing, Carson is at my side, tripping over himself as he hopped off of his vehicle. Once his feet were firmly on the ground, he folded himself ninety degrees, hand clasped against his chest as he huffed and puffed to catch his breath. I stared at his pathetic form, half wishing he'd stop being so dramatic, and half wanting to push him off balance to laugh at him.

"I…got here…as fast as I could!" Carson gasps.

"Perhaps you should've left earlier. That would allow you to pedal at your own pace." I slap him on the back and then wheel my bike onto the entrance trail of the forest. I feel his eyes on me, probably giving me an annoyed look, before he began to follow after me.

"So how long do you think it takes to get to 'your home'? Where is it anyway?"

"No idea," I shrug, "but it must not take *that* long since it seems that River woman has been there and back in a short amount of time."

"Okay but where is it?" he asks again. "Like what is it called. Is it a city? A state? Are we going to like…Ohio? 'Cause that definitely doesn't take too long. I can get back to moms later tonight then."

I look over my shoulder at him. I was sort of thinking about how to answer. Yes, I knew the name of the place, but I had no idea whether or not it was some kind of city. And I might not be perfect at geography, but at least I know the surrounding states of Michigan and not one of them is called Obscura.

Carson stares at me, gesturing for me to hurry up and answer. "Well?" he says.

"Somewhere called Obscura," I say finally. "But I don't know where it is."

Carson tsks and shakes his head as he immediately moved to pull his phone back out of his pocket. He seemed to be searching it up online. Why hadn't I thought to do that?

We were coming up on the spot we agreed to meet Rose at. I didn't quite remember which tree it was, but my eyes had caught some markings at the base of a particular tree's trunk. I pushed my bike through the leaves and then let the kickstand down before going to get a better look.

There were scuff marks, like something made from a shoe. I remembered that Rose had been kicking at the tree yesterday, and this was probably why. I stare at it close, and in the pealing bark I see a carving of a rose. My eyebrow raises at this. When would she have time to do that? Or maybe she had already planned on having me meet her here and had done it before.

But the most important thing was, we made it to *rendezvous point* with five minutes left to spare.

"Dude," Carson's voice draws my attention away from the tree and back to him, "literally nothing comes up."

"What?" I watch his thumb scroll almost frantically and he's shaking his head.

"Look, there's nothing." He shows the screen to me and he was right. Nothing came up for a place called Obscura. It even tried showing different suggestions of words he meant to say. "Ethan, seriously, what if she's a loon!"

"Don't say that," I snap, "she wouldn't be, that doesn't make any sense. River said so, that that is the place that I'm from. Gramma said so too. And in my uncle's journal it even shows—"

"BOYS!"

Carson and I screech at an embarrassing pitch, flinching backwards as Rose seemed to have appeared from absolutely nowhere; jumping from behind the tree we stood beside.

"God! A warning would have been nice!" Carson fussed as he shoved his phone back into his pocket.

"Sorry, I didn't realize you could be so easily startled." Rose is smiling and I catch it again, something strange about the shape of her teeth. But before I could zero in on it, she's spinning around to completely face me and I notice the different mood she's in today. Yesterday she seemed like she could break down in a sob at any moment, and today she radiated with happiness—excitement even. She wore the same cloak and shoes from yesterday, but she didn't wear her hood up. Her hair was gathered behind her in that same sad, tortured scrunchy that could barely contain the wild black coils that sprung in every which direction. "So, is he meant to be coming with us?" she asks me. I look past her at Carson who seemed like he was ready to throw a fit or start arguing his case.

"Well…yes," I say. I looked her in the eyes, and as strange as they were, the color was simply hypnotizing. She looked as though she were going to protest, and tell me he wasn't supposed to, but I spoke up again before she had the chance. "I'm not going without him," I tell her firmly. "Either he comes with us, or I'm staying."

Her lips purse and I almost regret being defiant. She turns to look at him. Her eyes rake him up and down and then she pauses to think for a second. Carson slowly moves to cover himself with his arms and he frowns a bit.

"That felt gross, is that what it's like to be on the receiving end?"

"Maybe you should think about your pick-up strategies," I mumble to him.

"Fine," she responds finally. "But you should be aware that people like him are strictly forbidden in Obscura. You will need to prepare to blend in as to not raise any suspicion. At least you're dressed better today, uhm…Camer—"

"*Carson!*" he huffs.

"Right, Carson. I apologize." I think everyone is glad he wasn't wearing what he was yesterday. That Great Aunt Tessie nightmare eyesore. Today he just wore sweatpants, and a matching gray hoodie. "Of course what the both of you are wearing is considered unique, so we will have to address this later. Anyway, we'd better get going, we don't have much time left. Follow me." She turns and begins to lead us deeper into the woods, ways away from any marked trail.

"Exactly how are we gonna get there?" I ask her. "Carson looked it up a moment ago and nothing even came up as a result."

She scoffs.

"You're not going to find it online, silly. I thought you would at least know that much." She looks up at me where it seemed like she was expecting me to take it as a joke. But when she saw my not-so-jovial expression, her smile faded. "Madame Grey really doesn't tell you anything, does she?"

"Not a thing..."

Rose sighs and looks ahead of her again. Her happy demeanor diminishes a little.

"I'm sorry. I really didn't know it was to this extent. No one does, apart from Madam River and your physician Dr. Valhera."

"Huh? You know who my doctor is?"

"Of course I do," she laughs, "well I mean, I wouldn't *know* him on any normal circumstance. But since he *is* technically breaking Obscura law to be here with you, I am aware of who he is."

"You mean...Doc V is from Obscura too?"

"Yes. Of course, he is. You definitely wouldn't be able to meet a regular doctor without someone trying to dissect you. Dr. Valhera is one of the most respected and talented doctors of the Druid class in all of Greenwood. They wouldn't have just anyone taking care of you."

I'm speechless. I didn't know how to respond or what to even make of it. But it wasn't farfetched. He was the first one I heard telling my grandmother to start telling the truth. I don't think I could blame him for keeping secrets that wasn't up to him to tell.

"I'm sorry, I just heard the word 'druid' and I'm unclear if we've changed the conversation to a game of some kind," Carson speaks up from behind, fighting with his bike to pass through a particular branchy spot on the forest floor.

"A game? No, we aren't discussing any game," Rose said.

"But druid like, old bearded forest dudes, right? I don't think Ethan's doctor looks anything like that."

Rose presses her lips together as she pauses to think about her next words. There was an awkward moment of silence before it seemed like she gave up all together to try and explain to him. Instead, she points ahead at a little tiny broken-down gate in the distance. Or at least what's left of one.

"We're here," she said.

Both Carson and I crane our necks to see exactly where 'here' was. But it didn't look like anything. We were still in the middle of the woods, surrounded by nothing but trees. And finally, as Rose comes to a stop, we all look down at this abandoned piece of metal.

It was in fact a piece of a gate or fence. It was metal painted in black, slightly rusted from rain and snow. It was no higher than Rose's knees, looking as though it had been cut off at the top. We look at the girl and she's staring down at the poor little fence.

"Ethan…" Carson mutters toward me, "I told you; she could be a very pretty loon."

I punch him in the arm and he winces with an 'ouch'. Rose then spins around on her heels to look at the both of us.

"Thirty seconds," she said, "just in time. Carson, would you please close your eyes, for just a moment."

"Excuse me?!" he glances at me to see if I agree or not but I only shrug at him. "Why's it just me, what about Ethan?!"

"Since you are the only outsider, it's only right. I'm sorry." She sounded genuinely apologetic but Carson wasn't having it. It wasn't until I gave his arm another punch did he finally squeeze his eyes shut in a huff. Once he had, Rose flashed a little smile at me before turning back to the gate. She reaches into her cloak and this time she pulls out a silver key. At the tip of the handle was the letter "O" with flower vines wrapped around it. It was then did I realize that the gate had a little key hole, and that was where she put the key. She turned it three times, and with each turn there was a clicking noise, each louder than the last. After the third turn she pulled the key out, tucked it away and took a few steps back, pushing Carson and I backward with her.

"Can I look yet?" Carson grumbled impatiently.

"Not yet," Rose answered.

I watched with uncertainty. It seemed like nothing was happening. But just as I drew in a breath to ask about it the gate began to vibrate and shake. There was an uncomfortable buzzing noise that reminded me of what I heard last night. The gate is shaking more violently as the seconds ticked by, and then there was a flash of white light, the sound of creaking metal, and next I couldn't believe my own eyes. The gate expands and doubles—no quadruples in size. As it once stood just below the knees, it now toward yards above our heads. It must have been a mile high and even a mile long. The bars of the gate twisted and tangled with each other in a sort of design, making it look much more sophisticated than it had just moments ago. It looked as if it were the grand gate to some sort of gothic, Victorian castle. But even though the gate had somehow grew the way that it did, there still seemed to be absolutely nothing behind it.

"Yo! What is that noise?!" Carson screeches over the rather piercing sound of metal on metal.

"Don't open your eyes!" Rose warns him and reaches up to cover his face.

I look at her and she looks back up at me with caution, as if gaging what I might say next. But I didn't say anything. I just watched for what she would do next.

The gate settles and quiets and we are left standing in front of the towering structure that now radiated with a blue and purple glow. Rose brings her hands down from Carson's face, grips him around the arm and then holds her hand out for mine.

"Are you ready to come home, Ethan?" she asks softly, her eyes glittering.

I draw in a slow breath and then I take her hand.

"As ready as I'll ever be," I tell her and look straight ahead.

Rose looks ahead and then she pulls the door to the gate open, revealing what looked like a portal. I had no time to react as Carson and I were both tugged forward.

"Rose—!" Her grip was tight, and a lot stronger than expected. I couldn't pull free even if I wanted to. She moves in one swift, rapid movement. And just as I was sure I had convinced myself I had been dreaming, there was a heavy gust of static-filled wind and then...nothing.

"...Am I dead?" Carson spoke up first and I could no longer feel Rose's hand, or the bike I was sure I let go of at some point.

"Oh, just open your eyes," Rose said.

I peak my own eyes open and I felt terribly dizzy. Once my vision cleared, I realized that we were still in a wooded area, but on the outskirts of it. There are trees around us but in the distance is a clearing of soft grass fields of vibrant shades of green. And beyond that was rows and rows of tall wheat plants. My eyes linger on this for a while and I'm suddenly getting visions of running and maneuvering my way through wheat taller than myself. Something is buzzing in my ears and it makes me feel light-headed. I blink away the vision and look passed the fields farther in the distance and I see a magnificent castle at the top of a hill. It was shades of grays and blacks with towers that ended in sharp points. It was very gothic style, like something you'd see in a Tim Burton.

The air was crisp here, certainly less windy than it was in Whitechapel. I couldn't even bring myself to ask how exactly any of that worked, being in Whitechapel one moment and in Obscura the next. But even so, my light-headedness was churning into nausea, and my brain started swimming.

"Rose…" I call her again, though I wasn't exactly sure why this time. Suddenly I couldn't focus, or catch my bearings. I blinked and my vision blurred. I blink a second time and there's flashing lights, and visions of running down corridors, and I could hear children giggling and screaming.

Rose is looking at me, worry all over her face as she reached out to touch my arm.

"What is it?" she asks in a concerned tone.

I reach up and press my palm to my head, and shut my eyes. I didn't have a headache which was definitely a relief, but I was having a hard time getting my head straight.

"He might faint," I heard Carson say.

"What? Does he do that often?"

"No, not often. …anymore at least. There was a time when we were kids where he fainted almost every hour of every day. His grandma never said what it was, but only recently has he fainted again."

I blink my eyes open and I hear Rose gasp.

"Holy crap…" Carson mutters.

My vision clears back up and I look at the both of them gawking at me.

"Your eyes…" Rose starts.

"What?"

Carson pulls his phone from his pocket and opens the camera before shoving it into my grasp. I raise the device so that the camera would focus and there in my reflection the color of my eyes was rapidly shifting between dark brown and neon green.

"Wh-what is happening?" I say more so to myself than to any of them. I blink a few times, hoping I was just looking at it wrong or it was a glitch on the phone or just something other than what it clearly was.

"I told you at the library, dude. Your eyes were green!"

"Ethan…I'm not sure why exactly your eyes are switching out of control like this, but the green color is natural." Rose takes the phone from my hands and returns it back to Carson. "Perhaps it's another side effect from the injection."

I suddenly think back to Gramma's eyes shifting to blue earlier and how I asked about them and her answer had been 'it runs in the family'.

"It's your S.E., Ethan. It's perfectly normal for people like you."

"What is an S.E.?" I remember hearing that before just earlier that day in that weird lucid dream or whatever it was I experienced. It was something my aunt had mentioned only briefly but didn't go into detail about it.

Rose looks almost exasperated and she rubs her fingers across her brow. I almost immediately felt sorry for having to ask so many questions but then again, why should I be sorry about that. I literally knew nothing.

"S.E.," she began, "stands for 'Soul Element'. Madam River would know much more about it than I would, but from what I know all Greenwood witches are born with one from the four elements we all know. Fire, water, earth, and air. Every witch's eye color seem to correspond with their S.E.. River's is water. How fitting right? That's why her eyes are so blue. Oh, and Doctor Valhera, his eyes are amber colored. His S.E. is fire. But actually, there is one more element than the four that I named. The fifth element of Spirit. It's the rarest of them all, and that is half of the reason why you are so special. Because you are the only Spirit element alive. Your green eyes are proof of that. But I would seriously talk to River about it, she can explain it loads better than I."

I blink at her, and I'm sure Carson and I wore the same perplexed expression. It was like I understood the words she said but I just couldn't wrap my head around them. My head tilts to the side and I draw in a slow deep breath. Carson looks between me and her, seemingly trying to decide whether or not he should say anything. But I speak before he does.

"I think you just told me that witches are a thing..." I say half-heartedly.

Rose blinks at me as if I had just said something stupid, and honestly with the expression she wore I could feel the color burning in my cheeks.

"That's...because they are. Witches are as real as the sky is blue."

"How on earth could that be—"

"So are elves, and goblins; werewolves, and vampires. Anything you can think of is true and more." There is suddenly laughter and both Rose and I turn to look at the skinny strawberry-haired boy hugging himself around the stomach, eyes squeezed shut and head shaking from side to side as he laughed. "Is there something you'd like to say?" Rose grumbles and crosses her arms over her chest.

"No, no, it's just," he began through his laughter, "ha ha ha—do you seriously think that we—ha ha—could believe something as stupid as that?! Ha HA HAA!!"

Rose is glaring, and suddenly I have a bad feeling. She uncrosses her arms and they drop to her side with a light *thud*. She steps up toe to toe with Carson who immediately straightened up and stopped laughing. His blue eyes widen as he looked down at her hazy lavender ones that gradually seemed to start glowing a piercing purple hue.

"Say that again," she dared him. "You question your own 'best friend's' existence. You question *MY* existence. You ought to be thankful to Ethan for allowing you such a *forbidden* opportunity to be here with us. Open your eyes, Carson! Because reality. isn't. a joke!" With every word she became fiercer and fiercer, and finally she was baring her teeth at him. Her teeth that consisted of two very real fangs. Although they were short and kind of round until they ended in a very sharp point. I knew I wasn't stupid; it was what I thought I had seen just last night when she smiled at me, and just a little earlier when she was all grins and cheeses.

Carson shrinks backwards, the color in his face had drained and left him pale and almost shaky. He held his palms out toward her to show he made a mistake.

"I-I'm sorry..." he stammered, "I didn't realize—"

"Of course, you didn't realize! You're a *nohab* without any idea of anything else outside of beings like you! If you can't control it, kill it, or understand it, you write it off and claim it doesn't exist! But we do! We're all right here!"

I step forward; obviously she was letting off a ton of extra emotion she probably didn't mean to be unloading onto Carson. I place a hand gently on her tensed shoulder and I feel her pause, before slowly relaxing. She blinked once and her eyes went back to…I guess we can call a dull lavender color normal. She eyes Carson who stood there frozen and then she turned to face me. She looked at me sadly and all of a sudden seemed to be fighting tears.

"I'm sorry," she said quietly, "I really didn't mean that…" I drop my hand from her shoulder and she rubs her arm sheepishly. "It has been very difficult here, more so than when you first left. But…" She looks down at that same funky watch that seemed to now be moving counter clock-wise. "We shouldn't stay here any longer. We have to get you home to Greenwood."

"And where is that exactly?" I ask.

"It's only the next district over. This place here is Lamia, and over there is Lamia Castle." She points over to the semi-far-off castle I had spotted before. "Lamia District is my home and home to the vampires of this land. But actually, Ethan you must know something. On the day you were taken to Whitechapel everybody believed that you had been killed. There are only a handful of people that know the truth of what happened to you, and there are also some who speculate the truth for ill intentions. Because of this we have to hide your identity until you are safe with Madam River. She can decide how we should move forward."

"Will my aunt and uncle be there too?"

"Yes," she says, "they won't be there when we get there, but they will come soon after to meet you. It's all a part of the plan. Now the only matter is transporting you over the district line. They will ask for ID."

"Like a license or something?"

"Well, we call them passports. Everyone has one, so if you show up to a boarder without one it would of course be quite alarming. I think the best way is to catch a buggy." She starts walking, not toward the castle but skirting around where we already stood and she expected us to follow. "The both of you will have to hide in the back of one. Perhaps one transporting goods, or bales of hay."

"And what about you?" I ask as Carson and I move quickly to keep up with her.

"Me? Well, typically the princess of Lamia shouldn't be crossing boarders without reason or escorts. But I can be quite persuasive. Just trust me. Do what I say, and we can get past with no problem."

Carson and I exchange looks but nobody dared to question her again. She moved swiftly, maybe too swift as it was hard for the two of us to close the gap between us and her. She maneuvered her way around trees and we continued avoiding moving any closer to the castle grounds. I watched us pass the massive structure in the distance. I could see where the front entrance was as it was guarded with tall black gates and two guards that looked like small smudges with how far away we were from them.

"Hey," Carson's voice brought my gaze over at him, "did I really offend her?"

"Clearly," I mutter plainly.

"I didn't mean to. But like, how does she really expect to say things like that and expect us to just go with it?"

I look at him for a moment before turning my head forward. "You know at this point we should just accept everything that's said. I mean I know you saw not just her eyes, but she literally has fangs."

"Okay…" he says slowly, "but she's out here in the sun. And I don't see no sparklin'."

I shake my head. "I don't think this is a joke, Carson."

"Stop." Rose halts after saying this and I realized we were now on the outskirts of a road where vehicles that looked like old-timey carriages were coming and going. Some were being drawn by horses while there were also engine powered ones. The road was rather busy with people of all sorts passing by. It was there first time we saw people since coming to Obscura. There was a man that caught my eye whose hair was white as snow. He sat atop a horse drawn carriage that had passengers on the inside. The man wore a long black coat and above him was a black umbrella that shaded him from the rays of the sun. His eyes were a striking shade of magenta and his skin was paper white.

Most people looked quite normal other than the crazy eye colors or the glimpses of very real fangs. I almost felt like I was in a crazy dream. But seeing as how most of my dreams were angsty abstract childhood related stuff…

Anyway, Rose is straightening out her cloak and "fixing" her hair that only sprung right back out in various directions. She then turned to the two of us and her expression was serious.

"I'm going to catch us a ride. Pay attention, because when I do you have to move as quickly as possible. Don't get caught and don't make a sound until we've crossed the border. Understand?"

"Sure," I answer for the both of us, "but I am just wondering…if we do get caught and they found out about Carson not being here, what would happen?"

"I'll just say it won't be good…" Rose answers with a deep frown. "That's why I wanted to tell you it wasn't a good idea to bring him!"

"But what about Ethan?!" Carson protests.

"Ethan isn't mundane, Carlson!"

"Okay, my name is *Car-son* for the last time. And I think you just called me a muggle or something." I shove Carson immediately. How embarrassing could he get showing off how much of a nerd he was. He trips over himself but he doesn't fall. "Ouch! That was unnecessary."

"A what?" Rose is stuck on the seemingly foreign word he used, her straight brow furrowing together.

"What? A muggle. Surely you know what that is! Haven't you ever read Harry Potter?" Rose stairs blankly as the blonde and shakes her head no. "I am speechless. Muggle is like a non-magic person. How could you have never heard of this."

"Oh. We call that a *nohabi* here in Obscura. Or *nohab* for short. It means 'a human with no occult abilities'. I suppose I should find out what a 'Harry Potter' is, since you seem rather bothered I don't know about it."

"Of course, I'm *bothered*. It's literally the only books I've ever read, *ever*!"

"*Shhh*." Rose suddenly shushes him as she's no longer paying attention to what he has to say. She pulls her long ponytail over her shoulder and takes a long step forward into the road. "Stop, stop!" She stepped directly in front of an oncoming wagon being pulled by a tired looking horse. The person on top was a man who didn't quite look like the other people I've seen so far. He was shorter and wore shades of browns. His eyes were a rather normal looking slate color, his hair curly and brunette. Upon seeing Rose appearing from nowhere in the middle of the road, the man yanked the reigns of his horse to a complete stop, mere inches away from colliding with her.

The man is heaving horrified breaths and he looked to be battling emotions that included anger, terror, and surprise.

"Princess Rose," he gasped first before straightening up and catching his bearings, "if I had run you over, Lamia would have my head!"

"I do apologize," Rose offers a little curtsy. I didn't know that she was actually a princess. Although I was still unsure if it were true or not. But then again, I had never met an actual princess before so it wasn't like I knew the traits of one. "Tell me, where are you off to?"

"I...well, I'm returning to Greenwood District, m'lady. I had an apothecary delivery up at the castle."

"Isn't it just my luck!" Rose lights up and her eyes dart over toward Carson and I who still stood hidden behind the trees lining the road before looking back at the man who looked just as nervous as before. "Do tell me your name, sir."

"Oh..." He adjusts the brown pelt vest he wore, maybe trying to seem a bit more presentable to her. "James Cobble, m'lady." Rose smiles sweetly up at the man; her little round fangs were more than clear this time.

"Mr. Cobble, I know I haven't got the right to ask, but won't you allow me to hitch a ride with you? You see, I was already on my way to Greenwood when I suddenly felt a little weak in my left knee. I'm sure it's from my ballroom classes. I would be more than grateful if you let me ride with you at least until Willow Way. I'd like to visit Juniper's Magic Shop before evening."

The poor man's eyes widened a little and he took a moment stammering over his own words as he tried to understand the reason why a Lamia royal would want to catch a ride with someone from the working class like himself.

"I'm sorry to ask, but I only wonder if it's truly okay that you travel without anyone to take care of you. If something were to happen to you, m'lady, I would be the—"

"Oh come now, there's absolutely nothing to worry about. Trust me when I say there are *always* people watching me, whether I have escorts or not. Now then..." Rose rounds the horse, gives it a little stroke on the neck before approaching the side of the carriage. Just before she was just out of view she motioned with her head to Carson and I to make a beeline to the back of the wagon. "Shall we be off?" Rose is climbing onto the seat next to the delivery man. He seemed shakier and more nervous than before to now have a princess trusting him to take her where she wanted to go.

"I think that was a que or somethin'," Carson said to me as he looked left and right for anybody who might see. When the coast was clear, Carson gripped my wrist and yanked me after him as he shot off to the entrance of the wagon. He hopped up into the enclosed vehicle and I stumbled after him as quickly as possible. When we were safely inside (and pathetically out of breath), we each found a seat on opposite sides of the wooden wagon. It was empty save for some open boxes with empty glass jars in and around them. "Woo!" Carson gasped a little too loudly. "This must be a sign to hit the gym."

"Hush," I whispered. "Remember Rose told us to keep quiet. If we get caught there's no telling what would happen to us."

"Sorry…" he grumbled sheepishly. I reached over to the two pieces of fabric that was draped over the entrance of the wagon. I pulled them closer together so it wasn't as easy to see the inside, but I still peeked through to see what was happening on the outside.

The wagon moved slowly over the bumpy dirt road, and it wasn't long at all before the wagon pulled to a stop and it looked like we were in a line of other vehicles and people on foot that were trying to cross the border. In the distance I could see a long black metal fence that looked similar to the one we somehow fazed through to get into Obscura in the first place. There were people who looked like guards that wore full body suits made from some type of woven material that also looked as hard as steel at the same time. They wore shiny metal helmets with a spike at the top and they all held long spear-like poles in their grasp. Our wagon inched forward and it seemed like we were closer to being next than I previously thought. The line wasn't that long and it moved rather quickly. I could hear the guard at the entrance of the gate talking to whoever was just ahead of us.

"Passports," I heard a deep voice say. There were other words exchanged, some that I couldn't exactly hear, and others asking why they were crossing into Greenwood District, and soon it was our turn.

"Passports," the same voice said just as deeply and just as bored as before. "Oh," suddenly there was more emotion in the persons voice and I was sure it was because they must have recognized Rose. I pull the fabric closer together again and I scooch further back into the wagon. If they were to round the back, I didn't want them catching a glimpse of two other people on the inside. "Princess Rose, what exactly are you doing?"

I hear her stifle a laugh before speaking up. Her voice was a lot softer and a bit harder to hear, but I could make out the conversation.

"I think it's rather clear that I am taking a little ride to Greenwood. Nothing out of the ordinary."

"Certainly, princess, but you don't seem to have any escorts with you. Does your father know where you are?"

"Why, of course he does. When does he not? Traveling with or without escorts is none of your business, however, I must say that. I'm only going to the magic shop as I usually do, and I happened to come across one of our delivery men who is going in the same direction. I can't say there's any problem with that."

"….no, princess, I suppose there's no problem with that." He sounded slightly defeated and there was a pause of silence before I heard his voice again. "I will have to see your passports, however…"

"Certainly." There is the sound of shuffling to where I assumed passports were being retrieved and checked before given back.

"Mr. Cobble, you were here on delivery, is that correct?"

"Yessir," the man answered a little uncomfortably.

"What were you delivering?"

"Apothecary items, sir. For the Elemalex Unit at Lamia Castle. Standard procedure, of course, sir."

"Yes, right. Shall we have a look in the back…"

"Oh, I don't think that'll be necessary," Rose's voice appears again and I look at Carson who stared back at me with wide eyes.

"It's only standard procedure, prin—"

"I agree, however I had the liberty of looking at it for myself. And while I only just met our Mr. Cobble, I dare say he has no reason for item smuggling.

As you may not know, he nearly ran me over earlier," I could hear that poor man make a small sound that was full of distress as Rose continued on. "Not to worry, though, it was entirely my fault. But you see, I reminded Mr. Cobble as I will to you, that there are always eyes on me. And should he be engaged in malicious activity he certainly would be found out. Anyway, I say all this to say, I do believe we've taken quite a bit of your time. Shall we move on?"

There is an incredibly long pause of silence and I was almost sure that everything she had said wouldn't matter. And that any second now someone would be at the back of the wagon, pulling open the drapes to see Carson and I hanging out like cowboys with wanted posters. I see Carson mouth a curse word at me and I shake my head frantically at him, holding my finger up to my lips and pray to everything above that he wouldn't make any sound. I hear some shuffling and then I hear the guards voice once again.

"Very well. But I will need to report that I saw you here today."

Carson and I untense and with a deep sigh, it was like my entire soul left my body.

"Of course. Standard procedure, right?"

I heard no response, but in no time the wagon is moving again. And thankfully we pass through the border.

"Bruh," Carson whispers to me, "could you imagine if they really looked back here?" I grimace a little and pull my knees up to my chest.

"I'd rather not think about the end of our lives, Carson."

6

The Genus Guild

I didn't know how long we had been riding in the back of the wagon. Carson had fallen asleep and I was feeling around for my phone in my back pocket. I was curious to know what time it was, how long has it really been since we left Whitechapel to come here—since I left Gramma there in the kitchen to sulk over her sujebi. When I turned on the screen, I was shocked to see the digital clock having a wicked glitch I'd never seen before. The time was changing rapidly; the minutes moving like seconds and the hours passing like minutes. The clock itself was flashing, appearing and disappearing. I put my phone back in my pocket and I shifted onto my knees to reach over Carson and take his without waking him. After successfully taking hold of the device, I pull it slowly into my possession and then retreat back to my side of the wagon. I turn on his screen, greeted by a rather risqué fanart of Marvel's Gamora. And once my eyes could focus off of…green…flesh, I noticed his clock was doing the exact same thing. I shook my head, not understanding what was happening with our phones. I look at the top right corner of the phone, and through the cracked glass I notice there's no service at all where we were. Feeling defeated I crawl back over to the other male and return his phone back to him, receiving a loud snort through his snoring that I took as a 'thank you'.

    The wagon jerks to a stop and I nearly lose my balance as I had been returning to my space again. I could hear Rose's voice thanking that Mr. Cobble.

As her voice started a little far away it became closer and closer until I saw her slender brown fingers pulling the fabric of the wagon back.

"—except I only want to check back here for real this time," Rose had been saying as she greeted me with a bright smile and was gesturing for me to wake the slumbering blonde and hurry out of the vehicle. My eyes widen as my brain stuttered before comprehending and I sprung into motion. I lunged forward and almost violently shook my friend to where I immediately regretted as I remembered how dramatic he could be. As he was waking, I slapped my hand against his mouth as quickly as possible. Carson jumps, his eyes fly open and I am muffling his rather unnecessary squeal as his arms fly up and swing around, connecting with me multiple times.

"Hush! Hush!" I hiss at him urgently to calm down.

"Well as I did tell that guard that I had already checked back here for any smuggled goods, you do know that it wasn't true. So, I thought I'd just do it quickly, even though I do not believe that you would," Rose called to the man at the front of the wagon while she frantically waved her hands around as if it would shut Carson up any faster. He must have been asking what she was doing back here. "As I thought, it is *indeed* very empty back here," she lies.

Carson finally relaxes and he's looking up at me confused as to why I was hovering over him. His ginger-ish brow furrows, and as if we were still kids, I feel his wet, slimy tongue connect with the middle of my palm, causing me to recoil backward.

"What are you doing?!" he whispers sharply at me.

"Eugh!" I'm wiping my hand on my pants to rid any remnants of his saliva, and I back up toward Rose. "Get up, we have to go," I tell him urgently before jumping down out of the wagon.

"Over there behind the tree," Rose whispers, pointing for me to duck behind the large trunk of a willow. Carson is up on his feet now after realizing we had stopped and it was time to move. He scrambled to his feet and stumbled out of the vehicle and after me to take cover.

"Is everything okay back there?" the driver asked, leaning over in his seat to see behind the wagon. Rose jogs around toward him and she stands there smiling up at him innocently.

"Yes, of course. It seems like everything is in order."

The man pauses as he analyzes her carefully. He nods after a moment, accepting what she had to say before asking "We're still a little ways away from Juniper's m'lady. Are you sure you're alright to walk?"

"Certainly," she answers. "I do it all the time, trust me. Now that you've let me rest my legs, I can make it there without a doubt. I'll be sure to put in a good word for you at the castle, Mr. Cobble."

"Thank you, m'lady. Truly. It was no trouble a'tall." He sounded genuinely grateful. It must be a big deal to have a good word about you in Lamia. After a sincere shake of the hand the man was off and Rose turned to face where she left us.

"Okay, boys," she began as she pulled the tie on her cloak loose and moved to join us, "it's not that much further now. Since we were able to cross the border no one should be able to tell any difference. People should simply assume you're witches. Which…one half of you actually is. But…" She's pulling her cloak off, revealing the entirety of her outfit. She's wearing an off-white long sleeve shirt with these thick black metal bracelets over the sleeves. Over her shirt she was wearing overalls, which I wasn't really expecting. But they weren't those really tight denim-type ones. They were made of a black thick woolen fabric, and it hung loosely off of her small frame stylishly. Around her waist was something that looked like a small utility belt to where she had some tools tucked away in them that I wasn't sure if I wanted to know what they were for. But…if I were to guess, one looked like the handle to a dagger, and there was a pocket with two empty vials tucked away in them. The other things I wasn't sure at all. I watch her little hands straighten out the silvery cloth in her grasp and then she's approaching me. "…I don't know the odds of people recognizing your face, Ethan." She's looking up at me with soft large eyes after moving toe to toe in front of me. She lifts her arms way up and wraps the cloak around my shoulders. As it was rather long on her, maybe ending at her knees, it reached only to my hip and didn't fit right around the shoulders. She lifts the wide hood up and places it gently over my head. Maybe it was the only part of it that fit right. "For me when I look at you, you look just the same as before. Just bigger," she giggles. "So just in case, we'll have you wear this. Remember, people think you're dead." She takes a step back after she finished setting the cloak to where she deemed it good enough and then she looks at Carson who was staring down at his phone wearing the same expression I wore before when I saw the way the clock behaved. "Carson has lovely blue eyes. Others should think he has a Water S.E. at best so that is perfect for us. Let's go."

She's turning on her heals and is moving out from behind the tall willow that provided us cover. I grip Carson by his hoodie and pull him along as I stepped quickly to keep up with Rose who seemed to walk the way a cheetah runs.

"Thank you," Carson suddenly said, eyes still glued to his screen. I wasn't sure if he was thanking me for not leaving him behind or responding to the small compliment Rose actually gave him. "Did you see this?" He's showing me his phone now. "Did I drop my phone somewhere?"

"Oh," Rose turns her head to look at the both of us, "did I not mention that your clocks won't work here?" Carson and I shake our heads at her and she shrugs a little in return. "Sorry. Your mundane clocks can't process the shift in dimensional time. It wants to keep up with the time in Whitechapel, but while you're here in Obscura…well there's too much of a difference."

"Speak English, Rose! I don't have service either. What if the moms calls?" Carson taps frantically at his data button but it doesn't change anything.

"You'll just have to deal with it. There is no way to communicate with your home from here."

Rose is a little firmer in her response, and although Carson's expression softened at this, he still looked rather annoyed that his phone doesn't work.

I take a moment to look around now that it seemed the cell phone topic had died down. We were surrounded by trees and there seemed to be nothing but dirt road until I looked up directly in front of us. Only a few yards away was a wooden sign strung up to two giant willows. The sign was crudely painted with greens and pinks over a carving of words that said: *Willow Way*. The dirt road branched off underneath the sign, fading into a pathway made with cobblestone. And that was where Rose led us to.

As we walked down this path lined with willows bigger than what I had ever seen, there were more signs of life coming into view. A stream was running on each side of the pathway, connecting at one point to where the cobblestone was raised into a small bridge to cross over it. There was a lot of chirping, humming and buzzing that I could hear, like there were many birds especially hummingbirds. In the distance there were tree branches with string lights hung upon them, and little buildings that looked like huts and little shops came into view. The closer we came to them the louder the sound of human chatter could be heard. And finally, there were people walking about as the path we walked began to branch off into many different directions as if we had entered a little town. There was a smell in the air that the moment it hit my nose my heart began to swell. It smelled of burning sage and sweet resins. There seemed to be a bakery nearby that added warm dough and butter to the air, along with other things I couldn't quite put my finger on. Rose said this place was my home, and something inside of me may have felt that way.

"Willow Way is one of the three best shopping spots in Greenwood," Rose whispered to me.

The people looked a lot more cheerful than the ones we saw at Lamia, although we didn't see many as we weren't in a particular town or city. Everyone here wore shades of greens and purples. Golds and silvers, and blues and browns. Some people wore very beautiful cloaks of many different shades and patterns. While some wore vests like that Mr. Cobble we met before, with little pointy hats to match. Many adults seemed to be adorned in jewelry made from stones, metals, or crystals. Like long beaded necklaces, rings on almost every finger, or bracelets of many sorts. There were even children who ran back and forth, chasing each other, laughing and playing. Mothers had baskets around their wrists filled with various books, bagged items, empty or filled glass bottles, and even sweets from the bakery. Fathers seemed to be with their children, teaching or playing. Maybe they were also out doing shopping of some kind. I look over at Carson who looked just as bright-eyed as I might have. It looked as though we had come to the Renaissance Festival or something. I wanted to take a closer look, explore, touch things, learn about what goes on here. But when I looked over at Rose, she kept her eyes forward and her step didn't stray off of the path we were on. We seemed to simply be passing through which was rather disheartening. We were walking toward a sign that read: *Holly's Grove* that pointed towards another tangle of trees.

Soon we were no longer around that community of people who all seemed quite content with their lives. We had entered a very wooded area that was much quieter than where we passed before. There was the soft trickle of the stream that flowed beside us, and there was a gentle breeze that rustled the oaks that stood tall and proud above us. I realized the deeper into these woods we walked there were more little hut looking structures scattered here and there that seemed to serve as homes. Some sat further into the ground than others. Some were elevated by wooden planks and stones. There were a handful with quite a bit of character, decorated with flowers and lights, or with pumpkins and figurines.

. . .

My head is aching.

There was something painfully familiar about the path we walked, and the more I wracked my brain to remember, the more unrelenting throbs panged through my skull. I groan to myself and shake my head as if it would rid the pain. But really it only made it worse.

"Is something the matter?" Rose is asking after noticing my behavior.

"Just my head," I answered with a frown.

I blink and there's a flash of light, and I can see a pair of small muddy boots walking on this same cobblestone path. I blink again and the vision is gone. "Rose," I call suddenly, turning my head to look at her properly. She hums in response but never meets my eye. "I was just wondering about something you said earlier…"

"And what's that?" she said gently.

"It's just…you said that everyone except for a few believes that I'm dead. Why?"

Rose is silent for what felt like an eternity, but then she finally draws in a breath.

"I'm not sure if there's a proper way to say it. But the short answer is because my aunt, Princess Annika, ordered your death. The reason's being you rank as the most dangerous oddity."

My brow furrows. "And that's related to my S.E.?"

She nods. "In Obscura there are all kinds of magical beings and creatures that live here. Witches, werewolves, vampires. Goblins, fairies, elves, and so on and so on. But it's easy to understand that not everyone can purely be one thing. A witch could fall deeply in love with an elf. Actually, that happens rather often. And what kind of child do you think they would have?" She pauses as if she were really waiting for me to answer, but even I have already learned that that is not the case, so I keep quiet. "It's neither one or the other," she continues, "they become a mix of the two. And could have certain powers and abilities from both parents put into one. But they are branded an Oddity because they are not one or the other. But something like this, a witch and an elf, is nothing really out of the ordinary. So, they are only ranked as a low-risk and can live quite normally. Others aren't as lucky, however."

I watch her and this time I see a small frown forming on her lips.

"Why?" I ask finally. "What happens if you rank higher than that?"

"Well…" she began cautiously, "all oddities, whether low-risk or high, must register as such, and it is something to be presented at appropriate situations for the safety of other citizens. Some oddities can't help some of the abilities that they have and hurt not just themselves but others, even on accident. This can easily get them qualified as a medium or even a high risk depending on the cause. There are also rare cases of beings that can appear into life from seemingly nowhere. And what they are and their powers and abilities are unknown and often times very dangerous. Just like the most famous case being your father. I'm sure you're wondering what makes you an oddity. Yes, it's true, you aren't just a normal witch like everyone else around here. And even the fact that you have the rarest S.E. that literally no one else alive has doesn't qualify you as such. You are mixed. Being a witch comes from your mother's side as you might can guess."

"And my father's side?"

Her lips pierce together and her expression was dark. That obviously wasn't a good sign at all. Especially since there is not a shred of evidence of who my father is. He has never once even come out in any of my suppressed memory dreams. I didn't even know his name. I sigh deeply and look away from her since she seemed to be avoiding my gaze. It was then that I realized we were approaching a little hut that looked half way buried into the soft damp earth. Bright green moss draped across the roof and blended into the ground like a thick blanket. There was a little arch woven from flowers and branches that sat at the entrance that also wore a sign that read: *Genus Guild*. My eyes widen a little as I remember seeing these words in the pages of my uncles journal. Genus Guild is an actual guild of some kind. I stop to stare at the structure in front of me and something about it radiated everything warm and happy. There were lights on through the windows, and there was the smell of something cooking coming from the inside. Rose stops and she looks up at me almost sadly.

"Welcome home, Ethan," she said quietly.

I look at her, and then back at the house. I wasn't sure who would be inside. My heart started to race and I felt nervous all of a sudden, like I was preparing for a public speech.

Carson pulled up his hood, stretched his arms and then walked past me.

"Let's hurry up. I'm hungry and somethin' smells good," he said as he hopped down the slope leading to the front door. Rose watched him, shaking her head but following after, and eventually so did I.

Carson is knocking on the door, and as I was expecting to see a familiar face, like River's, the door is cracked open and I see a bulky muscular frame that most certainly wasn't her.

"What d'you want?" a voice lower than the ocean said.

Carson took a wide step back and the door opened all the way revealing a rugged tough looking man with eyes that burned like a roaring flame. His short dark hair was thick and unkempt that added to the four o'clock shadow on his face. The energy he gave off was heavy with impatience and intolerance for any nonsense and I was almost certain we must have knocked upon the wrong door.

"Wooo," Carson sang, holding up his hands in innocence, "a good meal would be nice. But also, I think we're deliverin' somethin'—*someone* to you, but don't ask me 'cause I'm just as lost…or should I say *confused* as he is. Possibly more."

The man is glaring and narrowing his eyes at the blonde, and I was sure that the striking amber color of his eyes were literally emitting flames. The man seemed like he was picking something up about Carson that wasn't right. And seeing as how Rose mentioned earlier that normal humans were highly illegal in Obscura, it would not be in our favor if he were to figure that out. As Carson shrunk back further, Rose pushed her way passed the both of us, shaking her head disappointedly.

"Won't you get Madam River? She should be expecting us," Rose said as she came into his view. His eyes widened a little and that flame dissipated. "But not only her, all of you should be, really."

The man's shoulders dropped slowly and he seemed more in disbelief than as stern looking as he was before. He eyes Rose, then looks at Carson who was shoving his fists into his hoodie, and then his gaze lands on me. I still wore Rose's cloak over my head, not sure when it was deemed safe for me to take it off yet. Before I could gauge what the man could possibly be thinking, he is shoved aside by a mass of white. It wasn't until my eyes focused did I realize it was River who made her way to the door without being called. Her hair was loose and just as incredibly long as before. Her deep ocean-colored eyes smiled before she did and she clasped her ring adorned hands together against her chest.

"Oh, I just can't believe it!" she gushed. "Jem, move out of the way and let them in! There's no time for your attitude today!"

He frowned at the woman, seemingly losing interest in what was going on. But he didn't say anything in return and spun around to walk away.

"Come on, come on. You must be cold; it was very chilly today. Please, get warm, get warm!" She moved to the side, allowing us to shuffle inside one after the other.

Rose first, followed by Carson, followed by me. I smiled sheepishly at the woman from inside of my hood, and I moved to the side out of the way of the door so she could close it back. It felt good to see her. Something about her reminded me of Gramma, but just…a hundred times less uptight.

I take a quick scan of the inside, only to realize the place seemed so much bigger than it had on the outside. But then again, it was halfway suspended into the ground. The foyer had portraits of five people in them, including River, and that man who opened the door whose name seems to be Jem. There were others that I didn't recognize. There were plants and crystals everywhere, and on the back of the door was a big symbol of some kind written in white. On the left of the foyer was where the smell of food was coming from. The kitchen. There was an old-timey wood burning stove. On the walls and hanging from the ceiling were herbs of all sorts hanging to dry. There was a huge cast iron cauldron in the middle of the floor and shelves and counters stacked with books. On the little wooden table in the corner of the room was a pan of cooling cakes that Carson seemed to have spotted and was trying to get River's attention on whether or not he could have some. But as River's eyes landed on him, she seemed to take a little pause.

"Carson, you came too?"

"Oh," he snorts, "someone who can remember my name right."

"I hope it's not any trouble, Madam River, but Ethan was very persistent," Rose spoke up as she was readjusting her belt.

"Hmm," River presses her hand against her cheek as she waves for Carson to go on and help himself to any food, to which he escaped quickly to the kitchen, "it shouldn't be a problem as long you all are careful while he is here. And as long as he doesn't talk too much…"

Rose and I both share a look before River moves past us.

"What the heck!" We hear Carson shouting from the other room, two cakes in each hand. "There's meat in this! It's so good! Ethan where are you and eat this!"

Rose and I look back at River who only smiled back gently.

"Please eat as much as you'd like, there is plenty here for everyone." She begins to enter deeper into the home but looks back at us once more. "When you finished come join us in the den. We have a *lot* to talk about." After this she disappears around a corner.

"God, who made this, because they'll have to show my mom a thing or two," Carson was saying as Rose and I joined him in the kitchen. He was shoving his mouth full of the stuff and had already found a glass of water to chug after it. But then he nearly spits everything out as a hand grabbed his shoulder from behind. He jumps, spinning around and spilling water from both his glass and his mouth.

"That would be me, sweetie," a sultry voice had said. A woman that seemed to have come from nowhere (which seems like a trait of everyone from this place) stepped from out of the shadows of the low-lit room. Long legs, thin waist, a face entirely like a model. The woman smirked as Carson was rendered speechless upon getting a good look at her. Her hair draped over her shoulders in neat spiral curls. Her brow was as sharp as the bone of her cheeks and her heart shaped lips were painted a deep alluring red.

"W-woah momma..." Carson stammered through a mouth full of food. She giggles quietly at this as she circled around him, studying him, analyzing him as if he were a new thing in a store.

"You're very interesting. It's not every day we have a new visitor. Especially a young boy like you." She stops circling and rests her fingers on her chin. Her slate-colored eyes twinkled with mischief.

Carson swallows thickly and he's straightening up, trying to seem less caught off guard as he wiped his mouth from spilled water and crumbs. "Ohh, I could visit you anytime if you'd like," he said.

She chuckles this time and she reaches forward as if she were going to touch him, but instead she took the extra cakes in his hands from him and then offered it to me.

"Eat, honey; you look like you haven't had a meal in ages."

I look away sheepishly. There was probably some truth to what she said. Ever since the stress of my headaches and dreams started, I haven't really touched the food Gramma would slave over for hours. I reach out and accept her offer and she watches me pointedly until I have taken a bite. The bread was soft, flakey and buttery. It was stuffed with a delicious mix of meat, chopped carrots, mashed potatoes, and peas. It was like a portable shepherd's pie.

"How is it?" she asked, leaning against a counter and looking at me through her long lashes.

I look at her, nodding my head as I took another bite. I turned to look at Rose who seemed a little unimpressed and then back at the unknown woman.

"It's good," I say, "really." She smiles at this, feeling satisfied by my answer. But then I turn back to Rose to offer her one too. As I reached out to hand her one of the extra ones, she waved her hand and refused. "Why not? You must be hungry too."

"No, I can't eat that without um…" She looked embarrassed and like she was trying to come up with some sort of excuse, but she never finishes.

"She can't eat any *normal* food without any of the red stuff first," the woman explains for her. Something about her tone sounded more tantalizing than anything else, though. She twirls one of her curls around a finger and Rose frowns at her.

"I hope 'red stuff' isn't what I think it is…" Carson spoke up through another mouthful of cakes.

"Of course, it is, blondie. Didn't you pay attention in your basic human occultism classes?" She eyes him, and it seemed the rest of us held the same awkward wide-eyed expression.

"I—" he began, looking like he was searching every bit of his brain to come up with the proper thing to say. But thankfully we were all saved when River's familiar voice came to the rescue.

"Victoria, I hope you're not bothering our friends," the old woman said as she came shuffling into the kitchen.

"Oh, so your name is Victoria," Carson's awkwardness didn't last long and his lips turned up into a smirk.

"I guess I didn't introduce myself. But you seemed to be enjoying my food so much."

"When ya eat somethin' made so good, especially by pretty hands like yours—"

"Shall we move into the den? I don't want to rush you all as I know it was quite the journey to get here. But I do have to be back at Lamia later tonight to complete some orders." River interrupts the other male before he could finish whatever cringeworthy thing he was going to say. Rose and I were the first to agree that moving out of the kitchen would be most appreciated. When River saw this, she motioned for us to follow, and so we did. Carson of course was hesitant, torn between the food, the girl, and joining everyone else. I look over my shoulder at him before we rounded a corner and I gave him a look that said he'd better bring his butt on *or else*. To which he followed behind begrudgingly.

"Here we are, make yourselves at home." River smiles at us as we entered a large cozy room with a fireplace roaring, pillows and blankets everywhere. There were more plants in this room, semi melted white candles on every surface. There were sticks of incense here and there, all of which were burning and smelled of lavender and faintly of charcoal. That man from earlier, Jem, was sitting in a chair in the corner, working with his hands to fix what looked like a broken clock and seemed like he would very much like to not be bothered. To the far right of the room was another corridor that seemed to have stairs leading upward, which was a little strange since from the outside it didn't look like there was a second story at all. And if there was it must have been rather short in height. There was a little gray and silver cat perched upon a stack of pillows on the floor, its long slender tail swishing idly back and forth as it rested comfortably.

River smooths out the skirt of her long blue tunic, readjusts her thick brown cardigan, and then takes a seat on a big plush chair that seemed to be where she sat often. There was a basket sitting next to it full of yarn, thread, and tools to knit and sew. It seemed like a hobby she might be into. She then gestures eagerly for us to sit down and get comfortable.

Rose and I sat down on a couch opposite of River and Carson found a good place on the floor. More so to stare annoyingly at the cat that was minding its business.

"Her name is Yulie," River says almost back handedly as she watched Carson stick his nose in the creature's face. "I got her around Yule two years ago. She's nothing but sweet."

"Nothin' but trouble," the man called Jem grunted without moving his eyes from his work.

"Oh…you'd say that about anything and anyone if you could," River sighs back. Then her eyes meet mine and I feel unsure of what's to come next. "Ethan, I'm so happy that you're finally back. It's really all thanks to Rose."

"Oh no, Madam River, you know it was my father's idea." Rose shakes her head and pulls her legs up to fold in front of her.

"Ah right. Prince Aero was the one who came up with the idea. But he wouldn't have if Rose hadn't kept asking about you. Although not completely thought out or strategized, at least you were able to get here without any problems."

I didn't say anything. Actually, there wasn't really much to say. If I thanked them, I didn't really know what I was thanking them for. And what would be the point of saying 'don't worry about it'?

Victoria walks in with a metal tray that held glass mugs of an unknown liquid, and little wafer cookies. She set it down on the coffee table in front of us and gestured for us to take some before she found a seat in another corner of the room.

"Oooo what is this?" Carson was the first to lunge at the new items presented to him, startling little Yulie in the process, who went darting to another part of the room.

"Just an elixir I brewed up. Meant for anxiety and controlling emotion. I can sense it will be very necessary from the stories I've heard about your friend."

The blonde raises a brow as he looked down at the yellow-colored drink. I two picked up a mug, not wanting to be rude since she took the time and prepared it for us. By the word 'elixir' I felt a little offput, but with a slight sniff of the stuff, it smelled sweet and inviting.

"What's in it?" I ask before putting my lips to the glass.

"Goodness. Don't you know it's rude to ask a witch what's in her personal brews?" I turned my head to look at her the moment I heard the dramatic distress in her voice. I understand now, there was something about her that seemed a little familiar. But not in the way that Rose and River did. Somehow, she reminded me a lot of Carson in the few moments I have known her. I opened my mouth to say a quick apology, but she was suddenly laughing in a teasing manner. "I'm kidding," she says through fake tears, "although I wouldn't really recommend doing that often, 'cause you really could offend someone, sweetie. There's lavender and chamomile, milk, honey, cinnamon… and my love and support." She smiles, but something about it seemed a little ingenuine. I look back at the drink and it sounded like it was just a tea with milk in it. I took a sip after watching Carson gulp half of it down in two seconds. "See, it won't kill you. It's nothing fancy but it'll do the job."

Rose looks up at me and she offers a reassuring smile before she also picked up a mug and drank some.

"Well now that that's settled," River starts and looks at her watch, "you'll have some visitors here soon, Ethan."

"You mean my aunt and uncle?" I ask hopefully

She nods her head to my satisfaction and folds her hands in her lap.

"I just don't know where to begin with you, dear. Originally Cathy was meant to explain the majority of everything to you, then bring you here herself. But I'm afraid she became lost. So, we'll just have to make do."

"How about we start with this injection I keep hearing about," I say a little firmer than I meant. I watched the rosiness of her cheeks drain a little and she became silent for a little too long.

"Okay…" she says slowly, "I guess we can start with the hard part first." I watch her swallow hard and she broke eye-contact with me, staring at her hands like it would make it easier to say whatever she had to. She breathes out slowly and then starts again. "June 21st, 2009, also known as Litha day, the day Ethan goes to Whitechapel, the day of Jiah Grey's death, and or the day of Ethan Moon's death. Quite a lot happened on that day as you can see," she chuckles a little but it sounded more nervous than jovial. "This was the day you were meant to take a potion that would wipe your memory of ever having lived and grown up here in Obscura. Temporarily of course. But it hadn't really been done before, and it was created in a very small amount of time without any chance to test whether it would work or not. What the side effects were. And would your memory truly return in its entirety. And by the looks of it, over ten years later, I'm a little worried for you, dear."

I blink at her, not sure how to take in everything yet. "Could you tell me why it was needed in the first place?" I say a little exasperated. I run my fingers through my hair, the stress habit that might make me start thinning if I didn't stop.

"That's quite the story…" River was still trying to make light of the situation, her blue eyes twinkling with both hope and despair. "I'll just start from the very beginning. That should be easier on all of us." She straightens up in her chair, her fingers find a bead on one of the many long necklaces she wore, and this time she truly starts. "In case you are unaware, all witches in Greenwood are all born with a Soul Element. Or S.E. for short. All soul elements are one of five: Water, Fire, Earth, Air, or Spirit. Commonly you will see Water, Fire, Earth, or Air S.E.'s among people. And in a far-off past, Spirit S.E.'s were just as common. Well…more or less. Certainly, more common than today. If you read about the Greenwood witch history, you can learn why this Soul Element went extinct, only to live on in the blood of some. That is, until your grandmother was pregnant with her first born. You see, there is a little ritual we witches do in celebration of a new life, and during this ritual we are able to find out which Spirit Element the new baby will present as. The moment we found out Catherine would be having the first baby in centuries of Spirit, we had no idea what to do."

"Why not?" I interrupt. "Wouldn't it be no different than if you were anything else?"

"Not exactly," River answers. "Yes, we all are human and are similar in different ways, but when it comes to our elements, we are different, and it decides what education is necessary to shape the abilities you possess unique to the S.E. For example, our Victoria here has an Earth S.E. She can understand our land more than any of us could. She connects with it on many different levels and her abilities have everything to do with the Earth and what it offers. You can guess what her education consists of. And Jem, he has Fire. His abilities are as hot as his temper." The man grunts from his corner. "It's very important that these S.E.'s learn from a young age to control themselves and their abilities."

I hear Carson gasp and he's whipping his head around to me to mouth: *Avatar*, excitedly bouncing form his spot on the floor. I roll my eyes at him and turn my attention back to the woman. Obviously, it was much different than…that super awesome nickelodeon. River continues. "All of these S.E.'s actively has someone that can help them, coach them, teach them. They do not have to rely on books alone. But for your mother it was a problem no one had ever experienced before. She was the only one alive. And on top of that, Spirit is much stronger, much more powerful than any S.E., and plainly speaking, a lot more powerful than many beings that live here in Obscura. The abilities are so much more different and needs nurturing and coaching even more so than someone like Jem. When we realized this, that there was no one to help your mother, we had to bring her to the High Druid Order and explain the situation. At first, they were in disbelief when they heard Cathy was pregnant with a Spirit. But it all made since after understanding your grandfather's bloodline. He himself wasn't spirit, but he had many ancestors with this S.E. Therefore, he was one of few alive who still carried it within their blood. Once the H.D.O understood this and got over the initial shock of it all, we were informed to take good care of Cathy to be sure she has a safe delivery when she was due. It was ordered that she only see the most highly trained and respected medics, and that once born your mother should work closely with the wisest and most profound mystics of the Druid caliber in order to help gain control of her powers as quickly as possible to avoid any disasters. Word got out that Greenwood would have its very first Spirit in centuries. It spread quickly and people from all over our district wanted to bear witness to her. They were thrilled. At least most people were as there will always be those on the other end of the stick. But anyway, we did everything we were told and prepared ourselves to welcome a new member in our home and into our guild. Your mother had been born a healthy and beautiful little girl. But something was wrong."

I'm clenching my jaw a little too hard as I listen to everything River had to say. Something was wrong with my mother, and based on the little slips of the tongue here and there from before, I could only guess what she was about to say next.

"There is a very rare condition that affects one in one thousand people. Most people will refer to the affected as *'tapped out'*, but the actual name of the condition is called *extinguersis*. Unfortunately, your mother had been diagnosed with extinguersis after concerns of her not showing signs of magic as a toddler. We prayed that she was just a late presenter like some children can be, but by the time she was six and still couldn't tap into her abilities, we had no choice but to accept that she was tapped out."

"What's the cause of something like that? Does that mean she's just human? Can't it be treated?" I watch the woman, trying to understand what all of this meant in the first place. She was shaking her head sadly. So was Rose, and so was Victoria over in her corner flipping through some sort of magazine.

"It's still not understood why some people just can't use their powers," River answers. "We're all human, Ethan, but her condition did not make her a nohabi. She was still full of unimaginable power. But sadly, her condition blocked its flow. Tests have been done, potions have been attempted to find a cure or a treatment for it, but it's still unsuccessful as of now."

I sigh disappointedly. I couldn't help but wonder what kind of things my mother would have done or would still be doing had her life been different. "So, what happened after that?" I ask.

"Once the news spread that our one and only Spirit was tapped out, many were understandably disappointed. Of all things to happen, an incurable condition is what stopped the reawakening of an extinct S.E. A lot of people hoped that your mother would grow up and balance the disproportionate rising of Lamia District. At the time Lamia's king, King Xxavier, had been struggling with keeping the peace within the district. There were words going around, protests of ill intent about how the people of the district needed to show others that they weren't weak and shouldn't allow others to step on them. Because King Xxavier was a peaceful man and did everything to make sure Lamia demonstrated compliance and peace, people within the district began whispers that he was what was making Lamia 'weak' and in order to show other districts their strength they had to get rid of him. Not all people were like that of course, but there were enough people who thought that way that caused a problem." River's eyes shift to Rose who was staring down at the drink in her barely touched mug. Then the old woman looked to me with a sigh. "As of now King Xxavier is still missing…" her voice lowered when she said this.

I didn't know his relation to Rose exactly, but since she is a princess and it seems her father is still a prince, he could only be an uncle or a grandfather. I frown lightly and look at Rose who seemed to have sensed my gaze and looked up, caught my eye, and then looked away awkwardly. I was almost compelled to ask what happened to him, but seeing how Rose seemed a bit uncomfortable I refrain from this and urge River to continue passed it. She shifts in her chair again, now fidgeting with one of the millions of rings on her pudgy fingers.

"Under the current ruling, things have become quite…difficult for many. Particularly in Sierra District where people have been affected the worst by

Lamia. They want to take over every district and make it so that we are beneath them rather than equal." Rose shifts uncomfortably before moving to set down her mug, and River continues. "Many people wished that your mother still was alive. Because as I said before, the Spirit S.E. is one of the most powerful abilities anyone can have in Obscura. Perhaps she could have stopped Lamia from what they continue to do now. But aside from her, Ethan, everyone knows that she bore a child that luckily was passed her same abilities."

"Yeah," I say slowly, "what's with people thinking I'm dead? You guys call this place my home but so far, I've just been sneaking around like a stranger."

"Well, that relates back to the injection mentioned before," River answers. "Jiah became pregnant with a healthy baby boy, and when it was confirmed that you would be born under Spirit, people were hopeful once more. And of course, some not so much. Those who weren't, especially after you could present your abilities from such a young age unlike your mother, wanted you gone. The reason being because you were a threat to them. Mostly their ego if you ask me, but some don't like the thought of knowing there are others more powerful than them. This unfortunately includes the current ruling at Lamia Castle. And because of them they wanted to see you dead."

"What? How could they be so threatened by a child?" I ask in a vexed tone.

River goes silent for a moment. I even notice Jem glancing upward at me. River runs a hand through the ends of her hair and she looks to be mulling over how to say the next thing. "That is because your S.E. is not the only thing they were worried about…"

"Well what else is there to worry about?"

"There's a ranking system that exists in Obscura, to measure your potential danger level," she starts.

"I told him about it already, Madam River," Rose speaks up now as she was nibbling cautiously on a little wafer.

"Oh, then you must already know the rankings. Typical, Low Risk Oddity, Medium Risk Oddity, and High-Risk Oddity."

"And I'm a high risk for some reason. Rose didn't expand on that part."

"I should put it plainly," River says, "as your mother would have been ranked Typical, rare, but Typical, your father on the other hand was everything but that."

My heart skips a little. Never had I heard anything about my father. *Never*. These people even knew who he was, and I was jealous.

"What was he? I guess it's safe to assume he isn't a no…a no…a what?"

"A nohabi. No, he wasn't one of those in the least bit," River says. "Your father is a very rare and an extremely high-risk oddity. No one actually knows what he really is, not even him. But his powers and his abilities are far more dangerous, and frankly terrifying than any being that exists today. He is no witch; he is not of Greenwood. He is from a different district all together. So, you are mixed. And some of the abilities that you have presented when you were younger were very…er—" she pauses for a moment, mulling over the correct word to use. "…were very *aggressive*. After one particular incident is when Lamia decided that you had to be gotten rid of. And because of…some particular people from Artemis District, you were to be killed, and Lamia saw no problem with that. Of course, we as your family did not agree, and we all firmly believed that you just needed to focus on your training. Which you did very well! You studied as much as your mother did, and you were nothing short of an angel as you grew up. But some didn't see you that way, and some didn't see you as *just a child* at all. Your grandmother, Catherine, worked at Lamia castle as the Water S.E. for the Elemalex Unit. For some reason Princess Annika, the one who is—"

"—actually a demon from the pits of hell!" Victoria interrupted from her corner as she continues her browsing through a magazine. Rose glares at her from her spot and Victoria looks up and shrugs. "Sorry, princess, but even you can't deny that your aunt is crazier than crazy."

River continues, "For some reason princess Annika requested your grandmother to create a potion that would ultimately kill you. Of course, she didn't refuse to her face, otherwise she too could be punished. So, she came to me and asked for help… I suggested we create something that could temporarily wipe your memory, and you'd drink it and we could send you off to the closest port town until things died down here. But as you can see right now, things aren't quite going as planned."

"And the injection?" I ask.

"That would actually be the memory wiping potion. You were meant to drink it, but Annika had her children give it to you. On that day you weren't really willing to drink any random thing from the Earh siblings. And I wouldn't blame you. Especially since you had just seen your mother—well…instead of at least force feeding it to you, they thought it would be more entertaining if they bit you and forced the liquid through the wound like venom." The woman frowns deeply and looks as though she had a bitter taste in her mouth. "It was very reckless of them. It was lucky you weren't accidently turned, or killed."

I frown this time and my hand moves to grip the left side of my neck, feeling an imaginary sting.

"I guess I still don't understand how my mother died," I say next. River sighs at this but answers nonetheless.

"Because of some trouble you had gotten into with the Artemis District plus Lamia wanting to get rid of you anyway, it was decided you'd take a death penalty as I said just before. And as I mentioned, we wanted to do everything we could to make sure you'd live, your mother included. After spending months defending you and arguing with the Lamia ministry about how you should be allowed to live and the incident you were involved in was not your fault, it proved fruitless as particularly Artemis did not want to hear it. They wanted you gone. So, we made a plan to wipe your memory to protect your powers and send you to Whitechapel until things became better here. But on the night of the scheduled penalty, we had more trouble than we expected. Somehow Lamia found out about our plan to smuggle you out of the realm. There was a fight…and your mother took a blade meant for you. Sadly, we couldn't save her. Not with such high stakes. Your grandmother continued to follow through with the plan and Catherine, Doctor Valhera, and I took it upon ourselves to protect you until you were old enough to return here. As for everyone else, they assumed you had been killed as ordered because of the confusion and chaos that ensued."

Silence falls upon the room once more, and I am taking every bit of a moment to process everything River had said, and it was a *lot*. My head was hurting again, the more I tried to understand, and the more I tried to remember.

But it was the first time that I could say that I *did* understand. For the most part anyway. I know that I understood that this Lamia place will get hell now that I know they are the ones who took my mother from me. Them and whatever this Artemis District is. There was something I wanted to say, but I wasn't sure how to place my words and it was visible on my face. I couldn't stop thinking about that weird vision...thing that I had just earlier that day. I could hear myself asking if I was bad. I understood there was something that I had done that caused my mother to go through what she had. As I was fixing my mouth to ask about this, there was the sound of the front door opening and all of our heads turned to see who it could be.

There's the sound of the door shutting, then slow heavy shoed footsteps and bickering whispers headed in our direction. And then finally peering through the doorway was two sets of piercing yellow eyes through masses of shaggy dark hair. The first figure was of a woman wearing a black leather jacket and rather tight looking pants tucked easily in matching heavy boots. Her face struck me as it was the exact same as it had been in the vision from earlier. Aunt Nari. Behind her stood a cautious looking man, with nearly the exact same face, only sterner. His dark hair was pushed backward and he wore a heavy olive colored sweater that contrasted sharply with his pale skin. He steps in tune with the woman until they had entered the room completely.

They're staring at me, and I felt paralyzed under their gaze. It was strange, they looked a lot like pictures of my mother I had seen before, and seeing them here in real life was a little jarring. Actually, a little too jarring to wear the faint pain in my head grew, and I felt like I was shifting in and out of focus. I grimace at this, all the while trying to focus on the two sort-of strangers who have joined us.

I keep wondering if I'm bad...

It's my voice, but so much younger, echoing from ear to ear.

Bad? Oh no, no, no, you are far from it. Exactly the opposite

I blink and I see a strange image that was dark and full of trees. There is me, and who I assume is Rose, standing cautiously in front of something. But I can't tell what it is.

Ethan, stop!

This voice was urgent and it struck fear into my chest, even when I didn't know why. It was Rose's voice and I whip my head around to look at her. She seems startled by my sudden reaction, and she stairs up at me with her large doe eyes. And then she frowns lightly.

"…Your eyes are doing that thing again…" she said gently, placing a hand on my shoulder.

"What?" I turn my head again and I look at the two who still stood at the doorway of the den.

"Oh, my joka…" Nari sighs sadly. She takes a few timid steps forward and I feel compelled to rise to my feet. Her eyes are watering, and expectedly tears escape and roll down her round cheeks. She looked almost angry, or bitter. She approaches me, and the man behind her takes a few steps further into the room, but he doesn't move any closer. The room feels like it's vibrating, or maybe it was just me. I felt like I was slipping away from my own body, or like none of this moment was reality. But it was as the thin woman in front of me reached up and carefully cupped my cheeks in her hands, and looking up into my eyes that this time I could actually feel flickering the way the others had said that they were. It wasn't painful but I wince as the sensation was unfamiliar. "Relax," she whispers to me, "you're fighting internally. You have to relax."

I blink, not knowing what that meant. "What would I be fighting?" I asked her. But then again, the answer was probably clearer than I wanted to accept. I watch her breathe in and out slowly, and she shuts her eyes for only a moment.

"Ground yourself," she said instead.

I wasn't sure what was happening. The vibrations I felt before became more intense and I felt a little overwhelmed. I watch the woman who didn't once release my face from her grasp, and then I see a spark of light. Something bright and yellow colored that started at the feet for a split second. And then a second time where I watch what looked exactly like electricity shoot up from the floor and whip around our legs. I flinch and move to jump backward but Nari looked at me in a way that convinced me to stand still. I hear Carson whooping behind me, and by the irritable sound Rose had made I was sure he had migrated to cower behind her or something. What I thought might feel hot or shock me in some way didn't at all. The yellow light calmed and looked ten times less aggressive as it rose from the floor, thinned out and floated in a serene manner around the two of us. My chest felt light and something about the energy around us made me feel like I was floating in a warm body of water, or like I had all my thoughts and emotions sorted and that I was in fact grounded like Nari told me to be.

The woman releases me and steps back. The light floating around had dimmed and disappeared and then there was loud silence.

"That's better," the woman said with a little smile. "Your eyes have settled. That only happens when you fight yourself. Your body is reacting to the magic all around you. But your mind is still fighting to suppress it. Now…" she stretches her arms out wide, and she laughs through more tears, "come give auntie a hug."

I smile a little. She felt so familiar, and in my heart, I knew I loved her. I stepped into her embrace and wrapped my arms around her warmly. She squeezed me with all her might and I almost lost the ability to breathe, but truly I didn't mind.

"My, my, how did you grow so tall?" She huffed into my chest. "I guess you became a man."

I smile at that and say: "Well, I guess you can teach me about knives now."

She stops for a moment before she slowly pulls away and looks up at me.

"…What?" she sniffs. "You can remember that?"

I notice everyone in the room stopped to see whether or not I really did remember something like that. But I wasn't quite sure if what I had experienced that morning counted as a memory, even if it had been true. Who remembers things as a ghost sent to the past? Or if I can even explain it like that.

"I…" I start awkwardly, "Well, this morning I think I passed out." I drop my arms and shove my hands into my pockets. "When I opened my eyes again, I wasn't at home anymore, I was in another room somewhere else. And then I saw myself. Like another me, but a lot younger. And you were there, aunt Nari. You were sitting with me, trying to cheer me up about something. A-and then…" I trail off and my eyes move to meet the man who seemed a bit standoffish. He stood there in the dimmer part of the room; arms folded inwardly against his chest. The expression he wore unmistakably reminded me every bit of Gramma. Particularly when she had a lot on her mind and was in a poor mood. "...and then you gave me a locket. A locket that I think you have..." I gestured to the man, and he seemed just a little stunned. "After that I woke up to Gramma yelling at me, and I wasn't sure what happened. ...I'm still not sure."

The adults are looking between each other as if they were sharing their thoughts telepathically. But for all I knew that could very well be with the sudden reveal of magic and *mystical creatures* being a thing. A moment passes and River is next to open her mouth.

"It sounds like you went through physical projection, dear. Or in other words, you projected through the physical plane."

"Only someone with a Spirit S.E. can do it," Nari adds. "Going back and forth through time is impossible. Not without an epoch key. And definitely not without your own body..." Her head tilts a little as she looks at me. I didn't know what I could say in response to this, and I wasn't sure if I wanted to hear more about potential things I could do that makes me "special".

My eyes meet my uncles again, and I'm reaching into the bag across my chest. His journal, wouldn't he like it back? I pull it out carefully and I take a few steps toward him.

"This is yours..." I say quietly. It felt weird. He felt unreal even when he was standing there right in front of me. Everything about now still felt unreal. Honestly if I thought too hard I could convince myself I was back in my room in Whitechapel, asleep in some uncomfortable position, cold sweats and all.

Namu unfolds his arms and he stares down at the journal in my hand. I was reaching out to hand it to him, but he never takes it. He shakes his head a little and leans backward against a side table.

"Keep it," he said, his voice quiet like mine, his demeanor a little displaced. "It could be of use to you one day."

I swallow and then drop my arm. I suppose I hadn't even opened it yet. So, I didn't argue and stuffed it back into my bag.

"Oh my, I'm going to be late if I don't leave this second." River is looking at her watch, hand pressed against her cheek as she assessed the time. She then looked between the twins and me before saying: "I won't be back until morning. Nana and Namu can help you and your friend get settled in and—"

"Wait! I can't stay the night, dude, my mom will *kill* me. D'you hear me? *Kill*," Carson interrupts.

"It's okay. Time difference, remember?" Rose stands up and smiles a little at him. "I can help you back before your mother notices it's been too long. And…if not…well we have a spell for that."

Carson blinks. "Oh word?"

I wasn't sure how well he was digesting any of this magic stuff yet. I wasn't even sure how much *I* was. But I would trust that they wouldn't let my friend get into any trouble.

"Then if that's all settled, I really must be going. Everyone will take care of you so don't worry too much. If you're a friend of Ethan's then you're a friend of ours." River smiles warmly. She waves a hand and with a small flash of light she had conjured up a woven knit bag right there in front of our eyes. "Goodnight, everyone, see you tomorrow."

She leaves and we're left in the room without her. Rose is collecting our mugs and placing them back on the tray they were brought in on.

"I have to get going too. My father will be looking for me," she says. She stands up straight with the tray in hand and faces me. "Might I have my cloak back?"

"Oh…" My eyes linger on her. Even though I've been with her all day I still felt like I haven't really talked with her. There were still things I wanted to ask her. I wanted to get to know her (again). I look behind me on the couch where I abandoned the silver fabric and I picked it up and moved to hand it to her.

"Thanks…" She takes it and drapes it over her shoulder before she began to step to the side to pass me toward the kitchen.

"Wait," I stop her, "can I talk to you for a minute?"

I watch her hesitate and her eyes seemed to have widened with emotions I couldn't really read. Before she said anything, my aunt had moved to take the tray from her, and she gestured for her to go on for a short chat with me.

"Okay, but only for a minute," she answers…

7

Progression

We were sitting outside, Rose and I. Nari and Namu quickly learned that Carson wasn't Obscurian. Which with the more he began to talk (like River warned) the easier it was to tell. But they were inside setting him up with a room to sleep in. The sun had gone down, and as I stared up at the sky from my place in the soft grass outside of the cottage, I realized that it was much different than back home. The sky was full of stars and clusters that looked like they could be different galaxies. The moon was huge, but not just that, there was another planet just beside it that looked a lot like Saturn with its massive rings. But...there wasn't just one set of rings, there were three.

I was blown away by how beautiful it looked, even though it made me question whether or not this was still Earth. I look at Rose who sat beside me, legs crossed, leaning back on her hands as she watched the stars above as well. She looked deep in thought, and I was almost afraid to break the comfortable silence between us. But I brought her out here for a reason.

"What is that planet there?" I ask first, pointing toward the massive three ringed orb in the sky.

"Why, that's Saturn, of course," she answers casually.

"Saturn? Last time I checked Saturn didn't have so many rings."

She laughs at me, sitting up from her laid-back position. She pulls her hair over onto her shoulder and she idly begins to untangle the ends of her dark coils.

"You're in a different dimension than Whitechapel, remember?" she says. "Some things aren't quite the same as the mundane world."

"I think you mean *everything* is not the same," I grumble, folding my arms across my chest.

"Don't pout," she jives, "you like it here, you just don't remember."

"That's the thing. I *want* to remember. But it sounds like there's a possibility I might never…" I look away from her. I felt ashamed. Even there in front of my aunt and uncle back inside, there was nothing I actually remembered about them. Other than what they called "physical projection" that I did that morning, I felt like it wasn't exactly a memory of who Nari is. Just a memory of time that passed. Like something to pin point in my timeline. Speaking of which… "Rose, can you explain to me one thing?"

"What's that," she answers softly.

"There's something that really doesn't make sense. I understand that I had a life here once. That my family lived here together, and I was born and raised here for some time. But I am also under the impression that I spent my whole life in Whitechapel. Even…if I can't exactly remember that far, Carson does, and he agrees that none of it adds up. How could I have grown up in two places at once?"

"Oh…" Rose looks down and she's quiet for a moment, thinking over how she wanted to answer. Without looking at me she begins, "Of course, I don't *exactly* know all the details because I can't cast spells or anything, but I do know the gist of it. When you were taken from here to the nearest port town, which is Whitechapel, both you and Madam Grey had to fit in immediately. If you had just showed up all of a sudden in a new house, people would ask questions and either you'd be outcasted and couldn't stay, or…just that. Also, because your memory had been wiped, you had no recollection of magic, or Obscura… no recollection of your family outside of Madam Grey. Everything was wiped until the moment you woke up in Doctor Valhera's care in the hospital. It would be awfully strange if you went on like that with no memories or connections. You would have lived a terribly miserable life up until now, certainly." She glances over at me for a second to gage my reaction. "So, Madam River, Doctor Valhera, and Madam Grey decided it'd be best to create fake memories for the people in town. They cast a spell to bring forth the most compatible people to you and to plant memories of you growing up in Whitechapel all this time. That's how I assume Carson became your friend and is under the impression you grew up together. But I think…you can't say the same. Can you?"

I eye her, taking my time to digest what she's saying. Planted memories, which means, Carson and I didn't grow up together. At least, not from meeting as toddlers. And she was right, Carson is the only one who remembers such a thing, and as for me, my mind goes blank when I try to think that far back. It seemed unfair though, at least for him and everybody else I knew back home. They were manipulated to know me, to befriend me. But…does that mean our relationships were completely a lie? My lips press together at this thought. Certainly, it didn't. Even if we didn't know each other from such a young age like Carson believed, our friendship was genuine. Our memories after eight years old until now are real. My relationship with his mother was real. My stupid crush on Hailey…was real. I look at Rose again and I watch her hug her knees to her chest. She seemed bothered and like she was putting up a few walls.

"Tell me about you," I say this time. "Or tell me about us." I smile a little at her. I wanted to coax her out of whatever dark cloud that kept hanging over her head. It was so noticeable, and I hated that for her. Especially since so far, she seemed quite sweet. "There's a dream I keep having. I've been having it for a few months now," I explain. "In the dream there's a little girl, and if she's not running away from me, I'm running from her. It's always in this field of tall grass or…wheat or something. I never see the girls face, but I always hear her voice."

"What does she say?" Rose asks, her voice barely above a whisper.

"Just my name," I answer. "It's only ever my name. She wears this white dress, and her hair is so…curly."

"It's okay to say messy," she laughs. She looks at me now, her eyes teary like she could cry. But she doesn't. "Your mother always tried to help me sort it out. My hair, that is. My father is unfortunately hopeless. She would try to keep the pattern neat, but it's like it has a mind of its own. Sometimes it made me feel not as…*prim* and *proper* as the other girls around the castle. But your mother always reminded me that my hair is beautiful. Regardless of if it's hard to tame." She smiles brightly, showing off her little white fangs. It was warming to hear that my mother was kind and went out of her way to care for another that wasn't her own.

"So, what do you make of my dream, then?" I ask her.

"I believe it's a suppressed memory that wants to break free. A memory you must be fond of as am I."

"So, it's true. You're the girl in the dream. But why are we running? What happened or—we must have been in some sort of trouble?"

"Not at all," she shakes her head. "It's nothing like that. We were only playing tag."

"…tag?"

"Yes. Tag. Certainly, you didn't forget what tag is…"

"I didn't forget," I retort. "Just…wasn't expecting it, I guess."

"Well of course, what else would two children be doing? It was our favorite thing to do, especially when you mother was away in the castle somewhere. We played tag together, or we read in my father's library. We went on adventures as far as we were allowed to go within the castle grounds. And we always ended the day with tea and cakes. Or whatever dessert Madam Grey came over with." I watch her as she explained her memories fondly. I envied her memory and wished I could share them with her. She seemed happy though, thinking back to that time.

"It seems like we spent a lot of time together."

"We did," she replies. "If you or I weren't away for classes or training, we were usually together. I really meant it before. You were my best friend…" She trails off quietly and I hear the pain in her voice. "If only you could just remember. Maybe you would see me the way that I see you. You are my family, Ethan. And I am *thrilled* that you are here right now. But for some reason, it just doesn't feel like how I always hoped it would."

I look down at my hands.

"It doesn't feel like it's actually me…" I say. "I guess because in a way…it isn't."

Her eyes round and I almost regret saying what I did. But nothing about it was untrue. I'm not the Ethan she once knew. Or at least, not yet. Not until

I can finally remember this place. Remember my life. But for now, she was only a familiar stranger.

"Yeah…" Rose sighs for a final time and then she's rising to her feet, dusting herself off. "I really should go now. My father must be worried." I look up at her from my place on the ground and she's pulling up the hood of her cloak she now wore. "Remind Carson that time moves slower here compared to Whitechapel, so he doesn't have to worry about his mother."

I stand up this time. A part of me didn't want her to go just yet. I wanted to hear more of her memories. What we used to do together as children, how well did she actually know my mother. But it sounded like it would have to wait for another day.

"When will I see you again?" I ask her.

"I'll see you tomorrow. Later in the evening once I've finished my schedule." She offers a smile and she's readjusting the belt she wore. "Go get some sleep, Ethan, I can't imagine how it must feel to have so much information unloaded on you in such a short time."

I make a sound that was meant to be a laugh but it sounded more like I just caught myself from choking. With an awkward smile I wave to her.

"Bye then," I say. "Get home safe."

She waves back and then in the next moment she had darted off in the direction from where we came. It was like something from a movie, like The Flash or something like that. I'd never seen anything except a bullet train move that way. Perhaps she had been faster.

I breathe out deeply, having to remind myself that all of this was real. And even though just a week ago life was more or less normal and I was worried about tests and being dragged to whatever else Carson had gotten himself into, now it seemed life was flipped on its head and everything I thought I knew wasn't true at all. I frown lightly to myself and my thoughts drift to my grandmother. I wondered what she could be doing this very second. Was she still upset with me? Was she wondering if I was alright or worried I had gotten into some kind of trouble? Did she feel bad for how everything had been going between us lately? I could only imagine how she must be feeling now. I also wondered why she couldn't just come here with me. What was holding her there in Whitechapel by herself when her family is here. *I am here.* I shake my head at my thoughts and then turn around to go back into the cottage.

As I step through the door and find my way back toward the den, I hear people fussing quietly, and I peer around the corner to see who it could be. My aunt and uncle were leaning against the couch in the middle of the room speaking to each other. Namu seemed very unhappy with something and Nari seemed like she was trying to get him to see differently. It also looked like Victoria had disappeared somewhere, and Jem was rummaging through a drawer near River's old chair.

"It's *unbelievable*," Namu hissed to his sister. "There's no possible way that boy can stay here much longer. If anyone found out they would have *all* of our heads."

"No one's gonna find out," Nari responds, punching her twin in the arm repeatedly. "He can talk all he wants as long as he's here. He just can't go out and do the same. It'll be fine."

Namu shakes his head. "I just can't believe he thought it was a good idea to bring him here."

"He didn't know. How could he have, he doesn't remember a single thing. He just—" she cuts off the second her eyes meet mine and I flinch at the intense feeling her gaze gave me. "Joka." She smiles a little, gesturing for me to come into the room (and to stop lingering like a creep). I awkwardly shuffle inside, joining them at the couch and I feel a heavy energy around them both. "Why don't we get you settled in your room, huh? You oughta be tired by now."

"Oh…sure," I answer quietly.

"Then let me take you upstairs. Come with me." She nods in the direction of the stairwell in the corner of the room and I move to follow her there. I look back once at Namu who painfully reminded me of how cold Gramma can be with the way he folded his arms across his chest and turned away without even a glance. It wasn't at all how I imagined meeting my long-lost relative would be.

We step up the stairs and once at the top we were greeted by a long hallway. Long vined plants lined the walls. There were more portraits hung, some had my mother in them, some had my grandmother in them. There was a small side table against the wall a little ways down that of which had a small picture frame sitting on it, surrounded with tea lights and flowers. I stop for a second to examine it and in it I find that it was a picture of my mother, holding a boy no older than six years old in her arms. In the picture she smiled brightly, she seemed so happy. I notice the locket she wore was the exact same one I saw when I projected. I wondered why Namu didn't say anything when I mentioned it before downstairs. I look at myself and I looked nothing short of innocent. I smiled while being smothered in my mother's embrace. And then I notice that one of my eyes were a different color than the other. One was green and the other had been brown.

"We all missed you."

I almost jump out of my socks at my aunt's voice. She was looking over my shoulder after she must have realized I wasn't following her anymore. I step to the side a little to look at her and she was staring down fondly at the portrait in my hand.

"Of course, we knew you were safe with Mama but it really felt like you had died that day too. We lost the both of you at the same time." She sighs a little and gently takes the portrait from me and sets it back down in its place. "We were all as happy as we could be before what happened. There is not a day that has gone by where I don't hate how our family has been torn apart."

I watch her frown and the yellow hue of her eyes flicker with anger…and actually quite literally.

"Why does uncle Namu seem so unhappy," I ask her. Not that I was expecting a tearful reunion like everyone else have done so far, but he hasn't in the very least seem all that happy to see me. As much as I was excited to meet him, it's turned out to be not what I was hoping for.

Nari looks down and shakes her head a little before finally stepping away from the table and continuing her way down the hall like before.

"He's happy," she assures me. "It's just that he is having a hard time believing it."

"Believing what?" I'm following her again and she stops in front of a door on the far-left side of the hall.

She turns and looks up at me, putting her hands in her jacket pockets. "My brother has a thing where family is the most important. And of course, it is," she starts, "but he has always put himself in the position to take care of everyone…even at the expense of himself." She wears a sort of guilty expression that made me curious. "He did everything he could to stop what happened to our sister. But she made her choice to protect you, so when that time came, Namu did everything he could to make sure you and Mama would be safe. But he hated the fact that he couldn't actively be there with you and her to make sure nobody found you to hurt you. He didn't eat or sleep for a long time after everything. He worried about the both of you until he got sick. And now after ten years, here you are. Obviously…not like you were ten years ago. You're not a sweet little boy anymore. You're about to be a man in two days. And although I'd like to think your personality and temperament is the same as it was before, even you know that you aren't past Ethan. Now you seem…lost. And confused. You don't know who you are. We all can see that. But it's still so hard to believe that you really are standing right here with us all, after all this time."

I frown deeply at this and run my fingers through my hair as I felt like there's still so much I need to think about, or to take time and process. As of now I'm taking in so many missing parts of the story—*my* story, that not even Gramma would fill me in on. There're still parts missing, but at least I'm able to put some pieces together.

"I just wonder," I say, "why neither of you contacted us, or sent a letter, or anything. Our family was split up, but did it have to be entirely?"

"We did, Ethan," she says matter-of-factly. "We contacted Mama as often as possible."

"Gramma never spoke of you," I tell her. "Not you, not even Namu. I didn't know either of you existed till recently. So how could you have contacted her and I didn't know?"

She shakes her head at me, her expression riddled with frustration. "I'm sorry, Ethan, but we couldn't talk to you. Even if we wanted to. It was too dangerous and you had no memory of us to begin with. Say your memory came back because we were too familiar? We would all be in trouble then. It was hard, but we had to keep you isolated for your safety, and anyone in that port town you care about." I stare at her almost irritably. Even though I didn't have a response to her answer, I wasn't satisfied with it either. She probably senses this and she lets out another sigh before gripping the knob of the door we stood in front of, pushing it open. "This is your room," she says. "It's been cleaned up but otherwise untouched since the last time you used it."

I peered inside after she flipped on the light and notice immediately that it was the exact same from what I saw when projecting. It was the same bed, made up neatly with grey and white bedding, where my aunt and I sat upon having a conversation about I'm not that sure what. It was the same dresser across from it with the many melted white candles on top of it and around the room. The same weird looking clock on the wall with its strange symbols and extra hands shaped like moons. There was the case in the corner full of vials and glass jars holding things that I now saw looked like herbs and liquid stuff. The same potted plants and hanging ones too. The drying flowers hung up on the walls and ceiling. I sniff a little and realize that there wasn't the smell of lemon balm and chamomile like I noticed before. The energy in the room felt stagnant and heavy. With good reason I suppose if no one has been in it after cleaning it ten years ago. I step in side, but the moment my feet cross the threshold of the doorway I feel an uncomfortable wave of energy hit me, almost like vertigo, that knocked me back a little. My head starts pounding almost instantly to where I wince and palm my forehead in hopes it would make it better.

"What's the matter?" my aunt asks me as she steps into the room and by my side. When I didn't answer she reached up and grabbed my forearm, pulling it down a little bit. "Look at me," she says calmly.

I wince again, and I felt like things were starting to spin. But I move my hand from my head and I force my eyes to open again to meet my aunts piercing gaze. I hear her tsk and she shakes her head at me with a sigh. "Focus," she suddenly ordered. I grumbled as I took my arm from her grasp and looked forward at the room again which I realized was starting to blur. I groan and shut my eyes. I didn't know what came over me, but I definitely wasn't surprised, even though it's been a little while since the last time my head ached like this. I feel my eyes flickering and shifting causing me to cringe at the uncomfortable sensation. "Ethan, open your eyes," I hear my aunt say. "Open your eyes and focus, or it will only get worse." I force my eyes open again and I feel my knees buckle from a sharp thump in my head.

It's alright.

I shake my head from a voice echoing through my mind.

It's okay to cry, darling.

I feel chills run up my spine and I see a flash of light before me. There's long dark hair and a woman curled up on a bed with a small boy in her arms.

Shhh.

I hear her cooing and I know it's my mother.

"Ethan…open your eyes."

I didn't realize they had shut again and I open them to see my aunt staring up at me worriedly. I let out a breath and I'm sinking down to the floor to sit.

"Focus," she repeats and sits down beside me. "The pain will go away if you see through it. Don't let something like pain best you. It's most likely what is blocking you from your memories. If you see something now, focus on it. Don't let it show you bits and pieces, demand to see it in its entirety."

I wince at another sharp pain but I listen intently to her. I was tired of the pain in my head. I stare down at my hands and focus my thoughts back on the image that flashed by just a moment ago.

Shhh.

I hear again. I stare passed my hands and I find the image of the woman again. I feel my eyes shift and somehow, I know they're not brown anymore. There's another flash of light and I can see this room at night, lights off, and the woman who I know is my mother laying there in my bed. Her body curled warmly around my small frame. I hear hiccups and whimpers and I know that I am crying.

"*I'm so sorry, eomma,*" I cry into her breast. She strokes my hair and I can almost feel her heart wrenching.

"*Why are you sorry,*" she asks softly to me.

The image fades away and there's another incredibly sharp pain that radiates down my neck and into my spine. I groan and squeeze my eyes shut.

"Ground yourself," I hear Nari whisper. "Don't let the pain best you." She places a hand against my back and although I didn't see the light that had been there, coming right out of her palm, I felt a strange tingling sensation penetrate my skin, and something that felt warm wrapped around each tense muscle. "*Him pulgo,*" release the tension is what she said to me. The muscles in my back relax and the pain let up again.

I let out a slow deep breath and I focus again on what seemed to be a memory. What was I sorry for? It seemed to be a theme that kept repeating itself and I had to know why. I open my eyes and stare down at my hands again. I had to stay grounded like my aunt said.

Another flash of light and I feel like I am not just watching the scene but a part of it. I'm in my mother's embrace. I feel her chest rising and falling. I feel the heat her body radiates. I can smell her scent, like ginger and jasmine.

"*Why are you sorry,*" I hear her say again, her voice ringing in my ear. I'm drawing in a shaky breath, and I'm sniffling snot like a child. Well…I was a child.

"*I didn't control my powers,*" I cry, "*I lost control a-and, and I scared Rosie. Rosie g-got hurt *sniff* because of *sniff* me.*" I'm angrily wiping my face free of tears with my small hands, but hot streams continue to fall from my eyes. My mother frowns lightly and she gently moves my hands back down to curl into my chest. "*A-and,*" I continue bitterly, "*I heard Mr. Aero a-and Gramma s-say that I…that I k—*"

"*Shh!*" the woman interrupts me sharply, pressing her fingers to my lips. I look up at her with large eyes and I can see her anguishing. "*Never mind what you heard,*" she said quietly. "*What matters is both you and Rose are alright. And that we all know it wasn't your fault. Sometimes we do things unintentionally. And we know that you feel nothing but remorse, even when you don't know exactly what you did. There's no need to feel so sorry, my love.*" She's holding me even tighter and I can do nothing but have my face pressed into her chest. It was warm there. Comfortable, and I didn't want to forget the feeling. I felt a tear escape. A tear that was real and not just a memory. There's another flash of light and I see my hands in front of me, trembling with the mixed emotions I felt. I turn my head and look at my aunt who sat there with a soft frown. She reached up and wiped the tear away.

"How do you feel?" she asks me.

I assess myself and notice that the aching in my head had completely gone away just the way it had suddenly appeared. Although the ache in my head subsided, an ache in my chest took its place. More so because I had unlocked a memory. It wasn't a happy time, and this thing about something I had done as a kid is highly concerning to me, but I longed to be there in that moment for real. My mother wrapped around me, comforting me, assuring me that things would be alright. I frown, and even when I try to replace the sadness I knew was in my expression with something more neutral, I couldn't control the quivering in my lip. Nari sees this and upon watching another tear escape from my watery eyes she wrapped her arms around me and pulled me into a strong hug.

"You remembered something," she pin-points and pats my back.

"I think I did something awful," I say after a moment. I sniff and wipe my face almost as bitterly as I had done in the memory. "Won't you tell me what it was? I hurt someone. I hurt Rose too. But how?"

She's quiet and I pull away to see her face. She draws in a slow breath and I feel her hesitating.

"I won't tell you that," she said to my disappointment. "I'm sorry, but not now, and not yet. I know you're a big boy now and can handle it, so I won't tell you it wasn't…awful. What's more important is retrieving your general memories for now. Remembering who you are, and awakening your magic again. After that, understanding what happened that day will be much easier than if you were to find out now. Just know that it truly wasn't your fault." She presses her lips together, watching my expression carefully to see if I would fight her about it, or demand she give a better answer. But I don't. Why would I? Even if I would feel better if I could just know all at once, I imagine everything is being told the way that it should in a way that makes sense to me. … if that makes sense. I avert my eyes from hers and I relax my shoulders.

"Then tell me something else," I say. "Why won't Gramma come back here? I'm here and she's still there—in Whitechapel."

I hear her sigh and she's shoving her fists into her jacket pockets after tussling her short hair.

"Honestly, I don't have an answer for that. Mama was supposed to bring you here herself. Then we could all be here together. But I guess just like River said, she's lost. I think…she got too comfortable there in that place. Maybe she's scared to come back and you get hurt."

"But it doesn't make sense. I'm here now so I could get hurt either way."

"Just give her time," she sighs again. "She just has to remember what's most important. She spent all that time there to protect you. But she has to see that you aren't a child anymore and you can't stay in that place for forever. You just can't."

"I'll have to go back there eventually," I say. "I can get her to come back if I tell her I got to meet you all."

"Hmm…" She stares at me for a moment before she rocked her way up to her feet. "At least stay until your birthday. Namu and I can come back here on that day because of Samhain. We can celebrate your birthday and Samhain together. You'll enjoy it." She smiles a little at me, hoping I'll agree. I guess I didn't see any problem with it, so I nod my head to accept her offer—not that I knew what a Samhain was. "Good." She nods, satisfied by my answer and she moves toward the door. "Settle in. The bathroom is just down the hall on the right when you come toward the stairs. If you need anything Namu and I will be downstairs. But we will be gone in the morning. Jem, Victoria, and Autumn are here of course, so if we've gone at some point and you need something just let any of them know. And like River said, she'll be back in the morning. Don't be shy to roam around, this *is* your home after all."

I nod to her and push myself up onto my feet. I take a second, though, to think over what she said. She just named three people and I only knew of two of them. I didn't question her about it, however, and I just move to take off my jacket and the bag still across my chest.

"Okay. Then goodnight, Ethan." She turns and leaves the room, shutting the door behind her and leaving me there alone.

I sigh to myself and turn to take in the room for the second time. I still didn't like the stagnant, untouched feeling it had in it. But it was cute in there regardless. It was weird to say it felt like me, but it did in a way. I walk over to the tall dresser and I see little wooden figurines languishing in dust, the paint chipping and aging. One was shaped like a horse, another like a little wizard man. There was another shaped like a cat, and one more shaped like a little girl. I reach out to touch the horse, and once my fingers closed around it, there was a sharp pain striking through my skull, a flash of light and then a vision of a younger me playing with the toys. I blink and groan at the jarring experience and I retract my hand. I turn around again and I look at the bag I laid on my bed, and I moved to pull out the extra shirt I packed. I grumble a little to myself, wishing I brought an actual set of clothes, but at least I had a shirt to sleep in. I pull off my hoodie and throw it where my jacket was and I change my shirt. After I was a bit more comfortable, I took out my toothbrush and moved to find the bathroom.

I pull the door of my room open and I look down the almost empty hallway. There in the middle of the floor was that silver cat curled up on its side, nestled into the violet carpet. I hear some water running and ignoring the cat I move down the hall and toward the right side where Nari said the bathroom was. There's a door opening on the left, and I stop immediately in my tracks.

There's a girl stepping out who I thought was going to be that woman Victoria, but it wasn't. Pink fluffy pajama pants step out first in fuzzy blue bunny slippers. There is a slender frame that is uncovered from the door and a girl who seemed less than aware of anything that had been happening outside of her room had appeared. Her hair was black and tied behind her back, but it was messy and sticking up in different places on top of her head. She wore large circle rimmed glasses and she seemed as if she had just woken up because she was yawning her entire soul out. In her arms was a stack of books chin high, and her blush-colored sweater was falling off one shoulder. She looked no older than me.

She didn't notice me standing there as she moved out of her room and toward the stairs, but then the door on the right swings open. A wet-haired Carson with a toothbrush hanging out of his mouth came waltzing out and it seemed neither of them saw each other. But somehow the blonde saw passed her at me and his eyes blew wide with what I assumed was going to be a tsunami of words. He opens his mouth, and as he takes a quick step toward me, I brace myself for the collision that was about to happen. The girl is basically walking with her eyes closed, still yawning. And then, as Carson is pulling the toothbrush from his mouth, both of them smack into each other. Carson spits everywhere as he fumbled backward onto the floor. The girl's books go flying and I'm strangely reminded of Patty that day at the library. Both of them groan after impact, and Carson nearly snaps at the girl to watch where she was going until he realizes it's a new face.

"Heyyy..." he whined and rubbed his bottom.

"Ow..." The front of the girl's hair had completely come loose and covered her face. She pouts and lifts herself onto her knees to start collecting her belongings. "I'm sorry, I didn't even see you," she apologizes.

"Hm? I haven't seen you before. Where have you been all this time?" Carson moves to help her and I eventually join them, collecting some of the books and handing them to the girl.

"I've just been in the study; I didn't know we had any guests." She pushes her hair out of her face, readjusts her glasses so she could see properly and she accepts the books from me. And then she notices that I am also a new face. She gasps a little, however, upon looking at me. She scrambled up onto her feet, abandoning the books in a pile on the floor and she fixes her sweater as to look less.....frankly a mess. "Are you *him?*" she asks me suddenly. Carson and I shared the same puzzled expression.

"Am I who?" I take an awkward step back as she took a step a little too close.

"*Him,*" she repeats frantically. "*Specturum Child*. Ethan Jaehyun Moon. The only Spirit S.E. alive! You look like him, just older—bigger, but like him. Is it really you? I heard sooo many stories and I just—"

"Autumn!" A familiar voice snaps and the three of us look over at the stairs where Victoria was emerging. She approaches us all but she never stops, walking past a drooling Carson, in between the one called Autumn and I and toward a corner to where the hallway branches off. "Don't be annoying," she calls. "Nobody likes strangers in their personal space." And with that she disappeared around a corner.

The girl in front of me relaxes and she takes a shy step back, twiddling her fingers.

"I'm sorry," she says. "It's just I heard that you were coming back after all this time. Only I seem to have forgotten when that would be." She drops her arms and she bends down to pick up her stack of books. She looked well awake now than she had before. "I'm Autumn, by the way. Autumn Feng. New addition to Genus Guild and Air S.E. It's really nice to meet you." She reaches out one hand and slowly I take hers and shake it.

"It's nice to meet you," I assure her. "Did we know each other before?" I let go of her hand and rub the nape of my neck sheepishly and she shakes her head in response.

"No, I'm only just now getting to meet you." She smiles a little. "When I joined the guild just last May, they told me a lot about you, your mother, and Mrs. Catherine. I hope I get the chance to meet her too one day. I hear that she is one of the strongest Water S.E.'s around. Even stronger than Ms. River! That's why she was asked to join the L.E.U."

"The what?"

"L.E.U. You know, the Lamia Elemalex Unit. Only the most powerful S.E.'s are invited to join. And what an honor! I hope that I could study enough to be worthy of such a position." She bounces a little in excitement and then she turns around to acknowledge the blonde who was now standing and brushing his teeth as he listened to what she had to say. "Who is this then?" she asks to no one in particular.

"I'm Carson," he answers muffled by the toothbrush in his mouth, "Ethan's *best* friend, and also even cooler than him. I have a band," he whispers the last part, wiggling his eyebrows at her.

"A band? That's nice. What S.E. are you?"

"Huh?" He sucks at his teeth and he looks up at me for help but really there was no point in telling her something different. My aunt and uncle already figured out he wasn't from here, and River already knew too.

"Is it Water?" she asks innocently after he doesn't answer. She adjusts her glasses and then looks between me and him. "Because of your eyes..."

"Actually," I speak up, "he's a special guest from...out of town."

"Out of town? Like from another district? Are you from Lamia? That can't be right, you don't seem like it..."

"No, no, I mean...*out of town*, out of town."

She pauses as she seemed to be turning the wheels in her head. Her eyes widen and she spins around again to gaze at Carson.

"You mean you're not from Obscura? Are you from another dimension?"

Carson scratches his head and shrugs a shoulder. "I guess," he answered plainly.

"Then what sort of being are you?"

"He's just a nohabi, Autumn," I say a little exasperated. "He's from Whitechapel, like me—I mean…like where I was before I came back here."

"O-oh." She's staring at him with wide eyes, and she had gone a little rigid. "Everyone else knows that right? It's really illegal…"

"Yes, everyone else knows. Just don't tell anyone outside of the guild, okay?"

She nods her head slowly at me and then her eyes go back to Carson who seemed to be wiping his shirt free of dribbled toothpaste.

"It's nice to meet you, Carson."

He winks at her and then moves passed the both of us after gesturing that he wanted to talk once I was done.

"If you'll excuse me," I say quietly and start to side step passed her.

"Oh yeah, of course. I'll see you around then." She offers a smile, readjusts her glasses, and then turns to continue her way to the stairs.

I breathe out once I enter the room. There were eucalyptus bunches everywhere (which actually smelled pretty nice). The mirrors were tall on one wall with a counter that stretched from corner to corner of the room. Two sinks and four racks for towels. The shower was really spacious and the room was big enough to hold a bath as well. It was really impressive, for what the house itself looked like on the outside. I step in front of the sink and stare at myself in the mirror for a moment. I looked like—well I looked *disheveled*. I looked like I haven't slept in ages, even when I thought I was pretty well dressed this morning. But even so, no amount of clothes can hide the status of your health. I frown a little bit but go on to wash up. When I was finished, I leave to reconvene with Carson. I find his room and knock on the door until I heard a noise that sounded like it was okay for me to come in.

I open the door and it's another spacious bedroom with sleepy blues and purples everywhere. There were candles burning on some shelves, and it smelled like lavender. I realize there's incense sticks burning in here like downstairs in the den. The room was lit by the soft light of candles and small lanterns strewn about the room and Carson laid across the queen-sized bed, playing a game on his phone. I'd almost say the mood in there was sleepy romantic. You know…if only Carson wasn't a part of it…

Anyway, I shuffle across the room and I climb up onto the bed with him where I bring my knees up to my chest. I sigh deeply and watch whatever RPG he was able to play without any wifi or data. He grunts, huffing and puffing as he fought off whatever enemy there was. That is until he died with a wail of defeat. I give him a slow clap as he rolled over onto his back, glaring up at me from where he lay.

"Shut up," he grumbled.

I chuckle at him and lean back against the headboard of the bed.

"What did you want," I ask.

"To hear about your talk with that girl, Rose. Also…how are you feeling, by the way? Like…even I still don't really…*get* what's going on here. But I've gathered that these folk are the family that's been missin' all this time."

I'm quiet for a moment as we share pointed looks with each other, his round blue eyes staring up into my (I guess) brown ones. I am hesitating to the point that he asks again. He rolls his eyes at me and sits up, setting his phone aside and folding his legs together. I frown a little, averting my eyes from his. The first and only thing I could really think about from the conversation was about the planted memories thing. How could I even begin to tell Carson something like that? And even if he believed it, how would he feel being manipulated all this time? So I decide not to bring it up. At least not yet. I look up again and instead answer:

"She knew my mother well. She didn't really say much but she said that she was really nice to her when she was younger. She was gonna tell me more but she said her father was wondering where she was." Before he can respond to this or ask any digging questions I change the subject, hoping to not bring up any trigging words that had to do with the strange timeline. "Anyway, after she left me and my aunt talked for a bit…after I had a little episode…"

"Again?" Carson grimaces at me. He really didn't like to hear about my headaches and anything that came with them. It always reminded him of when

I had been in the hospital just after he lost his father. Which then again, now I can't help but think about how this emotion is completely fabricated. Although I was in the hospital at that time, now I know we were complete strangers. We didn't know each other before that moment. How weird to even imagine it. I felt guilt churning in my stomach. I felt like I've been lying to him all this time even when I didn't know about it until now.

"I don't know, it was something about the room she took me to. But that's not really important. The important thing is there's something I did as a kid that caused all of this to happen."

"What d'you mean?" Carson asks slowly.

"I mean all of this. Literally *all* of it. The headaches, the bad dreams. My family splitting up, my mom dying. You heard the things River said earlier. Not that I think you were really listening but, all of *this* seems like one huge ripple effect from something I did a long time ago."

"Something like what? Like what sort of thing could you have done that would get your mom killed?"

It was a good question. What could a child have possibly done to get their parent killed? Or *sacrificed*? I sigh heavily and straighten out my legs on the bed.

"That's what I think I need to find out," I answer finally. "I asked my aunt but she straight up told me she wasn't going to tell me. At least not yet anyway. She said I had to remember everything first before she told me. It also sounds like even when whatever it was happened, I didn't even know I did something wrong at first, or…" I pause. "I dunno. But whatever it was, was bad."

"That's crazy." Carson pouts a little and looks down, fidgeting with a loose thread on the comforter now. "Do you think Rose knows what happened?"

My brow raises. I guess I haven't considered asking Rose yet, even when I know somehow that she was a part of it. That I hurt her in some way. I sit up some.

"I think she does," I say a little too quickly. "I know she knows about it because I saw it in a dream."

"A dream?"

"Well not exactly a dream. Just like one of those vision thingies. I was telling someone that I hurt her by accident.

Carson stares at me silently for a moment before drawing in a breath.

"'Kay well, maybe you should work on that memory problem you got goin' on. It'll be like figuring out your origin story or somethin'." He chuckles a little. "Oh, and that thing your aunt did when she came in—that sparky, sparky, electro-lightening whatever? So, can you do that too or what?!" He's suddenly excited and he's bouncing a little as he watched me expectantly. "I can think of a few things we could do with that. Think of the people we could freak out!"

"Carson," I grumble, wanting him not to make a joke of this.

"I'm just sayin'," he shrugs. "Well, even if you can't, that weird thing you've been doing with your eyes recently is probably enough. You're lucky I'm such a good friend or I would have dipped out the second I saw that freaky mess. I mean at first, I was like 'no way, hard pass'. But then I thought about it and realized that I am the chosen one."

"…" I blink stupidly at him, not sure what exactly he is going on about all of a sudden. "…what?"

"No, look." He leans forward a little, and I lean backward as if the next thing to leave his mouth would actually physically hit me in some way. "*This is real life.*"

"…yeah?"

"Yeah," he nods, "and, like, clearly Ethan is havin', like, this weird 'calling to adventure' thing, like the story arch—no, story…" he's snapping his fingers as if it would help him remember what he's trying to say, "…well you know, that thing we learn about in English class! Anyway, so that's what all of this is somehow in real life. Like we're in a literal movie, and *I* am the chosen one."

"How would *you* be the chosen one?"

"Because! I'm your best friend, stupid! Which means I have to be here while you figure out whatever magic powers or…shape shifting thing you're obviously 'bout to go through! And then when you figure all that crap out, *I* will have the *power* to have you do. my. bidding. I was chosen to have a WIZARD as my best friend! Isn't that great?!" He clasps his hands together, grinning like an idiot while I stare back at him dumbfounded. "Best friend privileges, obviously."

My mouth drops a little. Perhaps I shouldn't have been so surprised. Carson somehow always managed to shift any sort of conversation into … whatever *that* is.

I swing my legs off of the bed and stand up without looking at him. Despite his cheerfulness I feel like I have to go and get my thoughts straight.

"I'm going to bed," I say awkwardly as I head straight for the door. "And I'm not a wizard."

I left him there without waiting for any kind of response, and I hoped he wouldn't get up to follow me. When I shut the door behind me and spun to the left to go back down the hall to that room of mine, I didn't realize the fuzzy pink pajamas bending over in the middle of the hall. In full stride I completely run into Autumn, basically mowing her over before I went stumbling onto the floor.

I hear her squeak as if someone had just stepped on their dog's chew toy, and I open my eyes after processing why there was a terrible pain in my right knee.

"*Ow!*" I semi (but also not really) fuss at her. I see her across from me lying on her side now on the floor. Whatever it was she had been picking up was now strewn everywhere. They looked like blue berries from an open jar that was also lying sadly on its side.

"You're heavy!" she cries out as she sits up into a sitting position, rubbing her shoulder sheepishly.

"Well yeah, I can't be this tall and weigh ten pounds!"

"You could…if you were like…a tall body pillow."

My shoulders drop as I stared at her pouting expression. Her hair was still a mess, she still wore her large round glasses and everything about her seemed…child-like.

"I'm not one of those, now, am I?" I sigh. "You're lucky I at least didn't land on top of you. You would've been hurt." I'm pushing myself up to my feet and I step over to where her spilled berries were to help her pick them up. "What were you doing anyway in the middle of the floor?"

"I didn't realize the jar of juniper berries wasn't closed properly," she says shyly and crawls over to start collecting what I now understand aren't blueberries. "I dropped them by mistake and they went everywhere. I'm sorry."

I frown a little at her as I grab the glass jar and drop a handful of the collected berries into it.

"Why are you apologizing to me about that? I'm sure it was just an accident."

"I…yes, it was an accident," she starts slowly while she too put a handful into the jar. "But I'm always doing stuff like that. Victoria says that a good witch would never be so clumsy. No matter how hard I try, I'm always making such stupid mistakes."

"Autumn…" I watch her throw in another handful, her body going rigid with frustration. "Hey," I reach out and stop her as she scooped up some more, making her meet my eyes. Her demeanor softens and she looks up at me for only a second before her face went red and she turns away. "It's okay to be clumsy. I'm sure there are a lot of successful people who are clumsy too. I don't know what kind of things Victoria tells you but don't let her make you feel bad," I tell her.

When she didn't respond right away, I moved to gather up the rest of the juniper berries and I pour them all into the jar, closing the lid tight and standing up to my feet.

"Thank you, Ethan," she says finally. She picks up the jar and stands up as well. "You're rather kind. I've heard that you were like that before."

"You heard that I was kind before," I ask to clarify.

"Mhm." She nods her head and looks down at the jar in her hands. "They, said you had always been kind to people. I'm glad you still seem to be that way." She stares awkwardly passed me, avoiding my gaze for a moment before asking: "Where were you headed by the way?"

"Just my room," I answer and turn toward that direction. "If you don't need anything else I'll just go there, I guess." I shrug a little, and I guess something about my body language hinted to the fact that I wasn't really all that thrilled to go back there. Yes, I most definitely wanted to sleep or lay down, and even though I thought the room itself was cute, I just didn't like the way it felt when I stepped into it. Autumn picks up on this somehow and she's clutching her jar close to her chest as she finally meets my eyes with her innocent ones.

"Maybe you'd like to have the room cleansed," she suggests, her voice going quiet as if she were almost too shy to say so.

"What does that mean?"

"Ah right, your memory. Here, I'll go run to my room and grab some things and I'll meet you there and show you." She smiles but doesn't wait for me to answer before spinning around and jogging off to her room. I stood there as I watched the orange scrunchy hanging on for dear life at the very end of her "pony tail" swing and eventually slip off once she rounded the corner into her room. I shake my head but turn the opposite direction and head toward my own room.

The moment I pushed open my door and I was greeted by that stagnant, empty feeling, I hear slippers sliding across the carpet and something rummaging around. I turn to see that Autumn moved a lot quicker than what was probably necessary, and her glass jar of juniper berries was replaced by a small wooden chest with the moon phase cycle carved into it.

She almost seemed excited until our eyes met and she immediately went shy. She draws back a little after realizing where she stopped had been a little too close and then she gestured into the room.

"After you," she says timidly.

"What did you bring?" I step into the room and cringe inwardly at the shift in feeling the room had. At first, I didn't exactly know how to describe it. But as I stepped in there a second time I now think it feels like walking into a room who you know belonged to someone you once knew who has died.

I look over at Autumn who was moving toward the bed side table. She sets the box down and then corners the bed, crossing the room and over to the window where she unlocks a clamp and pushes it open.

"Let's let some fresh air in here," she says without answering me. I realize she must have found her scrunchie as her back was turned to me, she had her hair tied again with it already falling loose like before. "Do you know what it means to be a witch born under Spirit," she suddenly asks, turning once more to look at me.

I shrug and shake my head a little in response. I expect her to make a sort of annoyed or frustrated expression like Rose does whenever I admit to not knowing anything, but she only smiles at me as she crosses the room again and goes back to her little box.

"It means," she starts, "that you are in tune with the energies of everything. Literally everything." I watch her open the box and she pulls out a lighter, a fresh white candle, and what looked like a toothpick. She carves three symbols into the base of the candle with the tooth pick and when she finishes, she sets it down on the bedside table, picks up her lighter, and lights it. After this she goes around the room and starts lighting the candles that were already there. "I hear it could be quite burdensome," she continues, "because tuning in to so many things at once is very draining. All Spirit S.E.'s are empaths. Other S.E.'s can be so too, but not all of them are like people like you. Clairvoyant, clairaudience, clairsentience—which is very similar to being empathic; and mediumship are all gifts that a Spirit S.E. has. So naturally you would be able to pick up on the energies people give off, animals, nature, and even objects." She stops and meets my eye again after she finished lighting the last candle on top of the desk in the corner of the room. "I assume you must be picking up on residual energy left in this room since the last time you were in it. No one else has been in here since you were taken to the port town to change the flow of energy. Even I can feel that it's quite uncomfortable in here."

"Glad it wasn't just me…" I mutter. "Why do you all keep calling Whitechapel a 'port town'? It's not even near any ports or…big bodies of water (I think)."

She turns and goes back over to her chest and this time she pulls out a small bundle of sage. She lights the tip of it, lets it burn for a few seconds before blowing the flame out and letting smoke billow out from the end.

"That's not what 'port town' means," she answers and starts waving the bundle around the room. "We call it that because in order to leave and enter Obscura you have to use portals. There are only a few that actually lead from mundane Earth to Obscura. And Whitechapel was the closest portal from where you were that night on June 21st. It's a port town because it's where the portal leads to once you leave Obscura from Lamia. I assume when you came back here the first District you were in was Lamia, right?"

"Yeah, I think so," I answer.

"Right. So that is why you've been in Whitechapel all this time. So that you could live close enough to come back. And, well, now that you're here…" She trails off and looks at me as she's waving smoke over my bed. "Maybe I have no place to ask this, but I've always wondered, maybe you'd want to help Greenwood keep its independence."

My head tilts to the side and I rub the back of my neck. "Whuduya mean 'keep'?"

She bites her lip a little and she walks over to the desk where there was what looked like an ashtray. She sets down the bundle of sage as its smoke was dying down.

"Perhaps…" she starts off hesitantly, "Princess Rose could tell you about it more accurately. Even though I hope to be strong enough to be invited as an Air Elemalex witch one day, I really don't want to work in Lamia while King Rhyland is still ruling. It'd be nice if King Xxavier could be found alive and well…"

"But what does that have to do with Greenwood's independence? I guess I didn't realize all of the districts were independent."

"Well, they are. But they're also meant to work together in order to keep peace throughout Obscura." I watch her walk over to the tall shelf case in the room and she's looking through the assortment of jars. "Oh, it looks like you used this mixture the most," she says and picks up a jar with a mixture of herbs that was almost empty. I walk over to her and peer over her shoulder at it. There was an aged sticker across the base of the jar, and written in cursive it said: **E. Jaehyun's Relax Blend**

I watch Autumn flip the lid open and she reaches up on one of the top shelves and pull down a tiny cast iron cauldron. She pours some of the contents into it, closes it, puts it back in its place, and then moves over to the desk where she left her lighter.

"Anyway," she continues, "of course, through history Obscura has had its ups and downs, but most of the time we have been at peace. Only recently Lamia District has been crossing lines that it shouldn't be allowed to ever since King Xxavier went missing and his nephew took over. Lamia is trying to rise up higher than the laws already set in place. They want to take over all of the districts, and unfortunately, they already won over Sierra. Their next target is Greenwood…" She's lighting the dry herbs and almost instantly there is a lovely scent of chamomile and lemon balm that breaks through the sharp smell of sage. I breathe in deeply and there's a sense of calm that washes over me. "Oh…"

I look at Autumn as she had turned to look up at me.

"That's strange. Your eyes are…"

"Flickering or something?" I finish, not surprised anymore by this. I watch her nod a little and she steps to the side passed me to go back toward her little box.

"I've never seen that. Sometimes it happens in children but it's really a rarity. It must have a lot to do with an inner stress."

"Yeah, my aunt told me earlier."

She hums a little bit as she puts the few tools she took out back in their box. She closes it and then crosses the room to close the window. After this, she faces me once more.

"One of the biggest reasons why Lamia wanted you gone was to stop a powerful being from messing up their plans. It's probably more obvious than they intended it to be. But since you're alive, maybe you can stand up to them since you're more capable than others." She sighs and plays with a string on her sweater, looking down shyly. "I probably had no business saying anything like that. But actually, I'm a little scared. Victoria told me if I admitted something like that I should go back home and leave the guild…but it makes me wonder how could she not be even a little bit worried about what could happen when they start trying to take over the H.D.O?"

I frown a little at her. I wished I could understand her feelings entirely, but I just didn't know enough about Obscura and the actual situations going on. Maybe it would be better if I could restore my memory. Though I didn't understand why I should be responsible in standing up to an entire district of people, but then again maybe something about these powers people keep claiming that I have could make a difference. If something was going to happen to Greenwood, the district that is my family's home, I should care enough to want to stop it. I sigh and I reach out, placing my hand on her shoulder.

"Don't be afraid," I tell her. "Maybe one day I can help. I don't want to see anything happen to this place either." I smile a little and she smiles some back before taking a deep breath and letting it out.

"That incense smells really good. No wonder it's almost used up. Also, what do you think? Does it feel any better in here to you?"

I take a moment and feel the energy around me, which is kind of a weird thing to say when I think about it. But the room didn't feel stagnant and heavy anymore. It felt clear and just about inviting. I nod at her and draw my hand back, putting it into my pocket.

"It does, actually," I admit. "I guess you'll have to teach me about what you did."

She giggles quietly and picks up her box. "Sure. But I think when your memory comes back, you'll remember how to do it. It's only the basics of cleansing. Anyway, I'm sure you want to get some sleep now." She's moving toward the door and I turn to watch her.

"Yeah, thanks. Goodnight, then."

She offers a smile and pulls open the door, and without another word she left, shutting the door behind her.

When she was gone I breathe out, and then take in the scent again that was filling my room. After a moment I move over to the mirror that leaned against the wall and I watched as my eyes shift between brown and green over and over. I cringe at the strange feeling and try to remember what my aunt said about focusing and grounding myself. But I seemed to not be able to work it out this time. After giving up I move to my bed, drop the stuff that was on it onto the floor and crawl into it. There were too many thoughts going on in my head and I wanted to just drift away at this point. Maybe in the morning I could see some changes.

• • •

I didn't know what time it was, and I still couldn't read those stupid clocks. It was dark in my room except for the beam of moonlight that poured through my window. To my surprise, however, I had fallen asleep not too long after Autumn had left my room. My bed was warm, comfortable—unlike mine in Whitechapel which was often cold and hard. And that cozy smell of chamomile and lemon balm beat the old moldy wood smell in my room in Whitechapel by a long shot. For a moment I could say I felt content. In the right place.

Until I felt something cold and heavy jar me awake.

My eyes fly open after feeling that cold and heavy something gradually weigh down on my chest until I realized I was struggling to breathe. But as I looked frantically around the room, gasping for air, I didn't see a single thing except the fact that everywhere I looked was an eerie shade of purple. I look around for a light source that could have been making the room look this way, but when I saw none, I blink my eyes rapidly, hoping it was just a dream, or maybe I was half asleep so things didn't look quite the way it should. But nothing changes and the heaviness in my chest doesn't change, causing me to panic.

I scramble out of bed, tripping over the sheets and the bag I left on the floor. I gasp for another breath and press my hand against my chest to try and feel what's going on, but there still was nothing that could be identified. I hear something outside my window and whip around to see, but the weird shade of blacks and purples before my eyes made it hard to make out any detail. I then stumble my way across the room to find the lights and struggle to find any switch. A frustrated grunt leaves my mouth and then I'm gasping again for air, the heaviness in my chest worsening. As I went through my head trying to figure out if this was what a heart attack feels like, a stroke, or some other awful thing, I came to the revelation that going to find some help was probably the most useful thing to do. As I skirt across the wall to find the door, there is suddenly a burning sensation starting in the tips of my fingers; the complete opposite feeling of what feels attached to my chest. My hands draw back from what I thought was the door. I was sure I was touching something hot, but there was nothing that I could see that would've been.

I look through the dark and the blacks and purples at my hands. Still nothing seemed abnormal about them, but the burning I felt was spreading, traveling from the tips of my fingers to my palms, up to my wrists and sizzling its way through my arms. A loud groan is ripped from my belly as it felt like actual fire was coursing through my veins. My eyes tear up at the pain and I gasp again. The icy feeling in my chest churned into something hot and electric. Help…I needed help.

I lift my arms through the pain and find the door knob, pulling the door open. I trip out of the room, gasping at the spreading heat from my arms and chest to my neck and down my spine. There was a light on in the hall but everything still looked purple and dark. I open my mouth to call out for someone, but a sharp ringing in my ears silences me.

"Come."

A loud deep voice booms at me in what sounded like two languages at once, and I was sure others should have heard it too. I jump and look around through my blurring teary vision to see who it came from. There's no one.

"Ethan, follow me."

My skin is burning and the air around me is buzzing. The voice(s) ring terribly in my ears and I reach up to cover them, but then I catch a glimpse of something at the end of the hallway. A black shadow slithered like a snake along the wall. Dark smoke billowed from it, and it left a stench of burning coal.

It wanted me to follow. But did I look that naïve to do something stupid like that? HA HA! No. I needed to get to Autumn; her room was closest. I groan again at another wave of hot pain sizzling through my body. I hug myself around the middle and my feet drag as I moved down the hall toward Autumn's room.

"Come."

I hear it again. Something about the voice made me feel nauseous and dizzy. I turn again to see where that shadow had gone. There are clouds of thick black mass stuck to the ceiling, slithering around like worms and filling the room with its awful smell. I gasp again, each breath becoming much harder and slower than the last. I take a few more heavy steps toward Autumn's door.

My feet are moving toward the stairs. Step after step as if I were sleepwalking. I pass Autumn's room. I pass Carson's room. The mass at the stairs draws backward the closer I came and I find that I'm following it downstairs, into the den and ultimately out of the house. Faintly I hear doors opening, and maybe muffled sounds of talking, but I can't focus in on anything else.

"Let…go…" I'm mummering hoarsely. To who I don't know. As I step outside, I'm greeted by a brisk gust of wind. I feel the damp, freezing earth under my bare feet and step after step I'm walking away from the house. There something darting through the sky, another dark mass. On the ground a smokey shadow slithering through the dirt from behind a tree toward me. "L-let…go…" I mummer again.

I'm out of breath and I can't breathe in anymore. My eyes shut and for a moment I felt absolutely nothing anymore. Everything was dark and felt like the state of sleep you're in before you start dreaming.

For a moment it was okay.

"ETHAN!"

I hear a woman's voice this time, breaking through the thick silence that was plugging my ears.

"Ethan, wake up! Wake up!" I feel slapping on my face, I feel my shoulders gripped and shaken.

My eyes open, and still through shades of blacks and purples I can see my aunt hovering over me. My uncle at her left, Jem on her right. As my mind was trying to focus in on them, and my mouth opens to speak, my body is suddenly tensing. My back arching as my voice is ripped from my throat in excruciating pain. Tears escape my eyes, and I'm unsure of what's happening to me.

"Ethan, what's wrong?!" I hear my aunt cry as her hands recoil.

My eyes blink away a few more tears and I catch a glimpse of a huge black figure standing behind her. Its eyes were nothing more than tiny golden lights, and upon looking at it I feel my body seize up and words spill from my mouth that I don't even understand. I couldn't tell if I was speaking English, Korean, or something else.

"Someone call, River. NOW!" I hear Nari order urgently.

"What's going on?" I could hear my best friend's voice this time and he comes into view for a second before he's quickly pushed away.

"Stay back," someone tells him.

My vision goes completely black now, I stop speaking, and I'm unsure if I had fainted or not, although I was still aware of the amount of pain I was in. This went on for a long time. Even when I tried to open my eyes again, they just wouldn't. My body was limp and at this point I could hear nothing outside of an irksome buzzing sound.

• • •

When I was finally able to open my eyes and see, the sun was already halfway across in the sky. I was no longer outside and was laid on the couch in the den. Carson was asleep on the floor next to me. Jem was in his corner flipping through a pile of books. There was a pungent smell of cloves and black pepper coming from the kitchen. I groan at a terrible pounding in my head and move to sit up but find my body was sore and weak all over.

"Don't move," someone says from behind. I turn my head to the side and I see River standing behind the couch, a mortar and pestle in her hands as she grinded something inside it up.

I take in a deep breath and realize it was easy to breathe again. I take a few more deep breaths just to be sure and then open my mouth to test my voice.

"What…happened to me?" I ask her, my voice hoarse. River frowns a little and shakes her head. She was wearing her crescent moon glasses, her long wavy hair was tied behind her in some intricate kind of way and she wore an orange floral apron over a blue and grey dress.

"We don't really know, dear," she answers finally and then rounds the couch. There was a medium sized cauldron hanging over the fire in the fireplace and she poured whatever she was mixing into it. Smoke billows out from it and a bitter smell comes wafting out. After this she comes back over to my side, stepping over Carson still slumbering on the floor. She presses her hand against my forehead, and then against my cheek. "Still warm," she mutters, mostly to herself than to me. "But…at least your eyes aren't purple anymore."

"Purple?!" My neck jerks a little as I tried to get a better look at her, but I wince at the shooting pain in my spine.

"Don't move," she repeats. Her hand leaves my cheek and she's stroking my bangs backward out of my face before she pulls back and stands up straight. "Did you see anything last night? Anything strange or unusual?"

"There were these black shadow things. They were like…smoking. And they smelled really bad…like burnt barbeque or something." I look at her again, expecting to see her judging me somehow. "They covered the ceiling upstairs in the hall. And some were sliding across the floor. A-and there was this figure outside. When Aunt Nari was checking to see if I was okay. I saw it standing behind her. But other than that, there was nothing else. Just…a lot of pain."

River is silent for a second.

"We can only assume that with the same way your wiped memory is blocking off your powers on the witch's side, it would equally affect your powers on the…on your…" she pauses and grimaces a bit, "on the other side. Exactly how, we don't know. We don't understand that part of you. Now rest."

8

The Reason Why

The rest of that morning I stayed glued to the couch. I was in and out of sleep. When I was conscious Carson talked my ear off about I don't know what until someone told him to shut up (which was always Victoria whenever she left the kitchen). River came in and out to check on my condition and even Autumn had come by a few times from wherever she hides to sit with me. I was a little upset that my aunt and uncle had gone, but they promised they would come back again on my birthday. Which was actually tomorrow. As of now, however, I had woken up again from another (thankfully peaceful) sleep. Carson was playing with the little silver cat that begrudgingly allowed him to touch her, and Autumn had been told to rub some sort of salve over my upper half. Kinda weird, I could've done it myself, but if I protested, I was immediately shut down.

"What time is it?" I ask as Autumn rubbed in the stuff that smelled strongly of rosemary into my arm.

"It's nearly half past 1," she answers through her intent focus. She looked a lot more put together today. I imagine since yesterday she was a little caught off guard when she found strangers in the house, she wasn't prepared to look her best. Today her thick hair was brushed and neatly rested over her shoulders. She wore an old-fashioned, blush-colored baby-doll blouse and billowing wide-legged pants. She didn't have on her glasses; her lips were painted with a natural pink tint and she had on a necklace with a piece of what looked like selenite strung into it. She was pretty, now that I could clearly see her face.

My ears perk at the sound of the front door opening and closing, and all of us but Autumn turned our heads to see who would be walking in. We could hear River exchanging words with someone for a little while, but it was a little too muffled to make out. And then after a moment Rose's small frame comes traipsing into the room. She was pulling nervously at the ends of her hair that lay loose around her shoulders. She wore a white lace Edwardian-style dress that somehow accentuated how delicate and feminine she looked. Her eyes almost immediately meet mine and her gaze shoots guilt and apprehension into my gut. She rounds the couch and she sees Autumn now rubbing some of the thick opaque paste into my chest and stomach. My nose turning up at the strong smell. I see her make a look and I feel my face flushing and I'm almost compelled to cover up my naked upper half. After gazing at Autumn and watching what she was doing, she skirts beside the couch and sits down on the coffee table.

"How are you feeling?" she asks, her voice soft and gentle. I look away feeling embarrassed and I stare over into the fire of the fireplace.

"I'm better now," I mummer. "I got some sleep so my body doesn't ache as much anymore."

"That's good." I watch her eyes land on Autumn again and she watches her hand rub into my chest. Something about her felt sharp and I think back to when Autumn explained my susceptibility to energies. The heat rises in my cheeks and I move to sit up some. "I think," I start a little too hastily, "you've done enough, Autumn. Thank you, truly." Her eyes meet mine and it felt like she was reading me. After a second, she closes the jar in her hand and then she stands up.

"I'll be back with some tea," she said quietly before disappearing out of the room.

Rose looks at me again and I awkwardly move to pull my shirt on.

"There's something you should know," she says cautiously. She pulls out a rolled-up piece of parchment from the tie in her dress and she hands it to me. After adjusting my shirt, I take it and look over the words inscribed on the side of it.

Sierra District Correctional Department

"I heard what happened from Miss Nari earlier this morning," Rose says. I look up at her as I'm unrolling the parchment and her nervous expression returns. "We have a record of just about everything at Lamia Castle. After my schedule ended, I went to the records room and took the latest record on your father. I think regardless of the family you have here, no one can help you understand the other half of you but him. Last night sounded rather serious. Before anything worse happens, perhaps you should finally meet him..."

I stare at her a little dumbfounded. To meet my father? The person I was sure doesn't even exist. I didn't even know what he looked like, even from an image. I didn't know his name; nothing at all. Slowly I look down at the open parchment and I feel my heart thumping in my ears.

Sierra District Correctional Department: Inmate **17-♭♀☿-2901**
Name: Yohan Moon
Dob: May 23 (year unknown), Mt. Fichik, Sierra District
Status: High-risk Oddity (Tier 2)

About: A rare high-risk with abilities yet to be understood. Born in Fichik seemingly from the shadows. There seems to be no parents but inmate continuously mentions "Darkness" personified. Two previous accounts of hostility have been recorded. Inmate is father to the Spirit Boy.

Sentencing: As of Jan^{uary} 3rd, 1999, Yohan Moon is barred from crossing Sierra boarders and is sentenced to life for the murder of 5 Lamia officers and severe injury to Lamia Military First Sgt. Henri Gualtiero.

As of today (J^{uly} 17th, 2008) inmate remains sedentary, doesn't eat and has had few visitors. He is to not meet with anyone from now until the end of his sentence. He will continue to be held in Carrier 22215 lined with sunstone unless action is necessary.

Note 1: Sunstone and Calendula seems to weaken him.
Note 2: Extremely cunning and highly powerful, do not let him trick you.

S.D.C.D
Eustace Odoardi

My teeth clench and I look back up at Rose.

"We can go there together if you want. Just don't tell Madam River. And certainly not your grandmother, she'd lock me away somewhere," she says.

Carson is looking over at us from the floor. After a bitter slap to the face from little Yulie he shifted his attention over to what was happening over here. He crawled over and was reading the parchment from my side.

"My father is in jail somewhere?" I ask her. "He murdered some people?"

Rose nods her head and then hugs herself.

"I never met him either, Ethan. He's been in jail since before we were born. I once heard that Lady Jiha visited him after finding out he'd been put in prison. Told him she was pregnant and left him. They say he did a lot of terrible things even while imprisoned until he heard of yours and your mother's death. After that they said he was no different than a whiffling stump."

"A what?" Carson questions before I could.

Rose looks between us at our puzzled expressions and she shakes her head.

"It's a sort of rock creature that mainly lives in Sierra," she explains. "Anyway, the only matter is letting you travel freely around Obscura. Which means people will have to find out that you're still alive. I've done some thinking about it. Whether they do or don't you will run into problems either way. Now that you've been brought back to Obscura and into Greenwood safely—after your passport is renewed, you'll have a sort of immunity from any severe action against you. The druids will protect you from any made-up legal trouble Lamia may want to enforce against you. We'll just have to avoid going into Lamia too often to stay on the safe side."

Autumn enters the room again and she approaches and sets down a tray of tea. As she's pouring cups for everyone, Victoria is strutting into the room from the kitchen. Her lips still deep red, her hair pulled up into a spiraled ponytail. She had on trousers that puffed around the knees, and she wore an off the shoulder blouse, all covered up with a frilly pink apron. She also came over and set down a tray of little sandwiches and a gravy boat with something golden colored in it.

"You forgot the honey, Autumn. I can't keep telling you that a good witch never forgets simple instruction. Right?"

"I'm sorry…" Autumn basically whispers as she stands up straight and lowers her head submissively.

"Sorry doesn't fix it. Come back into the kitchen so you can show me the charm you studied last night. Hurry up, I've got lots of other stuff to worry about." She's striding away, only to stop in the doorway for a minute to look back at me. "The tea is ginger. It'll help break your fever, sweet pea. Keep eating so fangs can see you get big and strong again." She winks and she's gone. Autumn awkwardly shuffles out of the room after her and I turn back to look at Rose whose eyes had disappeared to the back of her skull.

I sigh and sit up completely. Aside from the light throbbing throughout my neck and spine I really did feel better. Better enough to get up and move around. I gesture for Carson to hand me one of the tea cups, but Rose moves before he does, too slow to figure out what I meant. She pours some honey into it, stirs it up and then hands it to me.

"So, I don't have to worry about sneaking around then?" I ask her before taking a careful sip of the hot liquid.

"Right," she starts and gives a pointing Carson a sandwich from the tray. "For the most part anyway. We just didn't want to be seen before the druids were aware of your return. As long as they know, Lamia won't be able to react to your return unlawfully without Greenwood stepping in on your behalf. So first thing is heading to the H.D.O and getting your papers updated and your passport renewed. And then also alerting the archdruid of your return while we're there."

"Then we can go find my father after," I say with a little more enthusiasm. "And finally get some answers about my other powers."

"And more importantly learn how to understand and control them," Rose adds. "That way, as your memory is coming back and your powers return, we don't have any… uhm… accidents."

Her words instantly remind me of the vision I had yesterday. She must know that whatever these "other powers" are, they're dangerous. After all, because of *those* powers, I hurt her, and also got my family in trouble in the first place.

"What is it," she asks.

I take a second, wondering if now was the time to ask her about it or not. But before I can say anything, Carson speaks up with a mouth full of sandwich.

"What about my mom?" he asks. "I mean I know y'all said it'll be fine but I have to go home at some point, right?"

Rose and I look down at him. He wasn't wrong. I was certain the both of us would need to go back home at some point.

"I guess that depends on what you want to do," Rose tells him.

Carson turns around and looks at me, seeing if I had any input. But when I didn't say anything, he shrugs his shoulders.

"As long as I don't get into any trouble, I don't care," he says. "I mean, this definitely beats any test, amaright?" He's laughing and raising his hand up for a high five. But Rose and I still only stare at him. His laugh slows to an awkward chuckle until he's completely quiet and puts his hand down.

"When I go to check up on Gramma you can check up on your mom," I say finally.

"Madam River stopped by Whitechapel earlier to put a spell on your mother. Currently she thinks you both are away on a school trip for a week. So that'll buy you plenty of time before you might want to go back there. As long as we can get you a passport at the H.D.O. then there should be no problem with you staying here."

"That's fine, I guess."

River walks into the room now with a tiny jar in her hand. She approaches us and sits beside Rose on the coffee table.

"Since you're sitting up you must be feeling better," she said and reached out, handing me the little jar. I take it and examine the thick blueish liquid in it, then I look back up at her with a raised eyebrow.

"Drink that," she told me.

"…um sure…but what is it?" I give it a whiff and there was a sharp smell of orange peel and something unpleasantly sour.

"It's been ten years since your memory was wiped. I'm worried about whether or not it'll come back completely. I thought I'd try a little experiment to see if I can help…Now drink up."

My mouth turns up but I wouldn't dare protest. There was no telling who would force something down my throat next.

I hold my nose and gulp down the stuff in one take. As it went down it left a terrible bitter taste in my mouth, enough to make me shutter. The three in front of me stare at me expectantly, but nothing happens.

"Well," River starts after a moment, "I guess we'll just have to wait and see if it does anything."

"River," Rose speaks up this time, turning to look at the woman as she took the little jar from me, "what do you think about us going to the H.D.O. today?"

The old woman's eyebrows raise and she pulls off her glasses, letting them hang down by their beads.

"The H.D.O.? What for?"

"I was only thinking that Ethan couldn't possibly just remember everything should he stay here within four walls. He has to see his home in its entirety. Or at least, familiar places. If he's going to do that, I believe we'll have to break the secret that he isn't dead."

River pauses for a moment, thinking over Rose's words carefully.

"I agree that keeping him inside won't be doing him any favors. Scott should be back in town today as well. You should stop by his office just so he can make sure you're actually alright." She looks at me this time. It's a little strange to say it would be nice to see a familiar face like my doctor's. But I was happy to say the least, other than feeling like I had a bone to pick with him about keeping secrets. "Take Jem with you. I trust you Rose to be able to hold your own, but it'd be better to have someone else with you that's familiar with everything. Particularly in our district."

I see Jem lift his head from over in his corner and he looks over with a face less than happy to hear River volunteering him as chaperone. He speaks up for the first time since he opened the door for us yesterday but is almost immediately shut down.

"I would rather—" he starts with his low voice.

"You would rather help our one and only Spirit and family of this guild travel safely through the district until he's back home with us," River says sternly. "I'm only asking you this once, Jem."

He frowns deeply at her but says nothing else. He shuts his books a little too aggressively, stands up with a huff and stomps off.

"He seems thrilled," Carson mumbled as he had taken the last sandwich from the tray Rose and I didn't even get to touch.

"He'll be fine. But listen to me now," River seems to be directing her speech to Rose and I and her expression is more serious than before. "Greenwood has been seeing a lot more Oddity Hunters recently. I would strongly suggest you stay clear of them as much as possible. Particularly the ones from Lamia. There's no telling what they're truly up to around there. It's okay if you are seen, Ethan, but try to keep a low profile. Don't make a spectacle of yourself. And although I'm not any of your mothers…I'd prefer you all be back before dark."

"That shouldn't be any problem, Madam River," Rose responds and rises to her feet.

. . .

After Carson and I showered and dressed, we joined Rose down in the den where she waited with a little book in her hands and a thick woolen cloak around her shoulders. Jem was also there, leaning grumpily against a wall with his boots laced and a coat on, collar hiked high. As Carson and I entered the room, we also heard the 100 percent one sided bickering that was coming from Victoria. She stood there by River's chair, her palm was facing the ceiling and there hovering just above it was a cloud of what actually looked like soil, spinning rapidly in a sphere shape.

"Just concentrate, Autumn, it should be the easiest thing for an Air S.E. to do."

Autumn held her palm up and her eyes strained at her hand. One second nothing was happening at all, then the next there was a wild gust of wind that sprung from her palm. It flung upward like a whip and slashed against the wall behind her, causing the portraits and other things hanging to come crashing down.

"Stop! Stop! Stop!" Victoria demands urgently. Autumn closes her fist; her eyes were flickering a greyish color and then the wind fades into nothing. River was peeking her head into the room from the doorway and we all stared at the mess that lay around the two girls. Autumn drops her arm and her face is riddled with remorse. "How many times will you let that happen, Autumn?" Victoria snaps. "You could've hurt someone. Particularly *me*. I just bought this top!" She's gesturing to her blouse and River is stepping halfway into the room shaking her head.

"Please, be kind, Tori," she tells her. She waves her hand and the mess is rising into the air. Everything gives a spin before finding their original places once more. The portraits fly back onto the wall, the shattered glass pieces itself back together again. The lights that had been knocked over replace themselves and then everything looks just the same as before. Like nothing ever happened.

Carson stares wide-eyed and mouth opened. And I suppose I looked no different. River steps back out of the room and silence had fallen for a moment before Autumn speaks up.

"I'm sorry," she says immediately, "I should have practiced this last night… I was too busy working on the charm bag you asked me to make."

"Sounds like an excuse," Victoria sings. "Go back and practice and we'll try again at dinner." She walks away. Autumn frowns deeply to herself before flashing an awkward look to the rest of us shocked at what we just witnessed. She turns glumly and makes her way toward the stairs without another word.

"Well…if that's the end of that we ought to be off," Rose says while closing her little book and placing it in a pocket on the inside of her cloak. This one was made from a thick wool, and it was a lovely shade of sky blue with white accents. Rose is closing the fabric around her tighter and she turns and leaves the den, headed straight for the door. Jem follows after her almost immediately, then Carson and I follow.

As we step outside a crisp wind hits our faces and I feel my body shutter. Oddly not from the cold, but instead from the sudden memory of last night. As Carson said I looked possessed, I *felt* possessed and I remember it in its entirety. That is until I passed out, of course.

"So where is this place we're going?" Carson asks as he pulls up his hood and tightens the draw strings.

"The H.D.O is located at the heart of Julieth's Quarter. It's also another popular place for shopping and leisure in Greenwood. You were also born there, Ethan." Rose looks back at me for a second before looking ahead again as we walked along the trail we used to get to the cottage. "Though, it's quite far from here, so I think taking the Faerie Ferry would save a lot of time. What do you think, Mister Jem?" She turns again to see the man's response, but he doesn't actually respond, unless you call a forceful breath through the nostrils one. He looks mildly annoyed, and I am almost convinced that his face is stuck that way. He had also fallen behind Carson and I and was lagging at the back of our weird sort-of line we were walking in. When he made no other identifiable sounds or movements Rose turns again as she leads us along as quickly as usual. And as we were approaching the pole with many signs leading to different paths that branched from the one we were on, including 'Willow Way', she turns left down a path called 'Sidhe' painted in pink and yellow with hand-drawn flowers bordering the word.

We're moving down a winding path. As many trees as there were there also became many flowers that lined where we walked. They were all in bloom somehow, even with the frigid weather, but the wind did blow many petals away and they scattered prettily over the ground. Mushrooms were growing here and there, and it seemed the farther we walked the more that we saw. That little stream appeared again as well, and trickled quietly passed us on its own path. Frogs were singing and buzzards were chirping. I can see deer grazing on grass, and then my eye catches little brown rabbits dashing about. And then—

Slow down, Ethan!

I wince sharply at the sound in my ear. As the familiar voice disappeared it left a terrible ringing sound that had me rubbing at my ear like a crazy person.

"Ethan? Are you alright?" the same voice says. The same voice, only older. I blink and look up at her, slowly dropping my arm as the ringing began to fade. Rose is staring at me with her large doughy eyes as she's basically walking backward to do so.

"I'm fine," I lie, which must have been terribly obvious because the face she pulled in response felt like a cold slap across the cheek. "I mean…" I start to say, feeling as though I should fix my response, "let's just…talk about it later?" I show her my teeth, which was actually meant to be a smile but it was absolutely not that. When her expression didn't change, I opened my mouth to continue adding nonsense until it was deemed good enough, but I was stopped when some sort of village came in to view, and a light that seemed almost rainbow colored zipped directly passed my face.

The path widens into a clearing and there is a large sign that reads "Sidhe: Cathair an-áthas agus an tsolais".

There is a bridge and as we cross there are more little zips of light of all shades and colors passing by, high and low, zig-zagged and diagonal.

"What is that?" I ask Rose since Jem is basically a walking brick. In the near distance there are a number of treehouses with bridges connecting them here and there. I notice people walking by—*flying* by. All of them wore strange clothing, some of which looked made from leaves or flowers. Their ears were pointed; they had translucent wings of different shapes, sizes, and colors protruding from their backs like fine silk.

"This is Sidhe," Rose answers. "This is where the people of the Fae live. You will see them in a few different forms. These small orbs of light you see everywhere are fairies traveling. I believe they find it faster and easier to fly when small like this. But as you can see, fairies can also choose a larger form. Typically, no taller than five foot six, however."

There are mats on the ground where larger fairies are sitting. Some seem to be selling things like glass china and silverware, or mushrooms, rocks, and moss. As we walk into town, people are looking at us. Perhaps upon noticing a whole princess passing through. Or was it for another reason? I notice there are more than just fairies around. There are some people with those pointy hats and long iridescent cloaks like in Willow Way. They were perhaps witches. There were smaller looking creatures hobbling about as well. Things with grey-ish skin and pointy ears with sharp teeth jutting up from their bottom jaws. Like a goblin of some kind. I was almost compelled to scream at it, feeling like the laws of nature have played a crewel trick on me. I look over at Carson who seemed to be having a much harder time holding back any reaction as he was swallowing a squeal after seeing the small grey-ish creature hobbling by. His finger flies out to point at the thing and I swat at him to stop before we call attention to ourselves.

Rose whips her head around, glaring at us both as we quickly brought our hands to ourselves. We smiled at her awkwardly before she turned away to where I glared sharply at the blonde.

A shimmer of pink and yellow light flits over our heads, and then it makes a spiraling zag back to where it could hover just in front of Rose. Its light grows brighter and brighter until I'm almost blinded, then the silhouette of a girl with greenish skin (like she had been dusted with spray paint) and curly brown hair comes into view. She's wearing something almost completely made of bright green leaves that wraps around her right leg and continues its way up in a spiral on her body until it spirals out over her left arm, wrapping around her middle finger.

…I thought maybe she should be cold…

"Princess Rose, is that you?! What brings you all the way here in Sidhe? Have you come for the Toadstool dance tonight? You're certainly much too early!" The girl is speaking a mile a minute. Her eyes glittered with shimmering golds and blues as her tall silken wings flittered behind her. There were patterns in them of spirals and swirls to which her wings ended in not a point but a curl. She was standing on her toes, or perhaps hovering on them as she seemed to not be using her long slender legs at all. "Who are your friends, by the way? They're both wonderfully handsome. Except that grouchy old man back there, why did you bring him?" Rose doesn't even get to respond before she's dashing over to Carson and me, circling around us with both her feet and her wings. "These two would do lovely at our dance tonight, they could be very popular. Yes, that's it, you shall be my guests! Hello, hello, *día dhuit*! My name is Pepper, and who are you? Who are you?!" she questions, her nose now inches away from Carson's.

Rose spins on her heels and she waves for Pepper's attention.

"Actually," she says to her, "we are just passing through for now. Perhaps we can come to the next dance; there are plenty of them. We're just looking to use the ferry."

"Ferry? The Ferry? Faerie Ferry? Ah yes, I should take you there. It's a shame you won't be to the party, though, it should be great fun. Lots of fun. I could have you meet my sister, Ivy. She would love to meet new friends like you. She spends too much time too herself. Much too much." She's flying her way passed us all and I suppose she expects us to follow. But as Rose continues to act as our leader, we only move the moment she does. "Well, maybe she wouldn't *love* it. But she should certainly appreciate it." She stops, hovering just above the ground before she turns to face us again. "Perhaps, when you return, you will stay for a while, right? It's been a while since we had you around, Princess," she says with a bright smile on her face. I looked at Rose who seemed a little hesitant to answer, but after a pause that seemed like forever, she says:

"There's a number of things I must take care of, Pepper. But once they're finished, I promise to return for a visit," she assures her.

Pepper grins (if she wasn't doing that enough already), and with a swing of her arms she spins rapidly up into the air, a trail of literal "pixie dust" or fairy…glitter, or whatever you call it was left behind until she glided back to the ground.

"That would be wonderful," she tells her before continuing her way forward.

We're winding down a path that led to a more congested area of people and creatures of all sorts. There's a smell of something sweet like syrup in the air and someone somewhere was playing an ocarina. I notice coming up out of the ground are huge, oversized mushrooms here and there. I was convinced they weren't real until I reached out and touched one, feeling its soft delicate flesh identical to the fungus of normal size. Rose and Pepper were engaged in a conversation that I tuned out of, and Carson must have been stunned and or confused because he was quiet the entire time.

"Fine jewelry! Fine jewelry crafted from the shards of a dyolre!" a man is shouting from a green mat on the ground just to the side of the path.

"From the shards of a what?" Carson huffs as he peers passed me at the ivory-colored jewelry.

"A dyolre," I answer without thinking, "it's a small creature with sharp points all over its head called 'shards'. They typically live in deep wooded areas in Greenwood, and are usually aggressive and feel threatened easily. Their shards are shed and grow back due to them being worn down or broken often from attacking."

Carson stares at me for a good minute. He didn't even have to say anything for me to realize that the words that came tumbling out of my mouth was not a conscious effort. I didn't even know what I said until I repeated it a few times in my head.

"...how do you know that?" Carson asks me skeptically, half feeling like I made it up, half recognizing my memory problem.

"I...don't know," I tell him and look over at Rose to see if she might have an answer. But she hadn't been paying attention as she was still conversing with that Pepper girl. I turn my head behind me at Jem who was staring back at me with his bright amber eyes, but he didn't say a single word.

"Candied plums this way at Madam Hickory's tavern! Fresh dandelion tea this way at Madam Hickory's tavern!" A younger looking fairy was calling from in front of a bustling little tavern, wearing long sleeves that looked woven from both wheat and wool.

There's a crowd of people coming in our direction. Some were very short with pointed ears and thick sharp nails. Others were tall and wore rather beautiful clothing made from a soft looking material. They all spoke and laughed with each other until someone's eyes met mine and their face had gone pale, like they had seen a ghost. I watched them and their eyes never left mine until they completely passed us, but they never stopped to say something.

"Watch where you're going!"

I'm stumbling a little after someone moving rather quickly had run directly into my shoulder. As I turned to look at the person who had a very strange hue of red eyes and paper white skin, they were snarling at me until they looked me directly in the face. It was almost the same reaction of having seen a ghost, but then they had sped off, just like Rose had done yesterday, moving impossibly fast. Maybe they had been a vampire like her.

"Here it is, here it is!" Pepper is cheering as she points to a tall staircase leading up to a platform of cars that looked like little ferry boats. Except there was no water. I stared up at the contraptions, trying to find a wire or a track that they were on. It seemed like one of those people movers you find at an amusement park, except it was attached to nothing. There was a long line of people waiting to load on to these boats, and I wondered how long would we have to wait. "Oh, Uncle Yucca is helping out today!" Pepper exclaims as she flies a little higher to see above the platform. "He can get you a car quickly, princess. Let's go up there." She's flying away, seeming as though she forgot that the rest of us were floor bound. Rose is shaking her head as she watches her while moving her way toward the stairs, and then the young fairy stops midair and spins around. Her shoulders drop as she realizes the fact that we can't move like her and she flies over to the stairs, gesturing for those in line to move over some so we all could get by. "I simply hate to climb this dreadful thing," she complains as her feet land on a step.

"Don't worry, moving slow with these guys is also a pain," Rose tells her as she shoots a playful look at us three.

"Excuse us for not having wings or super speed like The Flash," Carson shoots back at her, only to receive a puzzled look from both girls.

"What is a 'the flash'?" Pepper asks as she climbs the tall green staircase.

Carson and I share a look and suddenly Jem is pushing passed the both of us.

"I would stop talking if I were you," he grumbled lowly to the blonde without even sparing a glance.

"Just a sort of…" I began to say to cover for Carson, "…flashing light… thing."

"You guys talk kind of weird," Pepper says as we finally reach the top of the platform. "Dress kind of funny too. And you," she's flying backwards so she can look me in the face, "you look strangely familiar. What did you say your name was?"

"Oh, that's not—" Rose began, trying to say it wasn't important, but she was cut off by a man with tired looking wings and hands dusted with blue.

"Ethan," he calls clearly, his eyes directly on me as he completely stopped helping a family of elfish looking people into a car. "How can it be true? It's you, I know it is." We approach him and he's scratching his head full of curly almost purple looking hair. His eyes were glittery like Pepper's, with golds and blues in them. Except they were full of confusion and disbelief.

"Uncle Yucca, d'you know these friends?" Pepper asks as she stops beside him and turns to look at us again.

He steps forward without acknowledging anyone else and he stops directly in front of me. He stares me down, circles me once with brows knit tightly together. He stops again in front of me and he shakes his head a little.

"But you died…" he says, seemingly to himself than to anyone in particular. "Didn't you?!" He stares directly into my eyes and I know they're flashing green.

"I-I..." I felt like I needed to say something, but what could I possible say? Hey, hello, I'm alive I just don't know anything. Long time no see, though, L.O.L.

"Mr. Yucca," Rose starts, stepping forward and placing a light hand against his shoulder, "Ethan didn't die. Something terrible's happened to him, however, and he's lost his memory." Her voice lowers as she seems to be trying to make sure only he and Pepper can hear and not the people standing in line who may or may not be paying attention. "It's not really a secret anymore, but please...don't spread the news around. Not until his memory has returned."

"This is Lamia's doing. Isn't it?" He looks over at her, resentment in his eyes. She doesn't answer, but her eyes give away her response. His hand swings froward and he's gripping me around the arm, pulling me forward a little as he stares back up at me. "My family always welcomes you, my boy," he says. "I knew you since you were born. When you disappeared, we were devastated...Pepper's a little too young to remember. What about Jiah? Is news about her also untrue?" He looks at us all with hope, but when we all remained silent for too long, defeat was quick to fall on him.

"Unfortunately, it is..." Rose says.

"*Ró-donna*," he bemoans. "I am so sorry...but I am *so* happy to know that you've been alive all this time. If there's anything I can do for you, anything at all, just let me know. Where are you all headed?"

"We're on our way to Julieth's Quarter," Rose answers. I'm staring down at the man and I feel my cheeks heating with embarrassment and shame. Nothing about him rang any bells but I was sure he had all kinds of memories of me, memories of my family. "We must get Ethan's papers renewed so he can travel about the land. Hopefully it will help jog his memory."

"You mean he can't remember a single thing? Not even me?" He turns from her to look at me once more and his eyes are searching mine. But I'm sure it was like staring at a blank canvas.

"Sorry..." I say slowly. "I will do my best to remember again." I didn't know what else to say but that. It must be very hard to know someone well and they don't recognize you at all. I couldn't imagine the extent of anguishing someone could go through for that reason. My eyes trail over to Rose at this thought and I frown a little upon looking at her. What sort of anguishing did she go through because of me?

Yucca is patting my back and he presses his other hand over his heart.

"Don't apologize. I don't know what those twisted people in Lamia did to you—no offense, princess," she shrugs a shoulder in response, "but I believe in you. Come back soon when your mind has been restored. And even if it doesn't come back, I'll have fresh piffim root made for you. Last time I checked it was your favorite thing to eat when visiting Sidhe." He smiles brightly at me but I could only give an awkward one back. "Now, let's get you off to Julieth. Come, step over here. I'll get you the next car."

We step in front of people queued up for the next car. No one questioned it like I thought they would, though. I assume because most people seemed to recognize who Rose was. Though if it were me, I would wonder why a princess could just cut in line just because she was a princess. But it probably wasn't about that. We knew Pepper who knew Yucca who seemed to run the ferry. Or at least…Rose did.

"It was good to see you today, Princess Rose. Please don't be too long again!" Pepper waves as she was up in the air again. I couldn't stop thinking that she was too lazy to use her own legs. Even Yucca stood this whole time, his wings folded neatly against his back. But then again, he was a very large looking man (particularly in the middle), and I couldn't help but wonder if his wings could carry him. But maybe that thought is a little rude…

A car decorated with flowers and long thick blades of grass comes floating toward the threshold of the platform. It moved slowly up and down as if it were riding round waves. Yucca moves forward and reaches down to open the door of the vehicle for us and gestures for us to step inside. Rose was first, then Carson and I, and Jem (who I often forgot was even there) last. We settle into the firm benches inside, and I feel a little afraid of heights. Mainly because my brain could not handle the fact that what I was sitting in was literally attached to *nothing*. I was sure at any moment we would go hurtling three stories down to our doom.

"Please be careful," Yucca says as he shuts the door firmly. "I will not say a word about today, those oddity hunters would really pose a threat to you.

Farewell, my friends. *Slán-leat.*" He turns to a woman who seemed to also be working. "*Tóg Julieth's Quarter iad, Betony!*" he calls to her before turning back and smiling as the car jerks and moves forward. I wave a little back until he's turned away.

The car is slow at first. Slow enough to make me wonder why Rose thought it was the fastest way to get to where we were going. But gradually it moves faster and faster until we were riding what felt like eighty miles an hour. (Though it could've been less than that.) I was almost afraid to look out of the car, knowing that if I saw how far from the ground we were again, I'd pee my pants or something. But as my eyes wandered and saw the vastness of the district we were in, the absolute fantasy dream we were in of houses in trees, impossibly sized mushrooms and strange looking trees outside of the oaks, willows, and elders. Things that I didn't notice were flying in the skies like fairies, other ferries, and other flying creatures of some sort. I was in awe.

"Ethan, how do you feel?" Rose asks after a while. It seemed like it was becoming her habit to ask every so often. I would find it annoying if I didn't think she was sweet for caring.

"*Dab-dab-hae,*" I respond in Korean without thinking.

"What?" she's looking at me with her head tilted.

"I mean, it's a little…" I'm tapping at my chest as I try to find the correct word that expresses what I said the first time, "…suffocating."

"What is?"

"Meeting people that know me is really hard," I tell her. "They always seem hurt when they find out I can't remember them. Also…" I look over at her as I remember something Yucca said, "what is piffim root?"

"It's a plant creature," she says. "It starts off a seed in the earth, and as it grows it becomes an animal similar to what the mundane have called an opossum. As it transitions from plant to creature, it sheds its roots and they're often harvested and considered a delicacy to many people in Greenwood—mainly Sidhe."

Carson and I both hold an expression that embodies both terror and intrigue.

"That can't be true…" Carson shakes his head. "I couldn't even imagine something like that existing."

"Well, it is," Rose says plainly. "Don't look so appalled. You used to eat dish after dish of them, Ethan."

Carson looks at me, face unchanging as he eyed me up and down.

"You're gross. Hard pass."

"Well, anyway," I grumble, wanting to change the subject. "How does he know me?"

"Mr. Yucca is one of three brothers to the Bhanríon, Áine. She's like a queen to the people of the Fae. Or at least anyone who lives or is from Sidhe. My father and I know her and her family well, naturally because we are royals too. All leaders meet in order to keep Obscura running right. Your mother of course was good friends with my father, and as he and I are often invited to festivals and celebrations by the Bhanríon and her family, my father would invite you and your mother as well. Also…" she shrugs a shoulder and she reaches into her cloak, digging around for something, "they were interested in both you and your mother's status. Not maliciously, of course, but they were extra friendly to you and your mother because they knew of the potential you had. Or…*have*."

"I see…"

"Mr. Yucca, Pepper, and her sister Ivy, though, they are all genuinely kind people. Their father, one of Mr. Yucca's brothers, however, is a little…" She frowns but never finishes her sentence. She looks as though she's found whatever she was digging for and she pulls out a small glass jar, shaped like a mini milk jug. However, the contents inside definitely weren't milk. It was thick and red, and I could only guess what it actually was. I notice the way she avoids everyone's gaze as she seemed to have pulled out a small metal straw to use after opening its lid.

"G-*girl*," Carson stammers as he eyeballs her all too hard. "You just gonna pull that out like *that*?"

She frowns as she sips the stuff, staring at her feet. I punch Carson in the leg, he was obviously making her feel bad about it, though I wasn't sure exactly why if it seemed this has been her life for as long as she's lived. (Which I wondered how long that's actually been.)

"*What!?*" he hisses at me and shoves me back.

"Unlike you who's eaten already, I haven't had anything since last night!" Rose snaps at him finally, red coating her teeth.

"Fine, sorry," he says. "So, since you're a vampire, or whatever, I'm just confused how you're just out here in the sun. I thought vampires turned to dust or somethin'."

"What? Turn to dust if I'm in the sun?" she asks.

"Yeah. Like why aren't you barbeque right now?"

She gives him a look that entirely read 'you're stupid'. I felt embarrassed since I was sort of curious of the same thing. I was glad he asked before I got up the nerve to, which I can always count on him to do.

"Vampires don't turn into dust if they're in the sun," she tells him. "That's just silly. It is true that we have sensitive skin when it comes to UV rays, however, and we can easily burn if we aren't careful. But there are plenty of products available that prevent that from happening. Sun screens, soaps made with UV ray protectant, lotions, and body sprays. Instances where vampires burn are very rare. If you were to see that today, you can say that that person was extremely careless to have let that happen to them."

"Okay, but what about sparkling." Carson leans forward toward her, and I almost wasn't sure if he was serious or just being annoying.

"Sparkling?" Rose questions, her face riddled with confusion.

"Yeah, you know, like—"

"*Stop*," I groaned irritably at him. "Don't listen to him anymore, he isn't asking anything important."

She takes my word for it and relaxes back against her seat. She's sucked down the red liquid rather quickly and she was storing the bottle back into her cloak. It almost seemed like her pockets were never ending.

Not too long after that the ferry was gradually slowing down and I look back out below us.

"How does this thing move by the way?" I ask. I felt a little better about being up in the air but I was still a bit freaked out by it moving by itself.

"Faery magic," Rose answers simply. "The fairies can bend light and harness its energies. During the day the ferries glide over sunlight. At night it glides over moonlight."

"What happens if it's cloudy," Carson asks.

"Then the ferries cannot fly."

"So, what if it's clear one moment, then cloudy the next? I would crap my pants," he says and presses his hands against his cheeks.

"Fairies are particularly talented at understanding weather patterns. They know exactly when the sun or the moon's light cannot shine properly. During this time, they do not operate the ferries. Obviously because it would be dangerous. You can trust them to operate safely."

"I guess…" Carson grumbles.

"It looks like we're coming to a stop," I say and look behind me to see the ferry approaching another tall platform with people loading and unloading from their cars. We continue to slow down until we're gently rocking up to the platform and a tired looking fairy is approaching to secure our vehicle and unhitching our door.

"So, is this whole thing like a subway system?" Carson asks.

Our heads turn after being startled by a loud snort that came from the man that's easily forgettable. His arms were across his chest and his face was hidden by his collar. But he doesn't actually say anything.

"I suppose you can say that…" Rose answers finally.

"Princess Rose, welcome to Julieth's Quarter," that same fairy says upon getting a good look at her. He reaches out his hand after opening our door completely and naturally she takes it as she rises to her feet. He helps her out of the car but stands to the side out of the way for everyone else. "Should I call a carriage for you, my lady?" he asks and adjusts the little green hat on his head.

"That won't be necessary," she tells him. "I will walk for now, thank you." She's readjusting her cloak, taking particular care to shield her chest and neck from the cold wind. The rest of us hop out of the car up onto the platform and the man ushers us toward the stairs that lead down to that ground I was starting to miss. She leads us as usual and we follow her directly into the bustling road.

"But the ferry only goes so far. It really only touches on the most crowded areas. It doesn't even go to Willow Way and it's quite popular. I know that a subway usually has many types of stops it makes, right?"

"Sure," I answer with a shrug.

"Well, anyway. Do you see that building over there? That's where we're going."

She's pointing to a tall golden building just a little ways away peeking over a bustling town that felt a lot like a fancy European city. The road was made from a white stone and parts of the sidewalk was made from matching white marble. Most buildings that lined the road was just as white and quite impressively molded. I thought the roads in Sidhe had all sorts of people in it, but here was much different. There were witches here, vampires there. Fairies in big plush looking coats and people with glowing eyes of all shades and colors. Some of which were dressed in very high-end Victorian looking clothing. Top hats, golden chains and all. There were more goblins here, creatures slithering about the ground, some flew just over head. I'm almost afraid to say they looked like tiny dragons, but that's exactly what they were. There were others who looked very unique with different colored hair, skin with rainbow hues and patterns. There were people who looked like soldiers or guards standing here and there, with staffs similar to the ones we saw in Lamia, except they were silver in color and they were spiraled into a point unlike the black ones that just looked like poles. They wore olive-colored uniforms with silver buttons on them, along with matching top hats that strapped around their chins.

"And there," Rose points east of the tall building that stuck out the most from everything else to a dark wooden building that poked out just a little above the tidy white ones, "that's where Dr. Valhera should be. We'll go there as soon as we finish at the H.D.O."

"What is the H.D.O exactly?" I ask as we push through a crowd. "It's like a government building or something?"

"The Druids are who take care of and run this district," she answers. "That is of course with the addition of the Bhanríon of Sidhe and the Lady of the Lake. Them and the Druids of the highest caliber make up the High Druid Order. So yes, they have to do with government. Especially when it comes to legal matters, the H.D.O is who you should consult. Keep that in mind, Ethan, because you are native to Greenwood."

"Right."

We soon approach the building that was even more impressive up close. Golden statues stood tall in front of the entrance. One of which was of a bearded man in a sort of robe, holding a large book in one hand and his other was outstretched toward the sky as he stared upward in a valiant manner. The other statue was of a tree that looked similar to the Celtic "tree of life" symbol with seven rainbow-colored crystals built into the trunk. There were plaques for both statues but they were in a language I didn't understand or recognize. There are two guards standing outside of the building as well, wearing the same uniforms as the others here and there on the street.

"Princess Rose," one of them spoke up as we came toward the very large golden double doors. "What brings you here, my lady? We aren't aware of any business between Greenwood and Lamia for today."

"I am not here on business," she answers. "It's only a personal matter. I am just accompanying a friend of mine have some paperwork done. Nothing more."

They eye her and she doesn't waver. Actually, I thought she was rather impressive. The way she carried herself was always strong and poised. At least for the most part. And just about everyone seemed to respect her.

"Certainly," one of them says. "Do come in."

Rose takes the first step after giving a little curtsy and we follow after into the impossibly large building. The first thing we are greeted with is a massive statue made entirely of marble and gold. It was of a witch in a cloak raising a staff up in the air. Just beside them was a fairy in a long flowy dress. On the other side sitting on its base was a mermaid whose tail dipped into the fountain the structure stood over. Her hand was up and out of it came water that arched back down into the fountain. It was awestriking.

There were workers in cream-colored uniforms with gold accents. The floors were made of white marble and the walls were all some sort of white stone or concrete. There were people walking around as well in brown robes with books and files in their arms. When you look up it seemed almost impossible to find the ceiling as it was floor after floor after floor.

"May I help you find something?" a woman says suddenly wearing a cream-colored blazer and matching skirt. She had on gloves and a handkerchief like a stewardess. Her eyes were amber, similar to Jem's.

"Yes," Rose answers and suddenly grabs me by the arm to pull me up next to her. I stumble a little bit by the amount of strength I was not expecting. "We'd like to renew a passport, but first, would you please direct us to the H.D.O headquarters?"

"Is there any reason?" the woman asks.

"We, or *I*, would like to speak with an order member. I didn't schedule any appointment, but with the news I've brought I don't think it should be any issue."

"Right this way, miss." I suppose she just takes her word for it. She's leading us down a hall full of portraits and paintings of symbols I didn't understand and people I didn't know. She stops suddenly for a second as a man is flying by without looking where he's going, too invested in a book he's flipping through. When he was out of the way the woman continues and she leads us to an elevator. She presses the down button and in no time a lift comes and we're piling inside along with all sorts of other beings. One of which had a crate full of something that was making a strange screeching noise and was rummaging around frantically. Another was a woman with scaley orange skin, yellow hair, and yellow reptilian eyes. She caried a stack of books and stared sharply at the blonde beside me ogling at her as much as I was guilty of doing. I shove my hands into the pockets of my jacket when he starts slapping at me to see if I'm seeing what he is. Rose turns around as the woman who was leading us to wherever had hit a button and we started moving down. Rose gives Carson a look a tested mother would that must have sent chills down both of our spines as he went rigid and stared ahead of him.

"Floor negative 603, H.D.O Headquarters," a voice from the elevator said after a short while. The door opens and we're greeted by reds and golds everywhere.

"You should find the Order down the hall to your left," the woman said. "As for renewing a passport you will find that on floor 212 B, directly to your right." The woman doesn't exit the lift and the doors shut not long after giving us direction.

"Did she just say *negative* big numbers?" Carson inquires, scratching the back of his head.

"Yes, there has to be about two thousand levels in this building," Rose answers and begins down the hall.

"*What?!* That's entirely impossible. That's—"

"So was that lizard lady but there she was!" I huff at him.

"Alright, you right." He throws his hands up. "I said I'd stop questioning stuff and go with the flow."

"Great," Rose says, "now please be quiet while I figure out what I'm going to say to these people."

"Wait, I thought you said that the H.D.O was a part of the plan to bring me back here," I say.

"They were, but we never told them exactly when we'd do it. Honestly, we didn't even know when exactly we'd do it until that day I—" She cuts off and I'm wondering what she was going to say, but she never finishes. She turns left and there's a big door that reads *"Headquarters"*. She pulls it open and inside is as sort of lobby. The walls were silver tiled and the floor was made from a dark wood. There were long grey couches on two walls opposite each other and there was a narrow rug that led up to a desk where a secretary person was sitting, their head buried in some sort of…what I thought was paperwork. But as we stepped closer, I realized this young man was flipping through something that I would have assumed was a golden hologram if I didn't have an understanding of where I was. Symbols floated around and he seemed to be calculating something much worse than the dreaded algebra. Rose clears her throat a little as she approached the tall desk, and the man lifts his head almost immediately.

"P-princess Rose…" he starts, as panic is filling his mismatched eyes. One was golden and the other was turquoise. A quarter of his face was dusted a purple color with a pattern similar to a fish's scales. But otherwise, he looked quite normal. (Not that I could see the rest of him behind the desk.) "I couldn't have possibly forgotten about any appointments, my lady. I know for a fact that your next appointment isn't until the end of February…right?" He's quickly swiping through what I will call a hologram for now (because it makes my brain happy) and symbols and numbers are spinning around frantically.

"Do stop what you're doing," Rose says, placing a hand on top of the desk to get his attention. "I haven't any appointment set up for today; I've come unannounced."

The man's shoulders relax and he sits back slowly against his chair.

"Then..." he starts, searching her expression carefully, "what can I do you for?"

"If you wouldn't mind, I must urgently see the Archdruid and the other Elders of the Order. I'll only be a moment."

"I'm sorry, Princess, but I cannot let you back there now, the Elders are currently in a meeting. If you could wait one hour more they should—"

"We do not have one hour to wait. Even they shall find my news profound. If you do not let me back there this moment, I'll be very sorry to have to go without your permission."

The man winces slightly as he measured what kind of trouble he could get in, either from her or from whoever he works for. After what seemed like a long silent staring contest between him and the princess, he finally straightens his back and picks up something that looked like a wand. When I expected him to start waving it around and doing some sort of magic, he instead holds it up to his ear and speaks into it. He mumbles into it so quietly even I couldn't pick up anything that he said. Then he places the device back down and a loud clicking noise pops from somewhere to the right of us. I turn my head to see a large crack in the wall that I was certain wasn't there before. And then before my eyes the wall splits and the bricks are sliding and shifting until they've created a little hallway.

I could feel my geek radar tingling and my head turns to see Carson literally doing the potty dance as he was about to explode with any sort of fanboy passion that filled his boyish heart.

"Ethan...*Ethan!*" he whispers harshly at me, his hand moving to slap at my arm for the second time today. "*When they make a book about you, I'd better get all the merch!*"

"...Okay buddy," I whisper. Anything to make him stop geeking out the fastest.

Suddenly I felt extremely nervous. My heart had sunk down to my stomach and all of my muscles were tensing up. I felt like something was about to change. I felt like my own life was slipping out of my control. Or…did I ever have control over it to begin with? I swallow hard as Rose thanked the man for finally complying and we go to follow her through this red hallway lit only by torches protruding from the walls. I jump a little at the sound of the walls moving again and I look over my shoulder to see the entrance closing. Only then did I realize Jem was no longer with us. Where did he go? I was just about to turn and ask this when Rose stopped abruptly and was swinging open a rather heavy looking wooden door. And then we enter a circular room completely made from stone. Lit by torches and lanterns. There was one long table at the very back of the room, lifted up higher than anything else and there were people in white robes sitting at it. There was another long table in front of it, sitting lower and vertical to the other one. There were empty chairs lining this one. Perhaps it was meant for when others came outside of the H.D.O to have a meeting.

The people in robes had been talking rather heatedly until they had all fallen quiet upon us entering. Their heads turned, faces shrouded in shadows their hoods casted. I felt something very odd in this room. The air was thick and my ears were faintly buzzing. My arms and legs suddenly felt like jelly and I thought I might collapse.

"Princess Rose," a raspy male voice inquires, staring across the room at her small frame and tied up coils. "Why have you disturbed this conference?"

"I deeply apologize, sir, but I would never have done so if it weren't essential."

Rose turns around to grab me and pull me forward, but then she finally notices that something has come over me. My eyes were flickering and my head had gone foggy. I was blinking hard to stop the room from spinning.

"Ethan…? What is it now?"

"I-I don't…" I reach up to hold my head and suddenly I thought I was going to vomit.

I hear chairs hastily scraping against the floor and every single person who was sitting in that room had stood up, leaning across the table to get a better look.

"Archdruid Bishop, do you see that boy's eyes?" A woman speaks up. All of them are pulling their hoods down and the man who was standing in the middle backs up away from the table and he folds his hands into his long billowing sleeves.

"Please!" Rose calls out as I bend over, fighting hard to not spew chunks all over their floor. Her voice had scared me more than whatever I was fighting with. Her voice cracked and every bit of poise and strength she held onto had unraveled in all of a second. She was gesturing for Carson to find a bin of some kind and he awkwardly bumbled around the room. "Help him! Please!" I could hear her choking up and I couldn't wrap my head around what came over her suddenly.

I was on my knees now, and Carson managed to have found something that resembled a garbage can, and that's what we're just going to hope that it was. Rose had taken it from him and was on her knees beside me holding it up to my face. I violently retch and I'm sick inside the bin. Rose was patting my back, sniffling as if she were crying. *Was* she crying?

"When did you find the boy?" the raspy voiced man asked calmly.

"I brought him over just yesterday afternoon," Rose sniffs. "He's been like this since then. Even longer than that, I've heard. And his memory…he still can't remember."

I groan a little bit and push the small can away. How embarrassing to throw up in front of a bunch of old people you didn't know. But maybe that shouldn't have been my focus. I stare forward, my hands bracing myself up against the floor as I continued to gather my bearings again. Rose is stroking the back of my hair and Carson was crouching beside me on my other side, staring at me awkwardly.

"There are…conflicting energies," the man says after a moment of silence. He then glides around the table and down the short little steps and begins moving toward us while the others stayed in their place, some gawking, all of them not knowing what they should do. My eyes zero in on his feet as he stepped in front of us, and then I follow the length of his rope up to meet his face. His beard was long and gray with what looked like twigs braided intricately into it. My vision clears up and I'm able to see the detail of his face. His eyes were small and sleepy, but a bright shade of brown. His hair was long and wavy almost like River's and it was tied behind his back. As he came closer the low buzzing in my ears grew louder, so much so that I could barely hear over it. I shake my head a little, trying to rid myself of the noise but it's unrelenting.

"Can't you help him, archdruid? Why should he have to suffer like this?"

The man raises his hand to silence her.

"I sense," he starts slowly, "that there will be no way for him to return to his original state."

Rose's eyes blow wide and I feel her hands grip tight at my arm.

"What?! That can't be! That's absolutely—"

"*If*," he continues over her, "he does not do the work for himself."

I groan a little once again and I rock back to sit on my knees. My hand is pressing against my head again and I feel it aching something awful.

"What does *that* mean?" I grumble up at the man.

"It means, my child, that if you do not believe in the magic and power within yourself, your mind and your soul will continue its feud, worsening until you can take no more. Your mind is the only thing that is holding you back. Your mind is what is causing your ailment right this moment. I can feel that the memory wiping potion used on you many years ago has long since worn off."

I blink and turn my head to look at Rose. Her face was streaked with tears and I was shocked to see that she actually had been crying. But why? She stares up at the man dumbfounded as her fingers were digging into my arm, so hard that it was becoming painful.

"W-worn off? It's worn off?" She turns and looks at me, her eyes desperately searching mine but still I was certain it was like staring into a blank canvas. "Th-then why can't you remember, Ethan? Why can't you remember anything, still?"

"There is trauma," the man speaks up again, reaching down and placing his hand on top of Rose's head. "He went through more than one trauma at once that dreadful night. Upon having his memory taken from him, I assess that he doesn't want to remember regardless."

"But I do!" I nearly shout, surprising even myself by the pitch of my voice. My eyes have stopped flickering, and I can see in the reflection of the metal pail that they have settled on the color that is unnatural to me. Bright green. I can feel every ounce of Rose's misery, of her pain, regardless of if I knew the reason behind it or not; and it was entirely overwhelming.

"You do," he says with a small nod of the head, "but only on the surface. You want this, not because it's what you feel deep within, but because you recognize the misery you have caused everyone else. *You* have to want to remember for *yourself*, not for others. *You* have to test your abilities and believe in them. And *you* will have to face the pain in *your* history. Only then will your fragmented memory return in its entirety. And only then will your continuous ailments end."

My shoulders drop in defeat and Rose finally releases her death grip on my likely bruised bicep. It was starting to look like my inability to remember was my fault. River's potion thing or whatever wore off as it should have a while ago, apparently, and if I had to guess it must have been around the time my headaches started up again. I draw in a slow deep breath and everything is clear. My vision isn't blurry or rocky, and the pain in my head dimmed. The buzzing sound in my ears quieted to the point where the silence between all of us was deafening. Rose sniffs. She's wiping her face with her hands before she pushes herself up to her feet. She brushes off her lacy white dress and readjusts her thick cloak before she meets the man's eyes.

"Thank you, Archdruid Bishop. What you've said has made many things clear for us." She does a sheepish little curtsy and then reaches down to pull me up as well. "Should he succeed in uncovering his memory, what then?"

Bishop folds his hands back into his sleeves and his eyes move over to me.

"A vision was bestowed upon me," he starts off just as slow and calmly as he has been. "*Dark times* shall fall upon us all. It is…inevitable. Should Ethan's memory return, I pray that you will return to us urgently so that we may prepare you for what's to come."

I frown deeply. What sort of "dark times" were we talking here? I am a pacifist, which is also Ethan for: *do I look like I'm prepared to throw hands?* Carson is up on his feet again and he's staring at the floor rather sullenly.

"I understand…" Rose answers, her expression solemn. "There's also the matter of Ethan's passport. If we are to travel outside of Greenwood, it will be necessary."

"Certainly," he answers. "There should be no problem to renew it."

"Actually, I bring it up not because of him, but for his friend…"

"Friend?"

His eyes trail over to the mundane boy who was now looking around a bit confused.

"Yes. You see, Carson is a nohab. He's from the place from which we recovered Ethan. I understand that it is against the law for him to be here, but Ethan refused to come without him."

"A mundane human?" a man speaks up from behind. "There simply can't be any such thing on Obscura ground!"

"Yes, but as you can see from the situation, it was the only way I could get him to come home. If he could just get a passport as well, just so that he might—"

"*Out of the question!*" a woman snaps. "It is absolutely ludicrous to have a mundane human even the slightest bit aware of—"

"Silence!" the man called Bishop calls, his voice raising the loudest it has been since we've been here. Everyone fell quiet immediately, no one even dared to move as they waited for what he would say next. His eyes meet Carson's for a moment, and the blonde starts shaking his hands innocently at the man.

"Fo' real, I won't say a word. I wasn't even here. Obscura? The freak is that? I don't know! Where was I this whole time? Just a bro trip. A bro trip wit' my bro. To Germany? No, Korea! We were livin' it up in Seoul this whole time, I swear to God."

I hold my breath and Rose and I were staring completely embarrassed at him as he spit out any and every word that came to mind. Someone scoffs after a pause of silence, shaking their head in disbelief.

"He couldn't possibly—"

"I will grant him a passport," Bishop interrupts steadily with a nod of the head.

"But Archdruid—"

"A single mundane human in our realm is the very least of our problems. As long as he sticks with the Spectrum Child and keeps silent about his origins, there should be no issue. Take this."

His hand swishes through the air and with a little puff he is suddenly holding a rolled-up piece of parchment tied shut with a black string with a tag hanging off of it that said: *H.D.O H.Q.*

Carson reaches forward and takes the object from him and looks down at it curiously.

"You will present this to an officer when going to renew the boy's passport. Then you should be able to receive one yourself."

"But Archdruid!" the same person speaks up again, simply not having any of this. "Should someone find out, what then? He should be in continuous danger should he stay! It is the law for a reason."

Bishop breathes out from his nose, before turning to the side to see who was speaking. A man with glowing grey colored eyes and brown hair that spiraled over his shoulders stood his ground against us.

Bishop folds his hands together again and every bit of his energy felt wise and balanced.

"Friendship," he began, "is a strong and powerful bond second to love. To love a friend purely, however, is equally as strong. The strength and power of such a bond is stronger than any challenge, any evil, and certainly any law. To lose a bond such as this over something silly as a law made out of fear and spite, will undoubtably snuff out the small glimmer of hope and comfort for any capable of making change." Bishop's eyes challenge the man to respond, but he does not. He lowers his head a little in defeat and backs down. "Now then," he turns his head to us again and waves for us to go, "be off, we must continue our conference. Do not forget what I said, the both of you." He looks between Rose and I. "If you find your memory, return to me. But in order to do so, *you* must want it for yourself."

9

The Sickle Wielding Hunter

We thanked the Elders before we left. Particularly the one called Bishop since he was the only one of any help. Although when we left the floor and found Jem wandering the halls, I felt like I had a good slap to the back of the head. Something about my memory was an error on my part and it seems like a good reevaluation of myself was more than necessary. I look over at Rose as we piled into a lift, headed to floor 212 B. She hadn't looked at me or spoken to me since I had gone and rid myself of my insides in a group of government officials' bin. She was very stiff, and kept her eyes either on the floor or in front of her. The elevator rose quickly, floor after floor until the numbers on the screen of the elevator read 212. Suddenly we lurch to a stop, and I can feel the lift spin around. And then instead of moving up or down like any normal elevator, we are being propelled forward. Both Carson and I go stumbling into other random people, while everyone else who seemed to think this was normal were planted perfectly still in the spot they stood in.

"*212 A,*" the elevator voice said as it made another lurching movement and spun around again. I go twisting, squealing embarrassingly as I smack directly into Carson who hopped down, spreading his long legs wide in order to have a firmer way of standing.

"*Now approaching 212 B,*" the voice announces. The elevator doors slide open and I feel a bit too jarred to want to move. Carson stands up correctly as

Rose steps out and Jem silently pushes passed. Carson presses his hands against my back, pushing me out of that death machine.

"Oo-ah!" I heave out as I stumble forward.

"There, there, big guy. You survived, we both did," he purrs.

I frown at him but trust my own feet to carry me down the new hall we arrived in. This floor was very busy with people dashing, sprinting, and flying about with arms full of all kinds of things. Something is chiming and I jump out of the way when a small black thing shaped like a crate is hobbling by with little feet. It was carrying stacks of files and books inside of it as it passed by me and around a corner.

I shut my mouth after finding it hanging open. Rose leads us around a corner in the opposite direction and here we see a line of people that looked similar to a bank or luggage check-in at an airport. There was some man screaming about something as he waved around some stack of papers in front of another man with wings behind a counter, looking as though any and all cares have gone out a window ages ago. There was a woman in a far corner smiling as her photo was being taken by an elfish looking person, holding up a tall ancient camera.

"Princess Rose," someone calls out and stops her in her tracks, almost causing me to run into the back of her. I was beginning to understand that she is recognized anywhere she went. A person no taller than four feet is standing now in front of Rose who seemed like she was almost completely out of it. Her head slowly tilts down to see this person wearing the same cream-colored blazer as everyone else and they smile up at her. "Pardon me, Princess, but what sort of business do you have on this level?"

"Oh…" she starts, her voice quiet, "I…I just need to have a passport renewed is all."

"I see…" the small man analyzes her a little and then looks passed her at me and the others. After this his eyes meet hers again which were no longer looking at him but at the floor. "Sorry, but are you alright, Princess?" he asks cautiously. She was clearly not in any good humor.

"Fine," she answers and takes in a deep breath. "Please, I usually wouldn't mind waiting in line, but if there is a way to fit my friend in as soon as possible, I would be very grateful."

He blinks and then looks back at me once more, analyzing me this time for a moment before turning around seemingly searching for something or someone else.

"Sure," he said and gestured for us to follow.

In no time he was able to set us up with the next available officer, which I felt quite thankful for as well as I was beginning to feel tired of being out and about. My people bar was running low. A woman is flipping through the same hologram looking thing like what we saw the secretary down stairs with. After a few swipes of her finger and numbers and symbols go spinning and jumbling around, she looks up to see us.

"Oh!" she starts, having not realized the princess standing before her. "Princess Rose, what brings you here?" she asks.

She doesn't say anything this time and instead she pulls out a folded-up file from the inside of her cloak and sets it down on the counter in front of the other woman.

The woman's eyebrow raises and she picks up the file and opens it, taking a look through what looked like a profile from where I was standing. I could see a little black and white image of myself between the ages of six and seven. And then my ears perk at the sound of a sharp gasp. I look up to see the woman with her eyes blown wide as her gaze was directly on me.

"I—" she starts off, looking as though she was fighting being flustered, confused, and being in denial all at the same time. "But this simply can't be," she says and holds up the page with my photo on it and compares it with my face. "Princess—"

"It's true, he's standing just right here in front of you," Rose quietly snaps. She takes a step back and she wore an apologetic expression. Her eyes go to the floor.

The woman is frozen for a moment too long before she picks up the entire file and stands it up to where no one could see.

"W-well I'll just have to ask some security questions…" she stammers. "Uhm…first name?"

Rose pushes me forward so that I was standing directly in front of the counter. I stutter awkwardly at first, rubbing my arm sheepishly before I can gather my brain cells to answer properly.

"Ethan-Jaehyun," I say barely audible over the loud commotion of the room.

"Last name?"

"Moon."

"…Soul Element?"

I blink stupidly for a second and look at Rose for help but she only gestures for me to hurry up and speak.

"Uhm—uhm Spirit?"

"Well don't sound so confident about it," Carson grumbles at me like he knew what was going on more than I did. I shoot him a look and he shrugs.

The woman rubs her neck for a second and then looks back up at me.

"And date of birth?"

"October 31st, 2000."

The woman sets down the file and I notice her hands shaking.

"I-it looks like you need your oddity registration card renewed as well as your passport. In the meantime…p-please come with me, Mr. Moon," she says and stands up walking to the end of the long counter toward where others had been taking photos. When the people there now finish, the woman says something to the little elfish looking man who had been taking the photographs and he looks up almost instantly at me. I look at Rose again but she's still avoiding my gaze. "If you would just stand over here. The camera will shutter twice. On the first shutter you will face the camera and look as plain as possible for a second. Then turn left, then right, and then face the camera again by the last shutter. Most people like to make a pose on the last shutter. Feel free to do so if you'd like," she explains and gestures for me to stand in front of a wall with "*Greenwood District H.D.O Center*" plastered on it in big golden letters.

I run my fingers through my bangs, and hope I didn't look like crap before stepping on the little 'x' that was on the floor. I feel a little pressured to do as she said correctly the first time but I go for it the moment the little man counted down from three and a big light flashes from the camera he held up. I turn left, then right, and then upon facing the camera again I throw up a peace sign because why not.

I step out of the way when it seemed like I finished, and then I see Rose handing something else to the woman. She's unrolling the parchment that was given to Carson and she reads over it for a moment before leaning down and telling something else to the little man. He then turns around and grabs at Carson's pant leg, spooking him a bit as he dragged him over to the 'x' and gesturing for him to stay before going back to his camera and counting down from three. The camera shutters and the blonde turns left, then right and then as he turned back to the camera he sticks his tongue out and gives two 'rock on' hand signs or 'I love you's' or however one would like to interpret it. He steps out of the way and the woman turns back to me.

"The passports should be only a moment to print, and I will have your new registration card ready," she says before clasping her hands together awkwardly. "E-excuse me, Mr. Moon. Perhaps it's inappropriate to ask but where have you been this whole time? The whole of Obscura knows you to be dead." I look at her, unsure of how to answer. And when I took too long, she draws backward. "It's none of my business," she says. "But I hope this means that our district can be left alone now that you've grown up."

My head tilts to the side as I wasn't quite sure how to respond to that either. As one awkward moment passes, she disappears for a second before she comes back with two tiny envelops. She hands one to me and the other to Carson and then looks at me. I wasn't sure if she was expecting anything or not, but I could feel my ears going red. I bow my head at her as a thank you but I also cringe inwardly at having done that rather than just saying the words. When no one else said anything Rose pushes passed and I hastily spin around to follow after her.

We step outside finally, and although I was happy to see the sun, I was less than so to feel the cold air again. No one says anything as we leave the building and cross the road, until Carson is opening up his little envelope. Inside he pulls out a card that almost looked no different than a driver's license. Except the only difference was...

"Whoa, sick!" Carson bellows and pulls the card out completely

...the image was moving. Carson was turning left and right and then his little pose he gave at the end.

"They put a boomerang on it!" he laughs.

I tilt my head a little and then go to pull out mine to see my image doing the same thing. The card itself was white with gold accents all over it, and a small golden symbol stamped on the lower left corner. And then I read the text.

> **Passport of Obscura**
> **Greenwood District**
> **Name: Moon, Ethan-Jaehyun**
> **Birth: 10312000: Julieth's Quarter**
> **Occult: Witch (Spirit) | Unknown**
> **Status: High-Risk Oddity (Tier 1)**
> **Citizen Code:** ۞ - 朱凸 - 2199

"Weird..." I mumble. "What does yours say if you're not from here?"

Carson shows me his but it almost looked no different.

> **Passport of Obscura**
> **Greenwood District**
> **Name: Foxx, Carson Leroy**
> **Birth: 09282000: Holly's Grove**
> **Occult: Witch (Water)**
> **Status: Typical**
> **Citizen Code:** ۞ - ∧\/ - 4126

"I guess that man lied for you," I say and pull my wallet from my pocket, tucking the card over my Michigan identification card. I then go to look at the registration card that I had received as well.

> **Oddity Registration Card**
> **High-Risk Oddity (Tier 1)**
> **Offenses (out of 3): X X X**
> **Name: Moon, Ethan-Jaehyun**
> **Birth: 10312000: Julieth's Quarter**
> **Occult: Witch (Spirit) | Unknown**

District: Greenwood

Description: Half witch, half unknown being originating from the Fichik Mountains, Sierra district. Is the only known witch alive possessing the Spirit soul element. Moon has demonstrated an inability to properly control his powers which have shown devastating and murderous capability. Beware as Moon is the highest ranking (and most dangerous) oddity to date in all of Obscura.

Citizen Code: ☀-⚒☐- 2199

My lip turns up at it. I already had two offenses apparently, and according to my description I am "murderous". Wonderful.

"Duh," Carson replies and interrupts my train of thought, "obviously they can't slap on here 'basic b human creature'. I guess Rose was right that people would assume I'm a water bender. Although I always thought of myself as the next super rad Fire Lord. But things change. Life doesn't go as planned."

I roll my eyes, but I guess he wasn't wrong. As I'm stowing my wallet back into my pocket, I'm suddenly running face first into a very solid figure. I stumble backward and eventually collapse onto my hind end. After wincing at the blunt pain in my tail I open my eyes to see thick black leather boots with chains woven into them. I trail my eyes upward and there's a huge man (who I could swear wasn't there before) wearing a long black coat and a belt strapped crisscross across his chest with vials and scary looking tools sticking out of it. He stood tall over me and I notice his piercing burgundy eyes that glowed in the shadow he casted. He had a sharp, jet-black beard and his hair with a streak of white was tied behind his massive back. He had a long scroll in one fist and in the other was what looked like a big hook or sickle of some kind. A deep low growl rumbled through the man's chest and I'm slowly backing away as nothing about him seemed as though he would be willing to help me up and dust me off.

Jem and Rose had stopped and they turned to see this colossal titan reaching down and fisting the collar of my jacket and pulling me effortlessly off of the ground. We were nose to nose and I notice the double fangs he had as he snarled at me entirely like a dog.

"What on earth do you think you're doing!" I hear Rose calling. "Unhand him this instant! You have no right to—"

He turns around without letting me go and he's baring his teeth at her, growling louder than before without any words. Rose looks taken aback for all of a second before her hazy lavender colored eyes glow a bright purple and she's hissing back at him with her own set of fangs. Jem steps in between them immediately and he gives a challenging look to the man who suddenly relaxed his muscles and let out a tantalizing chuckle.

"Jem Magno," he says with a voice that could quake the earth. He finally sets me down to where my feet could touch the ground, but he still doesn't release his grip on my collar. He's dragging me around as if I were a rag doll as he completely turned to face the others. "So, you decided to show your face again after all this time? Perhaps you need another public humiliation like before." He's smirking and Jem's eyes start glowing. No, they've turned into flames just like I thought I had seen the first time I saw him. His fists are clenched at his sides but he doesn't move.

"Release the boy," he warns, but the man is only chuckling again before he turns his head to look at me.

"I've never seen this one before," he says and stows his big silver sickle behind his back. "But if you're associated with a freak of nature like Jem Magno, I should suspect that you have to be the same."

"I demand you release him, or else I should make Artemis officials aware of your doings today!" Rose is yelling now as she was trying to get passed Jem who was blocking her way.

"Let's see," the man says as he ignores Rose's threats, "do you have a passport or not?" He's reaching into my pockets and I squirm around trying to pull away.

"What is your problem! Let go of me!" I shout. His grip was strong and his arms were like logs. As I tried to wring myself out of his grasp his grip tightens and he lets out a harsh bark directly into my face that sent my body rigid.

Upon searching my pockets, he finds my wallet and turns it this way and that, wearing a quizzical expression. He flips it open and see's my passport but still seems to be almost perplexed.

"What sort of gold pouch is this?" he asks, though I wasn't sure if it was directly aimed at me.

He pulls the card out and he's reading it over. After a few seconds his eyes are growing wide and he whips his head around to look at Jem and Rose who had gone quite still. He didn't say anything to them and neither did they as they watched for what he would do. His head turns back to me and he's scanning me up and down.

"You're the one who killed her," he says out of nowhere. I stare up at him not sure if I just misheard him.

"Me? Killed who?" I ask while tugging at his fingers to escape.

He's suddenly snatching his hand away from me and he tosses my passport and wallet at my feet. He reaches over his shoulder and grabs his sickle again and I jump backward, afraid he'd swing the sharp thing at me.

"You're meant to be dead. Just to have your head is worth a ton of money. Aside from your freakish father you're the only tier 1 around. Just you wait." He grins darkly and steps passed me. And without another word, he walks off just like that.

I look up at Jem and Rose. Rose is shaking and I don't think it's from the cold or fear. Carson steps over to me and bends down to pick up my things. He tucks the passport back into its place and then hands me my wallet.

"Something tells me we're gonna see that thing again."

My teeth clench as I take the wallet from him and put it back into my pocket. I readjust my jacket on my shoulders and I push passed him.

The blonde is frowning and he throws his arms.

"And then I was gonna say, we gotta get you suited up for battle. Y'know like a first boss fight!"

I ignore him and continue walking. When Rose and Jem turn to walk after me, Carson does so too when he failed to lighten the now very heavy mood.

• • •

"Doctor Valhera will see you now," a woman at the front desk of the hospital says as she went to pull open a door. We're all stepping inside Doc V's room for where he met patients after a little while of waiting in the lobby of the medical center Druidic Scholars Institute of Medicine. We all pile inside the fair-sized room after falling a small green colored goblin down a hallway. It gestures for me to sit down on the examination bed and for the others to have a seat on the other side of the room.

After I climbed up onto the bed, the little goblin comes hobbling over to me. He hops up onto a stool and with its long cold fingers it unzips my jacket and pulls it off without any warning. He hops down and crosses the room to a table where he retrieves a little white basket, and then he returns to my side, hopping back up onto its stool. He's wrapped something tight around my arm and it swells up without any pumping like a blood pressure thing. He pulls it off after a moment and then takes out another tool that looked like a little ball. He presses a button on the top and it sprouts legs. My eyes widen as he puts it directly onto my shoulder. I hear Carson laughing at me as the thing crawls over to the back of my neck and up onto the top of my head to my forehead. It suckers itself between my brow and I'm unsure how to feel as the little goblin is pulling out something else that looked like an ordinary jar. He holds it up to my mouth and then gives two strong slaps to my back.

"Cough," he croaked out to me.

Confused, I give two little coughs and he closes the jar and labels it with something. He then pulls the thing off of my forehead finally and he reads some numbers that were on its back. I scratch my head and watch him put it back into the white basket and then he hops down again, hobbling toward the door.

"Dr. Valhera should only be a moment," he said just before leaving.

"...What just happened?" I question and look over at the others. Both Jem and Rose were staring at the floor and only Carson looked alert and amused.

"You just had a goblin nurse give you a weird check-up," he's beaming.

I sigh and look down at my hands. My mind was being overrun by thoughts again. I thought back to that big man outside who must have been one of those Oddity Hunters River was talking about. Who not only assaulted me for no reason, but also accused me of killing someone. I rub the back of my neck and also remember him being able to identify Jem. I looked over at him, eyeing him up and down. He called him a freak of nature but nothing about him looked out of the ordinary, except the weird thing he can do with his eyes. But he was a Witch of Fire, so I didn't see why that would make him any different. But by what that man had said, Jem was apparently an oddity of some kind. But I wondered how, and I wondered what sort of thing happened to him for him to have said the things that he did to him.

I'm frowning deeply until I hear the click of the door being opened. I look up and see that familiar salt and pepper hair and thick black rimmed glasses. But instead of a white doctors coat he's wearing a brown and green robe. He peeks his head into the doorway first before stepping all the way in with a cautious smile on his face.

"Hello," he greets in his sultry voice. "Ethan, I'm so happy to see you've made it home safely."

He steps into the room and as much as I wanted to smile and tell him how happy I was to see a familiar face from home—the home I knew (aside from Carson's), something was bugging me.

"How have you been feeling?" he asks me.

"…when did you leave Whitechapel?" I question instead, not having the energy to beat around the bush.

He tilts his head a little, his handsome smile fading gradually.

"Well, I actually just arrived earlier this morning," he answers.

"Then did you talk to Gramma before then?"

I watch him draw in a deep breath and he pulls over a little chair before taking a seat.

"I did," he confirms. "I spoke to her just last night before returning. Since you are here now there is no reason for me to stay in Whitechapel. But I hesitated to leave because your grandmother is unwell."

My head tilts to the side, and I see Rose and Jem looking up at the doctor. I blink stupidly for a moment as if it were hard to digest his words properly.

"She's unwell?" I repeat. "So suddenly? What's the matter with her?"

"She isn't unwell from any illness," he assures me and folds his hands together in his lap, "but she is unwell in the mind and heart."

"What does that mean?" Carson speaks up. "Like she's depressed or somethin'?" I shoot him a look and he shrugs his shoulders at me. The doctor looks at him for a second and then does a double take.

"Carson, what are you doing here?"

The blonde shakes his head and leans against the wall behind him.

"I'm accompanying my buddy at a doctor's appointment, I guess," he replied.

"Well, I… that's not exactly what I meant." Scott turns his head again to look at me now and he leans forward onto his knees a little. "I suppose it's something like that, being depressed. I tried to convince her to come back with me but she just wouldn't have it. Catherine has always been a stubborn woman, however. But she's afraid of something, I know that much. I just don't know of what exactly. Perhaps if she could see that you're doing just fine she would get up the courage to return. I know her family misses her. And she must miss them too."

I hum out a sigh and think for a moment. Going back to see her is definitely something that needs to happen. But I know that I can't stay there in Whitechapel, as much as I would be comfortable in doing so. What's going on here is much more important to figure out rather than ignoring it like my grandmother has been doing all this time.

"I will go the day after tomorrow to see her. I'll try to convince her to come back myself," I decide aloud.

"But Ethan, you can't travel back and forth by yourself. You could get into a lot of trouble if you do not do it properly."

"That's alright, doctor, I will accompany him," Rose speaks up.

"Yeah, and me. Gotta go see the moms." Carson raises his hand up and smiles at the man who was still quite puzzled in seeing him here.

"I won't be alone," I say finally and straighten up a little.

He's mulling this over before he accepts this and moves on. He stands up from his chair and approaches me. He waves his hand and there's those golden symbols appearing and floating midair. He flips through them, numbers spinning and letters flying. After a moment he waves his hand again and they've disappeared.

"I heard something happened to you last night," he says. "How are you feeling today?"

"I feel fine," I tell him, though even I wasn't too convinced by it.

"Any headaches recently?"

"Well…here and there," I say. "Not that long ago I vomited in the H.D.O Headquarters place. And last night…I'm not sure if I was hallucinating or possessed or what…"

"Yeah, his eyes were scary purple, doc!" Carson adds.

Scott is analyzing me now, picking up my wrists and I guess was measuring my heart rate.

"Did you see black shadows and was your vision sort of purple-tinted?" he asks.

My eyes widen and I start nodding frantically.

"Yes! I also could barely breath and—"

"You felt like your body was on fire," he finishes.

"…yeah…but how did you—"

"It's not your first time to experience this," he answers. "Just before June 21st you had this happen to you a couple times that year. Unfortunately, we don't understand why that is. Aside from you there has only been two other reports of this sort of occurrence. One of which is your father. And another is of an oracle who lives east of the Grey Meadow. But both of which are oddities who originate form Sierra District. Which means…it's possibly a hereditary case. It could have everything to do with the abilities you've inherited from him."

"Which are what exactly?" I stare up at him expectantly and I watch him hesitate. He lets go of my wrist and he's made those symbols appear again, flipping through them, searching for something. Then after a moment he makes them go away again before meeting my eye.

"It's hard to say exactly as he too is a high-risk. The both of you are the only two alive that rank so high. Or, at least the only known two. There are reported cases of your father using a sort of dark magic, something no one has ever seen before, that's why it's so hard to say. When asked directly what sort of things he experiences—well, he's simply never answered the question. The only strange thing that anyone has ever kept track of with him is the way he uses the word 'darkness' as if it were a person. But we don't understand what that means."

"Then I should go meet him," I say, now feeling more emboldened to do it than earlier when Rose and I talked about it. "If he doesn't answer any other person, he couldn't keep that sort of thing from his own son, right? He should tell me."

The doctor rubs the back of his neck sheepishly which already hinted to what he was going to say.

"I don't think that's a good idea, Ethan," he tells me. I'm almost rolling my eyes at him.

"Why not? If no one else can tell me about it, and say something happens to me worse than last night, then what? He's the only one who would know."

"That might be true, Ethan, but your father is currently unreachable as he faces his sentences. You might not be aware but he's been imprisoned for numerous amounts of crimes. I hate to say it but your father is a very unstable man, and there's no telling what sort of mindset he'll be in *if* you were able to see him any time soon. I couldn't in good conscious let you meet him. At least not without Catherine's approval. All this time you've never met your father, so he might not even have sympathy for you. I'm warning you, Ethan, do *not* go looking for him."

. . .

I'm going to go looking for him.

Regardless of if he has sympathy for me or not, and regardless of if he's dangerous or unstable, if I talk to him while he's behind bars I couldn't see any harm done. He might say something that could help, and if he doesn't I'll be back at square one but at least I tried. I look over at Rose who was watching me until our eyes met. She immediately looks away. I don't know what that's about but I do know that if she still believes I should go too, then I can do it more confidently.

When I didn't respond to the doctor, he sighs a little and from his robe he pulls out something that this time I was certain was a wand. He adjusts his glasses and measures me, and then points the wooden thing at me. I brace myself, sure that whatever he was doing was going to hurt.

"Wait, wait, what're you doing?" I question.

"I'm just going to check your vitals," he answers calmly. "Your magic ones, obviously. It might sting a bit since we already know you're having complications."

Was that obvious? I squeeze my eyes closed, not sure what his idea of "stinging a bit" was going to be. As he aims directly at my sternum a bright white light shoots from the end and straight into my chest. Upon impact to say I felt like I had been hit by a truck would have been an understatement. (Or perhaps that's just me being a bit over dramatic.) I double over with a groan that had all of the air leaving my lungs. And although that pain didn't last long, a series of other strange things occurred directly afterward. I can see my hands glowing green and it was radiating up my arms and across my body. My eyes flickered a few times like an old lightbulb before they shifted green entirely. I felt woozy and light-headed like I could faint at any second. As I look around the room, I notice that everything was tinted a deep turquoise color and my ears had plugged as if I were under water. When my eyes land on Doctor Valhera in front of me, I notice a light that shined as bright as a red flame burning in the middle of his chest. Around his body was a steady pulsating light that was blue in color that felt serene and nurturing. I whip my head around to see the other three—their auras, all different colors and soul elements. Jem has the same fire-colored light burning in his chest, but the light surrounding his body was a sharp red, pulsating jaggedly around him. It felt passionate, it felt angry. I look at Rose whose light in her chest was a cool toned purple. Surrounding her was a dim pink light, but circling this was a gray colored light, vibrating at a depressing frequency. Lastly, I look at Carson who only had a bright white light shining in his chest. Around his body was a yellow light that circled him at an energizing rate. My head tilts to the side when a golden orb zips passed me from out of nowhere and disappears through the door. I see a few more of these travelling through the air. All of which held my attention until I tuned into Doctor Valhera's muffled voice, calling my name. I look over at him and I can barely make out that he's waving his hand in my face.

"Snap out of it, Ethan," I hear him say.

I blink my eyes a few times and as my vision is starting to clear and the array of colors I could see started to dim, there was suddenly a harsh buzzing noise in my ear. I wince at this and I can feel the air around me starting to sizzle. I look down at my hands and that glowing green light shifts into a deep purple. The veins in my hands darken unnaturally and the very second I felt heat growing under my skin, I panic, hopping up to my feet as I'm reminded instantly of last night. My breathing picks up and I hear the others calling for me to focus and snap out of it, but I was afraid to feel and see what I did last night. There's that same icy feeling creeping over my chest, my vision bleeds purple and black. I look up and I can just see my reflection in a mirror across the room. My eyes had gone purple and the whites were black just as Carson described this morning.

"W-what's—" I start with a pant, but I don't finish. I shrink backward as my eyes trail up to the ceiling where I see a black shadow slithering about. I'm pointing at it, hoping the others could see it too, but they don't.

Doctor Valhera is grabbing me by the shoulders now and he's raising that wand, pointing it between my brow. He whispers something I couldn't hear and then there's a flash of a lavender colored light that sends a wave of equanimity over my mind. My eyes roll back a little before my muscles go lax and my vision clears up. I stumble forward a bit into the doctor and he holds me up until I'm balancing again on my own.

"Focus, Ethan," I hear him say. I blink a few times and then look at him, maybe my expression was riddled with annoyance or disdain because he looked back at me with a deprecatory smile. He pats my back and squeezes my arm but I wince and draw backward.

"Ow!" I pout and rub my arm.

The man tilts his head and he moves to roll up my sleeve.

"Oh my, what's happened here?" he asks after seeing a green and purple bruise wrapped around my bicep in the shape of a certain someone's hands. My eyes dart over at Rose who was on her feet now. She looked at me puzzled before coming over to take a look herself. She rubbed her own arm sheepishly and took a step back.

"Sorry…" she apologizes and looks over at the doctor.

He shakes his head and I pull my sleeve back down.

"Well, Ethan, I can tell you that your vitals are operating in a more fluid way than before, that's for sure. But you don't need me to tell you that there are still many problems going on here. You're not able to induce your own abilities by yourself, you're not able to control them, there's still bits and pieces that are blocked off, almost like extinguersis, and you're not able to turn it off. Now that you're back in Obscura I would highly recommend you start exercising your powers. In moderation, of course as it could be very draining and unfortunately dangerous given your status. I'd have River help you with the basics since she is a fairly powerful witch herself. Aside from that and that rather painful looking bruise on your arm, you are healthy."

I push my bangs back out of my face and I turn away after he finished speaking. I go to the examination bed and pick up my jacket, putting it back on before turning again to face the doctor.

"Thanks," I say in a rather bummed tone. "I'll talk to River about it. Is there anything else?"

"No..." he says, eyeing me carefully. "Not for now, at least. I'd like to continue monitoring your progress, however, so come back once a month. For us witches our vitals are very important to keep operational, otherwise we can become ill with a condition known as degeneration. The older you get the easier it is to develop it. If you have no other concerns then you're free to go."

I look over at the other three who all seemed to be collecting their things (not that they really had any), and then I nod at the doctor. I walk out without another word and he's waving and bidding farewell as we all leave the hospital.

We step outside and Carson is checking his phone out of habit, forgetting that nothing can come through, and not even the time shows up properly. He sighs a little and then nudges my arm.

"Cheer up," he said to me almost at random. "It's cool that you got magical powers in the first place. And when you can finally figure them out, you'll be the most dangerous thing around. That big scary guy from earlier? You could crush him by just blinking your eyes! Right, Rose?"

He looks over at her who kept her eyes forward. I was starting to hate how glum she seemed (but maybe that was a bit hypocritical of me). She shrugs a shoulder but doesn't answer him. He scoffs a bit in response and spins around to look at Jem, but upon remembering that he probably would never even try humoring him he turns forward again and shakes his head.

"You too huh? I don't see why either of you are all bummed out right now. Ethan, you might not be able to remember anything yet but at least you've got a few more answers and clues than you did before. And Rose, even though E can't remember anything still, especially you, at least he's here right now with you. Not to mention talking to you. As his bestest friend, when I say Ethan gets physically pained from talking to new people you can believe it. He's comfortable with you already. So, cheer up."

Rose slowly turns her head to look at him, and I was bracing for her to bear her fangs or snap at him or something, but she doesn't. If anything, her face looked even sadder than before. I sigh and reach up, patting Carson on the back so he wouldn't continue his way of lecturing.

"Alright, bro," I say, "we got it. And you're right. Let's just get home and we can figure out what to do next."

10

18th Samhain

"You're back! How did it go? I hope there weren't any issues. And how about Jem? Did he behave himself?"

River is speaking a mile a minute the moment we stepped through the cottage door. Jem shoots her an unamused look as he pushes by and disappears somewhere toward the den. Rose stops in the doorway and Carson is sauntering off to the kitchen to find something he can scarf down.

"How about your passport? Did you get it renewed? And Scott? Did he make it back okay? It's his first time to return to Obscura in five years. He's only been back once the entire time you've been in Whitechapel." She's grinning ear to ear as she shuts the door back behind us, locking it by a wave of the hand.

I pull out my wallet and I show her my passport so she could see. She takes it and smiles down at the looping image.

"Look how handsome you are, even photographed. I find that if I take a picture, I look very square," she laughs.

"That can't possibly be true," I say quietly with a small smile on my face. It felt good to be around her. Her energy somehow made everything feel better.

"It is! Or at least I think so. Now come in, come in, and tell me about your visit to the city. Did you remember anything while you were there?" She looks at me hopefully, gesturing for us to move to the den but Rose doesn't move from her place. "Rose, what's the matter?" she asks her.

"I'm terribly sorry, Madam River, but I shouldn't stay. My father will be wondering where I am by now. I'm also feeling a bit tired so I should go now while there's still a bit of light out. I'll be back tomorrow for the Samhain celebration."

River eyes her for a moment before nodding and moving in to give her a little hug.

"Alright then, I can't argue with that. Thank you for your help today, dear. We'll save most of the festivities for when you get here." She pulls away and gives her a sincere smile. Rose smiles back and gives a little curtsy.

"Goodnight, Ethan," she says to me and then turns to leave without another word.

"I saw Jem headed to the casting room, did they all make it back?" Victoria is quickly rounding the corner and she stops when she sees River and I still standing at the door.

"Yes, they're all back," River says and begins her way to the den.

"And what about fangs? Did she go back already?"

River shoots her a look but goes to have a seat in her chair.

"Yes, *Rose* has gone on home. What are you asking for?"

"Oh no reason," she sings, folding her hands together in front of her as her slate eyes meet mine. "I just didn't want her to see me give you this." She snaps her fingers and there's a flash of white light before a small cutely wrapped box appears in her hand. "An early birthday gift."

I tilt my head to the side, firstly wondering why she would care anything about my birthday let alone giving me a gift, on top of it being *early*. I felt a bit suspicious not that I had any real reason to. I take the gift from her and watch her expression, trying to watch if it were some joke or prank of some kind, but she only smiles back at me with her red lips and sultry eyes.

"Well go on and open it, surely they give gifts on mundane earth!" she demands.

I unwrap the gift and open the small cardboard box. My head tilts a little bit more upon seeing something shiny inside. I pull the small delicate object out and examine it. It looked like a tiny music box with a glass figurine on top. The figure was of a creature with a body of a snake, or a dragon, coiled up in a spiral as it sat up. Its head was of a swan with its eyes shut in a peaceful manner, laying atop its coiled body.

"Well?" Victoria asks expectantly as I was not reacting fast enough for her.

"Thank you," I tell her, turning the thing around in my hand. "But…what is it?"

Her shoulders drop a little and she points to the little crank on the side of its base.

"You turn this thing here," she says, "and it plays a little song."

"Like a music box," I confirm, but she shakes her head.

"No. It plays a song and gives a little show. But if you bury it while the music is playing it will summon a raxon. So not only am I gifting you an incredibly valuable tool, that I *cough* made myself (not to brag or anything), I'm also gifting you something educational. When you finally stop thinking you're too special to study like the rest of us, you can go and look up what sort of being a raxon is and how it could help you in the future. You know, because I'm a *really* good guild mate." She flips her hair over her shoulder and then does a little wink that I wasn't sure of.

I look back at the small object and I'm only imagining what sort of "being" it would summon, and for what purpose. But regardless of its purpose it was somehow a rather thoughtful gift (I think).

"Well give it a try," she said suddenly, waving her hand around frantically.

"In here?" I ask, afraid of conjuring up something huge and recking the place worse than Autumn had done that morning.

She rolls her eyes at me and she snatches the gift away from me, pulling it back out from the box and then turning the little crank a few times. A soft tune starts to play and gradually the glass figurine starts to glow a light blue color. The glowing grows brighter and brighter until the whole thing is engulfed in a bright light. This light then shoots up into the air and disperses into a shower of falling embers, like that of an exploded fire work. Something zips out of the top of the figure that was shaped like the creature that I will assume is called a "raxon". Its body slithers through the air like a miniature dragon and it swirls around with a little dance to the peaceful music. This goes on for a few seconds before everything dims until its disappeared altogether and the music quiets.

"Wow!" an awestruck Carson revels from the doorway with his hands and mouth full of something he found in the kitchen.

"Was that the—" I begin, but Victoria shakes her head before I could finish.

"No, I just told you, you have to bury it for the real thing to appear. But I would study it first before using it that way. But in the meantime, you can enjoy the little show whenever you want. Happy birthday, Specturum kid!" She grins, hands me back the gift, and then struts off faster than I could register.

"Well, that was nice of her wasn't it," River says from her chair. "She can be a bit harsh but she is a very talented young lady. Very good with her hands."

There's frantic coughing from behind and I turn again to see Carson in the middle of a red-faced coughing fit.

"Oh, is he alright?" the older woman asks as she watches him beat at his own chest.

"He's fine," I say quickly with a disappointed sigh. "Anyway, River, about my trip to the H.D.O…"

"Ah, yes. How did it go?"

"Not really the best but not bad either, I think."

"Did you remember anything?"

"No," I shake my head and go to lean against the back of the couch, "but specifically, about that, we met some H.D.O Elders or whatever they're called. And a man called Bishop, he basically told me it was my fault that I can't remember. And more specifically he said that your potion wore off a while ago already… He said it wore off and due to trauma or something subconsciously I don't want to remember. If that's the case then what do I do?"

The old woman's bright blue eyes search mine for a moment and it seemed she was taking time to mull over what I said. After a long pause she folds her hands together in her lap and averts her eyes.

"Archdruid Bishop is the wisest man that lives in all the realm. If that is what he said then it is true. Although a little disheartening, it is wonderful news to hear. The reason is because we now have a different way of looking at your memory problem and how exactly we should be targeting it to fix it. It means that it is possible for your memory to be restored and it is not an error in my brew. Good thing because I was truly worried I had taken your memory from you for good." She presses her lips together and looks at me apologetically.

"But River, I think if we're to change how we look at my problem, shouldn't I be facing whatever trauma you all keep mentioning? I should know it. Earlier I ran into one of those oddity hunters. He said something to me about murdering someone. A 'her'. What does it mean?"

I can see her swallowing thickly and I almost felt bad for asking. But on the other hand, I couldn't see any other way to unlock my memory if I don't exactly understand what truly happened to lead up to that day when I lost it.

"My dear," she starts off slowly, "even if I did tell you I'm not so certain it would be any help. The only reason why I say that is because when…*what happened*, happened, you couldn't remember it afterward. You were quite sick for over a month following the incident. You were able to recover bits and pieces but overall, you had no recollection in the first place. So, I don't know if…trying to relive any of that will do any good. But maybe I'm really saying that because I really hate to see you so beaten down."

I sigh heavily trying to keep my frustration levels low.

"I think I just want to know," I say finally. "Everyone else knows but me, and it's literally about *me*. I would like someone to tell me, regardless of if it helps my memory or not."

River gives me a hesitant look for a good minute before she leans over the side of her chair and picks up her basket full of yarn. My shoulders drop as I watch her gather her needles and an unfinished knitted something, feeling defeated by her distraction.

"Ethan, let's celebrate Samhain," she says instead. "It should be good fun, especially since it's your birthday as well. I couldn't possibly describe that sort of thing just a few hours before a celebration like this. You're back home with all of us, and although Cathy isn't here to see it, you'll get to celebrate your birthday the proper way for the first time in a long time. Let's do that *and then* I'll allow that story to be told."

I ruffle my hair and turn away from her to look at Carson who was sitting much closer than I thought he was. He looks up at me and smiles.

"I'm down for any shindig, E; let's do that before getting bummed out again," he tells me.

"Fine," I grumble and turn away from him as well. As I take a step toward the stairs, before I could properly lift my foot from the ground River stops me.

"Where are you going, you haven't eaten yet. Dinner is in the kitchen. Eat and then you can go to your own devices."

I frown. That's right, she was almost just like Gramma. Maybe that's why they were such close friends.

. . .

After eating something I couldn't name if I wanted to, washing up and finding my way to my bedroom, I was up late staring at that clock I was beginning to resent. I could feel that it was late; my eternal clock said so, and so did the moon as bright as it was pouring into my window. But exactly what time it was, I didn't know, and I hated not being able to read anything. My eyes eventually pull away from the device and trail up to the ceiling where I was afraid I'd see those scary black shadows. But there was nothing. I had been almost too afraid to come into my room at all that night, afraid of being alone, afraid of what my body might turn around and do next. But as time ticked by painfully slow, I eventually had fallen asleep. And although I didn't feel anything icy weighing at my chest, or my skin burning, there was something about the dreams that I had that night that was very off putting.

I'm running, and Rose is chasing after me to keep up. Weaving through trees and hopping over rocks and slopes, I can see something small in front of me. Something I was chasing.

Please! Slow down!

We shouldn't be going so far, Ethan! Wait!

There's a flash of light the images are fragmented, broken and skewed. I can feel myself stirring in my sleep, but I never wake up.

I see teeth, sharp and menacing like that of a large predator. There's a flash and I can hear Rose crying. She's tugging at the back of my shirt and I feel a raw anger building in my chest. The image fades and all I can hear is a young Rose's sobs.

I hurt Rosie...

"Ethan! Get up! Wake up, dude, are you gonna sleep the day away or what?"

I'm being shaken violently by an excited blonde and every bit of his voice was grating. My eyes squeeze open and I stare up at Carson groggy and very unhappy that I was awoken before I could get up by myself.

"Ew, you look terrible," he says and crawls off of me and stands up on the floor.

"Thanks, bro," I grumble sleepily and sit up a little.

"You're welcome, bro. Victoria told me to come wake you up. She said River's got somethin' for you in the den."

I stare blankly at him, his words jumbling together the moment they hit my ears. He cracks his head to the side, asking me if I was paying attention without having to say so. My eyes roll shut in response and I fall backward into the bed again.

He's huffing and reaching over me, grabbing the pillow beside me and dealing a hard wallop across my face with it.

"Get up!" he yells until I'm groaning and pushing him away.

I'm up after a slow start and Carson has disappeared in the bathroom. I'm stepping down the cold wooden steps with my bare feet and I'm listening for others, but I don't hear any sound. As I enter the den, I'm greeted by a warm scent of pumpkin and cinnamon that piqued my interest. I look around, but I still don't see a single person other than the cat that has found a comfy spot in the middle of a couch. I step toward the kitchen where I was expecting Victoria or River to be, but neither of them was there. But there was a tall vigorously boiling pot that sat atop the stove, along with various other things cooking and baking. As I leave the doorway of the kitchen, I turn toward the foyer and I'm approaching to peak out of the window, but before I get close enough the door swings open. River is hastily walking in carrying another large pot like what was in the kitchen. She almost didn't see me even when my face nearly connected with the door had I not dodged out of the way (with…how swift and cool I am). It wasn't until she heard the little (*manly*) squeak I made out of shock did she turn her head and see me.

"Ethan!" she exclaims and kicks the door shut behind her. "You're finally up, good morning! Oh, and happy birthday!" She smiles and gestures for me to follow as she continued her way to the kitchen and set the pot down into the sink. She runs water into it and now I see that it is full of bright red apples. "Did Tori tell you? I've got something for you. Well, something outside of your birthday gift of course."

Ah, so it was Victoria's job to relay this message, but she sent Carson instead.

She doesn't wait for me to answer. She's turning off the water and she's walking full stride out of the kitchen and into the den. She spins around upon entering the doorway, and I hadn't noticed a long black bag hanging up on the wall.

"It occurred to me that all of your clothes are far too small for you here. Have you taken a look at them?"

I shake my head. I haven't actually touched anything except the toys that gave me a harsh flash back and my bed. I haven't even opened any drawers or taken a closer look at the many strange jars shelved against the wall.

"I guess I haven't," I answer quietly.

"Well, no matter," she says and reaches up to unzip what was clearly a garment bag. "I can't afford to replace your entire wardrobe, but I at least thought it would be lovely to get you an outfit for today's celebration. It's a bit traditional, but you can wear it to other places if you like. Your grandmother, however, would put you in something from her own tradition but since she's not here, the choice was mine." She smiles brightly as she's pulling out an entire set that I would honestly *kill* to wear at the Renaissance festival back home. It was a linen shirt with the crisscross tie collar. There were those puffy brown medieval pants with matching leather arm guards, vest, and traveler's pouch. River then waves her hand and there on the floor appears the matching boots and a folded up thick brown cape. My eyes light up and I'm completely stoked to wear it immediately.

"Wow!" I say and reach out to feel the fabric of the clothing. "You got all of this for me?"

"Of course, dear. Not only do you need a change of clothes, but I just thought you should own something nice after returning home. That's why I got you a good cloak too. Oh, and that friend of yours…I didn't leave him out and got him a little something as well."

Almost right on cue, Carson is high kicking his way down the stairs. He with a spin and a strut as if he were on a catwalk approaches the both of us and then throws his arms out wide to display his new clothing.

"Do I look pretty, boss, or don't I!" he exclaims with a huge grin. He's wearing a white linen shirt similar to the one River got me, but this one has ruffling down the collar and around the wrists of the sleeves. I only thank the universe that it actually looked pretty okay on him, very much unlike that awful costume he wore at Eric's party. His pants were loose but gathered together by the rather nice boots River was kind enough to get. He has on a thick leather belt that had a travel pouch attached to it, with a cloak (that grant it wasn't as nice as mine but nice enough) clasped around his shoulders.

River approaches him and she's adjusting his collar and brushing out some wrinkles with her hands.

"It's not bad," she tells him. "You could really pass for a Holly's Grove native. Ethan, go and dress up quickly so you can help us set up."

"Set up?" I say and peak passed her to the window that I couldn't quite see.

Her hands move up to her hips and she looks at me with eyes that read: *do I have to say it twice?* My lips press together, I nod and I take the clothes from her, pick up the boots and cloak from the floor and I take them upstairs to wash and dress up.

After a while I am coming down the stairs and entering the den as I'm adjusting the guards on my arms. I only stop when I nearly run into Victoria whose back was turned to me as she was rummaging through a big storage box that she had propped up on the coffee table. She was wearing a black and purple layered skirt with an embroidered bodice laced up over an off the shoulder black peasant top. Her hair was pulled up in a ponytail that she had straightened and she was ladened with crystal jewelry.

"Can I help you with anything," I ask, startling her a bit as she jumped at the sound of my voice.

"Oh, Ethan!" She stands up straight and spins around but pausing at the sight of me. "Well," she sang and placed her hands on her hips, "don't you look rather *attractive*. Very festive, very…western woodsman." She smirks and I notice the paint on her lips was not her usual velvety red, but instead was a daring shade of purple. Her eyes were dusted with a smoky black that brought out the flecks of green in her grey-ish orbs. Even with the complete change in style she still exuded an alluring charm. "I was just looking for the stand to one of our lanterns, it seems to be missing. But never mind that, they could use your help outside around back." She waves for me to get a move on and then turns back to her box full of many miscellaneous items. I go and step outside. It was pleasantly warmer than yesterday without any frigid winds, but instead a rather nice breeze. Upon taking my first step onto the soft earth, a wave of vertigo hits me and I have to stop for a moment.

You seem strange…

I jump at the sudden sound of a disembodied voice. I was almost certain that it wasn't from my own head. I turn this way and that, searching for where it could have come from but there is no one.

So strange… Very curious…

I sigh irritably. I was very much not in the mood to start hearing voices, but something about this one was very different. It was the voice of a woman that seemed to carry across the breeze.

Who are you? Can you hear me?

Hard no. Hard pass. I spin on my heels and take long quick strides around the side of the cottage. To see others, or *hear* others that I knew were directly in front of me would assist in retaining my sanity. As I'm cornering the back end of the house, I find that there is quite a sizeable clearing of bright green grass. Jem is shoving large poles into the ground using brute strength. River in clothing similar to Victoria's but with an apron wrapped over her was using magic to stir an insanely large spoon inside of the largest cauldron I had ever seen. It was sitting atop a makeshift fire all incased in the circle of large stones. Carson seemed to be helping her, throwing bag fulls of spices and herbs. Autumn was setting a long table with glass plates and fancy goblets made of silver. She's wearing something that was very different from the rest. She wore a red colored qipao-esque garment with long flowing sleeves of silk that reached the end of her golden embroidered skirt. Her thick black hair was pinned half up in an intricate bun with a ruby colored pin stuck into it.

I approach her, feeling like I'd do better helping her out than I would with whatever heavy thing Jem was doing. When she sees me walking awkwardly toward the table, her eyes light up and she smiles kindly to me.

"Ethan!" she calls out happily. "Happy birthday."

"Thank you," I return with a little smile. "Your dress is quite lovely," I say, "but I only wonder why you'd wear it for today?"

She's folding up a stack of napkins now, making them look nice before setting them at each plate.

"Do you know the significance of today?" she asks. "Outside of your birthday, obviously."

"Well, it's Halloween? Or something you guys keep calling Samhain."

She giggles a bit and somehow, I feel embarrassed by my answer, not that I thought that what I said was wrong. Or was it?

"You're right, it's Samhain, but also known as 'Halloween'. I've heard many stories about Samhain on mundane earth. But that on Samhain night children go out to beg for candy from their neighbors. Isn't that true?"

I snort.

"Yeah, you could describe it like that."

She looks up at me again and she hands me half of the napkins she had folded.

"It seems a little silly. I'm not sure what the significance of that is. But the true meaning of Samhain is to honor our passed loved ones and our ancestors. We celebrate the lives they once lived, remember them and the impact they had or still have on our lives. And then obviously the fun part is the *festival!*" She laughs a little and once she finished with her napkins, she's summoning lanterns from a pile of them that was on the ground somewhere. With her hand she beckons the objects and they slowly (a little unsteadily) float over and sit themselves onto the table. "I've been practicing that," she adds quietly after a successful job. "Anyway, so, I wear this gown in honor of my Taiwanese heritage. In Obscura it is tradition to wear clothing that symbolizes your family's tradition and background on Samhain. If you didn't know, in the past Obscura and mundane Earth used to be connected. We all originate from there and lived one with nohabs. That is until the Great Divide. But that doesn't stop us from carrying our past traditions from generation to generation."

223

"Interesting..." I say slowly as I listened carefully to her. It really was fascinating to me to hear what this day is meant for, at least to the people that live here. And what an honorable holiday to have, the meaning surely beats going around asking for candy... (not that...I wouldn't love to be out milking my age as long as possible right now *eh-hem*). "Then I guess I wonder why River put me in this," I chuckle, looking down at my western medieval clothing. Autumn smiles again and smooths out the skirt of her own dress.

"To her, you're a part of her family. Like a grandson. So, she's going to dress you up however she likes if you let her. But I do think it..." her voice hushes as it seemed she was suddenly remembering her shyness, "...fits you well. It's what people wear often today anyway...sort of." She shrugs a little and is rounding the corner. "Though, I am sure that if miss Catherine were here, she would put you in something from your own heritage. I have seen very beautiful Obscurian hanboks around where I grew up. I'm sure it would fit you just as well..." She presses her mouth closed and there was an awkward pause before she gestures to a pile of decorations. "Uhm...help me set these up, will you?"

The rest of the morning was spent decorating for the holiday. Victoria had finally returned after a while with the missing lantern she was looking for and she went around the yard hanging them on poles Jem propped up for her. Autumn and I set chairs around the table while River and Carson disappeared inside while the cauldron boiled frantically with something that smelled like cinnamon and cloves. Victoria had gone inside as well for a while before she returned with a hot pan and a tray of drinks floating behind her. She had approached Autumn and me, offering us quiche and cider for our hard work.

The sun was lowering in the sky, and by now we had finished the jobs we had been given. River had come out with Carson carrying pots and dishes of foods (a number of them floating behind them) as they went to wrap them all up to be taken somewhere. River repositions a center piece made from colorful fall leaves, twigs, candles, and what I hope was a fake skull, and then she stands up straight and smooths her hands over her apron.

"Everyone!" she calls out, her face full of joy and excitement, "let's gather around the table." Carson joins me by my side and we all make our way over to the table. After everyone gathers round, River gestures for everyone to sit and get comfortable. "Firstly," she starts, "I'd like to thank you all for your help this morning, I know it can be tedious setting up for holidays like this, but it makes it all the more fun, doesn't it?" She now turns to me and folds her hands in front of her. "The reason why we're out here today is because we thought it would be nice to celebrate the birth of our miracle boy who we are so grateful to have returned to us before heading off to Willow Way for the festival. Isn't that right, Jem?" She looks over at him and he's slouched down in his chair, manspreading to each end of the universe. He looked up at her, his eyes glimmering with embers and he gave a little grunt that was left up to us to interpret. "We'll take that as a yes. Either way, Ethan, we want you to have a happy birthday, and at least for today forget about the stresses we know you're facing. Although I'm unsure of where your aunt and uncle are…everyone, let's sing to our boy!" She grins and she's gesturing for everyone to start singing. Gradually everyone began to sing to me the happy birthday song (that is all but Jem but that wasn't much of a surprise). After the song had been sung, River snaps her fingers and there before her on the table is a stack of gifts. I blink my eyes rapidly, firstly trying to process that something just appeared out of nowhere, and secondly feeling like gifts were less than necessary.

"R-River—" I began but she cuts me off almost immediately.

"Now I know what you're going to say," she said. "'All of this couldn't possibly be for me', or 'you really didn't have to'. I know, you were exactly like that even as a child. But think of it as not just birthday gifts, but a welcome home gift."

"And a 'sorry you got your mind wiped and was kicked out of your homeland for ten years' gift," Victoria adds, earning a nudge in the arm from River. She shrugs and picks up a black and gold wrapped box. "I'll go first, it's your official gift from me." She's reaching across the table and handing me the medium sized box.

I look down at it curiously. I begin to open it, not wanting to keep them waiting, and there I pull out a brown leather leg holster first, meant to hold a dagger of some kind. Victoria eyes me expectantly and when I looked up at her, she gestured to the box again. "There's more," she said. I dig through the gift paper and find that at the bottom was a smaller black box that was where all the weight of the gift came from. I pick up, open it, and there inside was a dagger with a green marbled handle. The blade was inscribed with symbols I didn't recognize, and sigils I didn't understand either. But either way, it sure was cool.

"Thanks, Victoria," I say, looking back up at her proud smirk. "You really didn't have to give me anything like this."

"Sure, I did. You're a guild member, even for longer than me. I didn't get to meet you or your mother. And I've only met your grandmother once or twice. So, I'm giving you this to show you I'm not all that bad."

"Fair enough," I murmur and set the boxes down carefully.

"Autumn, why don't you give him your gift next," River suggests. She seems to have been snapping out of a daydream upon her name being called. After registering what was said, she perks up and reaches over to grab her gift, wrapped in light blue wrapping paper. It was a small square box that she handed over to me carefully.

"My gift was a little last minute," she says sheepishly and sits back down after I retrieved the item. "But I did put some thought into it, so I really hope you like it."

I unwrap the gift, opening the box to pull out quite a few pieces of jewelry. There were about three necklaces, all with some sort of crystal attached; there were bracelets as well made with crystals and metals like copper or silver. Actually, they were quite nice, and I wouldn't mind wearing them at all. I look at Autumn again and she seemed rather nervous as she tugged at her long silk sleeves.

"It's witch's jewelry," she explains. "As I'm sure you've seen, just about all witches wear crystals and metals for their magical properties. Each crystal has a purpose. I thought you ought to have a lot of obsidian and black tourmaline to protect you seeing as how you're…sort of popular among those who'd want to bring trouble. That and amethyst, to help with any anxieties you might feel while you continue to recover your memory. There're other bits in there as well. I wrote on a little card that explains each rock's purpose. I truly hope it helps."

"Thank you, Autumn," I tell her after she's finished. "It's really thoughtful of you." I take a bracelet that looked to have amethyst in it and wrap it around my wrist so she knows I mean it. That and any relief from anxiety and stress would be greatly appreciated. Autumn wears a relieved expression and leans back into her chair. River then turns, clasping her hands happily against her chest as she faces Jem.

"I believe it's your turn, Jem," she tells him. He looks up at her, and I wasn't sure if his expression read that he was annoyed or unamused, or…both. I surely wasn't expecting him to have anything for me at all. But to my surprise, he's reaching deep into his trouser pocket and after a bit of digging around he pulls out a little blue sack. He tosses it my way and I only just catch it. I didn't wait for him to say anything as I was sure he wasn't planning to anyway and I open it up. Inside was a coarse red powder that shimmered a bit when it caught the light. I dig my finger around in it, wondering if there was something else inside or if it was just the powder. After assessing that I didn't understand what it was, I look over a Jem who was yawning boredly. When there was too long of a silence, River is waving her hands around frantically, wanting to move us along (or maybe she was just excited to give me her gift). She's picking up a big box wrapped in floral paper, and she picks it up with all her might, slamming it down in front of me.

"Thank him and let's open the last gift!" she says sounding almost winded.

I give thanks, even though I wanted to ask what the purpose of fancy red dust was, but as River was excitedly egging me to open hers, I move on, stand to my feet and tear the box open. As I'm peering inside to see what she got me, I'm distracted by a familiar voice, coming from behind.

"Sorry we're late!"

I spin around, having been almost startled by the voice until I laid eyes on my aunt carrying a big cake and my uncle following behind her with a bag in each hand. Aunt Nari was smiling widely and she seemed in good spirits as she approached me and pressed a kiss to my cheek.

"Happy birthday, *joka*," she says quietly to me before moving to place the cake down. River waved her hand quickly, having to make room on the table for her by using magic. Uncle Namu moves passed me, and when I was sure he was going to ignore me, he sets the bags down on the table and then turns around, pulling me into a strong hug. My brow raises in surprise at the sudden gesture. He didn't even hug me the day I first met him. My hands close around his back until he pulls away, placing his hands on my shoulders as he looked at me with his strange yellow eyes.

"I'm sorry for the other day," he said unexpectedly. "Don't misunderstand me. I am very happy to see you."

I didn't know what to say to that. 'Don't worry about it, maaan.' That's something Carson would say. But it seemed he didn't wait for me to answer anyway and he was rounding the table to greet everyone.

"We were caught up in a conference with a few elders. All of which *weren't* the archdruid," Nari starts explaining as she finds a seat next to Carson.

"A conference?" River repeats, confusion twisting her expression. "There aren't supposed to be any Greenwood conferences at Lamia until November. What could it have been about?"

"We're not quite sure. We weren't supposed to have any involvement with the castle today at all," Nari says.

"We specifically cleared all schedules for today so we could come home early," Namu adds.

"Then all of a sudden as we were preparing to leave, Annika demanded we answer a few questions before we could go about our day."

"She had us go into a conference room where a conference was already meeting before we got there."

"What did they ask you," River asks.

"First, they asked our opinion on Greenwood and Lamia uniting as one district immediately. Asking how do we see citizens reacting to it being proposed or ultimately happening," Uncle Namu answers.

The girls are shaking their heads, and River presses her fists into her sides.

"And then," Nari continues, "they asked if we knew anyone by the name of Ernest Convel-Hildwulf."

"Who is that?" Victoria asks, wrinkling up her nose.

Nari shrugs. "Beats me," she said. "Someone who comes from Artemis. But both of us said—"

"—as rarely as we go to Artemis these days, how would we know?" Namu finishes for her. "And even if we did, what's the significance?"

"They didn't quite answer that question," Nari says. "But after that they went on with something about concerns with oddity imbalances and something called *'invictus'*."

River is staring blankly at the twins before she draws in a slow deep breath and takes a seat.

"Let's talk about it some more later," she tells them.

"Do you know what that is?" my aunt asks but River only repeats herself, shushing her with her hand.

"Let's talk about it more later. I'm not exactly sure what they might be up to, but I think it's safe to say that whatever it is isn't any good. But we don't want to shroud today's celebration with the ill will of others."

"Of course…then I guess that means I should give you this now." Nari leans forward to see me past Carson's big head and she points a finger at one of the bags set on the table in front of Namu. As she dragged her finger through the air, the gift slides across the table and stops in front of me.

"Now hold on just a minute! Ethan was opening a gift from me before you two came! Hurry up and look at what I've got you," River nearly shouts. I crack a smile and stand back up to my feet to see into the tall box. I am finally pulling out a medium sized trunk that didn't seem new at all as the evergreen-colored leather seemed to be wearing a bit on the corners. I move the box out of my way so that I could set the trunk down. "The case was already yours," River tells me before I had to ask. "I just filled it up with new stuff for you. Take a look." She's smiling brightly at me and I flip open each latch until I can raise the lid. Carson stands up beside me to peer inside as well and in it was quite a few items. There was something wrapped up in a thick brown cloth that caught my attention first. I pick it up and go to unwrap it only to reveal a wooden wand wrapped in a long cord of silver that simultaneously held a chunk of clear quartz and amethyst in place at the end of the handle.

I didn't dare touch it outside of the wrapping. I'd seen too many movies that taught me that nothing good comes out of such a tool if you didn't know how to use it. I turn it this way and that from within the cloth before I look up at River and the others who seemed to be staring at me expectant of a reaction or response. But when I didn't give one, River spoke up again.

"If you're to start exercising and practicing magic you'll need a tool that can help you control your power," she said gently. "Using your hands can be too dangerous when the energy isn't properly controlled. It was a pretty penny, but I had this one crafted for some of your specific needs. Whenever you'd like to start, I'd be happy to help you. And so is everyone else here. That is the benefit of being a part of a guild, dear."

"Thank you, River," I tell her. I suddenly couldn't help the looming guilty feeling. I wasn't quite sure why I felt that way, but it had something to do with how everything around here that's happened is because of me in some way. I carefully place the wand back into the trunk. I didn't feel like taking up any more time to go through the many things that were in there. I'd do it later on my own time. "I'm very thankful to you, River," I say with a little bow of the head. "I'll take a look at the rest later on. One surprise at a time."

"Then we can open up ours a little later. You seem a little overwhelmed. We still have the rest of the day," Aunt Nari tells me, standing up and taking her bag back. She pats my shoulder and then moves back to her seat. "I suppose we can cut the cake. Are we waiting on anyone?"

"Just Rosie," she answered. "But I'm sure she will eat with her family first before coming here."

"That's settled," Victoria calls out and stands up to her feet. "Let's get this over with." She straightens out her skirt and then she claps her hands together firmly. Slowly she releases her hands, waving them over the table. Candles appeared on the cake and all of the goblets on the table filled with cider and pitchers appeared filled with beer. Jem was quick to pour out the cider in his cup, right over his shoulder and filled it high with beer instead.

I'm asked to make a wish and blow out the candles. And as I close my eyes to think of one, only one thought came across my mind. I just wanted to get my memories back, and make things right. After this thought, I blew out the candles, and after everyone cheered, cake was distributed to us all. It was settled that we would wait for Rose to come before heading off to the Samhain festival I was eager to get to experience. The others talked amongst themselves merrily, and we all were having a good time.

After a while of eating and laughing and talking with each other, I couldn't help but start to tune out and feel withdrawn. There was something bothering me again, and at first, I couldn't put my finger on it. It wasn't until a particularly cold gust of wind passed by my side, hitting me in the face.

Peculiar...

I flinch at the sound of a quiet voice, turning quickly to see who it was but no one was there. I frown deeply and turn back to the table. The others were still talking, even Autumn was sharing a story about a trip around the district she took when she was younger. But I wanted to step away for a moment. I stand up and Carson looks to me to ask where I was going.

"I'll be back," I mumble to him. Carson watches me walk off and so did some of the others but no body called after me or followed.

Can you hear me? Please...

I ruffle my hair and try to ignore the sounds in my ear. I move far off from the others and venture off into the cluster of trees in the distance. I climb up a small hill and kick through the twigs and the leaves until I find a good spot to sit. I crouch down, feeling as though I had a low battery and needed to charge. The wind blows and leaves fall. I pull my knees up to my chest and I stare off into the distance.

What are you?

There was a different voice this time, one that sounded like an older man. It was frustrating to want to be alone but not feel alone. I look around me, but there was nothing but trees and land. I could still hear the others, and I wasn't too far off where I couldn't see them.

What are you, boy?!

The voice was louder and I flinch again at it.

"Won't you be quiet!" I snap at nothingness, only to jump at the sound of something moving rapidly in my direction. I couldn't see it at first, other than a blur of blacks and browns.

"I didn't know my running was so loud," Rose's voice says.

I peek my eyes open, leaning way over on one leg while the other and both my hands were held up to "protect" myself from whatever danger was coming at me at high speeds. But when I see Rose standing above me, my muscles relax and I feel my ears burning.

"That's not" I started to say, only to get distracted by her choice of clothing for today. She wore a long black gown that trailed behind her a little. Her sleeves were of a sheer material with a design of roses crocheted into them. A black corset hugged her around the rib cage, clasped together in the front by silver fastens. The collar of her dress was made from the same sheer material that covered her neck and shoulders. She carried a closed parasol in her hand, a small basket in the other, and her hair was tied behind her back. She wore a black lipstick and her eyes were painted with smoke and glitter which brought much attention to her smokey colored eyes I find myself closing my mouth and Rose is crouching down beside me.

"I was only joking," she said quietly with a little pout, nudging me in the shoulder. "But who were you talking to?"

I shake my head and look away. I was suddenly reminded of the end of yesterday where her entire demeanor had changed. She barely even spoke to me until now.

"No one," I say. "I was just practicing…my…assertiveness." My lips press together and I give a nod to really assure myself of the lie while Rose only watched me with an eyebrow raised.

"Sure," she says, "because we all know you're too soft."

"There's nothing wrong with being soft." I frown and fold my legs together.

"No, there isn't. It's a good trait to have, being empathetic. But it can also make trouble. You wouldn't have to practice assertiveness if it didn't, would you?"

I rub the back of my neck. Even when I was lying in the first place, she still made good points. I didn't respond though, and instead dug into the ground with a small stick. Rose watches me for a moment, and she shifts from crouching to sitting, her legs bent to one side. She smooths out her skirt and she stares ahead of her.

"Happy birthday, Ethan," she said after a long pause of silence and set the basket she had with her in front of me. "Although I can do it myself, my father wanted to help." She gestures for me to look inside and so I do, moving to open the lid. Before I could see what was inside there was a sweet familiar smell that warmed my chest. I glance up at her but she's still staring ahead of her. I reach inside, first pulling out a sizeable jar full of a red tinted liquid. Setting it aside, I look into the basket.

"...Goguma," I say quietly as I identify the smell. Inside wrapped carefully in red and white cloth were tarts. Some were made of egg, and the rest were all sweet potato. Goguma. My eyes flicker and it felt a bit difficult to think. As familiar as these desserts were, I could even taste them in my mouth, I knew that Gramma had never made any for me before. I'd never eaten them. Yet, I know I have. I look over at Rose again whose gaze had fallen. She didn't have to say anything for me to pick up that she was waiting for a certain reaction from me. My eyes flicker again and I can see a faint image of myself sitting on the floor of someone's house, shoving as many of the tarts (only the sweet potato ones though) into my mouth as I could. With someone every so often saying

"*I think you've had enough, Ethan.*"

A shiver runs up my spine and I'm closing the lid of the basket.

"That jar is Rose's Tea. It's something your mother made up. She left me the recipe before she...erm." She rubs her arm a little and then gestures to the basket. "You didn't read the letter," Rose tells me, turning now to look at me.

I didn't notice the letter. I open the basket again and see a little folded piece of parchment tucked to the side. I pull it out and open it.

> *If you ever find yourself in Lamia soon, won't you stop by so that I may lay my eyes on you once again? Rosie's told me everything, and I want nothing more than to express my deepest remorse to you in person about the pain my family has caused you and yours. That, and there's something I'd like to give you that once belonged to your mother, that belonged to your grandfather.*
>
> *Happy Birthday, Ethan.*
> *And P.S...*
> *I did most of the work on the sweets. :)*
> *Kindest Regards,*
> *Aero Ncuti*

"My father is lying!"

I didn't notice Rose hovering over my shoulder until her voice nearly burst my eardrum. She takes the note from my hand and she's reading it over again and shaking her head.

"He most certainly did not do most of the work, don't believe that," she's telling me.

I eye her, obviously not believing her, but also not focused on that part of the letter like she was. That man had something that belonged to my mother, that also belonged to my grandfather. I didn't even know who my grandfather was which I found rather strange. Rose finally meets my eye after fuming over her father's note and then she sets it down.

"Sorry," she says.

I shake my head and take the note back.

"No. I'd like to meet your father one day if I can."

"The annual masquerade ball is coming up at the castle. It's meant to celebrate the transition of fall to winter. I was thinking of not going this year, but perhaps…it'd be fun if—"

"No," I interrupt, shaking my head frantically at her, my hair flying.

"No?! What do you mean no? You'd be wearing a mask, so no one would know who you are and neither do they have to. Which is sort of a win win because we would rather people within the castle not see you anytime soon. That and you're an incredible dancer!" She's grinning widely to which I had almost forgotten about the pointy feature in her mouth that could probably kill at a moment's notice. I blink at her stupidly and screw up my face.

"Dance? HA HA. That's funny, because I hate nothing more than trying to *dance*."

"What? Oh, don't be silly. You know that you are a fantastic dancer. You were top of the class! Even when you weren't meant to be in it anyway. You should have lots of fun. You used to look forward to the ball when we were… I mean—"

Her excitement dies down and my face relaxes as I watch her brightness fade again. I hated that; God did it make me feel beaten down by guilt. She's turning away and hugging herself around the middle.

"I-I just mean that…It could be something to remember about the past. Either way you do not have to go if you really don't want to. If everyone is at the ball, it'd be easier to move around the grounds and get to my father."

I frown a little and look up to the sky. The sun was going down now; it was close to sunset.

"I'm sorry," I apologize. "I didn't mean to make you—I mean, I didn't want you to—" My shoulders drop and I shake my head. It seemed like I could never say the right thing.

You've done it now.

Poor boy.

I jump at two voices now, searching around me frantically for the owner but there's no one.

"Don't you hear that?" I ask her, and she looks at me sideways.

"I think you have to be more specific…"

"People talking. It's been happening all day."

She blinks at me and then looks past me toward the others far off in the distance. I was sure she was going to ask if I was talking about them, but instead, she says something different.

"Ethan, it's Samhain."

My brow furrows at this random comment and I run my fingers through my hair.

"Yeah, I know that. What about it?"

She's shaking her head this time and she shifts, folding her legs together and readjusting her skirt to lay properly over them.

"The veil between the living and the dead is very thin, right now. Usually, you can see the dead quite clearly on this day. But it seems like you can only hear them instead. That must be what you're hearing, right?"

I scrunch my nose as I'm unsure how to process this information. I should feel relieved that I'm not going crazy and hearing voices in my head, right? Or should I feel mortified that I can hear dead people?

"Well why are they talking to me? Can't anyone else hear them too?"

"Not many people have that ability without any form of magic or divination tool to help," she explains. "It's a gift that all Spirit S.E.'s have exclusively."

And since you're…the only one…" I frown and when she notices this her eyes go back up to the sky. She never finishes and I don't say anything else for a while. Until my mind drifts back to yesterday. I draw in a breath and I dare myself to ask a pressing question.

"Rose," I call and she only hums in response. "Yesterday, when we were at the H.D.O, what happened? Why did you start crying? And why after did you seem so…stand-off-ish?"

She's quiet, and I was almost sure she wasn't going to answer until she leaned back on her hands and sighed.

"I can only imagine what you must be going through," she says. "So, I feel it must be selfish of me to speak on how unfair it is that I've been completely wiped from your mind." She looks at me and something about her gaze felt melancholic. "It might even be silly to feel that way. We were only children, so how much could you or I even remember of each other after so long? But if I think hard enough—at least for myself, I remember quite a bit, and I remember every emotion we shared together even that young. So, when I look at you this way, lost, confused, not yourself, it's very painful to see. You suddenly fell ill yesterday and I couldn't help the panic that was displayed. But then, after the archdruid said that you cannot remember because internally you choose not to, I felt…defeated. Angry, almost. Because not a day went by since you left that I did not think of you, or your mother, or Madam Grey. If you were okay, if you were well, if you were happy. You never thought that way about me. Or my father. And it hurts to think about it, even when I understand that it isn't your fault." She presses her lips together and she looks down at her lap. "Is it silly of me? Selfish of me?"

"I don't think so," I answer quietly, and lay backward completely on the ground. I'm watching the sun as it slowly goes down and there's an annoying voice beside me whispering along with the wind:

You don't want to remember. You must be selfish

Stop. He is honest

I knew he was peculiar. The last Spirit boy.

I roll my eyes and start playing with the string on my shirt.

"If I were in your position, I'd probably feel the same way. But about what the archdruid said, I don't understand it, because I feel like remembering and trying to remember are things that I have been doing all this time." I sigh. "I'm going to ask River for help. I will try my best to remember, and that's a promise. And Rose," I wait for her to acknowledge me. She turns her head to look me in the eye and I continue. "It's not true what you said. You weren't completely wiped from my mind. All this time it's been your voice that I hear when I try to sleep. And it was always the one memory of us playing as children that I would see when trying to sleep. I might not have known what the significance of it was, but a part of me somewhere did."

Her eyes are welling up and she was opening her mouth to say something but she never does after River's voice was calling after the both of us.

"ETHAN! COME BACK OVER HERE! THE DAY'S NOT OVER YET! YOU TOO, ROSE, I KNOW YOU'RE HERE!"

Rose cracks a smile and sniffs before she moves to push herself to her feet.

"Come on then," she says gently and lends a hand to help me up too. We walk back to join the others and upon meeting them Carson is jumping in front of us, staring down at the basket I carried in my hand.

"What's that? More food? Let's see it!"

"It's not for you, Collin!" Rose snaps. Carson's eye blow so wide that I was sure they would pop like balloons. His chest was filling with what was going to be an angry tirade until Rose stops him.

"HOW MANY TIMES DO I—"

"Relax," Rose says with a taunting smile on her face. "I was only joking. I *do* remember your name, Carson. Ah, but I wasn't joking about Ethan's gift though, it's not for you."

Carson's chest deflates and he's crossing his arms.

"I was going to complement your Sa-lloween outfit, but you bullied me just now," he pouts. "Maybe next time when you're nicer to me."

Rose snorts and River and the others join us.

"Let's head off, the festival should be well started by now," the old woman says with a smile. Victoria makes a beckoning motion behind her and those big pots and cauldrons of food that had been wrapped up are being levitated and moving over to float behind us. Carson and I shared an excited look before we followed behind the other five who had begun their way to the front of the house and to the path that would lead us to Willow Way.

After the fair walk into the center, we were greeted by flaming torches that led the way into the heart of the area. High energy music filled the air with string instruments and flutes. We could hear the excitement of crowds of people before we could see them. People were dressed in all sorts of clothing. Some like what I wore, some in very interesting variations of traditional cultural clothing. Some people wore masks, and others wore cool make up and face paint. There were sparks of fireworks shooting up from someone's wand. People were dancing, others singing old songs together. As we walked further together into the crowd of celebrating witches and other individuals who may have just come for the festival itself from other parts of the district, I spotted a long table full of all sorts of delicious looking foods and deserts. There was a huge pumpkin sat in the middle. Smoke billowed out of it and people were using magic to ladle out whatever drink was inside into silver goblets. It seemed just as I had noticed this, Carson had too, and without hesitation his feet carried him over there to get his hands on food. Jem was close behind him as it seemed he was going right for the pitchers of beer.

"Come this way." I heard Victoria's voice in my ear as I felt her grab my arm and pull me in the direction of people clapping and cheering. Rose and Autumn followed as River had gone to follow Carson—I suppose to supervise his actions. As we approached wherever Victoria was dragging me off to, I stood on my toes to peer over the crowd to see a woman in intricate clothing, bells jingling from the fabric they were sewn into. She danced and her eyes were alluring as they glowed like that of Jem's when he was particularly moody. Her arms twisted and twirled as she conjured dancing flames and shot them up into the sky with her hands and feet. Another witch, wearing draping fabrics that seemed to repel the moonlight, was twirling around until the fire was high enough in the air where he used his wand to shoot shards of water, like ice but not frozen at all into those dancing flames. The water shot through the flames until it began to take a different shape, twirling and twisting itself around them to make fascinating shapes. Shapes that were abstract until it morphed and took the form of a fierce hawk. It screeched as it dove toward the ground, causing the crowd to both cheer and gasp as it flew just over head until it burst into little particles of embers and water droplets.

"Woah!" I clapped my hands along with the others.

"Fun, right?" Victoria calls out over the cheering, looking back at me with a grin. "I bet they don't have anything like that back in your nohab town."

They certainly didn't. Unless you count fireworks or something. But I didn't quite answer her as my attention soon shifted toward a booming sound of drums and mysterious music coming from behind. I feel Rose grab my sleeve and she's pointing in that very direction.

"Ethan, look," I heard her say.

I turned around to see a man wearing a dark mask. He walked barefoot on the cold ground, contorting his body to the sound of the drums. Behind him was a parade float with the largest jack-o-lantern I've ever seen. It was enchanted to make different faces. People gathered to watch it go by as another float followed with witches with tall pointy hats dancing on top, throwing treats and baggies of goodies as other people danced with silk pieces.

"Ethan, Ethan!" I turn my head to see Carson pushing through the crowd, holding two wooden cups of in each hand, reminiscent of the Halloween party in Whitechapel. Only this time Carson was handing one to me. "You have to drink this right this second! I had like *hic* ten already!" He hiccups, and I was almost sure he had found some alcohol until I smelled the beverage he gave me. But it wasn't alcohol at all.

"Oh, you found gourd stew!" Autumn exclaims after getting a look at what Carson brought over.

"What? Is it soup?" I ask her, turning up my nose as I examine it closely, to which Victoria laughs and Autumn giggles.

"No, it's not stew," Vicotira shouts over the noise. "They just call it that for fun."

"But it's got *gourds* in it?" I raise an eyebrow at her, not sure how appealing squash in a drink would be.

"Gourds as in pumpkin," Autumn corrects with another laugh. "It's just pumpkin, some spices, and sweet cream. It's really good!"

"Oh...so like...a pumpkin spice latte?" I watch her but Carson is making a face as he looks down at the drink in his hand.

"Uhh...I'm lactose intolerant," he voices with an uneasy expression. All three girls look over at the blonde staring down into his mug, and no one says anything for a full minute before he shrugs and takes another big swig of the stuff. "Just stay out of the bathroom tonight, ladies," he professes as he turns around to wander back toward the food table.

"That's...disgusting," Rose mumbles as she turned to face the rest of us. We all laugh with eachother as we enjoy the rest of the festivities. There were more fascinating displays of magic, potions were being brewed to share with everyone there. More dances, more laughter. It was good fun.

As it got later and the sky was dark, I began to feel strange vibrating in the air that was very much not the sound of music. As I was being forced to dance with Victoria near some band of people in a very grunge get-up (giving her my grandpa dance), I couldn't help but get distracted by the sudden sensation. I turn my head and look around toward the sky to which Victoria stops and pushes lightly at my shoulder to get my attention.

"Hey, what's wrong?" she questioned, but I don't answer her.

He knows.

Someone is whispering, but I knew it didn't come from anyone at all.

He's very strange.

I look off into the distance and gradually little balls of light started to appear. At first I thought they were lighting bugs, but considering the weather, that's not what they were at all. The balls of light grew into fist sized orbs and they were everywhere, surrounding the crowd of people, floating in the sky and down below.

"What is that?" I gasp, waving my finger everywhere as I try to get a fast response from Victoria who seemed confused for a second.

Carson, Rose, and Autumn all look over from where they danced and I was preparing to hear that I was the only one seeing things but when a big grin grew on Victoria's face, I knew they could see it too.

"Woah!" Carson awes as the lights seemed like stars that fell too low from the sky.

"They're souls," Autumn says with a smile. I wasn't sure if that was something to be happy about... "It is said that on this day new and old souls meet to journey off to their next life. Or...whatever business they might want to take care of before passing from this world to the next."

"That sounds...kind of dangerous, doesn't it?" I look over at her and Carson seems to agree.

"Yeah, like what if one of them was a criminal and has some unfinished business?"

"You'll certainly know about it if one was," Victoria is laughing to herself.

"That's not something to worry about. Typically, the dead has no real interest in the living. That's unless they're related to you somehow," Autumn says.

"Or if you've sought them out yourself. Or pissed one off somehow," Victoria adds and earns a sharp gaze from Rose who stood beside her. She shrugs a shoulder and goes back to dancing, swaying her hips to the music. My eyes turn back to the orbs of light and I watch some float in the air, some gliding up or sinking low. Many of them drifted east. I would say it was beautiful if I didn't know what they were exactly. Carson and I watched them until we were dragged off to something else entirely.

At the end of the night, many people were gathering around a large bonfire. I was almost afraid of what were going to do, but as we met up with River, my aunt and uncle, and even Jem, I was assured that whatever it would be would be painless. River took the time to explain that it was tradition to throw in the names of our passed loved ones to honor them. That and an herbal mixture of some kind. As I watched others do it, calling out the names of their loved ones, pleasant scents filled the air and the color of the fire changed with each unique name. The others found pieces of paper to write on, and River was the first of us all to finish. She folds up her piece of paper and she calls out the name "Calder Dallas" and says:

"This year I'd like to remember that old fool. My dear brother. He passed away over a decade ago, but he was older than many of the trees around us now. He could bicker and tease until he turned blue, but no matter my weary nerves, he will always have a big place in my heart." Her smile was bright as she spoke and she didn't seem sad at all. She seemed happy to remember him and I suppose that's how it should be. She kisses her folded up note, grabs a handful of the herbal mixture and tosses both into the fire. The fire wooshes, and for a brief moment the color turned light blue, the flames swirling until it's settled again back to normal. Carson and I jump backward a little bit, standing a little too close to the flames that burned violently until it settled back to normal. Jem is next, quickly making his move to get it over with. His face was dark as he folds up the paper in his hand.

"Aislinn Elswyth." He grunts and tosses the name and herbs in. The flames grow almost instantly, wild and nearly out of control. It turns a deep red before it settles back down. My aunt leaned in close to me as we watched Jem back away, taking a big swig of beer before leaving entirely. Perhaps heading home just like that.

"He says the same name every year," she whispers to me, wearing a solemn expression before turning away and focusing on her own piece of paper. Aunt Nari goes next, calling out my grandfather's name, "Minhyun Lee". She said a few interesting words about the adventures he used to share, and learning her Earth magic from him. My uncle follows directly after her, wearing a complicated expression as he calls out my mother's name and tosses everything into the fire. He didn't say much about her, but it was clear in his face that he missed her and he was still very much sad about the loss. The fire turned a melancholic blue, and he shoves his hands in his pockets and moves on. Victoria was next, mumbling something back handed about her cousin "Dalia Star," and tossing it in, causing the fire to glow forest green before it went back to normal. Then it was Autumn's turn as she steps hikes up her skirt and approaches the fire. "A-yen Zeng" who she explained was her grandmother who passed away last year was the person she picked. She looked a bit sad about it as she tosses in a handful of herbs and the name. We watched the fire turn light pink, flares sparking this way and that, swirling around magically before simmering back down. Autumn hesitates to step away briefly before finally doing so, going to join River by her side as the remainder of us took our turns.

Carson is moving around awkwardly when he decides to go next. River told him before hand that he didn't have to participate but he insisted since it was a tradition and he was a guest.

"Okay," he stammers a little as he attempted to start, his words quickly turning into a ramble. "Well, my pops uhm…well his name was Curtis. Curtis Foxx. And he was super cool. And smart. And took care of me and the moms well…" He frowns a little. I was actually surprised. Carson rarely—almost never talked about his father. He hated it and I didn't blame him. Being too serious was hard for him, but on top of that, the loss of his father still affected him and his family today. He throws in the name after not coming up with anything else to say along with the herbs. Then he jumps backward, ready for the fire to change, but it doesn't and only the fragrance of the herbs could be detected. He dropped his shoulders as he came back to my side, a look of disappointment on his face.

"Aw man, I did all that and got nothin'?"

"Sorry, dear, but that requires a little touch of magic," River imparts. "But regardless of magic, your loved ones can always hear you when you call upon them." She offers a sincere smile and Carson pauses after those words. Seeming to seriously consider them as he slowly moves out of the way.

I guess it was my turn, as I looked beside me at Rose who didn't seem quite ready yet. I wasn't sure if I was either, but I took the chance. I slowly moved closer to the fire, staring at the flames that roared and danced around. I knew my uncle had already said her name…but she was the only person I could think of, regardless of if I could remember her. My mother. I look down for a moment at the paper folded up in my hands and then I speak her name: "Jiah Grey", before tossing in everything. I didn't have anything to say about her, but I knew I loved her, and I wanted to respect her. As the paper and the herbs hit the roaring embers, it was slow to react. And I was almost certain it would be just as ineffectual as Carson's was. But then the amber color shifts into an unnaturally bright green, and in the next second, the flames shot up high into the air. I jump backward, and I hear other's gasp at how high the fire reached, spiraling up into the sky. I gazed at it in awe until my eyes caught something off in the distance. I could see a silhouette of who I was sure was her, far off near a group of trees. Squint my eyes to be sure, and before I could make any hasty decisions, I flinch at a voice in my ear.

"*My Hyunni,*" the voice sings, causing me to flinch and swivel my head around. But I don't see anyone. And when I turn to look for the silhouette again it is gone and I'm left seriously questioning if my eyes and ears were playing tricks on me.

Rose steps up now, looking a little nervous or unsure of herself as she approaches the fire, staring down at the piece of paper in her fingers. She takes in a deep breath as to calm her nerves and then she began.

"Neveah Ncuti. My mother," she murmurs quietly. She takes a pause as if she were trying to find her next words. Her eyes shift and catch mine for a moment and I'm staring over at her, having no idea that she was missing a parent. She looks ahead now, staring into the flames of the fire deeply. "I-I didn't know my mother. I didn't get to meet her before she died. But my father has always spoke highly of her. I wish to speak that way as well, but truly there is nothing that I can say. All that I know is that wherever she is now, she must be watching me, and expecting that I do her proud. So, I will. I will try my best." She tosses in her note and her herbs. The fire turns a deep purple like the color of her soul and then after a moment it goes back to normal. She comes back to my side, avoiding everyone's gaze as she smooths out her skirt.

"Well, that was lovely," River sings from where she stood, gathering all of our attention for the moment. "It can be hard to do that sort of thing. Recalling our memories of loved ones we can no longer see anymore isn't easy, but it's important to remember the people who have made us who we are today, and respect the memories they left on this Earth. We certainly don't have to wait till Samhain to do so." She clasps her hands together and she gazes at everyone who seemed to have bored expression at her speech. As she realizes this, she throws her hands up and laughs. "Alright, don't let me put you all to sleep. Let's head home, shall we?"

And on that note, we all returned home. The festival was over, and it was enjoyable. It was definitely a fascinating way to celebrate my birthday. As we arrived home, Rose, Carson and I remained outside for a while longer, peacefully watching the orbs that traveled through the sky until we had enough. It was comfortable, but even if for the moment it felt that way, I had to start thinking of tomorrow. I would need to travel back to Whitechapel.

11

Return to Whitechapel

Upon returning to my room that night, I found that all of my gifts had been moved from outside into a corner near my bed. I guess I didn't even think about where my gifts had gone after helping clean up before we all said goodnight. Carson had gone off to bed after being allowed a small cup of ale. Not only had his face flushed red immediately, but he also began slurring his entire life story to the others who frankly could care less. By me saying he had gone off to bed, I really mean that he was forced to bed by the others. Rose didn't say much to me before she left. Only to wish me happy birthday again and that she'd meet me tomorrow morning to help us get back home. And then she was gone. After a shower that felt almost pointless when putting back on the clothes I wore yesterday, I'm pulling back the covers to slip into bed until there was a little knock on the door and Aunt Nari is peeking in. She gave me a sideways smile and then her eyes trail from mine down to her unopened gift on the floor.

"*Seon-mul*," she says quietly and then steps into the room. I look at her for a moment until I've gathered that she wants me to go get it and open it. As I move to do so, she's crossing the room and takes a seat on my bed. I pick up the bag that I remembered was from her and I go back to sit beside her. She waits for me to open it, and as I do I find that I'm pulling out a long box similar to the one that had Victoria's gift in it. It's wrapped with a shiny purple bow. I pull it loose and open up the top to reveal two sharp knives with handles made with beige ceramic material. I stare down at them, first wondering what I could possibly use such weapons for (don't answer that) and then I remember back to the vision I had where I asked aunt Nari about learning to use knives like her. I look up at her and she's wearing an unreadable expression.

"You didn't have—"

"I will teach you how to use them," she interrupts and pats my hand. "I told you to wait till you were a little older and well…you're a *lot* older now. The next time I can come back home, we'll start. But only if you're still interested."

My lips press together and I close the box and set it down beside me. Sure, I'd learn to use them, if that's what young me wanted and what she wanted… but wait. I *have* to stop thinking like that. The archdruid said specifically that I am too focused on what others want rather than what *I* wanted. Perhaps thinking of my past self, the self that was knowledgeable of this whole world, counts as an "other". Of course, I'd still be interested to use something cool like *knives*, I just only wished there would be no reason to have to use them. She's eyeing me and I find that I'm drifting off into the rabbit hole that is my thoughts. But then something else occurs to me.

"Aunt Nari, do you live at Lamia castle?"

She seems a little hesitant and her eyes diverge from mine.

"Yes. Namu and I live at the castle."

"But why? Whenever you talk about coming back here it sounds like you don't get much choice in the matter. That and Aunt Nari…I can't help but notice uhm…well your…" I'm gesturing at my teeth, making the "EEEE" face. "Are you a—"

She clears her throat loudly and she's standing up to her feet.

"Ethan, that is—that's…I can't talk about that." She frowns deeply and I instantly feel bad for asking.

"I'm s—"

"No. Don't be sorry. Just…" she sighs and gestures to her gift, "…when I come back, I will teach you to use those. Goodnight, Ethan, happy birthday." She's quickly crossing the room to leave but she turns around once more. "And tomorrow…be careful. I miss Mama, but if she continues to refuse, please don't wait for her. At this point you are safer here with us than you are there, okay?"

I nod slowly and she's stepping out of the room.

"Okay…the faster you come back, the better." She wears an expression that seemed both worried and deeply bothered. I could only wonder what it was she must have been thinking. She leaves without another word, closing the door behind her and leaving me alone again.

・ ・ ・

"I don't see how any of that's important. He's just a boy." Through the crack of the door, I can see a man in a long black coat. His hair was cut short and his skin was warm like mahogany. He was tense, and he stood in his study, back facing me as he frowned upon whatever the old woman whose grey hair curtained around her shoulders was trying to explain to him.

"He is. But it's beyond that. He will grow up and will no longer be 'just a boy'. What then? There's no way we can protect him. And when I say 'we' I mean me and MY family. Frankly it's none of your business." The woman is protesting.

"But it is, because I care about him as much as Ji-ah cares about Rosie."

"Then should you care about him so much, you ought to care that he puts Rose at risk. Every day I have no choice but to study him, research him like some science experiment. My own grandson! But today what the Elemalex found in his DNA is more dangerous and more profound than anything our realm has ever seen. Not only is he a danger to everyone, he's a danger to himself. Any day now he could explode with a catastrophic amount of raw power. And what are we supposed to do?"

"Are you proposing we just…lock him away, and pretend as though he's an animal and not human? Guidance is what's important. Not fearmongering. I am horribly surprised at you, Catherine."

"That is NOT what I am proposing! What I am telling you is that maybe not today, or tomorrow, but someday it is likely that Ethan will change. He will lose control of himself, and he could become haunted much worse than his pitiful father. The magic that is spirit and the magic inherited from his father will begin to clash, and it will tear him apart. I only wish I meant it figuratively." The woman is hugging herself and turning frustratedly toward the window, and the man seems unsure of how to respond or even react.

"Can't it be prevented?" the man is asking, his voice dropping to a cautious tone. "It hardly seems fair. Perhaps the Greenwood Druids could—"

"No. There is little to nothing any druid can do for the boy. That is how severe this situation is. It is entirely up to him and his strength of will that comes between potentially destroying everything in sight including himself, and completely harnessing control over the juxtaposition that lives inside him. But how is anyone supposed to deal with that?"

The image is fading, slowly at first then all at once. I feel my hair stick to my forehead; I feel my shirt clinging to my chest. Then I feel my entire body being shaken.

"Ethan! Ethan, wake up, you've over slept!"

My eyes fly open and I'm jumping at the sight of Rose hovering over me. She flinches backward and watches as I quickly move to sit up, but I can't focus on what she said. I was still trying to wrap my head around what I had just seen. I press my hand to my forehead and my eyes close tightly.

"A-are you alright?" Rose is asking, taking a cautious step forward.

After a moment I've opened my eyes again and I turn to look at her. I looked up into her eyes and she seemed wary and unsure until I swung my legs over onto the floor. I didn't notice Carson standing a few feet behind her.

"Ethan, you're all sweaty…" Rose is saying as she watches me stand up. "Did you have a bad dream?"

I frown immediately. It was a dream. But I wasn't sure to what extent. I look at Rose again and my frown is churning into something that resembled anguish.

"Am I a juxtaposition?" I ask suddenly. I wasn't particularly looking for an answer, but it was what was ringing through my head the loudest.

"What? What does that me—" Rose stops herself and her face almost completely goes pale. She clears her throat after a quick pause and then takes a small step back. "W-what does that mean?" she finishes, but something about her tone sounded like she already knew. I eye her skeptically, taking a step forward to approach her.

"You tell me," I challenge. "'The magic that is spirit and the magic inherited from his father will begin to clash, and it will tear him apart.'" I quote, taking another step. "'I only wish I meant it figuratively.'"

"Where is this coming from?" Rose is waving her hand at me, backing up now until she's run into Carson.

"Ow-ah," he whines dramatically and pushes her forward a little off of him.

"I saw it. That's what I saw last night. My grandmother said it, but why? There's something else you all know that I don't. Tell me!"

"It all doesn't matter unless you recover your memory. Otherwise…the status of your magic, it doesn't matter."

"But then…is it worth it to remember and then put all of you in danger again?"

I watch her and she bites her lip, her body tensing and her mind clearly racing. Carson is looking between us two and rubs the back of his neck.

"I'm sorry," he butts in, "but what exactly are we talking about? I thought we already understood that whatever kind of wizard Ethan is, is crazy dangerous somehow."

"*I'm not a wizard!*"

"*He's not a wizard!*"

Rose and I snapped at him at the same time and Carson throws his hands up in innocence.

"Sorry. But whatever he is, we already knew that he was threatening enough that people'd wanna kill 'em. That's literally the whole reason why we're in this mess. So, what's suddenly the problem?"

I'm clenching my jaw, trying to find the correct answer but there wasn't one that I could find. He was right, that was something we already knew. But I think what was bothering me was the fact that whatever it was that I am could hurt everyone around me the second I lost control. That's what it sounds like and that's the part that seems like people want to sugar coat.

"Ethan…" Rose begins carefully, "I understand what you are saying. But don't you think we all know that risk? I was there that day, when my father and your grandmother went to his study to discuss the risk you pose to not just everyone, but particularly me…she came that day to tell him to stop letting you around me. Because there would come a time where you might hurt me. Both you and I were spying on them at the time, and from then I watched how you became so cautious and afraid of your own self. It probably hurt you more to see and hear what your grandmother had to say than the cold fact itself. It's true that you are like a juxtaposition. Your spirit side and your father's magic are both incredibly rare and powerful forces. But the problem is that their energies are completely the opposite of each other. That's as much as I know. Your grandmother would know more since she had to study you. Perhaps even River would know since she was called to take her place. I know the risk. But we all love you enough to help you survive and live the life you deserve."

My shoulders drop. It seemed it was time to accept the facts. Whatever this is now is real, and nothing can change that. If I thought things were hard before with the headaches and the voices, oh boy was I sure it was about to get real tough real quick. But I wanted to be prepared for it. Suddenly I knew what needed to be done.

"I'm sorry, Rose," I say sincerely. "I shouldn't have come on so strong. I think what we need to do now is talk to Gramma. And *you* need to be there. So, she can see you, and talk to you too. We can try to get out of her what we can, and if that doesn't work, and if she doesn't want to come back with us, we have to leave her." I'm thinking of what Aunt Nari said last night. "We'll come back here as fast as possible, and then let's make a plan for heading to Sierra District to find my father. If neither of my flesh and blood can help me, then it looks like it will just be up to us."

"To do what exactly?" Rose asks slowly.

"To get my memory back. And to figure out how to control myself when I can finally…understand how to…"

"BE A WIZARD!" Carson shouts.

Rose and I glare at him and he shrugs.

"Someone's gotta lighten the mood," he grumbles and spins around. "Hurry up, times a-wastin'!" he walks out of the room and Rose turns to follow after him.

"He's right. The portal closes in the next hour." She looks down at her watch, the watch I wish I could understand, and then she walks out. "Please hurry up, Ethan!" she calls before the door shuts behind her.

In no time, I've dressed back into my normal clothes. I strap the bag I brought across my chest, and just as I'm about to head out of the door, my eye catches the gifts in the corner. My mind began to race with all the things that could happen traveling back through the district that tried to kill me once. I couldn't use magic like the others and relying on Rose's quick wit all the time would most likely tire quickly. In a second I'm rummaging through the boxes and I find the dagger Victoria gave me with the holster she was even nice enough to include. I strap it around my leg, tuck the weapon away and then I jog out of the room to join the others. As I enter the den, Rose is pulling on the white and silver cloak she wore the first day we met, and Carson is in a mirror trying to sort out his hair. Jem sat in his corner, working on broken things, and Victoria was cleaning up the room.

"Are you ready?" Rose asks when she saw me. "Now that the both of you have a passport, I think going through the boarder properly is the right way this time."

"What about hiding my identity?" I ask her.

"Your identity is no longer a secret," she answers. "But the important thing is to avoid those of whom that we *know* will cause trouble. That includes all oddity hunters, the Lamia military, my aunt, and…probably my cousins Ryland and Fey. Staying far away from them as long as possible for now will keep things in our favor."

"Right, you don't wanna run into Fang's crazy part of her family," Victoria chimes in from behind the couch.

Rose gives her a look that she doesn't see and Carson spins around to face all of us. Victoria stands up after using a dustpan and she gives a little smirk, her lips back to their usual crimson shade.

"You know, I hate for you all to leave so soon. It became much livelier in here with all of you. Blondie, will you be returning?" Victoria faces Carson and he swallows dryly before reaching up to lean against a wall that was not there and nearly falling over. When he caught himself and repositioned his posture with a clearing of the throat he says:

"Sure. Someone's gotta be there when Ethan finally levels up—er, I mean *cough* when he can do magic or…whatever."

Rose is facepalming and rightfully so as it was rather painful to watch. But Victoria finds it amusing and she approaches the three of us.

"If you come back, I'll make sure to fix you whatever you like. It seems like you Nahabi's eat more than your own weight."

Carson holds up his finger to dispute but she laughs at him and turns away.

"Where's River?" I ask her, and she turns once more to look at me.

"She had to go to work today. I hear they're working on a big project so she might be gone for more than a day."

"We really should be going, the both of you," Rose interjects and turns to head for the door.

"Right…" I wave Victoria goodbye and I'm following after Rose who was already stepping out of the front.

"Until next time…" I hear Carson sing before he jogged to catch up with Rose and I. As we start down the path that was becoming more familiar each time, Carson is pulling up the hood of his sweatshirt and singing something that I know was a song he wrote. Rose was tapping at her watch and she seemed a little irritable. I wasn't sure if it was because of Victoria or something else.

"Why does Victoria treat you like that?" I ask before thinking first.

"Why does Victoria treat anyone the way that she does?" she grumbles back without sparing a glance.

"Fair point," Carson chimes. "I just hope she stays sweet on me. Hoo hoo."

"She will until she gets bored. You're just a new toy to her."

"Ow, rude."

"But what does she have against you? She's always taking jabs at you when she gets the chance."

"She's like that simply because of what I am. Where I am from. It's childish but childishness isn't exactly below her."

"Are a lot of witches like that?" I ask. "I mean, disliking vampires?"

Rose spins around and she's walking backwards to look at me directly.

"Vampires have always been disliked," she answers plainly. "Even the dogs in Artemis are more acceptable than being human with sharp teeth. Vampires have always gotten the short end of the stick all throughout history. We were finally getting to a point where we weren't treated like monsters when my grandfather was in charge of things. But unfortunately after he…um *dis-*

appeared the people of my district thought it would be better to embrace the monster narrative, and try to take control of everything as a sort of revenge."

"But other people, when we go around Greenwood, seem to recognize you and treat you with respect. I guess I don't fully understand."

"That's thanks to my father," she answers and turns once more to face the front. She's looking up now at the sky and clouds are racing by. "He was meant to be king after my grandfather, but he turned the position down directly after he went missing. I don't completely understand why he made that decision, but he's always told me that doing the right thing can sometimes be hard and sacrifices would have to be made. He said by not taking the throne he would be distancing himself from the problem. He would have no part in the corruption in the castle. All this time I had no idea what lead him to that sort of conclusion. But I find that as I grow older, I just might be getting a glimpse of where he's coming from. Either way, his actions didn't go unnoticed. And although he might not be all that welcome around Lamia, others outside of our district were aware of his choice, and they respect him for it."

"Then what about you?" Carson asks. "If your father turned down being a king, are you still treated like a princess at home?"

Rose turns right as we approached the fork in the path. We were entering Willow Way but we weren't headed directly out of it like the way we came the first time. Rose falls back a little and she was no longer walking fast enough to lead, instead she walked between Carson and I. I couldn't read her expression, but the energy she gave off vibrated uncomfortably. I blink harder than normal and my eyes shift from brown to green, and suddenly I was able to see the aura around her wobbling around weakly and dimming into a dismal shade of gray.

"Don't read me," Rose sighs. I flinch, blinking again and my eyes go back to normal. I wasn't sure how she knew, but on top of that I wasn't sure how I did it in the first place. "It's a little complicated," she answers Carson. "I am regarded as a princess even with my father dropping his title. I still must attend schooling and practices of a princess, and engage in courtly affairs. But of course, on the other hand there are people who will treat you poorly based on their personal views. My father is sometimes seen as a traitor. So sometimes I am treated as a traitor's daughter."

I watch her carefully and she seems to be drifting farther into thought.

"Do you resent him?" I ask her, curious to know how she dealt with being treated poorly. But she shakes her head no.

"Not at all," she says. "I believe that my father made his choice for a good reason, and I will stand by him."

That is fair. I look up to focus on where we were walking to and it seemed we reached another area that resembled a road. This one was much busier than the one we took to get to Greenwood before. There are people bustling and scurrying about. Some were loading and unloading cars with cargo, some were being dropped off or picked up. I look at Rose again as she starts to speed up and she approaches the street. She waves her hand high back and forth, seemingly flagging down a cab. And by cab, I mean an old-timey horse drawn carriage. Soon a man pulls over to the side in front of Rose and he quickly hops down off of his bench to greet her. Carson and I catch up quickly and the man is pulling down his hat and bowing a little to Rose.

"Princess Rose, what's brought you here to Greenwood?" he asks and scratches the side of his beard.

"I was only doing a bit of shopping," she lies. "But I didn't quite find what I was looking for. Perhaps I'd be a bit more successful at home if I go into town. If you could just take me and my friends down to the boarder it would be greatly appreciated."

"Certainly," the man agrees and quickly steps backward to pull open the carriage door. Rose steps up inside and the man politely helps her along. Carson follows after her and I do so last as the man bows his head a little as a sort of greeting. After we were all tucked inside, he shuts the door and climbs back up onto his bench, and we were off.

"We'll get to the boarder much faster this way," Rose tells the both of us as she peers out the window. She checks her watch after a moment to check the time. "Yes, we've still got a little over half an hour before the portal closes."

We nod our heads to acknowledge her, and Carson sitting across from Rose and me is staring thoughtfully at her. As I anticipated something coming out of his mouth, I deeply hoped it wasn't something embarrassing.

"So, what happened to your grandpa, Rose?" he questions. I wasn't sure if I should feel relieved or frightened that Rose would become any more upset.

She looks up at him, folding her hands neatly in her lap as she seemed to be filing through her mind for a way to respond. After a moment she shakes her head.

"I don't know," she answers calmly. "I didn't get to meet him. He disappeared before I was born. Perhaps five years before? It is only said that he went missing one day, and royal guards and the Lamia military went searching for him—even Lamia oddity hunters were sent to find him, but he was never found. Not a trace. So, he was never pronounced dead, either. No one knows what happened."

"Hmm, a mystery," Carson ponders, stroking his bare chin like a beard. "Doesn't anyone think it's kinda sus?"

"Kind of what?"

"Suspicious," I clarify and Rose looks at me sideways.

"Yeah, *sus*. Suspicious. I mean he was there one day doing whatever he does, and gone the next. Without a trace. It's a mystery."

"Well of course. I like to think many agree that it's rather suspicious. There's a rumor going around that my aunt had something to do with it. Killing him in secret so that she could take control somehow. Now, I might think my aunt can be a little cold and stubborn—"

"A little? Wasn't she the one who wanted Ethan dead?"

"Well, yes…but I'm not entirely sure if it was out of ruthlessness or fear. My aunt can be cold, but I don't know if she would go to the lengths to kill her own father. Ethan isn't even related to her, even if it was out of ruthlessness. She has no ties to him so to her killing him wouldn't have mattered." She frowns a little and looks up at me. I can't say I knew exactly what expression I was wearing, but the face she made in response was full of guilt and remorse.

"I don't know," Carson shakes his head. "I don't think that's enough to rule her out, aunt or not. Sorry, Rose. Who's in charge now?"

"My cousin, Ryland. He's the king now but—"

"But?" he eggs her on.

"But, he's a bit of a push-over if you ask me. It seems like my aunt does most of the work."

"So how is it her son is king, and she didn't become queen? Isn't she your father's sister?" I ask this time.

"In Lamia there is a specific rule—although a very old-fashioned one, it's what technically keeps my aunt from being queen. If there were to be a queen the person must have been the first-born daughter. For example, if my father had been king, I would have been next in line to be queen. Otherwise only the son can take the throne. In terms of how my cousin got the throne instead was a very unusual occurrence. No king or queen has ever gone missing before. Murdered, yes, but never missing to never be found. And on top of that a refusal to the throne which is also something that has never happened before. When my grandfather went missing my father was still too young to take his place so my grandmother took over his work until he was. At 21 my father was asked to take over but he asked for more time. By 22 he made his decision to refuse the position. So, my grandmother had to continue running the district until the eldest grandchild was old enough to take her place. The position could not go to my aunt because she was a second-born daughter rather than a son. When my cousin Ryland was old enough, he took my grandmother's place."

"That's messed up," Carson frowns. "I don't even think the English do that. Right, E?"

"Sure," I mutter.

"It is quite unfair, but I suppose it's also a good thing. My aunt might be pulling the strings in the background, but imagine if she had complete control. Things would probably be much worse."

I pull at the fabric of my jacket as I'm contemplating Lamia's effect on the other districts. It certainly seemed like whatever was exactly going on was bound to be much worse. And that everything that I've learned about so far is connected in some way. My mother's death, my banishment, the missing king mystery, and the suffering of other districts. At least within Sierra.

"What about Artemis District?" I question, trying to understand their relation and how they might be affected.

"What about it?" Rose asks.

"Well, I know you said before that Lamia has gained control over that other district, Sierra. And currently they're trying to do the same with Greenwood. But what about Artemis? Do they want control over that one too? There was something else you mentioned once that makes me think that maybe they work together somehow. They had something to do with my mother's death as well."

Rose is looking out of the window again and we're passing through a quaint little town surrounded by those tall magical looking mushrooms and unique colorful trees. There were people of all sorts walking about. They looked like elves.

"I-It…wasn't Artemis as a whole that had to do with her death," she starts. "Only a very powerful family. The Blackclaw's. Either way," she sighs, "Lamia and Artemis are actually notoriously rivals. There is a long history of fighting between us and them."

"What sort of creatures live in Artemis?" Carson asks, narrowing his eyes as he's expectant of a certain answer.

"Majority are werewolves. Why?"

"Mhm, yeap, that's what I thought." He leans back in his seat and clasps his hands together.

"What?" Rose tilts her head, confused by what he's getting at.

"Duh, vampires and werewolves never get along. Don't you watch movies?"

"…movies?"

Carson's eyes pop out of his head.

"Are you serious right now? You've never seen a movie? Ethan, when we get home, please God let's take her to the movies. What's out right now?" He pulls out his phone immediately and goes to search the current movies out, but is painfully reminded of the fact that there's neither Wi-Fi nor service. He pretends to throw his phone across the carriage before stuffing it back into his pocket with a huff.

"Uhm…anyways," Rose continues. "I am under the impression that Lamia eventually will want to target Artemis. But they would be the most difficult. Lamia and Artemis might not be the most agreeable with each other, but they do have one thing in common, which Lamia will want to use to their advantage as long as necessary."

"Which is what?" I question, staring at her maybe a bit too hard. Her mouth closes and she turns to look up at me. She searches my eyes for a moment before answering:

"Getting rid of you," she finishes. "When they find out you're still alive and have returned to Obscura—if they haven't already, there is no doubt that both districts will team up to find you and make sure you stay dead this time. That's why we really should be careful, especially since you can't use your magic. The longer we stay out of their sight, the better. ...Because I'm sure at any time now shit will hit the fan."

"*Rose!*" Carson gasps at her. "*Language!*"

"I learnt that phrase from a book," she chuckled lightly.

"Hey, you sure do know a lot about everything that goes on around here," Carson points out.

"Yeah. After I found out Ethan was alive, I did a lot of snooping around the castle. There's almost always some sort of meeting going on, and usually those meetings have to do with plans for Lamia's future, or measures for if 'the Spirit Boy' wasn't killed properly."

"You mean you thought I was dead too?"

She looks at me and she seemed like she was ready to call me a moron or something. But instead, she throws her hands up and shifts to lean against the wall of the vehicle.

"Of course, I did," she said matter-of-factly. "You were attacked right in front of me."

"You *saw* Ethan get his memory wiped?"

She nods and crosses her legs.

"I saw everything…until my father took me away. I thought they were killing you, especially when the day after came there was news everywhere that you died. Until my father finally told me what actually happened to you, I believed it."

"*Damn*," the blonde whispers as he sits back again against his seat.

"Language," Rose jokes. I'm frowning. But the more stories Rose tells, the more I am able to piece together what happened and what's currently happening. The only thing left that I didn't understand was what happened in the first place to knock the first domino down. There was an accident. And Rose got hurt. I look at her, prepared to finally ask her how I hurt her before, and as I open my mouth the carriage jerks to a stop.

"Oh, we made it," Rose is saying as she looks out of the window. "We'll get out now so we don't have to wait in line. Let's go." She pushes open the door and she hops out before anyone else could say anything. Carson follows her lead and eventually I make my way out to join them. "Here is perfect, mister, thank you for your help!" Rose calls up to the driver who seemed a bit confused why we had gotten out. She approaches him quickly, steps up a step and hands him a few gold coins before hopping back down. He looks down at the coins and he's suddenly very lively and excited. She must have given him extra.

"Oh, no trouble at all, princess!" He smiles, pulling off his hat and waving it at her. "Take care, now." He yips for the horses to go and he leads them out of the long line of vehicles.

Rose gestures for us to follow her and she turns to head toward one of the two line full of people. One of the lines moved very quickly, while the other one stood still and trailed on for ages.

"What's with that?" Carson asks, gesturing to the two lines as he must have been noticing it too.

"One line is for Lamia citizens, and the other is for everyone else," Rose answers with a frown. "It didn't used to be this way, only at the Lamia border are they making it very difficult to go in and out of the district. It started recently."

"So, do we have to wait in that line? If we do, that would suuuuuck."

"No, because I am with you. Come on, and hurry up." She breaks out into a little jog and she moves quickly to the front of the citizen line. She approaches the gate and the four guards standing in front of the entrance. "Excuse me, I must get through," she calls out and stops beside the next person in line. One of the guards look down at her seemingly surprised to see her.

"Rose," a deep voice sounds. "Why have you been travelling without your escorts?"

"What? Why should I always need an escort only to engage in leisurely activities?"

The guard frowns. "Because it is the rule you must follow. Where have you been?"

"The only place I ever seem to go these days," she answers with an annoyed frown. "Would you let me through, or are you going to continue wasting my time? You are in fact blocking the way of a princess from her own home."

The guard is silent and he stares down challengingly at Rose until he stands up right and turns to look at the others, exchanging looks before they all turn to look at Carson and me.

"Who are these two?" he asks.

"My friends," she answers quickly. "Father summoned them for tea…"

"Passports." He holds out his hand expectantly and Carson and I share a look.

"But—" Rose starts but she is cut off.

"They are not special just because they are your friends, Rose. Show me your passports."

Carson clears his throat awkwardly and starts feeling around for his wallet. I sniff dramatically and do the same until I'm pulling out my wallet and pulling out the card. I'm reaching out to hand it to him until I realize at the last second that it is my Michigan ID card and not my passport.

"*Oops*," I say and draw my hand back quickly before he can take it. Carson hands him his passport and after finally retrieving the right identification I do the same.

The guard is reading each one carefully, starting with Carson's.

"Your name is peculiar," the guard sniffs and turns the card over.

"Thanks," Carson shrugs.

The guard eyes him but returns the card back to him and then he looks at mine. It took a moment, but after he seemed to have finished reading what he needed to he quickly looks up and compares my face with my image. After assessing that it wasn't fake, he turned to the other guards, motioning them over to take a look. Rose takes a few steps back to fall in line with Carson and me.

"From now, Ethan," she whispers up to me, "Lamia will have proof that you're alive."

I nod slowly. I guess that is supposed to mean that starting now Lamia should want to finish what they started regarding my death.

Oh boy.

The guard faces us again, waving around my passport.

"What game are you playing, Rose," the man says irritably.

"What are you talking about?"

"Date of birth!" He ignores her and barks the next question at me. I blink a few times before registering that I should probably answer.

"October 31st, 2000," I say quickly. "But what—"

"This is a lie," he says sternly, looking back down at Rose and waving my passport around again. "Obviously it is when the real Ethan Moon is dead."

"But it's not a lie," Rose tells him and then glances down at her watch. "He's standing right here in the flesh!"

He looks at me again. It seemed like he wasn't sure if he should believe his personal preconceived notions or his own eyes. He looks at my passport once again, turning it this way and that.

"What was the name of the water Elemalex witch ten years ago?" he interrogates. It seemed he was testing me, to see if I really was who I say I am. It was lucky that I had a good memory (which is ironic since I've been battling a sort of amnesia). I remembered the job Gramma had when she worked here. The job that River has taken over since she's been gone. I knew the answer.

"Catherine Grey," I say confidently.

He frowns deeply and the other guards are looking between each other. Rose checks her watch again and she sighs heavily.

"Are we done here?"

The guard hands me back my passport and I quickly take it and put it away.

"Does King Ryland know about this?" he asks.

"I'm sure you can ask him yourself. Now if you don't mind, we really must be going." Rose grips mine and Carson's arm and she pulls us passed the guards and across the border. When we take our first steps on Lamia land Rose is suddenly walking the way a cheetah runs. Carson and I hurry to keep up with her as she takes a dirt road path in the direction of the castle grounds. The presence of vampires was quite unnerving, although they seemed normal enough as some were driving by, riding on horses, or walking along. On this path there were huddles of guards with their tall spears marching in different directions. The road Rose led us down branched off from the castle to the woods and she swiftly moves us through.

"Are you okay?" I ask her winded, nearly tripping over a stone in the road.

"I'm fine," she says casually. "But they took up a lot of time. We have only fifteen minutes to make it to the portal before it closes."

She suddenly dips off of the road and into the tangle of trees. She was just about running and Carson and I had to chase after her.

"Won't you slow down!" Carson puffs, dodging a tree before running shoulder first into it. "It's like gym class all over again."

"No! We need to hurry. Remember what I said about the time difference between here and Whitechapel? The faster we get there, the more daylight we'll have left."

We're headed to the outskirts of the district and a little ways ahead was a sort of garden arbor, leaning lamely to the side, made from an old rusted metal, painted black like the gate used to get here.

"And forward! Pick up your feet, Maier!" a loud voice is calling. The three of us whip around and Rose is rising up on her toes to see over a slope at the group of soldiers of some sort marching through the woods. They were carrying spears like the guards at the border and they wore similar looking armor but in colors of greys and reds. Rose gasps and swiftly ducks behind a tree.

"*Don't let them see you,*" she whispers to us. Like a reflex our knees fold and we drop down low, hoping to not be seen by chance by the people marching in the distance. "*Come on,*" Rose waves us forward and we scuttle across the shrubbery to reach her.

"Sir! I hear something from the west!" a man shouts. The group of soldiers halt to a stop and the person that seemed like the leader of some sort is circling over to the one who interrupted. Rose gestures for us to stop and to be still as the rustling of the shrubbery beneath us could be too loud.

"Is there a reason you've spoken out of turn, cadet?" we hear the leader ask. His voice was much farther away as he was no longer shouting. He towers over the seemingly young soldier and drops his head.

"Permission, to speak, sir!" the soldier calls out almost half-heartedly.

"Sure. Only if you have a good excuse. And trust me if you don't you can expect a hell of a night in the dungeons."

Rose is waving around for our attention. As I turn my head to look at her, she's throwing a small rock at Carson's shoulder. He whips his head around and mouths an 'ow'. Rose whispers for us to slowly close the gap between the three of us but to stay behind the cover of a tree.

"There was movement, southwest, a few yards away, sir."

"There's movement all the time, cadet. Ya ever hear of something called a deer? Or a hogmink?"

"B-but sir…"

SNEEZE

"SHHHH!"

"SHHHH!

Rose and I shush Carson frantically as he suddenly lets out the worst timed sneeze imaginable. Carson snaps his mouth shut, but it was a little late as the one who seemed like he was in charge had turned around, looking left and right toward our direction. Carson ducks behind a tree and I try to make myself smaller, praying to anyone who'd listen to not let them see us. The man takes a few steps closer, moving down the slope they were on. His face became more visible and it was…well let's just say Carson's disgusted expression said it all. Half of his face was shades of pinks and greys with horrendous scar tissue that trailed down the entirety of his neck. There was no telling how far it went with the clothes he wore. Even his right hand looked as though it had been burned, tossed in a pot to boil, and then grated a few times for good measure. His right eye was a ghastly milky white color with a very obvious purple vein crossing over the middle where a pupil should be. Whatever happened to him must have been awfully disturbing.

"COME OUT!" the man shouts with a bold commanding voice.

I turn to look at Rose and she shakes her head so that we would stay put. The soldier frowns and he turns toward the closest tree. Reaching up, he tears off a branch like it was nothing but paper. He turns around again and hurtles the limb far with the strength of five men in our direction. It lands a few meters away from me in the brush of the earth. I hold my breath to avoid a startled yelp, and to our luck a fluffy gray creature with horns coming from a very slimy looking snout jumped up from hiding, squealing very much like a hog. It runs in a different direction, occasionally jumping up on the trunks of trees as if it were doing parkour.

The man throws his arms up and turns around to face the other soldiers.

"A hogmink," he says. "MOVE! That's a night in the dungeons for you, Maier!" At the boom of his voice, the soldiers resume their marching and we could breathe a sigh of relief. Rose is looking at her watch with a worried expression and then she gestures for us to keep moving. We follow her quickly toward the old little garden arbor, and soon we were finally approaching.

"We must hurry, there's three minutes left," Rose rushes as she's digging around in her cloak pocket for something. After a moment she pulls out the key that brought us here and I notice a little rusty lock hanging off of the side of the arbor. "Carson, close your eyes."

"But—" he began to protest.

"Hurry up!"

He squeezes his eyes shut and Rose is jamming the key into the lock. She gives it three quick turns, a clicking sound was made, each louder than the last, and then the arbor begins to vibrate and shake. The metal creaks and scrapes against itself as it began to morph and reshape. The arbor grew four times its size. There was a wind moving at high speeds and a bright golden light that started from the middle of the structure.

"WHY IS IT SO LOUD?!" Carson yells over the noise.

"Let's go!" Rose tells us and steps through first. I frown a little, remembering how the first time she had to pull both Carson and I inside. Well, I don't blame her now and going through a weird vacuum of light the sun threw up doesn't sound that appealing. I grab Carson by the wrist, and with a deep breath and a few encouraging jumps, I move through the portal, dragging Carson along. He's screaming and I'm only trying to fight the feeling of suffocation. After a moment, it was all over, and the sound and the lights and the wind had all vanished like it never happened. I let go of Carson after feeling the ground again under my feet and I turn to look behind me. There looking lame and out of place was that little black gate from before. It was weird, I couldn't understand how any of that worked.

"AAHK!" I spin to see Carson falling over, hitting the ground hard enough to make me wince in pain for him. He catches his breath and rolls over. "Oh, look, Ethan." He points down at what he's tripped over. "It's our bikes."

Well, that's nice. No one stole them. I bend down to help pick them up. Rose is checking her watch again and then after a moment she turns to face us.

"What are you doing?" she asks. "We should get going."

"Rose, who were those solider guys? Dude looked like Hulk's arm after snapping."

Well, that was one way to put it. Rose reaches out to help him up to his feet and he picks up his bike.

"That was a group from the Lamia military," she answers. "The ones we should definitely stir clear of."

"And the guy with the messed-up face?" I inquire as we began our walk out of the woods. "What happened to him?"

"He's the military general. Henri Gualtiero. I'd strongly suggest to never approach him, Ethan. He has—er…he's a part of Lamia's problem."

"Yeah, but the face! You seem to be avoiding that question!" Carson presses, screwing his face up as he said so. "Literally just awful. And I can say that since we must agree he's bad news."

Rose closes her cloak around her, taking her time to find the right way to describe whatever terrible incident that must have happened to him. After a minute of pondering and weaving through the trees with Carson and I wheeling our bikes beside her, she draws in a breath and says:

"He was attacked by Yohan Moon. It's ultimately what landed him in prison."

"You mean…" I begin almost untrusting of what she said, "my *father* did that to him?"

"Ethan's baby daddy turned him into a walking dead zombie?!" Carson borderline shouts as he steps up a little closer to see Rose's expression. Though I'm sure she didn't quite understand by the way she turned up her nose. I reach behind her and shove Carson in the arm.

"That's not how the term 'baby daddy' works, idiot!" I hiss at him. He trips but catches himself before falling. "What could he have possible done to literally disfigure him that bad?" I frown deeply, feeling guilty for my father's actions, not that I even knew who my father was. But whatever it was that he did to him seemed beyond harsh no matter what reason there could have been.

"He used magic," Rose answers casually with a little shrug of the shoulder. "Of course, I don't know the details of that bit, but we already know that whatever your father is, is very powerful. And dangerous. That's why he was ranked tier one for years until you were born. There was some kind of fight one night in Lamia Common. Your father and some of his followers along with Henri and some military were all involved. It's not clear whether the fight was just over something Henri and his friends said, if it was just because Yohan initiated it, or if it was over politics."

"Politics? That's lame," Carson grumbles.

"Yes, but remember, there is unequal treatment between oddity citizens and pure-blooded citizens. Yohan was an oddity and he lived a poor life when he was young. At least that's what I've heard. And at the time of the fight, Lamia began their plot for revenge and triumph. It's no secret that Henri believes that vampires should be seen as better than everyone else rather than equal. He is loyal to the corruption in the castle, and his father was the exact same way."

"Ah…so that's why he's bad news."

"That, and because he gets off on the thought that Yohan's lover and only child is dead. So, *when* he finds out you aren't—which he will, he will most likely want to kill you himself because you're an oddity, because you're the son of the man who disfigured him, and because originally the castle ordered your death."

"That's great," I mutter.

Finally, we're on a normal path in the Whitechapel Forest, and in no time, we're exiting and approaching the street. It was refreshing to return to someplace familiar. Carson and I walked beside each other and it took a minute to realize Rose had fallen behind. At one point we both stop to look behind us at her dragging her feet as she took in her surroundings.

"Why are you all the way back there?" I ask her. She turns her head and blows a long coil of hair that had fallen loose out of her face.

"I don't know where we're going," she answered. "You two should know this place better than me, right?"

That was true. I smirk a little at her and wave for her to catch up and walk between us.

"It'd be quicker if you had a bike too," Carson says as he's mounting his only to push it along with his feet. "Gramma's house is at least ten minutes from here."

"You can ride," she tells us, looking between us both. "It's okay."

"But we'll leave you behind if we do that…" I stop, and she's shaking her head.

"Don't be silly. I can walk faster than you can ride your bike," she laughs.

I'm opening my mouth to protest but Carson is already fixing his feet to the pedals.

"Alright bet!" I suppose he's taking it as a challenge. He kicks off and goes to ride his bike at full speed. Rose smiles up at me and gestures for me to hurry before she's suddenly speeding off, passing Carson almost as soon as she started.

I follow after them, standing up on my petals to catch up. Rose slows down the moment she's gotten too far ahead. She probably wouldn't have if she knew the way. I catch up with Carson and he's already panting and gasping to fill his lungs.

"Geeze *wheeze* I really thought I could *cough* keep up with her."

"Better luck next time, buddy," I laugh.

Rose completely stops, turning to face us and throwing her hands up.

"You guys are terribly slow!" she calls. "Which way should I go?"

We were approaching a crossroad. Before either of us could answer there was the sound of a bumping radio growing louder from behind. Rose peers behind the both of us and Carson and I slow our bikes to turn around. A black Chevy was rolling down the street, and with everyone knowing everyone in this small town, I prayed that at least whoever it was didn't have time to stop. But to my dismay the SUV is slowing and the back seat window is rolling down.

"Hey, Ethan!" I look up, hopping off of my bike while trying to place the familiar voice. The car stops in front of the three of us and Hailey is popping her head out with a big grin on her face. "How was your trip to Miami! Why didn't you call me when you came back?"

I was muttering a confused *"what"* to myself when Rose moved a little closer to whisper:

"River has been manipulating their memories so no one in Whitechapel will ask questions. Mainly for your friend here…"

I guess I took too long to answer since Hailey was now climbing over someone and pushing open the car door. I caught sight of Julia who was waving sheepishly and I waved back. Hailey steps out and she's wearing a long soft looking cardigan. Her twisted hair was hanging loose over a shoulder.

"Who's your friend?" she asks innocently, approaching all of us and looking between Rose and me. Rose seemed to have gone a bit stiff, as if she became anxious or something. Hailey was eyeballing her hard for some reason and I watched as Rose drew backward some. "Woah, your contacts are really cute," she says, while pointing at her own eye. I'd forgotten that Rose's eyes were entirely an unnatural color, I was just relieved for her sake that it was assumed to be contacts. "I've always wanted to try contacts, myself. Like hazel, or maybe green. But thinking about touching my eyeball to put them in and take them out gives me the creeps." She shutters, continuing on as the three of us stood awkwardly in silence. She then holds out her hand for a handshake. "My name is Hailey, what's yours? You're really pretty, too, by the way. Your hair is just gorgeous. How do you get your curl pattern like that? What products do you use? I'm looking to get a new leave-in because the one that I have doesn't seem to, like…*define* my curl pattern like I wish it did."

Rose seems completely taken aback, unsure of how to exactly take in this new personality. She looks down at the waiting hand and finally she reaches out and takes it, shaking it gingerly.

"Oh, your hand is really cold," Hailey points out, looking down at the girl's hand carefully. "It must mean you have a warm heart, too. That's what my grandma would always say. Cold hands, warm heart." Her eyes are smiling as much as she was. She could get really excited over very small things, and even while meeting someone entirely new she still gushed kindness and enthusiasm. I feel the tips of my ears heat first, and directly after I know my entire face is going red. I look away embarrassed by the way she effortlessly affected me.

Rose pulls her hand away, and I suppose she gives a little curtsy out of habit without thinking about it first.

"...It's a pleasure to meet you, Hailey," Rose says slowly, sounding almost unsure of her voice. "I must say you are rather vivacious. I am pr—um... I am Rose. My name, that is."

"That's a nice name. It fits you." Hailey smiles sweetly and drops her arm. "So where are you all coming from? Rose, your outfit is very..." She takes a step back and tilts her head to the side as she examined the unique clothing Rose wore. I was just glad she wasn't in a full-on 18th century get-up. "Actually, it's super cool. It's like...vintage, laid-back sexy, almost. Did you guys come from the Renaissance Fair? I was just trying to convince Eric—er..." Hailey closes her mouth suddenly and looks up at me apologetically. Her demeanor shifts almost instantly and she clasps her hands in front of her to close herself off. "I mean, I've been trying to go before it closes. I'll probably just go with Julie. But...if you all don't mind going a second time, you're free to come with us."

Rose is analyzing. Her eyes almost seemed robotic as she must have been reading anything she could about her. After a moment she takes in a quick breath.

"Are you friends with Ethan?" she asks.

"Hm? Yes, we're friends. We've known each other since elementary school. Of course, we don't hang out as often as we should, but I've always thought of...him—uhm...you...as..." Her eyes drift from Rose's up to mine and she seemed almost shy which was out of character.

"...a...friend," I finish for her awkwardly.

"...yeah." She rubs her arm sheepishly and Rose stares up at me for a minute before turning to look at Carson who seemed to be grinning like the Cheshire cat.

"Aye! Hailey, let's go, you're wastin' my gas!" I look up to see Eric rolling down his window. When he caught my eye, he sneered as a "friendly" greeting. "Say goodbye to the dorks already!"

"Uh-hum excuse me!" Carson shouts back. "Is that *thing* in your backseat not considered a dork?" Julia's mouth drops and she flips the bird at him.

"Uh, yeah," Eric nods and ruffles his hair. "But she's Hailey's 'bestie' so..."

"Figures," Carson mutters.

"What is a dork?" Rose asks, looking up at me for an explanation. I suck at my teeth. What a weird question to ask if you didn't understand her circumstance. Hailey didn't seem to hear it though as she was turning around with a small frown.

"Sorry," she apologizes to us. "I don't know why I—...I mean..."

I frown. I know what she was going to say. I reach out and squeeze her shoulder a little and she looks downcast.

"Don't worry," I tell her gently. "I'll see you later."

"...and tell me all about Miami?" She looks up again hopeful, a small smile creeping back into her expression.

"Uh, yeah. And tell you all about Miami."

"Anything for you, Hailey," Carson chimes in, coming closer to make a kissy face. "And he means *anything*..."

"*Ugh*." I push him out of the way and he stumbles over his bike.

Hailey smiles at me and waves.

"See you later, Ethan. It was nice to meet you, Rose." She's turning but stops to eye the blonde. "Later, dork."

"See ya, brah," Carson waves and she's turning to get back in the car.

I sigh as I watch them pull off. I was pretty sure I just lied to her face. If I go back to Obscura, would I ever see her again? I frown at the thought. There was probably no one else in Whitechapel that I would miss enough to want to come back. (Aside from Carson, but luckily, he's been with me all this time.) Hailey was...Hailey *is* someone I care about. Maybe a bit too much for as little as we actually engage with each other.

"You're in love with her."

I flinch harder than I should have at the *L* word. I look down, brought completely out of my thoughts at Rose who was staring up at me almost emotionlessly. She then turns away and starts walking and Carson follows after her.

"What?" I start and hop back on my bike. "I don't love her. How could I love her? She's got a boyfriend already. They've been together since freshman year."

"You keep telling yourself that but we all know it's a lie to help you cope," Carson says and shakes his head. "Even Rose figured it out and she just met her just now."

"Pretty girl," Rose acknowledges with a little nod of the head.

"Ethan definitely thinks so. He doesn't admit it now but he does in his dreams."

"I don't know what you're talking about," I fume and shake my head.

"*'Oh, Hailey, you're so beautiful. Let me treat you better than your ass-hole boyfriend. Come here, let me kiss you.'*" He's tonguing the air and I'm compelled to inflict violence. But I settle for calling him childish instead. He laughs and is lifting his feet to ride the downward slope of the street. "Sleeping Ethan betrayed you. He tells all. Remember the last time you were over mine for a slumber party?"

"A slumber party?" Rose narrows her eyes at him quizzically. "Are you both children?"

"Huh? What? No, it's not like that. Just a bro sleepin' at a bro's house." He watches her but she doesn't say anything. "You wouldn't understand. You're too young."

"Too young? I suspect I'm only a year younger than you!"

"Exactly. Too young."

She rolls her eyes. Both of us do actually. I think that Rose is learning now that the less you respond to Carson, the quicker he'll stop talking.

We're finally turning onto my street and the neighborhood was just as I remembered. (I say as it's only been four-ish days.) It was quiet, and dull, and the houses were old. Some in need of repairs. Rose looked around her, her head continuously on a swivel.

"I've never been to a place like this," she says quietly. "It's a little less cheerful than it seems in the books I've read."

"That's just Whitechapel. Probably Michigan as a whole," Carson tells her. "Maybe we really should take a trip to Miami and have a hot-girl summer. We'll take you to the beach. Or better yet, Orlando!"

"What's in Orlando?"

"UH-HUM! WIZARDS! And uhm…SPIDERMAN!"

"…A man made of spiders? That sounds rather horrible…"

"Gi—…no, that's not—"

"Shh." I shush them as we approach my house. Gramma's car was in the driveway but every single light was out inside. The curtains were pulled closed and it seemed not a soul was there. How odd.

"Is this where you lived?" Rose asked. Although I thought the past tense was odd since I haven't officially moved anywhere else…to my knowledge. I don't answer her. I'm kicking down the stand of my bike and I jog up the stairs. I dig around in my bag for my keys and upon retrieving them I quickly open the door. Rose and Carson follow close behind me and we step inside.

There was a strange smell, almost like mold or water damage. The kitchen was empty except for the mountain high dishes in the sink. The tap was running for some reason. I kick off my shoes and enter the kitchen. I reach over the dishes and turn off the faucet.

"It feels creepy in here, dude," Carson whispers to me as he and Rose still stood at the door. Rose looked around unsure and also trying to take in her surroundings, and Carson bent down to unlace his converse. I keep going, slowly moving to the hall way while trying to hear any sort of noise that indicated someone was here. There was an unsettling feeling in the pit of my stomach. I could only imagine how much I would hate to find my grandmother hurt in some way. I peer up the stairs, wondering if there were any lights on or people up there, but it seemed quiet and empty. I turn and start heading toward the living room.

"Ah!"

"What?" Carson had caught up and was backing up as I flinched backward into him. I look down to my feet and the bottom of my socks were completely wet. The floor had a good two-inch layer of water standing over it and it bled into the carpet of the living room. I look back at Carson, unsure of what to make of it but he only shrugs back at me. I continue. I step into the living room, the carpet squelching uncomfortably with cold water. I take a look around the room. Outside of the wet floor I didn't notice anything out of the ordinary. At first. Until I notice the figure standing in front of the curtained window. My brow furrows as my brain was trying to understand whether the figure was real or not; whether it was an intruder, a person, a *ghost*.

"G-ma?" Carson questions before me, pushing passed me a little to get a closer look. He was right. It was Gramma. I think. Her back was to us, and she was wearing a long night gown. No apron. No bun in her hair. It rests loose around her shoulders.

"Gramma?" I question this time. But she doesn't move. I frown deeply. Never have I seen her…or *anyone* like this. I step further into the room, approaching her, but I don't get too close, afraid of if she lashed out, or wasn't who we thought. "Gramma," I call again. "What's wrong?" There's no response. I feel the room start to buzz and I am slowly coming to learn that whatever that buzzing was continuously brings unwanted strange occurrences. And not soon after the buzzing started, my head began to ache. I wince a little at a throb in my temples but I wouldn't let it distract me. I step closer and Rose is joining me at my side. "Gramma…" No answer. "*Halmoni…dab-hae-jwo, jom.*" I'm resorting to begging as I ask her to answer me. To respond, to say *something*. I come closer and I notice that the sleeves of her gown were soaked and dripping water. Her hair was wet, the bottom of her skirt was wet. "*Halmoni,*" I call again, "*wae i-rae?* ….eodi apeo?"

"*Jaehyun-ah…wa-ni?*" Finally…she says something. I stare at her cautiously and it seemed she was drawing in a very slow breath. Her voice was weak and was barely over a whisper.

"*Eung…wasso.* Is there a reason you're standing there like that? *Issang-hae.*"

She's slowly turning around. I was almost scared to see her face. Rose grips my sleeve and Carson is basically hiding behind me. She faces us and her eyes were glowing blue. Her face was tear-stricken and her skin was pale with a greyish hue.

"Gramma, *appa?* Are you sick?" I ask her a second time but she doesn't answer.

"*Bap meokeoss-eo?*" she asks instead. She looks at me first, and then looks past me at Carson. "How about you? Did you eat today?"

"Um…sure," Carson replies slowly. "How about you? What's with the water on the floor?"

Well, that's one way to get to the point. Gramma looks down and she's studying the floor as if it were the first time she had seen it.

"Ah. The water," she says. But she doesn't say anything else on that topic. She looks up again and her eyes train on Rose. As Rose locks eyes with her and she remains silent, the girl bows her head and gives a cautious curtsy.

"Madam Grey," she greets, watching for any negative reaction to her presence. But Gramma bows her head a little back to her.

"My, how you've grown into a young woman," she says slowly. She takes a step forward, the carpet squelching under her bare feet. After a step she pauses and we were expecting her to say something else. But she doesn't. Her eyes flicker a few times until they've rolled back into her skull. She wavers and then collapses. Rose was the fastest of us all to react, just catching her before she landed on the floor. Carson and I spring over to the two and I'm unsure of what to make of it. Her eyes were leaking. Tears? Water? It was pouring from them unnaturally, like little streams. I'm kneeling down and Rose pushes the woman's hair back out of her face.

"What's wrong with her?" I try to ask as level as possible to avoid panicking.

"I'm not that sure," Rose answers. "Though, I'm suspicious of if she had a burn out."

"What is that?"

"Witches who go through a large amount of emotional stress or trauma can lose complete control over their powers," she explains. "It might explain why there's water everywhere. If only Doctor Valhera was here, he could help her."

"Should we call an ambulance or somethin'? Is she gonna be okay?" Carson asks and kneels beside me.

"No." Rose shakes her head frantically. "If any nohabi sees her like this there would be trouble. I think getting her to a bed would be best. Let her rest for a little while and maybe she'll wake again to tell us what's gone wrong." Rose shifts into a squatting position and she's moving to support the old woman's back and legs. Carson and I move to help her, but Rose is already standing up with the woman in her arms, lifting her as if she weighed nothing.

After bringing the woman up the stairs and carefully placing her in her bed, we notice that her bedroom was as much of a wreck as it was downstairs. When I pulled back the covers, I notice a small portrait on the bed along with various torn up pages of something. I pick it up to see a picture of Gramma, my mother, Aunt Nari, Uncle Namu, and a man I'd never seen before. I stare at him; his eyes were slate and he had long black hair woven into an intricate braid that rested over his shoulder. After Rose was finished tucking my grandmother in, she peered over my shoulder at the image in my hand. She looks between it and my face that clearly read that I didn't recognize everyone, and then she turns away.

"That's your grandfather," she says nonchalantly as she reached up and opened the blinds a little to let some light in.

"How do you know that?" I ask her without looking away.

"Aside from him being a part of an obvious family portrait?" She must have been rolling her eyes. "Mattias Grey is actually rather famous in Obscura."

I look at her this time before turning to set the image down on Gramma's dresser. I'm then gathering up books and folders that had been scattered around the area, and I stack them up neatly for the woman.

When I didn't question her more, honestly assuming that she would continue on her own (which she does), Rose pushes the not-so-helpful Carson out of her way so she could start collecting the torn-up bits of paper and scattered images around Gramma's bed. And then she continues:

"He was an adventurer," she tells me.

"Was?" Carson asks before getting the hint that he should help tidy up the room as well.

"I only say was because the last adventure he went on he never returned. I guess much like my grandfather no one knows whether he died or not. But Mattias Grey wrote many books about his adventures and experiences. He also would get into a lot of trouble. He even ended up having to change his name."

"To what," I ask.

"…to Mattias Grey," she answers. "His name before was Minhyun Lee, but don't go around saying that, I'm sure he changed it for a reason."

After I finished tidying up what I could, I turned to face Rose again and she was focused on placing the images she collected into a nearby envelope. I sigh a little bit, causing the other two to look over at me.

"How do you know he changed his name?" I ask this time.

"From my father, of course. I don't know everything. I imagine my father knew from being friends with Lady Jiah."

"It seems like you know everything," Carson muttered and took a seat in a chair near the window. "So, what now?"

"I guess we just wait. Carson, if you'd like to see you mother I'd go now. And if you're returning with us then just meet us back here."

Carson looks over at me as if he were asking for permission. I frown a bit and put my hands into my pockets

"Are you good?" he asks. "If you don't want me to go back with you, I—"

"I thought you wanted to be there when I 'evolve' or 'level-up' or whatever you said."

He chuckles a bit and stands back up to his feet.

"Uhm, of course." He pulls out his phone and he checks both the time and the billions of notifications he must have gotten. "Just text me and I'll come back. I'm just worried that my mom will freak out or somethin'…"

"Don't worry about your mother. Remember she thinks you went on a trip. Apparently to somewhere called Miami. When you're ready to leave her just give her some other excuse and River will fix it for you," Rose explains to him.

"Right. I don't know how that works but got it." He gives a little wave and after a "see ya" he's gone.

After nearly an hour of awkward silence between Rose and I having been left alone in the house waiting for any sign of Gramma waking again, Rose is digging through the cloak she had taken off and pulling out a familiar small glass jar full of a thick red liquid. I couldn't help but to stare as she opened it, put her little metal straw into it and sucked down the stuff as she staired out the narrow opening of the curtains. After the stuff was gone, she was pulling her hair free from the bun on her head and began struggling to use her fingers to detangle the mass of curls. It was a little weird to me that she was so normal but casually drinking what I was sure was blood at random. She was muttering to herself now, maybe regretting taking her hair a loose as she moved over to see herself in the mirror. Watching her suddenly became entertaining as the time went by.

"What are you smirking at?" Rose grumbled. I must have been a little too entertained as she glared at my reflection in the mirror. I shrug and kick my foot idly.

"I just wonder why you don't just cut it off if it bothers you so much," I say and pretend to look away.

She pouts and winces when her fingers get caught in a knot.

"It might be a pain but I do happen to like my hair," she says. "Father typically helps me if it gets too out of control of course…" She gives a sheepish expression and I approach her from behind. Don't ask me whether or not I knew what I was doing but the poor girl looked like she was having a hard time. I gently pull her fingers free and she watches me cautiously as I part the thick locks from their tangles. After a bit the hair is more or less manageable. I pull the scrunchy from her wrist and before she could stop me, I'm already pulling her hair back up into a bun for her. After I finish and turn her around to admire my own work, smirking proudly like a world-renowned hair stylist, she pushes a little at my chest so that I would give her space. She turns again to see her reflection.

"Where did you learn to do hair?" she asks me skeptically, but I only shrug and place my hands back into my pockets.

"Nowhere. I've just seen girls do it a lot at school." I say, but by "girls" I just might have *possibly* meant Hailey. *ehem*. Rose narrows her eyes at me a little before turning once again and leaving. "Where are you going?" I call after her.

"To explore," she answers and exits the room. "The least you could do is give me a tour of where you've been all this time."

My eyebrows raise at this but I hurry to follow after her and she's already crossing the hall toward my bedroom.

"Wait," I call but she's pushing open the door.

"Is this your room?" she asks and pokes her head inside. I jog up behind her and peer inside myself. It was just how I left it…a bit of a mess.

"Uh…yeah, but—"

She steps inside, the floor creaking embarrassingly loud. She looks around curiously at all of my things (not that there was much). She eyes a poster on the wall of Pennywise and grimaces.

"What a hideous creature…" she says, though I wasn't sure if it was to herself or directed at me. Probably both. She turns to all the clothes on the floor that I dug through before leaving to go to Obscura in the first place.

"Uh…I'm usually really neat," I tell her, "I was just in a hurry the last time…"

She shakes her head and moves over to my dresser where there's trinkets and images. Stuck to my mirror is an old photograph of Carson and me when we were about ten. We were wearing matching overall sets that Mrs. Foxx had put us in as we stood three feet apart in an awkward hug in front of a very creepy mascot for the city's annual book fair. Rose looks up at me quizzically and I peer over her shoulder to get a look at it.

"Aha," I chuckle a little at it. "It's a good laugh," I tell her. "We look pretty silly, right? It took Carson's mom a good two hours to get us in those terrible outfits. I think at the time I regretting going over his house."

"And you remember that?" Rose asks almost hesitantly.

"Of course, I—" I watch her expression and then look away. "…yes, I remember," I say. She turns to move on and she picks up the Lego replica of the Millennium Falcon that sat at the end of my desk

"What's this?"

"*Don't!*" I began urgently, but I was too late as she was turning to face me, she drops the figure and a good chunk of it breaks into pieces. I swallow my lungs as I was sure I'd throw them up. Rose sucks at her teeth and bends down to start picking up the pieces.

"Sorry…" she apologizes sheepishly.

"No worries," I croak to keep myself from cursing her entire family lineage. "It only took me almost a week to build." I choke down my tears to help scoop up the pieces and place them onto my desk.

After a moment of silence and the pieces being collected, Rose stands up and goes to sit on the bed.

"Did you enjoy living here?" she asks.

I sit in the chair at my desk and watch as she takes in the room entirely.

"Did I?" I question. "I haven't stopped living here yet…"

"You have after coming back home. Here is not your home. It's more of… a safe house."

"Except it's not," I say. "Regardless of the reason I came here, I still grew up here. Really, I've lived here longer than I did in Obscura, even if I do or don't remember it."

Her shoulders drop and she lays back on the bed.

"I suppose you're right…" she says. "But did you enjoy it? It's rather different than back home, isn't it?"

"Sure, I guess. It's not like I really have much to compare it to, given the whole…memory…issue. Though I once took a trip to L.A. with Gramma a few years ago. I thought that Whitechapel was boring before but after that I was sure I'd go to college out of state to have a more exciting life. Maybe even out of the country. Like to University of Toronto, or Yonsei University. Which reminds me…do you know I'm supposed to graduate in the spring? I'm also supposed to start applying to colleges soon…so with this whole magical land thing…"

"Realm," Rose corrects casually. "I hate to say you have no place here on mundane Earth," she says. "I guess I never considered how much of this place you must be used to. No magic, no war—"

"Oh, there's war," I tell her, grimacing at the thought of politics.

"Wrong choice of words," she admits. "But you've become so accustomed to…living like a nohab. Anyone would believe you were one if it weren't for the immense magical energy you have sleeping away inside of you."

"Weird way to put it," I mutter.

She sits up and looks at me with a serious expression.

"You have to put away your nohab dreams. Perhaps one day in the future you could come back here and visit…but staying here will be impossible. I'm sorry, Ethan."

"What about school?" I frown. "I literally slaved away for forever and now with six months left of my senior year I have to throw it all away?"

"There's school in Obscura," she tells me. "School that will teach you more important things like…how not to kill people by accident because magic exploded from my hand."

My mouth drops a little at that, but now that she mentions it, "Speaking of killing people," I start, "the time that led me here in the first place. I killed someone, didn't I? And you were there. I hurt you. But how? What happened?" She pauses for a moment and looks down at her hands as she ponders her response. But as soon as she opens her mouth to finally help me understand this killing of someone business, we hear the sound of coughing from the other room. We look at each other, and then we're up to go check on my grandmother.

When we entered the room, Gramma was pushing herself up into a sitting position, looking around with a confused expression.

"Gramma!" I call, maybe a little too loudly as I approached the bed to sit beside her. Rose lingers in the doorway as the woman seemed to be trying to understand what was going on.

"Ethan?" Her eyes analyzed me frantically; they were stuck a very pale looking blue color. I reached out to hold her hand and she takes it, giving it a small squeeze. Then before anyone said anything else, the woman raises her arm and forcefully pushes her palm out at me. A gush of cold water rushes out and hits me directly in the face, drenching me completely. I spit out a good bit of water and push my soaked hair back out of my face with a frown.

"What was that for," I grumble and adjust the collar of my sweatshirt uncomfortably.

"For leaving!" she answers sternly. "How could you? You have no idea what you've gotten yourself into."

"I haven't even been gone that long, Gramma," I tell her. "And just look at me, I'm completely fine."

She eyes me for a moment and then leans back against the head board. Her eyes sadden and I'm unsure of how to approach her.

"Two weeks…" she whispers suddenly.

"What?"

"Two weeks," she speaks up. "You've been gone nearly two weeks."

"Huh? That's not true, Gramma, it's only been about four days." I look back at Rose for support but she only gives me an apologetic expression. I look back at the old woman and she's staring down at her hands, turning them over as if there was something wrong with them.

"Nearly two weeks," she repeats. "Whitechapel's time is much faster than Obscura's." She looks up at me this time and she seems like she was going to start crying. "I haven't heard a single thing from you for that long, Ethan Jae."

"Now…" I pull my hand from hers and put on a sterner expression. It felt wrong, but I had to remember that we're here for a reason. "That isn't completely my fault," I say. She looks offended like I was sure she would. "Why are you still here? Doc. V arrived in Obscura the other day, he told me he asked you to come with him and you refused. Why don't you go back? Everyone I've met asks about you. Even Aunt Nari and Uncle Namu…" I pause at the expression she makes. It felt…bitter. Resentful.

"You call them out so comfortably now?" she says, words laced with venom. I'm taken aback by this, unsure of what her problem was. I draw backward and my head tilts, balked, unwilling to accept what my ears had heard.

"Sorry? What would you like me to call them instead? Forgotten daughter number one and forgotten son number two?" Gramma frowns deeply and she's raising her finger to protest but I cut her off. "*Aunt Nari* and *Uncle Namu* still exist whether you like it or not. Your friends, your family miss you whether you like it or not. I came back here because leaving you behind is wrong. You're my family, and I'd hate to leave my family behind. But it seems like we have two different ideas about who ought to be left behind."

There's a sudden draft in the room that quickly churned into a strong wind that quickly turned into a large dark cloud over the woman's head. My eyes widened a little at the phenomenon occurring in front of me and the very real cloud begins to rumble and growl with threats of a down pour.

"That's not fair!" Gramma shouts, her voice cracking with pain that struck me in the chest. Her eyes flicker and tears tempted to fall. "I had no choice. Do you think I wanted any of this to happen?"

Rose is entering the room now and she was gesturing for me to tone it down a notch or two, but I couldn't help the frustration boiling in my stomach. It seemed like every time I talked to the woman things became very complicated and anger inducing. I hated it the most. I hated it mostly because it wasn't always like this.

"Regardless of if it happened or didn't, what's done is done," I say. "It happened and now here we are. I know just about everything now, no thanks to you, and I got the chance to meet the family that has been estranged to me for years. We could've gone back there any time!"

"Ethan…" Rose calls, trying to ease the situation, but we continue.

"No, we couldn't!" Gramma snaps. The cloud rumbles again and in no time, rain is showering over her head. "How could we? You've been reduced to nothing short of a tapped-out patient! It's been ten years and your memory still hasn't returned. The whole reason behind why we needed to protect you will probably never return at this point and it's all my fault!"

There's silence save for the rain falling in our house. She sits there, pale faced, defeated. My shoulders drop and Rose is joining me by my side, sitting down and placing a hand on my arm. My gaze falls as I think about the blame she seemed to have put on herself. But actually, none of it was her fault.

"Actually…" I speak up now, "it's mine."

"What?" Gramma gives a quizzical look.

"It's my fault," I repeat. "I know about the potion, Gramma. And I know you made it with River's help. The potion wore off a long time ago. I suspect sometime last year."

"…then you can—"

I shake my head at her, knowing she was going to ask if I remember things now.

"We went to the H.D.O. to get his papers renewed," Rose steps in, leaning forward a little to make sure the old woman saw her. "When we were there, we saw the archdruid who told us that due to trauma Ethan subconsciously doesn't want to remember. So, he…doesn't."

"Except I don't completely understand that theory," I mutter.

"It's not a theory," Rose says. "It's the truth. So, I'd really appreciate it if you'd…"

She trails off and doesn't finish. The rain slows to a trickle until it stops and Gramma stairs forward, still with a helplessly defeated expression. She blinks a few times before her eyes meet mine again.

"Gramma," I call, "come back to Obscura with us."

She slowly shakes her head, waving her hands around in refusal.

"I can't…I won't."

"But why? I'm sorry, but I won't stay here with you."

"Stay…" She sheds another tear and I felt a soul eating guilt. "B-being here…it's not so bad. The people here are friendly enough. What about th-the…friends you've made? The plans you have? We don't need magic, Ethan. Even if you never get your memory back…I will always love you. Here we can be safe."

I shake my head at her this time and I stand up to my feet.

"I think that isn't true. And I think you also know that. It really...*sucks* that all of this had to happen. That my friends lived a lie. That *I* lived a lie. I know that you brought me here to protect me, but there seems to be a crap ton of unfinished business where we came from. Even if you don't help me, I will figure it out with the ones who will. I want to fix things."

"What is there to be fixed, Ethan?" the woman frowns.

"I...don't know exactly, yet," I admit. "But I feel it. I feel that I need to be there right now. And should I recover my memory...well I'm sure it won't be great if I have an explosion of unexplained magic or whatever happen in public around here, will it? I'm going back, Gramma. I just wish you would too. There's nothing here for you when I'm gone." I start to turn away, but before I could take a step, Gramma stops me.

"Wait..." she says, her eyes begging. I turn to face her once more and I was sure she was going to say something else to try and convince me to stay, but instead she reaches up and grabs my arm. She pulls me down with a strong tug and wraps her arms around me.

I'm a little jarred at first by the gesture, but then I move to hug her back. "I'm sorry..." she apologizes. "I don't know when to admit my shortcomings." She pushes me away a little so she could see my face again. "I am afraid...and not just for myself. Your life could never be the same in that place. You have...you *are* more than you know." I frown a little but she presses her cold hand against my cheek. "Forgive me. I know I've treated you unfairly."

"No, you—" I begin to protest but she shushes me.

"Promise me something," she says. "*Please*. Don't go looking for your father."

My brow furrows as her words mirrored Scott's. I thought about pressing the matter, but I could already tell that she wouldn't have it. I pull away to stand up straight but I'm still puzzled at the reason why the two warns against it. Even River did. But what could he do locked away in prison? That and it seemed he would be the only one who would remotely tell me anything about *his* side of things. Trying to ask Gramma now didn't seem like I'd get anything out of it. I shift uncomfortably in my wet clothes and give Rose a complicated look. Finally, I look back to my grandmother and say:

"I'll be safe." I ruffle my bangs and turn around to face the door again. "And Gramma, whatever this wet house business is, could you stop it? You're causing a ton of water damage. *If* I come back, I don't want to find you buried under soggy house."

I hear her sniff in response, but I don't look at her again. Afraid that I might change my mind. About everything. Maybe I would just settle down here with Gramma. I mean it *was* just about all I knew. Carson was here. And maybe I would get a shot with Hailey someday. Or find someone else at a college I've been eyeing. Marry. Have normal kids and a normal life.

• • •

Or…would they be normal?

My eyes flicker and I frown as I move quickly out of the room. I couldn't stay there any longer.

Rose catches up to me after staying behind for a bit. They must have shared some words that I didn't hear. She followed me back into my room and I'm going into my closet to find a bigger bag or two.

"What are you doing?" Rose asks, watching me carefully.

"I can't quite fit an eight-year-old's clothes, now, can I?" I probably sounded a bit harsher than I meant to. I was stuffing as many things into the bags that I could, going through the closet and my drawers as well.

"Ethan," Rose calls and steps back out of my way, "maybe we shouldn't go to Sierra, after all…"

I stop and turn to face her.

"But we have to," I say firmly.

"Well…maybe we don't *have* to. Maybe there's someone else who could tell you more about him. Maybe River could since she's an Elemalex."

"But even she said she doesn't really know. Why are you suddenly backing down now? What could he do behind bars with security and all that stuff?"

"I don't know…" She shrugs a little. "But even Dr. Valhera said it'd be a bad idea. Perhaps we need to rethink it."

"I'm going there," I tell her, unwavering from my position. "Everyone's always saying what I shouldn't do and do I listen? Of course, I do! I'm the good boy that does whatever anybody says. You know, unless it's clearly wrong." I'm spinning around as I speak, continuing my unstructured packing. "I'm just *sick* of everyone telling me what to do all the time. What I should, what I shouldn't. Don't do this, Ethan, you could like…die or something. *Ya, mwo-ha-nya? Geu-ro-ji-ma!*" I tsk, and shove some underwear into my bag. "*Jenjang,*" I curse quietly. "I'm eighteen now, isn't that great? It means I'm an adult and can make adult decisions. I'm gonna go find the bastard, and make him talk whether anyone likes it or not."

Rose lowers her head a little, clearly recognizing that whatever she says now won't get through to me. After violently zipping my bags and throwing them over my shoulders, I pull out my phone and dial Carson's number.

He picks up after a few long rings.

"Yo," he answers.

"Are you coming or what!" I snap into the phone. By mistake of course, I was only feeling a bit too passionate. Heh.

"Woah," Carson responds. There was a lot of shuffling in the background but I couldn't make out anything in particular. "Who pissed you off, hot shot? How 'bouts ya open the door?"

My brow furrows and I look over at Rose who looks back curiously before I cross the room and go straight down the stairs.

"Kidding." Carson laughs. I was sure he was going to say he wasn't actually there, but upon entering the kitchen, I see the front door opening and his strawberry blond hair poking around the corner. "Door was already unlocked!" he laughs.

I watch him curiously and Rose is coming down the stairs, stopping just behind me. Carson stops just before the entrance to the kitchen and it seemed like we were all staring at each other, watching to see who would do something first. Then Carson hangs up the phone and throws his hands in the air.

"I don't know what y'all are waitin' for. I'm not takin' my shoes off again."

Fair. I move to join him at the door and I slip into my sneakers.

"So, did Gramma wake up? Is she okay?" Carson asks.

"She'll be fine," Rose answers and slips into her shoes as well. "She'd be better if she comes home and let Dr. Valhera see her. But, either way, she'll probably do okay now that she saw Ethan today."

"So, she's not coming back with us?" Carson frowns and he turns to push open the door.

"She's scared," I say. When we all exit the house, I lock the doors back so that she would at least have that much security and I turn to hop off of the porch. "Maybe there's something else she doesn't want to say. She's obviously used to just being here, but I think aside from me getting hurt, she must be afraid of seeing the others again."

"She might also be afraid of what could happen if she does come back," Rose adds.

"What do you mean?" I look at her as Carson and I are kicking off the stands of our bikes and mounting them to return back to the forest. It was dark out now; the sun was completely gone and the temperature had dropped significantly. I was glad I shoved a thicker coat into one of my bags.

"I mean, your grandmother was a part of a special unit at Lamia Castle. She was given an order to do something, grant it unthinkable and unfair, but she disobeyed that order to save you. Madam Grey has never been back to Obscura within those ten years you both have been here. If she comes back, sure she'd be safe around Greenwood, but she could never show her face again near Lamia. She'd be severely punished, I'm sure."

I frown at this. I didn't even think about that. Gramma did all of this to protect me, but it didn't go without a cost. It most likely cost her her freedom. I have to make things right, somehow. But…how?

12

Leisure and Leashes

"How is your mom?" I'm asking Carson as we took our time to ride back to the portal. Rose was saying that we had to wait a little while for it to open up again as it closed not too long after we passed through it a few hours ago. So, there was no hurry to rush anywhere.

"She's fine," he answers and adjusts the backpack on his back. He must have decided to pack some things too, but he definitely didn't have nearly as much as I did. I just hoped that meant he wouldn't ask to borrow clothes later… "Actually, she was on her way out when I got there. She was gonna bring some trays over to the country club."

"Grandfather throwing another party?" I ask.

He nods his head with a roll of the eyes. "Another party," he affirms.

"What's a country club?" Rose mutters almost half-heartedly as she focused on kicking a rock behind our bikes.

"A stuffy rich folk hangout," I tell her with a less than beautiful snort.

Her eyes widen a little and she looks up at Carson almost surprised.

"Are you rich, Carson?"

He laughs something painful in response and waves his hand at her.

"Ha. Ha. No," he answers. "Grandpops loves to keep his green to himself. I mean the least that guy could do for my mom is help her pay some of our bills for all the times she's helped him with his stupid parties and his…stupid social life."

"Oh, how pitiful." Rose wrinkles up her nose and then looks back down for the rock she lost a few steps away. "Why does he throw so many parties, then?"

"Bored," Carson tells her. "I guess he likes to think of himself as the modern-day Jay Gatsby."

"So, you do pay attention in literature," I tease and he sneers at me.

We move along the road that leads into the parking lot of the forest. As we approached the entrance, I couldn't help but to feel bad about not returning with my grandmother. If only she would just…listen.

"But anyway," Carson continues, "my mom kept talking about this guy she met a while ago. Said he was in town visiting some family member but he would leave after today. Recently my mom stopped bringing desserts and stuff to the country club but she was doing it for this guy. And when I helped her bring the trays over there, I met him."

"…What was he like?" I look at him cautiously. I remembered what Mrs. Foxx was telling me before that day we went to the Halloween party. It was weird, and I wasn't entirely sure if she got the story right in the first place.

"He said he knew you," he finishes, his words mirroring his mother's from that night.

"What?" I tilt my head and he's nodding up and down.

"Real tall, fancy schmancy hair. When he met me, he asked me all these weird questions about the bass." I clear my throat to stop an unwanted laugh, but actually it was kind of funny. "He was like 'your mother told me all about your musical endeavors' and blah blah blah. Then he looked pretty offended when I told him I didn't play an oversized cello, I play the bass guitar. Anyway, that's not important. After that he asked me about you, and said he knew you were my best friend. He asked me about your childhood, and your parents. And when I said your parents were dead, he asked me about your grandma. But then he said something *really* weird to me that made me think this guy must be bad news…"

Rose and I are staring at him expectantly. We've entered the forest and we're on the orange trail to our final destination. Carson pauses dramatically, or maybe he was just trying to put the words together right before saying it out loud. After a moment he says:

"He said that my life is an illusion or whatever. He said I would never even be friends with you if I knew you'd been manipulating me all this time." I swallow hard and look over at Rose who was looking back with a concerned expression. But Carson continues still. "Obviously that didn't make sense to me so I told him to piss off and to stop hitting on my mom. He must be a creep or a dirty stalker, right?" He looks behind him at Rose and I who had fallen behind. He narrows his eyes at our guilty expressions and then he stops walking altogether. "Is there something I missed?" he questions.

Rose looks away, obviously it wasn't her business to tell. I felt like I was breaking out in the cold sweats. Should I tell him? Should I let him know that hey by the way you were put under a spell or something to believe we grew up together. I mean aside from the fact that we did…after that day in the hospital, of course. There was no way to tell how he would react if I did tell him. Sometimes he was a bit unpredictable. I was taking too long to answer now and I could tell Carson was becoming suspicious. He adjusts the straps of his backpack and gives me a good stare down.

"Earth to Ethan," he calls. "I really hope you're not keeping something from me. I mean, you know all my secrets. Like that time in fifth grade when I ate some bad shellfish and threw up in Julia's gym bag." He presses his lips together and his eyes shift to Rose's who was now unsure of if she should ignore him or outwardly look disgusted. "Forget I said that, Rose, it wasn't meant for your ears."

She shakes her head and he turns back to me. Finally, I draw in a breath, take a step forward and wrap my arm around his shoulders.

I wouldn't tell him.

"Don't be silly," I say and pull him forward to continue our short journey back to the portal. "I don't know who that guy is but you're right, he's obviously bad news if he's even willing to…make up *lies*. I mean, 'your life is an illusion'? What does that even mean? I'm your best friend. I would never… *knowingly* manipulate you. Or lie to you. You know that."

"I guess you're right," Carson says after a small pause. He looks up at the sky for a moment before shaking his head again. "But you're wrong about one thing."

My brow raises and my heart skips as I quickly analyze what I just said a moment ago. Did I slip up or say something wrong?

"...I am?" I question after not pin-pointing where I could have been mistaken.

"Yeah." He looks at me and we meet each other's gaze for what seemed like a painful amount of time until he continues. "You're not my friend," he says. "You're my brother—eeehhhggk!" with a strange Carson sound and a positive laugh he throws his arm around my shoulders too and I'm breathing a deep sigh of relief. It probably does no good to continue delaying the truth he's bound to find out at some point, but for now I couldn't bring myself to tell him just yet. So, I've bought myself some more time.

Rose is passing by us now and soon enough we're approaching the little gate that is our entrance into the magical realm I'm unsure about calling "home" just yet. Rose looks down at her watch for a moment and then suddenly she's plopping down to take a seat on the cold ground.

"What are you doing?" I ask her. She looks up with an expression that was a mixture of exhaustion and annoyance.

"Fifteen minutes," she says simply.

There was nothing we could do but wait. Pulling out of Carson's grasp I take a seat beside her and he joins us as well.

"I'm hungry," the blonde grumbles and pats his belly.

"You seem to always be hungry," Rose answers with a pout.

"And weren't you just with your mom around a bunch of food?" I add.

"Yeah, but it's not like she let me take a lot. It was for those lousy club members."

I nod slowly. Makes sense. Who but Carson's mother knows him well enough to know that if not warned (or threatened) he'd eat up anything he could get his hands on? But now my mind starts to wander. I thought back to the strange interaction I had with my aunt last night. If she and my uncle live at Lamia Castle, perhaps Rose could shed some light on their situation.

"Rose," I call. She hums and looks over at me. "Are my aunt and uncle vampires," I ask, which must have been entirely random to her because her eyes blew up with sudden surprise. "And if they are," I continue, "how does that work? Because if my family are witches then how is it they're not? Or are they? Aunt Nari did magic the night we got there. Or does that mean they're some kind of hybrid or oddity, or however you call it. Does that also mean—" I didn't realize how much I was going on and on until Rose was threatening me with a fist full of soil. I shut my mouth and she cease's fire.

"Did you ask them yourself?" Rose inquires.

"Yeah, I asked Aunt Nari. But she got all weird and shut it down," I say with a small frown.

"Then it's not any of my business to tell."

"What? Why not?" I look at her and she seemed rather firm in her position.

"Because that is their personal business," she says. "I only know because rarely any secret gets passed me in the castle. Erm…mostly because I can be a bit nosey but that's neither here nor there."

"So, it is a secret," I clarify. "I just noticed their fangs, but also the fact that they seem to know a lot about magic too. I mean they must if Gramma's a witch and they grew up around it."

Rose hesitates after I confirmed that the matter was secretive to begin with. She's carefully choosing her next words and dusting off her hands after playing with the dirt.

"It's a secret," she acknowledges with a small nod of the head. "Which makes it all the more reason why it isn't my business to tell. I'll only say this, your aunt and uncle were born witches, and no person can just be born another occult without it directly being in their blood. As far as I know, no one in your bloodline is vampire. You come from a rather strong line of witches. I mean…obviously since you turned out to have an incredibly powerful element."

"So, they were turned then," Carson chimes in with a 'duh' expression. "If they were born witches and no one can just spontaneously change what they are, then someone turned them."

Rose shuts her mouth and sits up a little straighter. She looked like she felt like she said too much as she was now looking for a way to change the subject.

"Oh, how would you know," she mutters and looks away.

"Movie logic," he answers with a shrug. "And literally any common knowledge about how vampires work. But I'm still surprised you don't sparkle in the sun."

"Stop that," I scold.

Rose twiddles her thumbs and she was silent for a little while. I was still staring at her expectantly and she definitely sensed it. She lifts her head again and looks at me directly.

"Turning is highly illegal in Obscura," she explains.

"Darnnit. I was just about to ask if you'd bite me so I could get super strength!" Carson folds his arms and pouts like a two-year-old before Rose could continue.

"Since the Vengeance Cult's turning spree in 1652 turning was outlawed. Even if an individual gave consent a vampire who turns someone will be severely punished. Sometimes without trial."

"How come? I mean, not that I'm advocating for turning everyone. But if a person gave consent, surely it shouldn't be a problem," I say.

"Aside from turning being against a person's human rights if they didn't give consent, their life would change forever... But even if a person does consent to it, there is the matter of the 'oddity problem'. And of course, if just anyone was turned there's no telling how they'll manage the mixture of abilities, what their plans could be if they have some, and obviously where would they live? In Lamia? They'd be mistreated, and they certainly wouldn't know our culture and customs to fit in."

"There's culture?" Carson asks almost skeptically.

"What? Of course, there is. Vampires have been around for millions of years, how could there not be? But regardless that isn't a very important reason why turning should be illegal. It's mainly the abuse of the power, and the unpredictability of ability mixing. It's usually terribly dangerous. And those individuals are cast away. Usually to Sierra."

"Where the largest population of oddities are..." I connect. More and more things were becoming clearer and coming together. "Does that mean most oddities who aren't favorable where they live are sent to Sierra?" I ask.

"Precisely. It's common for oddities to be born or even just appear in Sierra. There is a lot of vast open land in that district. So, oddities from other districts are sent there under the impression that there is room for them and they should be accepted easily. But the truth is, Sierra is struggling with a population issue. 90% of the people there are oddities."

"What's the 10%?" Carson asks. "What's living there that isn't odd?"

"Trolls, minotaurs, oreads…uhm, there's a few others but many of them have been lost with time. Many of that ten percent are at risk of extinction. And I fear that with Lamia having taken over recently, they won't help their situation."

"Gurl, did you just say *minotaurs*? Like full on man body and head of a bull goin' on? I know you playin', please don't lie to me! I can get along with these whole magical powers and vampire what have you going on but a *minotaur*? I would hate to come into contact with any such thing!" Carson squeezes his eyes shut and shakes his head rapidly at the mere mention of such a creature. But I didn't blame him. I couldn't even imagine seeing something so *fiction* in real life. Not to mention how scary it could be…

"I apologize," Rose says and reaches out to pat Carson on the knee. "I apologize that you didn't know they existed. They're just as real as you and me." She stands up and dusts herself off with a little smirk on her face as Carson stared up at her in disbelief. "But lucky for you, you shouldn't meet one as long as you don't go adventuring in the deep caves of Sierra." Rose pulls out her key from her cloak and she turns to face the portal. I suppose that was enough of a hint to tell us it was time to go. Carson and I push ourselves up to our feet and I turn to look behind me at the path we took to get here. We were leaving Whitechapel again. But now I was wondering how long will it be before I come back. How long will it be before I see my grandmother again? What about Hailey…

"Could you explain to me why I gotta close my eyes?" Carson is fuming as Rose was turning the key.

"Because to see the transition between worlds is too much for the nohab mind. To see it your mind is at risk of snapping into a fit of madness."

Carson blinks a few times and gulps at the thought and then squeezes his eyes shut. I rubbed the back of my neck, curious of if it were true or not. But what would be the reason to lie? At the third clicking of the turning lock, the bright light appears, the buzzing vibrates the air, and the energy of the portal whooshes loudly. Rose steps through without hesitation. I push Carson in front of me and follow through as closely behind Rose as possible, afraid of getting lost somehow. Then after a short (slightly uncomfortable) moment, we were stepping on Lamia land again. But it was a little strange. It was just dark outside, the sun nearly disappearing behind the horizon, but here it was still day light. The time difference.

"Rose, what time is it?" I ask her. But it seemed there was no time to waste because she was already yards away, walking quickly through the tangle of trees.

"What?" she calls back. Carson and I have to jog to catch up with her and she's storing the portal's key back into her cloak.

"The time," I repeat. "And could someone teach me how to read the clocks around here?"

I bShe laughs a little in response and takes a look at her watch.

"It's nearly half past three," she responds. "We've been gone a little over an hour."

"Sorry, but I was with my mom almost two hours, ma'am," Carson puffs as he's struggling to keep up.

"Time difference. For the last time," Rose shakes her head.

"Hey, while we're over here, why don't we go see your dad," I suggest. "Then we don't…have to go to a party to do it."

Carson snaps his neck to the side, and I should have guessed what he might say. Almost immediately did I regret saying what I did.

"*Party?*" he questions. "A party? If we have the chance to go to some crazy magical party, we are definitely going, Ethan, what are you even saying!"

I press my lips together and look over at Rose for her reaction, but her expression was unreadable (from what I could tell).

"We can't," she says. "About this time the guards should be rounding the front grounds. That's where my father's cottage is."

"Sounds like to me party is first and then father. What party is it…?"

"The annual Masquerade Ball," she answers.

"Fancy costumes? When did y'all have this conversation and I wasn't there to hear it? Whatever Ethan told you, Rose, don't listen to him, we're going to that party. I'm invited to *every* party! That's how cool I am."

"That's a lie," I snort.

"Then if you both are truly going, we must get you the proper attire." Rose turns around to walk backwards and her face lit up again with a semi-hopeful smile. "It should be great fun, Ethan. Don't think about the dancing, just think of it as, um, another opportunity to learn about Obscura. Or remember it…"

"She makes a good point, brooo…" Carson sings. "Oh, don't make me beg you, and you know I will. How could you give up the chance to see a real-life vampire party? Remember all the kids in middle school who went through a phase of thinking they were vampires? They'd be incredibly jealous of us right now!"

"*Alright!*" I almost snap at him so he wouldn't go on any longer.

"Well, if I knew it'd be that easy to convince you I would have involved Carson the first time," Rose chuckles and spins back around. "The ball is always the first Friday of November. Wednesday is the last day I have any schedule for the occasion, so Thursday afternoon I'll come by so we can go shopping." I could hear the excitement in her voice which was certainly new. "If I spend the night then we can go to the ball together. No one should be looking for me so it's entirely possible. And Ethan, should you tire of the ball quickly then we can slip away to my father's cottage and stay for a while before returning home. How does that sound?"

"It sounds like you're eager," Carson points out first.

Rose is quiet for a moment as it seemed she was leveling herself and her excitement.

"Why yes…I suppose I'm more than thrilled by the matter," she responds calmly. She then shakes her head and frees her arms from her cloak, swinging them back and forth with a deep sigh. "Just wait, Ethan. You'll remember the joys we once had." She smiles to herself again but nothing else is said between the three of us.

· · ·

The journey back to the guild almost seemed like forever. Passing through the border was a pain again as we had gotten different guards asking the same questions about the veracity of my existence. And after that Carson and I had both fallen asleep on the carriage back to Willow Way until we had gotten rather heavy-handed shakes of the arm by our very strong vampire friend who seems to forget her strength from time to time. By now Carson and I should know how to get back to the guild from there. And if Carson didn't, I did. We said our goodbyes to Rose once the carriage had stopped and the driver turned around to take her back. With a sore-armed walk back to the guild, Carson and I finally could rest from our journey. Before we could even knock on the door, it was swinging open and we were greeted by a bright-eyed Victoria with too much energy that neither of us really wanted to deal with.

"Well, isn't this a wonderful sight!" she exclaims with a little bounce and a flip of the hair. "I almost thought blondie wouldn't come back, I'm shocked at your tolerance for the extraordinary."

"Well, you know me," Carson raises his shoulders, "I'm a bit extraordinary myself."

Her eyes shift without any response to him and she eyes me up and down. I could only stare back, wishing for the love of God that she would hurry up and move out of the way so that I could come from out of the cold. It was a shame that I didn't feel comfortable enough yet to just barge in passed her.

"I find the clothes you wear very fresh and modern," she says. "You've changed them from earlier." She reaches out and grabs me by the collar. She pulls me inside with a strong arm and I stumble into the warmth of the home.

"Tori, what is taking so long!" someone shouts from inside the den. I see my aunt coming over to see what was going on and she catches the woman man-handling me. "What are you doing?" she questions sternly.

"Oh, nothing." She releases me and smooths out the wrinkle in my collar.

And smooths.

And smooths.

Ah yes, she was feeling me up. I grip her wrist with only two fingers and pull her hand away from me.

"We were chatting but he was taking so long to come in, you know, so I—"

"That's enough, Victoria," Aunt Nari says and shuts her eyes.

She frowns a little in response but she doesn't say anything else and goes off into the den. Carson frowns deeply and turns his head to glare at me.

"*What does she see in you!*" he hisses before turning to go explore the kitchen.

Aunt Nari shakes her head and then steps a little closer to me and wraps her arm around my shoulders. She leads me over to the den as she gives me a good squeeze.

"I'm so glad you're alright, joka," she says with a genuine sigh of relief.

"Yeah," I frown, "but I couldn't get Gramma to come with us."

She's shaking her head again and we enter the warm and cozy den. Lanterns and candles were lit and Jem was in the same place we left him. River was in her chair stitching something up, and that little silver cat was rolling around the floor with some feathery toy. I take a seat on the couch and my aunt joins me, taking a moment to pour me some tea from the set on the coffee table.

"As much as I hoped she would, I am also not so surprised," she tells me calmly and hands me the tea cup. I stared down into its contents and the hot steam hit my face, filling my nose with the scent of apples and cinnamon. I don't think I ever drank so much tea in my life…but did I like it?

Yes.

"Then really what was the point of going there? It was almost entirely a waste," I tell her with a deep frown. "I mean I hoped she would come back and I was hoping she'd be a bit more open to talking about the past now that it's all out in the open, but she was almost exactly the same. Except…"

My aunt watches me expectantly. She had been tearing apart a soft piece of bread but stopped to listen intently.

"Except?" she questions.

"Just…when we got there, she collapsed. There was water everywhere and Rose said something about a burn out. I don't know what that means but she's fine now, I guess. She was up and talking before we left."

I watch her frown and she sits back against the couch. The entire room seemed to be quiet now. I noticed River looking up from her stitching and she was adjusting her glasses on her nose. And then my uncle walks in, looking around a bit confused why the energy in the room seemed to have shifted negatively.

"Ethan, when did you get back?" he questions after a moment, pulling his hands from out of his pockets. I look up at him and he comes over to join all of us on the couch.

"Just a moment ago," I tell him and look back down at my cooling tea. "Can I ask you all something? And please, don't give me the run-around, it's really frustrating."

Uncle Namu looked like he entirely regretted walking into whatever he did and the others continued to watch me carefully. Unsure of what I might say next, how to react, how careful they should be. I press my lips together for a moment, mulling over my next words until I finally just say what I'm thinking.

"I want to know about my father," I say plainly. "I know he's in prison, I know he is some sort of oddity. And I know that whatever it is that he is, is a part of me. And…and I worry that *if* I can somehow make magic work, that part of me is dangerous, and it's caused trouble before, it will cause trouble again. Isn't it only fair that I have some knowledge of who and what he is? There's something Gramma said once. She said that what's inside of me will inevitably take control of me. Haunt me like it does him. And eventually tear me apart. Isn't that a fun thing to hear without any real context?" I laugh, but it was full of stress and uncertainty. I couldn't tear my eyes away from the liquid in my cup, and I could feel that same anxiety I felt in Gramma's room washing over me again. At this point I just hoped that whatever is blocking my ability to use my powers now would stay forever. Then there'd be nothing to worry about, would it?

The silence is deafening in the room again. Not a single person moved. It even seemed like no one was breathing. That is until Carson comes sauntering into the room with a large bowl of something he found in the kitchen. He was shoveling big spoonsful of what looked like chili into his mouth until he was aware of what was going on. He gulps, looking around the room wide-eyed until he decided to spin around and go back to the kitchen.

After he was gone, Aunt Nari draws in a deep breath, and sets her piece of bread down.

"You know, Ethan," she starts off slowly, "none of us can truly say that we *knew* your father. We certainly didn't know him the way that our sister did. Though I was there the day she met him, and well, what they had in the beginning seemed entirely genuine, and sweet. I know for a fact that your mother loved that man deeply and perhaps he felt the same way for a long time until he started to change."

"He was obsessed with politics," Uncle Namu chimes in. "Or just fighting. …Or both." He shrugs.

"In the beginning what he was doing and what he was focused on was honest work. It was for a good cause."

"But that man was known for being short tempered and quick to act without thinking."

"He went from simple protests and leading innocent oddities like himself for fair treatment to fighting, to killing. We watched Jiah struggle with the way he went from soft with her to angry and difficult."

"They began to fight often, argue, and it always ended with Jiah coming home in tears while he went off to a pub or the streets. He was unhinged and we begged her to break things off with him."

"It was obviously hard for her," Aunt Nari says and shakes her head. "She loved him. *Too* much. But even she knew that there was no rekindling their relationship. He had gone crazy with this…thirst for rage and violence. She ended up too afraid to say anything because of how easy it was to set him off. It wasn't until the incident in Lamia Common with that…" She pauses and when I looked up to see her face she looked almost livid at the thought of whoever it was. Uncle Namu seems to notice this so he continues for her.

"Until the Lamia Common incident with some military when he was finally caught and imprisoned was she able to tell him they would separate from then on. And of course, by that time she had been pregnant with you. Either way, like we've told you before, Ethan, no one truly knows what your father is and what sort of powers he exactly possesses. We only know that they are entirely dangerous. It is said, however, that he is cursed by Darkness. And although he may have started off a normal bloke, his curse is what caused him to become unhinged."

"That's not entirely true," River steps in with a shake of the head. "It isn't a curse. Not a real one anyway. There have been other cases similar to your fathers, but of course not anywhere close to its severity. It is extremely rare, only five in history like your father's case where they were born to no parents."

"But how is that possible?" I shake my head, not even sure of how to process that.

"No one knows. There are many mysteries on this earth, and that is certainly one of them. Your father was born in the caves of Mount Fichik, completely surrounded by darkness. And the way he describes it, Darkness is not a just a thing. Darkness is a being that gave him life and his powers. The Elemalex Unit have tried their best to research the matter but there is little we truly understand about it. But we did find some truth to your father's explanation, and we believe that the negative energy that makes up darkness is what your father's powers are made from. And because of that, it controls him in a way that might not be who he is individually. His powers possess him, haunt him, control him. And that is why he has such a terrible streak of violence and negativity. Though it's only a hypothesis."

"There have been instances where you seemed possessed or controlled by something else in the past, Ethan," Aunt Nari adds and looks to me with a worried expression. I look back at her as I'm thinking back to the first night I spent here. I look back down at my mug and no longer could I see the steam billowing out. I couldn't help but think about the vision I had about crying to my mother about hurting people. About hurting Rose. About possibly killing someone once. I didn't have the energy to ask about that. My eyes shut and I sigh.

"I don't want to hurt anyone..." I tell them quietly. "And I definitely don't want what Gramma was going on about."

"Then the faster you let us help you face your magical ability, the faster we can help you to be strong enough to control it on your own. You *are* a good ten years behind," River says and finally sets down whatever it was she was stitching up. She waves her hand and it disappears into thin air. "But we can't do anything if *you* don't want to do it. You cannot force magic out. If you're looking to be serious about this then I hope to see you in this room tomorrow morning, seven a.m. sharp." She stands up and gives me an austere expression that felt strangely out of her character, or maybe it was too reminiscent of my grandmother. The woman leaves the room and perhaps she was off to bed.

"And perhaps later I could start teaching you to use knives, if you'd like. While Namu and I are still here."

I look at my aunt who in the eyes seemed hopeful but, in the face, seemed expressionless. She watched for my answer and I nod my head and give her an almost inaudible "okay". She offers a weak smile and reaches over and ruffles my hair. "Okay," she agrees and stands to her feet. "Because of the ball on Friday we're able to stay over for a little while. So, whenever."

My eyes trail back over to my tea and it's gone cold. I began to wonder if it would even be possible for me to use magic. It almost seemed like a joke. How could I, a boy from little ol' Michigan, suddenly start doing something so unreal. Except I knew it wasn't unreal as the few days I've been in this place has taught me that. But it still seemed out of reach. But if it were possible, if I was able to unlock this power within myself, perhaps I'd have a better voyage to find my father. Then should I run into another one of those hunters like what we did in Julieth's Quarter, I'd at least be able to stand up for myself. My expression softens at this thought, and I almost had a plotting smile on my face. I gulp down the tea in my cup and I stand straight to my feet.

"Alright goodnight. See you all in the morning," I say in a chipper tone. A complete 180 from just a moment ago. Just as I sat down the tea cup in my hand and slipping around the coffee table, Carson is walking in the room with a popsicle and he and the others are watching me basically jog over and up the stairs.

• • •

"There's nothing left of her," a man is explaining in a solemn tone. "Nothing but a puddle of blood, a tuft of fur, and one tooth. If he doesn't answer to it, someone else will have to."

"How could he? He's eight years old." I could see her. She was so close yet so far away. Just around the couch I could peer at the woman. My mother, standing there

in the foyer with a guard from Lamia castle. I couldn't quite see her face as her back was facing me. Her hair was long, straight, and dark, and she wore loose wide-legged pants that skirted around her ankles. Her feet were bare on the runner carpet that led into the den. "What was her name?" she asks after a slight pause.

"Viola Blackclaw," the guard answers. "Perhaps now you can see why it's a tough situation your boy has gotten himself into."

"But what was a Blackclaw doing that close to the castle? Or anyone for that matter?" The woman is pressing her hand to her forehead and she seemed overwhelmed. "I understand that what's happened to her was simply terrible, but surely, she is at fault as well. She had no business there where any of the kids were able to run into her. Shifted on top of that. Was she hunting vampires?"

"We're not entirely sure on that part. So far it sounds like she never realized she crossed the border. West of the castle is the most unmonitored and the least protected. Even still, to have been killed particularly in that manner is quite unforgivable. Child or not. Artemis and the Blackclaws won't let it go lightly. We can't cover this up."

"He had no idea what he was doing. He can't even remember it. Ethan was taken over; it wasn't his fault. He couldn't even hurt a fly on purpose. Surely there is something we can do…"

"Jiah, right now Artemis is asking for an even trade. I don't think it will be that easy to sway them. And I shouldn't tell you this, but I am fond of you. The castle is looking to get rid of him anyway. They are saying Ethan poses a threat to everyone. Including the integrity of Obscurian laws. They figure he would seek power. Though I am sure it is a projection of guilt on Lamia's part. The return of the King would fix everything. I think only he could find a way out of this for your son. But for now…" He's shaking his head.

My mother is sighing and wrapping her arms around herself. She looks to the floor and kicks her feet as she thinks of what to say next.

"So, what now?" she asks dimly.

"Friday Artemis officials, the Blackclaw family and the ministry are meeting to discuss how to move forward and compensation. You have been called to join. Think of it as an opportunity to plead his case."

She nods her head and turns her head back toward the den. I duck back behind the couch so she doesn't catch sight of me, but something told me she already knew I was there. She turns again to look at the guard and she stands up straight as she faces him.

"Thank you, Esad."

"Don't thank me." He places a hand on her shoulder and squeezes gently. "You and your boy deserve peace. I only fear the greed of my district will become more than us all."

They exchange sincere looks and I watch as my mother ushers the man out of the house. At the door he gives his tall staff two clicks against the ground, bows to my mother and then he heads off. I'm holding my breath now and I begin to draw away to run off as to not get caught spying on the conversation about me. As I'm spinning around on my hands and knees, I feel my collar hitch and I'm pulled backward into the shins of the woman who stood behind me.

"Shouldn't you be in bed, young man," I hear her say. Her voice, although stern, was sweet and comforting. I turn around after she releases my shirt and I see her standing straight and holding a hand out to me. I watch her as she offers a kind smile despite the stress in her eyes and I take it as she leads me out of the den and up the stairs.

"I feel better, eomma," I say to her. "I want to go see Rosie."

"Not yet," she tells me. "First, we have to be sure if you truly are alright. Which means I should call doctor Valhera. And second, we must let Rose rest. She had quite a scare, so we don't want to push her, alright?" I nod my head in response, trying to understand what sort of scare she must have had. I knew at this point it was because of me. But I wasn't sure what happened between running through the forest and waking up in my bedroom. "Ethan?" she calls my name, breaking up my thoughts. I look up at her as she takes me back to my bedroom. She lets go of my hand upon entering the room and she goes to straighten out the covers and pulls them back further for me. "Would you like to hear a story?"

"Is it true?" I ask hopefully and climb up into the bed. The woman tucks me in and sits down at my side. She pats my stomach for a moment before reaching over to the nightstand and rekindling the flame underneath a lantern.

"Yes," she answers finally. "This one is about a man named Balance."

"Do I know him?" I ask excitedly and pull the blankets up over my chin.

"No," my mother laughs and moves now to push my bangs back. "You never met this man. But I think his story is an important one. Balance is a man who, despite his name, struggled with the importance of balance."

The image is fading.

"Although Balance often preached about this, a sort of yin and yang of life…"

Her voice is fading.

Please, not yet.

"…he often needed another's help to remind him of what he preached. Balance lacked an element that is essential to balance."

"An element like fire?" I ask.

"Almost." Everything is growing dark, and her voice was barely a whisper. "This element is called love."

My eyes open, and I'm frustrated to see the sun pouring through my window. I roll over, pulling my pillow over my head and I squeeze my eyes shut, hoping to fall back into my dream. But to no avail. I had never seen my mother for so long before. Or heard her voice sound so real. I throw my pillow aside and roll back onto my back, frowning at the ceiling until I'm ready to accept that I could hear no more. But what insight to the past. It must have been what that was, right? I push myself up into a sitting position and I ponder over this new information. Who was Viola Blackclaw? And what had I done to her?

After unearthing myself from my bedroom and dressing for the day, I began my way to the den to meet River. Although she gave me a specific time, I *still* had no idea how to tell it from any of the clocks around. So, I just hoped she'd forgive me on that part. It was nice, however, to be able to wake up on my own without opening my eyes nose to nose with someone else. Before I started down the stairs, I peeked into one of the culprit's room. Carson was still asleep, spread out across his bed, blankets half on the floor, mouth wide open as he snored away. Actually, Carson was pretty good at waking up early, so he must have been tired if I woke up before him.

I shut the door and with a short skip-hop down the wooden stairs, I find I am now falling over something surprisingly hard. I'm bracing myself to smack my face across the floor, but I am frozen just centimeters away.

"Oops, sorry. I meant to move that so that wouldn't happen."

I peek my eyes open, half wondering if I had died upon the impact I never felt. But I lift my head and see Victoria and Autumn standing a few feet away, Victoria standing with her hands pushed out in front of her. She closes her palms and drops her hands and I am now meeting the floor and registering the slight ache in my foot and shins. With a grunt I roll over to see what I had tripped over. There in front of the steps was a small crumbling wall of vine and rock. Victoria turns her palm up now, rounds her fingers into claws, gives her hand a twist and the rock lifts momentarily before sinking loudly underground. I blink and push myself up onto my knees to see the damaged floor and the hole that remained.

"*Victoria*—" I began in disbelief, wondering why she would make a mess of the house on purpose like this.

"Autumn, would you please," I hear Victoria say before I could finish. I turn to see the younger girl pulling out a thin dainty looking wand and she gives it a quick twirl. The ground starts to shake and I scramble backward out of the way as the hole closes up, the wood flooring repairs and replaces itself, and the carpet is mended and laid back over the empty spot. It looked brand new.

I close my mouth and turn again to look at the girls. Autumn returned her wand back to her pocket and Victoria was checking her manicure.

"Not bad, buttercup. But we're weening you off your wand, remember?"

Autumn tsks and runs her fingers over her brow stressfully.

"Sorry," she says. "It's really become a habit."

"Well, break it." Victoria puts her hand down and instead places them both on her hips. "Is the floor comfortable?" she asks me this time. "Or did you get hurt?"

I stand up awkwardly, and put my hands into my pockets.

"Other than busting my shins, I'm fine," I tell her.

"Good morning, Ethan," Autumn says with a small wave.

"Good morning," I answer. "What are you girls doing anyway?"

"Tori was just demonstrating combination defensive magic. It'll be a while before I can start studying it, but I was curious to see it done."

"That small little wall was supposed to be defensive?" I raise a brow at her and she laughs in return.

"That was only what was left of it," she tells me. "Perhaps when you start using magic again, we could try practicing together. I wonder what a Spirit and Air combination would make…"

"Definitely a mess."

I turn my head to see Aunt Nari walking into the den, and she was pulling off a pair of dirt-stained white gloves. She meets my eye for a second but her expression was just as plain and somewhat tired as it usually was. "Aren't you late for your first lesson with River?" she asks me. I raise a brow at her and shrug my shoulders.

"Am I? Didn't she say to meet her here in the den?"

"You must be too late. You know how she can be," Victoria says and motions toward the stairs where I came from.

"I really don't…" I mutter.

"She must be already in the casting room. You should probably hurry before she goes off to do some other work," Autumn tells me. I look at both girls and I feel lost. I suppose my face made that clear as Aunt Nari seemed to shift the direction she was walking in toward the stairs.

"Let's go, joka," she says with a sigh. I pout a little and look between Victoria and Autumn one last time before turning to follow after my aunt.

"You'll do great, Ethan," I hear Autumn say. It was encouraging, but I had no idea what I was about to get myself into.

I follow Aunt Nari up the stairs and she leads me down the hall and then rounds the corner to the right. I had never gone this way before but I saw the girls coming from this direction a few times. This hall made the house seem even larger than before as it stretched on quite a ways. We passed room after room which I assumed belonged to Tori, River, Jem and so on until we reached the end of the hall to a round blue door with black markings and symbols painted on it. I look at my aunt but she doesn't say anything to me. She instead gives me a pat on the shoulder before moving passed me and going back the way we came. My shoulders drop and I turn back to the door. With a quick internal pep talk I push the door open and I'm blown away by what was inside.

The room was lit by candles and lanterns. The wall was made of stone and half the room was carpeted while the other half was of wood. On one side of the room there were rows and rows of book cases with tables and chairs for studying. A cozy fire place in the corner. There were large cauldrons here and there, a chalk board against a wall with symbols and letters I couldn't read or recognize. And then on the far side of the room on the wooden flooring was a huge white pentagram that intimidated me. Each point had a corresponding candle half burned and melted. There were shelves of certain tools that I wasn't sure of and then in the middle of the room seated on the floor was Ms. River, crisscross apple sauce and looked to be meditating. I gingerly step inside and the door shuts rather harshly behind me. After taking another second to take in my surroundings, I approach the woman, but I was too afraid to bother her. But before I could muster up any courage to reach out and tap her shoulder or call her name, she's drawing in a deep breath and then she rises up to her feet.

"Have you ever meditated before?" she asks me suddenly.

I scratch behind my ear as I registered what she's said.

"If you consider sleeping in yoga class meditating, then yes," I answer.

The woman shakes her head and turns around to look at me. Her eyes were strikingly bright. They were glowing, just like that time I saw her at Whitechapel Library.

"Magic takes a lot of focus, Ethan. Controlling your thoughts, emotions, and energy is entirely important. Especially with your Soul Element. 'Grounding' is your word of the day today. Understand?" I nod my head slowly in response and subconsciously press my hands into my pockets. But just as I do the woman slaps at both my wrists and I'm pulling them back out again. "We want to wake your powers up again, but we ought to do it slowly and carefully," she continues and circles around me.

I'm standing at attention as if I were a soldier in the military. I can see the woman contemplating and planning. She stops in front of me after a third circle and looks me in the eye.

"Close your eyes," she tells me all of a sudden. With no questions asked I do as I'm told and shut them. "I want you to practice something," she says. "I want you to practice being aware of yourself. What do you feel? And not your emotions, but your being itself. Focus on your being."

She's quiet now and I suppose I'm trying to do as she asks, but I just couldn't put together what exactly she's looking for me to do. What did I feel? Maybe a little hungry.

307

"What do you feel?" she asks again. I think now she was looking for an answer.

"I guess the blood rushing to my fingers," I say half-heartedly.

"Is it blood?" she questions. "Or is it energy? Is it magic? Search for your magic."

"And what exactly does magic *feel* like?" I asked. I could feel my ears burning. It felt silly to ask such a thing but I supposed I needed to take things seriously.

"It's different for everyone," she admits. "Magic is energy. Magic is *you*." She looks away for a moment and I was sure she was about to give up on me, but instead she waves her hand and the wand that was gifted to me appears in its wrappings. "Take this," she says, but I give her an uneasy look.

"I dunno, River, what if I blow something up or…"

"You could lose a few toes and it would be fine," she tells me with a chuckle. "This room is meant to protect everyone in it for training and practice purposes. The entire room is charmed and enchanted, so don't worry. Now take it."

I take the wand from her and I stare down at it, turning it over in my hands. River is eyeing me for a moment before she turns her back to me and continues.

"Do you know what a wand is, Ethan?" I shrug as though she could see me but she responds as if she did. But then again…for all I knew she had eyes at the back of her head. "Don't think of it as the tool that does magic. A wand is not magic." She turns once more and she's smiling kindly at me. She moves over to my side and reaches over to touch the wand. "A wand is an extension of your arm. Think of it like a lightning rod, except instead of taking the lighting from the end into you it's taking lighting from within you, out through the end. Components on the wand can also influence the strength of the magic you do. That's why some witches may have more than one wand customized for different reasons such as healing magic or banishing."

"But, River," I interrupt as I try to absorb the information as much as possible, "I thought that the wand was meant for like…beginner witches or however you'd call it. Don't you begin to use your hands after a while?"

"Yes, that is true," she nods her head, "but there will always be a sort of magic that could use an extra bit of help. The wand is a great tool for that. Maybe you're doing a particularly powerful banishing spell. If you don't feel confident enough to focus the magic through your hands, a witch is more than welcome to pull out their corresponding wand to help them do the job."

"I see…" I respond and look back to the tool in my hand. River runs her finger along the coil of copper and silver wrapped around the handle of the wand and she offers an encouraging look.

"Everything added to your wand including the type of wood is all meant to assist you in controlling the strength of your magic."

"I have a question." I drop my hand and I plop down on the floor. With a good scratch of the back of the head I wait of her to acknowledge what I've said before asking, "so every witch has their own element. I guess I don't know if according to the element you have is the only type of magic you're able to do? Like, if you're water you can only do water things. If you're air only…air things? Then what does a spirit do? Ghost things?"

River laughs but actually I was pretty serious. She leans against a small nearby table and readjusts the way some of her necklaces lay.

"No," she says first. "Every witch can do any kind of magic. Practical magic, defensive magic, charming, banishing, enchanting; all of those things are universal to all witches. Your element, however, only determines what element you naturally resonate with, but it doesn't limit you from using other elements. Personal Elemental Magic is the magic you think of when you think of a witches S.E. But actually, if you study and practice enough, you could use other elements that is not your own in PEM. However, some are harder than others, especially depending on what your S.E. is. Spirit on the other hand is next to impossible to master or even become fluid in unless you're born under it." River stands up once more and it seemed her focus shifted to something entirely different. She waves her hand and one tall wooden figure comes wabbling out from a corner as if it had come alive. It stops and plants itself down a few feet away from where we stood and River turns again to face me. "Back to our focus of why we're here today," she says. "Let's get your magic flowing. As long as you trust yourself you shouldn't have any problems. I want you to focus on this target here and envision a bright green light striking it down. You might not knock it down on your first try, but that's okay. We just want to make anything happen. Go on and give it a go."

I press my lips together, ready to complain or dispute her. Tell her there was no way I could do anything of the sort. But every bit of that would simply be my pessimism talking. I shut my eyes for a moment and let out a quick breath as I remind myself of what she said earlier about feeling magic within myself. I still wasn't sure what that specifically felt like, but I wanted to try my best. As I push myself back to my feet, I gather my thoughts and my focus and I feel a strange tingling sensation at the tips of my fingers. A sensation that was somehow different than feeling your blood flow. I felt my eyes flicker poorly like an aged lightbulb before shifting to that unnatural green color. I picture a strong green light shooting from my wand and when I somehow self-induced myself in a strange hypnotic state, I've raised my wand at the target and give it a flick.

. . .

...nothing happened.

My shoulders drop at the anticlimactic result of my first attempt at magic and River rubs at her chin as if she had a beard there.

"Sorry," I mutter. "I tried." My eyes flicker back to normal and River only shakes her head at me.

"There's nothing to be sorry for. There actually might be one other thing stopping you, I just thought of it." I tilt my head at her and suddenly she's spinning to completely face me and she's snapped her fingers. A big purple colored rock appears in her hand and she's slapped it smack into my forehead, perhaps forgetting a rock is a rock. Before I could react properly with a good high-pitched manly yelp, there was an entirely blinding light, and buzzing that filled my ears all at once, to the point that I couldn't hear anything outside of it. My eyes have gone green once more and I feel something warm travel from the slight pain in my forehead throughout the rest of my body. River is mumbling something, I couldn't hear it, or see it, but I just knew. I sort of felt like

I was slipping out of my own body. Like I was too aware of *me*. Too aware of my soul. I want to shudder but I find I can't move. Not until River has pulled the rock away and I'm left gasping for a breath.

"What did you do to me?" I pant and rub my forehead. River doesn't answer right away. She seemed to be waiting for something. I narrow my eyes at her skeptically until I blinked. Upon closing my eyes for that millisecond, I flinch backward at an image of a younger version of myself screaming. Filled to the brim with rage. The eyes were black, the skin was riddled with unsightly purple veins, tears were running down my face as I hovered in the air with an intense amount of energy pouring out of me.

I shudder and look back at River who seems to be pleased by the sudden reaction.

"What did you do?" I ask her a second time. She smiles at me now and she pats me on the arm.

"No one can make you remember anything but yourself," she answers casually. "However, I figured you'd have an easier time if your crown wasn't blocked."

I rub the nape of my neck and take a step back from her. I couldn't grasp what she was saying as I was still a bit jarred by the image I had just seen.

"I don't understand," I say and shake my head. River frowns in response and steps up to me again. She reached up and jabs her thumb into my forehead.

"Energy flow is important, remember?" she says with a bit of frustration in her voice. "Our bodies have specific points that controls specific energies within ourselves. A little depressed or frustrated lately, Ethan? Other than the obvious reasons, the energy flow in your crown has been blocked. Now try again."

"What?" I tilt my head and slowly push her arm away.

"Try to hit the target again. Try again."

I swallow, unsure if I wanted to anymore. But I do as she says and turn again to face the block of wood. I settle my breathing, and shut my eyes for a moment, but flinch again at the jarring sight of such an emotionally distraught me… My eyes open and I suddenly feel fear, but I give the wand a wave. The tip of the tool makes a poor sputtering sound and I watch little flicks of light try to escape, but ultimately nothing really happens. Except River seemed over joyed by this as she's jumping up as far as her little old knees would allow, and she shoves me in the arm, causing me to go stumbling in the other direction.

"Did you see that?!" she exclaims brightly, clapping her hands together rapidly. "Ethan, you did it!"

"Did what?!" I huff and rub my arm. It seemed all these Obscurian women were extremely heavy handed.

"You used your magic! Although terribly weak—that won't last forever. You just proved that your magic is still functioning inside of you! Now all we must do is a little coaxing, and your magic could be as strong and even stronger than before!" She's grinning ear to ear and I look back down at the wand in my hand. Was that little sad sparkling that significant? I suppose it was. I did something. Although, not sure what exactly, but if sparkles count as using magic, then I'll take it.

"So, now what?" I ask her, feeling a bit more confident after her rejoicing.

"We practice some more. If we can get more out of you, perhaps it'll give your magic a good jumpstart. But don't worry," she spins around and conjures up a few other various targets, "we won't go for too long. We don't want to exhaust you. Let's try again."

For the next thirty minutes or so, River encouraged me to focus on what I would have considered impossible only a week ago. But the more she corrected the grip on my wand, the way I stood, and easing the rigidness in my body, the more I began to realize how natural it felt—how familiar it seemed. I continuously saw images of myself. I'm not sure why, and what exactly was happening, but it was all the same one. Young and surging with energy. Although I seemed angry, or sad, or scared. Or perhaps, all of them at once. A lot of times I couldn't make anything happen. But the more I tried, and the few times little sparkles came out of the tip of my wand, the more I began to feel light-headed and overwhelmed. My eyes had completely zoned out and gone green; perhaps it was from focusing too hard. The room became hazy and River seemed to no longer exist the deeper I fell into a meditative state. The image became clearer and more intense. Instead of just seeing myself, I could see the surrounding area. I could see trees all around. I could see the night sky. I could see Rose…

My body is heating and as I'm aiming at the next target like River has been directing me to do there was a surging electric sensation that coursed through the length of my arm. As it left through the tips of my fingers, a bright green light left the end of my wand, exploding vibrantly and traveling a few feet forward against the bust of a dummy that sent it rocketing backwards.

I could see Rose. Crying. Pleading for me to stop.

But I couldn't. It was much too late. The creature before me had been decimated.

"*Ethan!*"

Someone was calling for me but I couldn't quite make out who it was yet.

Rose was injured. I never saw it but I could feel that she was.

"Ethan! Focus back on me, dear."

I blink hard and turn my head to see River, but all I could see was the night sky, and the haunting sound of Rose's cry.

"What did I do?" I whisper out, wishing I could go to the young girl and help her. I saw my small feet turning, preparing to lay eyes on what had been done to her, but then everything goes black.

I feel hands on my face and River is shaking me back to reality.

"Ethan," she calls again, giving my face a few light slaps.

I blink a few more times, and catch the breath I hadn't realized was trying to escape me, and finally I zero back in on my true surroundings. River stared up at me, her bright blue eyes searching mine and somehow it seemed like she knew what I was seeing. I swallow dryly and bring my gaze downcast, staring at the floor beneath us.

"What happened then does not define you," she tells me quietly, pushing my bangs back from my face. "I can see it, that you want to remember…but did you see what you just did?" She smiles gently and gestures over at the target that was now clear across the other side of the room. She then presses her finger into the middle of my chest and her smile widens. "Your magic has been there this whole time. Isn't that wonderful? But that also means from now on you must be extremely careful. *Please*. We know that you don't want anyone to get hurt. We all know that. That day you did hurt Rose. And another… But

Rose never once blamed you. And she never will, because she knows you had no control over what happened."

I frown a little at her but she's now patting me on the back. I draw in a deep breath and let it out to steady my nerves. I will have to accept the information I am given little by little. Because at the end of the day, what happened in the past, is in the past.

"Was it bad?" I ask her. "What I did to Rose, I mean."

River gives an awkward look and averts her eyes.

"Somewhat," she answers honestly. "It was not life threatening, and she wouldn't have lost any limbs. So, it wasn't bad in that sense. However, it was a terribly large gash. She was losing quite a bit of blood. But it was not long between the injury and us getting to the both of you to stop it."

"Sorry," I mutter sheepishly.

"What are you apologizing to me for?"

I grimace and pull away from River, but I stand up straighter. I wouldn't let the thought bring me down. Although it sounds awful, I was forgiven and it was in the past. I reach out and pat River on the shoulder this time.

"Thank you," I say to her. "For everything."

She smiles sweetly and moves closer to wrap an arm around my waist to lead me out of the room.

"Let's get you a cookie. It'll replace the energy you lost."

. . .

"Welcome back, tall, skinny, and handsome," a cheery Victoria says from the floor of the den. She was sitting with Yulie on her shoulder, Autumn huddled to her left and Carson huddled to her right sending her a sharp look as she held a large bowl of colorful, ornate looking candy. Or were they small cookies?

"You're just in time, Ethan," Autumn smiles up to me as I draw closer to see what exactly they were doing. "Tori said that we could show Carson Morphies! Come join us."

I turn to give one last look at River and she gives an encouraging smile in return before moving off to the left toward the kitchen.

"What are Morphies?" I ask curiously as I find a seat in front of the three.

Victoria gives the glass bowl a few tosses and shakes to mix up the contents inside, and now that I could see them up close, they were individually wrapped chunks of taffy of all shades and colors.

"Carson, why don't you go first?" the brunette suggests and offers the bowl over to him. I watch him scratch his head and draw backward some with uncertainty.

"Why me?" he questions cautiously. "Will it do somethin' to me? Is it really spicy or what?"

Victoria shakes her head and then pushes the bowl toward me instead.

"You go then," she said. "Unless you're chicken…"

My eyes trail from hers, down to the bowl, and then over at Autumn who gave me a look that assured me that whatever happens it would be fine. So, with Carson shaking his head at me to not do it, I put my hand into the bowl and randomly pick a color. I unwrap the sticky taffy and tossed it into my mouth.

Everyone is eyeing me hard with expectation and curiosity, and I wasn't quite sure what exactly they should be expecting. It was easy to chew and tasted reminiscent of blueberry yogurt. But nothing happened.

I shrug my shoulders at them and I suppose Carson decided it must be safe because once I had he was plunging his fist into the bowl himself. The other two girls were still staring wide-eyed and expectant, and once I opened my mouth to tell them it tasted fine and I don't know what fuss there was about it, there's a strange tingling sensation across my tongue. I almost thought I was having an allergic reaction until I looked down at my hands that were turning shades of purple and blue. My nails started to grow long and sharp, and in the next second my vision had blurred until it cleared up in strange hues of gray and green.

"…I can't see?" I say, half-way between panicked and complacent.

"Oh my god, what have I done?"

I look over at Carson who seemed to have swallowed a round pink one already. He flipped his hands back and forth, watching for what he could possibly turn into.

"Am I gonna look like that? Is Ethan dying? I don't wanna die! And I certainly don't want to become ugly like him!"

"U-ugly?!" I stand up to my feet and move to find a nearby mirror to see myself properly. My eye color had changed to some shade of gold and my ears went pointy.

...But I certainly wasn't ugly!

I whip around to the girls who were now rolling on their backs in a fit of laughter. Victoria had dropped the bowl and was squeezing herself around the middle while Autumn hid her face behind her hands as she giggled along with her.

"I'm not ugly!" I protest. "But what the hell happened to me?"

"Oh—Oh no! It's happening! I'm changing!" Carson had rolled onto his hands and knees and he looked to almost be in tears as he braced himself dramatically for whatever would happen to him next.

His hair goes pink and his brow grows hair longer than his face. His nose grows outward and dips down like a broken door handle, and his ears fly outward like Dumbo.

"HA HA!" I bellow, belly laughing at his misfortune. "You're the ugly one!"

Carson scrambles to his feet and runs over to the mirror on the wall. Upon seeing himself his jaw drops and this time he really did look like he'd cry.

"What have I done?!" he wallows. "I can hear space! I can French braid my eyebrows!"

I'm still laughing, working up tears in my eyes as Carson whined and tugged at his new features.

"Is it forever?" he cries.

"It isn't forever," Autumn answers. "You should be back to normal in the next few minutes or so."

"What is the purpose of this horrible candy!? To grant you the ability to never step foot outside again?"

"Why don't you girls eat one?" I say after having collected myself and wiped a few escaped tears away.

"Oh no," Victoria shakes her head and sets the bowl up right and away from her, "I was just giving you boys the chance to try something new. A popular candy amongst the children here."

"I think you should, Victoria," I dare her. "It'd be nice to see you step out of your comfort zone. It surely can't be as bad as Pancake Ears over here." I blink a few times and tilt my head to the side. "I'm pretty sure I have night vision now."

"I can *literally* hear space," Carson adds.

"It would be nice to see you try one, Tori," Autumn speaks up. "I'll do it with you."

"No," Victoria protests, crossing her arms against the idea. "I don't play childish games."

"You just provide them?" Carson inquires and plops back onto the floor beside me.

Autumn reaches over and brings the bowl back toward the two girls and she picks out a yellow piece and offers the bowl to the brunette.

"Come on," Autumn encourages, "it'll be fun."

We watch her contemplate for a good minute before she rolls her eyes and reaches hastily for the bowl.

"Fine," she says sharply and picks out a green and orange colored taffy.

"At the same time," Autumn says after unwrapping the candy. "Ready?"

Victoria flips her hair behind her shoulder and finally after the count of three the two girls pop the taffy into their mouths, and after a short moment they began to morph and grow new features. I would have thought it were painful had I not tried it myself.

I was already seeing clearly again and the changes I had gone through began to fade away and disappear. Just as I had gone back to normal the two girls became different. Autumn had turned red along the length of her neck. She opened her mouth and a puff of fire the size of a soft ball came billowing out of her mouth.

"Woah!" Carson exclaimed as he leaned backwards away from the very real heat. "How come she got something cool while I look like a Hobbit reject!?" he whines.

"Because you are one," I sneer.

"Rude…"

Our eyes trail over to Victoria now who had grown quiet since eating the magic candy. She sat there with her expression indifferent. Her long brown hair was now a shade of lavender and it had somehow straightened and shortened to the middle of her neck. Her eyes were turquoise and around her mouth and jaw was a long purple beard. We all stared at her silently for a moment, taking in her new appearance. But I was the first to snort and stifle laughter before we all started to laugh together. Even Victoria cracked a smile, pretending to not find it funny by turning her head away.

"Shut up, the three of you," she said below her breath.

"Lighten up," I return and reach out to touch the newly grown hair. "I think it suits you."

"Do you, now? Are bearded ladies what you're into?"

"Sure." I shrug. "As long as her heart is as beautiful as the hair on her chin."

More giggles and laughter erupt from this, and the four of us spend another little while trying more of the taffies and seeing what we'd turn into. It was good fun, and for the first time I felt almost entirely content.

13

The Deal

Aunt Nari has already spent an extended amount of time showing me the art of knives. And with the longer we stood outside—the sun descending, the air increasingly frigid, the more I understood that my aunt had a very strong attachment to her weapons. And that she felt the need to have and know how to use them was imperative to living. She focused hard on my grip and my footing that was reminiscent of earlier this morning when River was directing me on the use of a wand.

"You want to stay low," she would say. "You may not always be aware of who's coming at you."

She demonstrates to me sets of attacks and defensives. I watch her spin this way and that, like an intricate ballroom dance. She swings an arm into the air, the other follows right after. She incorporates her legs, kicking high and swiping low. I'm amazed (and maybe a bit hesitant to exert enough energy to move like that). With another spin she seems to be gathering her strength, and in a second, she has darted forward with all the speed of a bullet. She swipes her arm hard at the trunk of a nearby tree, and in the next second it's gashed and wounded deeply.

She's breathing hard and she straightens up after her sharp and measured attack. She turns around and her yellowy eyes were glowing. She seemed like her mind had wondered off somewhere difficult and her arms drop to each side. After a moment of collecting herself, she closes the space between us and places her hand on my shoulder.

"You can do that too…" she said almost sheepishly.

"What? Me?" I laugh in disbelief. "Impossible."

"Perhaps not exactly like that…" she says instead and cracks a small smile. She nods over towards the way we came and she begins the short walk home. "But with the powers you have, Ethan, cutting halfway into a tree is nothing compared to what you could do if only you learn to control it."

"…Really?" A brow raises and I look over at my aunt whose eyes were on the ground, watching her own steps. Although the idea of being so powerful seemed farfetched, the more encouragement everyone around me gave, the more I felt could be possible.

After arriving again at the cottage, we were greeted by a warm smell of boiling vegetables in a savory broth. Before I could even think to go running toward the kitchen after realizing how hungry I was, Carson had come darting in my direction, gripping me around the wrists and yanking me in that direction.

"WHOA!" I exclaim louder than I would have liked.

He's giggling like a child, and as he brings me into the room that smelled like everything anyone could hope for in a home cooked meal, Victoria is hovering over the stove and she flicks her wrist almost backhandedly over her shoulder. A long wooden spoon begins to float up into the air and glides effortlessly over to me. Without a second thought I've opened my mouth and the spoon stops where I can taste what was being made. And yes. It was *delicious*.

The spoon returns back to Victoria once I had finished and I go over to her side to see what she had been making. River was at the other end of the kitchen with a smaller cauldron that she was boiling something spicy in. She was focused on dropping measured dried herbs inside while Autumn had come in with an empty tray.

"While you were outside, I was in here making some…whatever this is." Carson grins as he hops up onto the table. "You're lookin' at a newfound chef! Real successful in his new line of work!"

"You barely did anything but dump in pre-cut ingredients," Victoria grumbles as she adds a few more odds and ends to the pot. "And if you were half a chef, you'd know this is *my* prized braised beef and vegetable stew." She finally turns to meet my eye and she flashes a quick smile. "How did it taste, Ethan?" she questioned.

"It was great," I say without any hesitation. I was just ready to have my own bowl of it.

"*Excuse me*, but I *did* do some chopping too!" Carson whines.

"Yeah. A single carrot. Less than half of it. *And* you cut yourself!"

My eyes trail over to Carson and he's frowning as he raises his index finger to show it wrapped tight in a bandage.

After more bickering between the two, Victoria had finished cooking and she made everyone a bowl of buttery mashed potatoes with the stew ladled over it. Once each bowl had finished, Victoria did some sort of incantation to wear everything began to clean itself and River had been pouring mugs of the stuff she had been brewing.

"What is this?" Carson asks before I do as he handed us each a mug.

"My healing potion," she said simply. "It's good to have it on lazy days like this."

Carson and I shrugged at each other and both took a big swig of the hot liquid. It tasted heavily of cinnamon, rosemary and other things I couldn't quite pinpoint, sweetened by honey. Carson was flicking his tongue in and out after he had swallowed, probably not enjoying the bitter notes of the herbs that had been used.

We all ate. Not together but in our own spaces in various places of the house. The few seconds I had seen Autumn earlier didn't last long and she had disappeared again somewhere. Probably to study. Jem had sucked down three bowls in a short time. I had been told it was his favorite meal, which was interesting to know that he actually enjoyed something. But he remained in his little corner, screwing together fragmented pieces of metals and placing in pillars of quartz while he ate. River has also disappeared somewhere with Victoria and Carson and I remained in the den for the remainder of the evening. We were the last two to stay down there that night as we had spent most of the time digging around for sweats and telling each other made up stories to pass the time.

After going to bed at some weird hour of the night, I had found that I was having a hard time falling asleep. And I worried that something may go wrong. It was interesting to me however that I hadn't had any bad headaches or something of the sort in a quite a while. Of course, I was glad, but it made me wonder what had changed. Perhaps the environment made a difference…

I was staring up at the ceiling in my dark room and as sleep refused to come over me, I decided to try my hand at using my magic. I look down at the dark shadow of my hands, staring hard at the middle of my palm. Obviously, I didn't know what I was doing, but I just wanted to make anything happen. See that amazing sign of magic again. I focused all of my energy on the palm of my hand, and hoped for anything. Even just a spark.

It wasn't working.

I frown to myself and then try to remember what River tried to teach me. I relaxed my body and I tried again, focusing intently on the palm of my hand. I feel my eyes shift from brown to green. I feel the energy around my room heighten like electricity. Then there is a small spark of green light from the palm of my hand. It sparks once. Then twice. And then it cracks into a strong glowing bright light.

I've almost startled myself, but I am holding onto my focus, wondering what else I could do. I slowly raise my hand and push it outward to which the light bends and swirls in that direction.

"Whoa…" I whisper to myself. I twirl my fingers around and the light dances around them.

There's a bright flash before my eyes and I'm unclear of if it was something I was seeing or a product of what I was doing.

"*How pretty…*" a voice says.

I am startled and I close my fist, making the green glow disappear. I listen for a moment for more words, but when I hear no more, I try again. I focus and turn my hand outward and try hard to make something happen.

And oh boy did it ever.

There's a flash of green much brighter than before that begins to fill the whole room. Within the light there were figures and shapes dancing about. And the longer I watched them the more it began to form an image. I tried to look closely and it almost seemed like one of my visions. There was a slender woman that I could make out through the bright light. Hair long and her movements swift as she crossed the room. I watched eagerly, amazed by what I was seeing, and curious to understand the image playing out in front of me. She glides this way and that, like a 3D projection. I try to make out her face, but the longer I stared, the more the image began to skew.

I flick my wrist, hoping that would fix the problem. I wanted her to turn around—to look at me. But she dodged any proper line of sight. I quickly slip out of bed, feeling as though if I come closer to this particular figure, I could get a better understanding.

My bare feet cross the cold wooden floor. Other shapes spun around me through the green illumination emitting from my palm. A tiny butterfly flitting above my head. A small rabbit dashing around my feet. But the only thing I was focused on was the woman. The closer I came the more the light around me began to dim. I moved faster, hoping to catch her before she's gone. But the more she and every other light animation faded, the darker and colder the room began to feel.

I hear buzzing, and the green light of my palm begins sparking in an unsettling way. My eyes leave the fading figure of the woman and instead focus on the power I knew I was losing control of. The green sparks are shifting colors and the air around me has become frigid. So much so that I could see my own breath.

I was beginning to feel light headed and the temperature of my body dropped so suddenly I thought I would have collapsed. I close my fist, hoping that whatever I must have been doing by accident would stop, but to no avail. My fist is smoking a deep black smoke and from within is glowing that purple I've come to be wary of. I spin quickly on my heels to the nearest mirror, and there I could see my eyes have gone from green to black and purple.

"No, no, no…" I'm muttering to myself as I cross the room, again unsure of if I should go get some help or if I can get it to pass somehow.

Ethan…

Something is whispering to me this time. A voice I haven't heard since the first night I arrived in this place. Its low, sinister tone forced every hair to stand on end and I was more than ready to flee for my life.

Wake. Up.

...What? Wake up? I spin once again on my heels and I look around my room desperate to make sure this wasn't a nightmare. Then again, to wake up from *this* would probably be better. But I knew for certain I was not sleeping. *I was awake.* My eyes trail up to the ceiling, and through my purple tinted vision I could see those same terrible, slimy, black shadows slowly crawling around up there. The putrid smell reached my nose and I nearly gagged. I quickly move now toward the door. I needed to get out of there because whatever was happening now was completely out of my hands. I needed River.

As I'm making a beeline for the door, I reach my hand out and just before my fingers could even graze the knob, I'm suddenly unable to move. I blink my eyes, confused at what's stopping me. But after a quick scan of myself, I see absolutely nothing.

Pitiful. You are WEAK.

I jump within myself, fear taking complete hold of me. I want to open my mouth and scream out, but in the next second I find myself being hurled up and back into the air. I was being thrown clear across my room, and as I was bracing to slam into the wall, I was jolted to a complete stop midair.

My eyes were squeezed shut in preparation for the pain that never came. But as I realized I was no longer moving I peeked my eyes open, hoping whatever this was had come to an end. But the moment my vision cleared I was met with a monstrous black figure just inches away from my face. I couldn't make out any features other than its piercing golden eyes that were illuminated like gems reflecting moonlight. I was petrified. Frightened to think that this could be the end of poor Ethan Moon.

It inches closer, its body radiating a freezing temperature. It stares at me, but it says nothing. It makes no noise. Something that resembled an arm raises, reaches up and captures me by the head. It's slimy icy fingers pressing uncomfortably into my temples. Before I could react with a warranted yelp, my vision blanks entirely and I feel my entire body go lax.

• • •

"...*My love...*" a man's mild tempered voice begins. "...*won't you look at me?*"

There's soft sniffling in the distance, but no response.

"*I had no other choice,*" he continued. "*I'm sorry that it turned out this way. But HE told me if I didn't make a proper decision, I should prepare to lose all that I love. And, well...since the only thing I truly love is you...*" He trails off and everything is silent for a moment or two. Then there is the voice of a woman, sad and distressed. Her voice I was coming to know and recognize well.

"*There is no justifying needless violence, you...you terrible fool.*" I could feel that those words were sharp and wounded him; whoever he was. She clearly knew it too by the way her breath shook and she stammered before continuing. "*I'm sorry,*" she says, "*but I cannot continue to stand by your side knowing that you will do the same thing over and over. You have lost your way...and I don't think I can help you.*"

"*But,*" the man began quickly, "*don't you still love me? As I do you?*"

"*Of course, I do...*" she affirms. "*I love you, and I always will. But perhaps that is the problem...I love the you who did right by himself and others. The you that focused on good. ...The you that wanted a life with me. But I don't recognize that man anymore.*"

He was becoming angry. Or it was the way his grief portrayed itself. I could feel it. It was horribly overwhelming, allowing his negative emotion to boil up, pressurize, and then explode in a manner least helpful to his situation.

"*I am that man!*" he shouts. "*I only do what has to be done! To protect you! To bring equity to the people born impure! Can't you see that? Why is it so hard for you to understand? If it weren't for HIM, I would never know what I need to do to fix things!*"

"*...Maybe you don't understand HIM the way you think you do...*"

There's silence. Like he didn't know how to digest what she said. I wait for a response, but it never comes. I am simply left with silent darkness.

A few moments later—at least what I felt was a few moments—my eyes are flying open, and I'm gasping for air in the middle of the floor of my room. I look around just to make sure that was where I was and then slowly after checking if I had all of my limbs, I sit up. It was morning now, somehow, which made me wonder if all that happened had been a dream. I look up to make sure those awful shadows are gone and then I rise up to my feet, realizing that my entire body was sore. I had no idea what happened to me last night, but I was glad, at least, that I didn't die. And with that in mind, I needed to go see my friends.

I cross the room and stumble through the door and into the hallway. I was a little more disoriented than I previously thought. In the next second, I'm running chest first into something small and boney, but it was still enough to knock me over.

"Ow," I whine and rub my bum. But it was when I opened my eyes and focused my vision that I saw what I had run into. And by "what" I mean "who". And by "who" I mean Autumn toppled over onto the floor with one fuzzy pink slipper on and the other across the hall somehow.

"Gosh, Ethan!" she cries out and rolls over onto her side. She fixes her crooked glasses and pouts at me.

"Sorry," I say sheepishly and scramble to my feet to help her up. "Really sorry. I was a little dizzy getting up this morning." I pull her up and awkwardly straighten her sweater to which she fanned my hands away so she could do it herself. Eventually her avoidant eye met mine, and her tired, slightly frazzled expression jolts into shock or surprise. I tilt my head in response and take a small step back. "What's the matter?" I ask skeptically.

"Ethan…" she starts, "did you go dipping into the Morphies bowl?"

My brow raises at this and as I shake my head no, I turn around to find the nearest mirror. She follows after me to the bathroom where the door was in mid swing and a sleepy Carson was almost trampled as I pushed passed him.

"What the—" he began and spun around; fingers stuck in his messy, honey-colored locks. "If you had to potty that bad, you could've knocked," he grumbled. "Good morning, Autumn." He blinked a few times as he watched me press my face into the mirror and Autumn joining me by my side until he got a clue that something wasn't quite right. He rubs his eyes and then he fully enters the bathroom to join us.

I scanned myself. And upon first glance my reflection seemed normal. But the longer I looked, I realized that the color of my eyes were entirely out of the ordinary. The pupil was split, half purple, half green with flecks of golds and silvers. They weren't glowing at all, just stuck. As if the two halves of my magic clashed somehow.

"Are you doing that on purpose," Autumn asks me as I am now blinking my eyes hard, hoping that it would make it go away.

"No," I tell her and now rub furiously at them.

"Whooooaaa." Carson finally got the sleep out of his eyes enough to see properly. "What happened to you?"

"Ethan, this isn't normal…"

"What do I do?" I feel like panicking, but Autumn gives me a reassuring look and places her hand gently on my back,

"I'm sure it will be okay. But I think we should be careful about your magic should you try using it again. …U-uhm, by we, I mean *you*."

I blink stupidly at her and then I look over at my friend who only shrugs his shoulders. It definitely wasn't like he could do anything about it. I sigh a little and we all head out of the bathroom. Autumn heads off the opposite direction to maybe sleep? Or study. And Carson and I start our way down the stairs to see if the others were up yet.

"Did something happen?" Carson asks quietly to me. I hesitate at first to answer. Especially because I honestly didn't know *what* had happened that night which was most likely the cause for the appearance change.

"I was just messing around with my powers…" I whisper back. "I did something really cool. I saw my mom."

"You *saw* your mom? But she's—"

"I know," I frown, "but I saw her. I don't know how, but I did something. I just couldn't see her face. But then I think I lost control." Carson eyes me carefully as we cross the empty den. Even Jem wasn't sitting in his normal spot for some reason.

"And then…" he says.

"And then everything went dark and cold…and this thing came out of nowhere and grabbed me."

"Grabbed you!?"

"Shhh!" I didn't want anyone else to hear just yet because I didn't want anyone to freak out. But it was too late as we had approached the kitchen and three women were sitting around a table. They had all turned their heads to see us.

"Grabbed you?" River repeats and eyes us both skeptically. "Who grabbed you?"

"W-what?" I stammer and push Carson forward so he'd step inside first ahead of me. "No one grabbed me. We were just talking about uh…a video-game…?"

I see Victoria who is sitting beside River raise an angular brow. And although she looked like she wanted to question it, neither of them did. Sitting at the front of the table with her back toward us, hair tied in a huge curly knot was Rose. Bright and early as usual. She shifts in her seat and finally turns to put her lavender eyes on us. She offered a small smile and then nodded her head over to the stove where there was a pan of warm pastries and glasses of flavored milk. Carson moves first, of course, and has crossed the kitchen in less than zero seconds to inhale everything. But I had only taken a step before I hear my name called urgently.

"Ethan!" Victoria nearly shouts. "What's happened to your eyes?"

Everyone turns again to face me, and as each of them were taking a closer look at my face, River has risen to her feet and made her way up to me.

"What have you done," she questions and grabs me by the chin, turning my face this way and that.

"I—I don't know!" I squeeze my eyes shut again, hoping that this time it would make a change, but I know that it hasn't. River's expression looks stern. So much so that I could see my grandmother in her. It made me feel small and child-like. I was ready to be reprimanded and sent to my room.

"I have never seen anything like this…" the old woman mutters. More so to herself than to anyone of us.

The other two girls had gotten up from their chairs and had joined the woman by her side to also get a closer look. Victoria looked like she was truly studying something new while Rose only wore a worried expression and chewed at her bottom lip.

"It's got to be a sort of overload. Right?" Victoria asks as she puts her face a little too close to mine.

"It could be…" the older woman responds slowly. She finally turns away, puts on her beaded glasses and conjures up a huge ancient looking book. "It'd best to not try to use any magic until that goes away, Ethan. There's no telling what that could mean exactly, and we don't want to take any chances. If someone gets hurt because of uncontrolled magic, oddity hunters will be on you faster than you can whip a wand. Rose?" She turns momentarily to look at the girl. "Where will you take them?"

"Just through Willow Way. I thought it's be good to keep them close to home," she answers.

River nods her head and goes back to sit down.

"Don't be long. If you can't get this under control by the end of the day you won't be going to that ball, Ethan."

I frown a little at this. Although I didn't even want to go in the first place, it just made me feel as though I had done something wrong.

"Right," Rose grabs her cloak from the chair she had been sitting in and pulled it over her shoulders, "let's get going. You two are never ready when I get here."

Carson shoots her a look over the edge of a big glass up against his face.

"If you didn't come so early," he gripes after swallowing a gulp of milk. "Or gave an exact time—"

"It's good to be out early, Carson," she replies, "especially when you're terribly busy like me, you learn to appreciate your free time." She adjusts her collar, glances at me, and then exits the kitchen.

Carson and I look at each other, but after a while we both have gone to prepare for going out. Not long after, the both of us are meeting Rose by the doorway and immediately she steps outside with the both of us following close behind her. It's exceptionally cold out today, and I was glad to have dressed warm. No one said anything for a while until we nearly arrived.

"So, I was thinking, maybe we could match," Rose says casually without looking at either one of us. I tilt my head a little, unsure of exactly what she meant, but then she continues. "I've already got a gown. It's quite beautiful. It's silver. So, perhaps we find you a similar suit. I've got some masks already, so there's no need to worry about that."

"Wait," Carson pipes in while stifling a laugh. "You mean you and Ethan match? Like a *date*?"

"Well yeah..." Rose responds to my surprise. I raise an eyebrow after having been glaring at the blonde beside me, and Rose shrugs. "I mean, everyone should have a partner. Of course, there are the odd ones out, but the elite especially are expected to...have a partner." She looks over her shoulder at me and then looks away faster than I could read her expression.

"But is it really a good idea to have *me* as a partner? Won't the people who basically ruined my life be there? Wonder who you're with? Won't they notice?" I stare hard at the back of her head but she never turns again to see me. She pulls her cloak tighter around her as a particularly frigid gust of wind blows by, and she kicks her feet with each step. Her muddied brown boots picking up the dust of the pathway.

"We can just avoid my aunt. ...And probably my cousins too. We'll have our faces covered anyway, so let's not worry about it too much."

"But let's say if we do," I press. "Let's say we run into them. Then what?"

"I'll think of something," she says. "There's been talk about you circling through Lamia, already, Ethan. I know my aunt already knows about you being here. But there is absolutely nothing anyone can do to you or me at the ball. Too many people. And she certainly wouldn't act so rash over it at first glance." She turns finally. She stops walking and looks me in the eyes. "I skipped the ball three years in a row already. My father stopped going with me after an incident with some townsfolk. The ball is good fun, but I just can't enjoy it knowing that the people that I love aren't there. When we were kids, it was so magical. I think you will remember if you just go and enjoy yourself..."

I watch her carefully. Although I felt like I didn't know what I was getting myself into, it also seemed like it would be important to experience something that I once enjoyed again. If I truly wanted my memory to come back that it. Rose and I stare at each other for a moment, and then I simply nod my head back on her direction. Okay. I'll just go with it.

"So, what about me?" Carson says finally as we turn into the small shopping town.

"What do you mean?" Rose asks and leads us to the nearest clothing store '*Emerett's Fabrics*'.

"I mean, if you two are supposed to be each other's dates, what about me? I'm just supposed to go it alone?"

"You have before," I offer.

"You're right. I have. *And* I'm good at it! But it'd be great if ol' Carson could meet a beautiful vampire princess!"

Rose and I stare over at Carson silently just as we had all entered the store. He stares at us both as well and then it seemed like finally understanding hit him.

"Ooh..." he said after his jaw dropped slightly. "I meant...uh, that's not what I—"

We shake our heads, and Rose and I walk off in different directions to browse the shop. There were endless racks of fine fabrics and accessories. There were capes and gowns of all shades and there were holsters for knives, wands, and vials. There were hats, and shoes, suits, and many other things in the old antique looking store.

My eye was caught by shiny jewelry that floated in midair in a corner of the room, attached to nothing and circling gently around each other as if it were on a carousel. I examined each piece. Some were golden chains with various stones in them, others were silver or copper.

"*Psst.*"

I turn around to catch Rose gesturing at me through rows of clothing. I cross the room to her and she's holding on to a bundle of black clothing that she has already found.

"You should try this on," she says quietly while visibly trying to hold back any excitement. She shoves it into my arms before I could protest and she pushes me toward a dark curtained corner. "I'll go find other options. If you need some help, just call and I'll send Carson." I whirl around, trying to warn her not to go overboard, but she had already flashed a smile and disappeared before I could even inhale. With a sigh, I go to change my clothes, and I find myself struggling through confusing bits and pieces of some sort of maestro ensemble. After a while of fumbling around with each separate piece I was finally dressed up in a very stuffy suit with a collar that was stiff as a board and held up my head like a neck brace. It didn't take long before Rose came back and was poking at the curtain to get my attention.

"Are you finished in there?" I hear her say. "Come out and let me see!"

I poke my head through the curtains first and I find her standing there with more garments in her arms. She eyeballs me back and then gestures for me to hurry up and come out. I sigh, feeling utterly embarrassed to show her the outfit that wrapped around my body *way* too tightly with purple accenting here and white swirled embroidery there. It was hideous. Rose does a once over as I had stepped out and held my arms up so she could get a good look. I hear her snort and she's swallowing an involuntary laugh.

"C-...can you breathe?" she teases and covers her mouth with the tips of her fingers.

"Don't laugh." I grumble and drop my arms.

"I'm not..." She paused but soon followed amused giggles. I sighed and turned around to go back into the changing room. "Wait!" Rose called through her laughter. "I'm sorry. Here. You might like one of these better."

I look at her again and take the clothing she gave me.

"I'd better. Or I'm not going," I say.

"Oh, stop it. We'll find something. We...we won't let you go looking like a dressed-up tooth pick." She bursts into more laughter and I scowl at her before disappearing again behind the curtain.

I tried on a few more. One of them looked like a whole magician's get-up. Another I could have sworn was a rip-off Dr. Strange costume. (Carson would've liked that one.) I felt like I was putting on and taking off so many layers of clothing I was going to get a baby rash.

Uhm, no I didn't admit that I have baby skin...

Finally, I put on something that looked halfway decent. Actually, I rather liked it. A black dress shirt and a black waistcoat with silver floral designs all over. There was a silver chain from the front silver button to the side pocket. The suit jacket was high-low and the black pants were crisp. There was a matching silver tie that I thought tied everything together very nicely. Was... was I in love?

"Ethan, how is it?" I hear Rose call as I'm straightening up the tie. I step out to let her see and she gasps a little. "Wow..." she began and slowly circled around me to see the back as well. "It looks perfect on you. How do you like it?"

"It's great." I smile.

"So, does that mean you're a bit more willing to go now?" she asks hopefully.

"Not in the slightest," I answer. She pouts a little in response and takes a small wounded step back. But I reach out and place a hand on her shoulder. "But I will go, Rose," I assure her. "I promise not to complain….too *much*." She smiles a bit at this and then nods her head.

"Get changed. You could go purchase your garments while I go back and help Carson."

"Oh, did he find something to wear?" I ask her.

"Uhm…sort of." She gives a complicated look but then reaches inside of her cloak and pulls out a small brown sack. "Take this, there's more than enough to buy yours with." She plops it into my hand and then leaves before I could say anything else. I shrug and return to the changing "corner" and put back on my clothes. I fold them up neatly and wander through the store to find the counter.

All the way in the back of the store was an old dusty wooden counter. There was an older woman with beads all over her hair and long draping purple clothing made from wool. Her back was to me and she was hunched over something behind the counter. I quietly set my things down onto the counter and after awkwardly staring at her and hoping she would just magically become aware of my presence I lightly clear my throat and she jumps, throwing something into the air.

"Oh!" she exclaims and spins around, beads clacking together. "Oh, my goodness. You certainly scared me, my boy." She presses her hand against her chest and heaves out to gather herself.

"I'm sorry…" I tell her. "I'd just like to buy these, please."

"Of course. Yes, of course. Let me just find something nice to put it in. Oh!" She picks up the pieces and grins widely. "My, doesn't this look darling. You're a handsome boy as well, I'm sure this would suit you perfectly."

Yes, I was blushing. Yes, I was trying to force away a smile. I tell her thank you and she throws out her arm behind her, almost nonchalantly while she refolded the clothes. A brown paper bag with the store's logo stamped on it rises in the air and so did some white and gray tissue paper. The paper unfolds itself and tucks itself away into the bag before coming into reach of the woman where she grabbed it and began packing away my items.

"That'll be 500 runes," she says.

"Uhh…" I look down at the little pouch Rose gave me and I open it, hoping that whatever was inside would make quick sense to me. There was nothing but large silver coins and smaller copper ones shaped like triangles. I scratched my head and the woman watched me expectantly after she had finished packing away my things.

"Are you alright, son? A little short?" she asks.

I shake my head and finally I just dump the contents of the pouch onto the counter. A little surprised, the woman tilts her head but picks through the coins.

"You must be from another district," she concludes. "Artemis? Or Lamia?"

I blink rapidly, feeling a bit embarrassed.

"N-no, I'm not from there," I tell her defensively.

"Oh, so Sierra then, that'll explain the eyes…" She points to both of her eyes and I'm reminded of their malfunction. "But they use all of the currencies there…you must not have ever had to go out and buy something." She shrugs and I frown. She takes all the money that she needs and pushes the rest toward me to put back into my pouch. "Well, you have a good day. Enjoy your stay in Greenwood." She smiles and waves a bit before turning around to go back to whatever she had been doing before. My shoulders drop in defeat as I take my bag to go and find my friends again. It just didn't feel good to be seen as a clear stranger in the place you're supposedly from. I sigh and make my way back, weaving through the many shelves and racks of the place. I could faintly hear Carson whining in the distance and Rose bickering at him in return. I couldn't wait to see what Rose put him in. I round a corner, bag in hand, and I can just see tufts of strawberry blonde peaking from the top of a large case. I'm headed in that direction until I feel my arm snag and my entire body is yanked backward, back around the corner I just came from. My back hits the wall and I drop my bag. I felt my heart race, hoping that when I opened my eyes, I wasn't faced with what I had seen last night, or one of those Oddity Hunters River warns about. I hear someone clear their throat and after peaking an eye open I am greeted by fiery amber orbs, similar to Jem's and a familiar wicked smile.

My eyes are wide open now and I open my mouth, ready to call out for Rose or anyone after realizing the tall man in front of me with salt and pepper hair and maroon colored trench coat was Julian Hickman from that night at the Halloween party in Whitechapel. He claps his hand over my mouth and shushes me with a finger before I could make any sound or protest.

"Relaaaxx," he coos. "I'm gonna remove my hand, and you won't make any unnecessary scenes, alright?" His brow rases expectantly and he slowly begins to move his hand away as I try to relax. "I just have a proposition for you. No harm, no foul. I'm *not* gonna hurt'cha."

I scowl at him, shrinking farther back into the wall as I watched him untrusting.

"What makes you think I want anything to do with you?" I whisper back, matching his lowered voice.

"I don't," he replies with a smirk and a shrug. "No one does. But maybe we can see eye to eye on something."

"Eye to eye? I don't want to help you. As I recall you tried to kill me not too long ago."

"What? Kill you?" he laughs and stands up straight. "I wasn't going to *kill* you, Ethan... Maybe wound you a bit, but not *kill* you."

I stare at him blankly but my lips were curled upward. His energy was a bit much for me. Something about him felt dark, almost soulless. It was very upsetting. I didn't notice that I was beginning to read his aura, my eyes are glowing (although still mix-matched colors) as I saw the weak energy around him wobble around and then spike outward here and there. The color was very dull and very gray. But there was something else...or *someone* else. I could almost make out a faint shadow of someone just beside him, and it—

He bangs on the wall beside my head with his fist and I jump in response as his gaze was more intense.

"*Stop that*," he warned aggressively. "Now, listen to what I have to say, because you may find it interesting." I watch him cautiously as he releases whatever sudden anger that was and he replaces the stern look he wore with another extremely fabricated and very creepy smile. "Now, you and I both know that there is a ridiculous amount over your clueless little head. People aren't looking for you now, but they will be soon. *I* serve as everybody's hitman, tip-man, or whatever have you. I know *everything* there is to know about *everyone* and I'll do anything for something worthwhile in return. Princess Annika of Lamia will be out for you the moment she see's you for herself. For now, you're just 'rumours'. She doesn't want to believe them. I could tip off any hunter that could be looking for you. That Ernest would be a very likely candidate." His smile twists into something more sinister and I'm unsure what to make of it exactly. He adjusts the collar of his dark blue shirt and stretches his neck before continuing. "I think you should help me with something. Now it's up to you whether you do or you don't, but if you *don't*, I just might decide to tip your whereabouts off for a profit. Or, hand you in myself. And if I do it myself, trust me it won't be gentle. I don't want to hurt you, Ethan. I know you have enough troubles of your own. Such as…Catherine refusing to return. Probably because if she's found out she'll be arrested. Or likely executed. *Or*, your lack of memories. I just might know a way to kick start that brain of yours…only if you're interested. And perhaps you may be stressed over the lack of knowledge of *who* or…*what* your father is. And what that means for you. And by the looks of it, you're already having issue with how ridiculous you look right now," he smirks. "I know it. I know it all. Ethan. All I want is a little help. Just a little help to find someone I lost."

"Who?" I question and eye him for any clue that he was lying. He straightens up again and I watch him swallow thickly. The crazy smile he wore melted away and the expression he wore now was so stone cold serious it sent a frigid shiver up my spine.

"My daughter," he replied in a deeper tone. "My Layla. I *need* to find her. To get her back. And you're the only one who has the ability to help me."

"But I don't know how to use magic," I tell him. "I can't see how I would be any help to you."

"Oh, you will be. If you agree to help me, I can get your memory back. At least enough to where you can remember your abilities. How to use them, and how to control them. Trust me."

I scoff at that. 'Trust me'. I look down and move to pick up the bag I had dropped from being surprised earlier.

"How do I know I can trust you? How do I know you won't just turn me in for that 'profit'?"

The man smirks and his amber eyes seem to glow brighter.

"Ethan?" I can hear Rose calling me from a ways away. She was looking for me.

"Turning you in will do me no good. I need you. I need to find my Layla. We can help each other, Ethan."

"Ethan!?" Rose calls again but she hasn't quite found me yet. Julian holds out his hand and he watches me expectantly.

"All you need to do is trust me," he reiterates.

I stare down at his hand, mulling over whether I should or shouldn't. Would it be worth my while? Will he really help me like he promised should I help him find his daughter? Finding a lost child seemed innocent enough. And Julian seemed as though he wasn't loyal to anyone but himself. Meaning that his ultimate goal was probably to get what he wanted. Perhaps he was less likely to break my trust if I carried out what he needed me to do in order to find his daughter. I stare at the hand, and I hear Rose's calls nearing after every moment. Then finally, I tentatively take his hand, and there was a burst of flames engulfing them both. It wasn't hot. Actually, it was quite cold. But as bright as any fire.

"Do something for me at the ball tomorrow," he whispers quickly into my ear as his hand firmly gripped around mine. "Watch for me."

"Ethan!" I jump and spin around to where Rose's urgent call came from. "I was looking for you everywhere! What were you doing? Did you purchase the clothes?"

"I—we—" I look behind me to see that the man was gone, as if he had never been there in the first place.

"What is it?" Rose asks and shakes my arm a little. "Did you see something?"

I blink a few times to process what just happened but then I shake my head.

"N-no…I just—I got distracted. It's nothing," I lie.

"Well come on then, Carson and I bought his things. Let's get back to the cottage."

She walks away and I follow after her listlessly out of the store. Carson was standing outside, foot kicked up against the building and chewing a little at his thumb nail. He didn't do that very often. In fact, he didn't usual bite his nails unless he was anxious. Which was uncommon for him.

"Are you good?" I ask him, squinting through the morning sun light.

"Hm?" he responded, taking a full minute to meet my gaze. He was thinking, which strangely wasn't a good sign. Something had to be wrong. "Oh, yeah," he answers finally. "I just—well, it's just this place catching up with me, I guess." He sighs a bit but puts on a small smile, drops his hands and kicks himself upright from the wall. "It's nothin'," he adds.

I hum a little in response and then I turn to look at Rose. I pulled out the money pouch she gave to me earlier and go to hand it to her.

"Here," I tell her to get her attention. She turns to see what I was handing her but then she shook her head and refused it.

"It's yours," she said matter-of-factly. When I gave her a puzzled look she continued. "River asked me to stop by the bank for you before coming today. I can show you how to get your money on your own later. But I withdrew that for you this morning."

"All of this is mine?" I ask and open the pouch to look at the money I didn't understand. "…however much this is," I mumble.

She nods her head in return and turns forward again as she leads us through the small shopping center.

"Obviously your mother left you with all she had," she told me. "It wasn't much…but certainly enough for you to get on." I took this information and saved it, understanding that my mother had a life here and I was well a part of it. Although I still couldn't remember her much, I felt thankful to her. "I suppose we ought to get you boys back home."

14

The Masquerade Ball

Nothing much happened for the remainder of the day. Although, Rose spent hours trying to crash course Carson on proper ball etiquette which I think he only listened to half of it while the other half he attempted an escape. I thought I'd go to the study to find some history books on my spirit element. I'd pass the time by replacing the knowledge I once had. As I entered that hole in the wall into the unbelievably massive room, I noticed Autumn tucked away in a corner at a desk, books piled high on both sides of her as she had her nose buried in one opened in front of her. I tilted my head curiously and approached her.

"Hey," I greet gently. But no matter how gentle I was the poor girl nearly jumped out of her skin, toppling over the stack of books to her right.

"GACK!" she hollers at both herself being startled and then the loud crashing of the heavy books. "Ethan! Goodness! How could you sneak up on me that way?!"

"W-what?" I laugh a little and shake my head as I go to pick up her books. "I did no such thing," I tell her. "What are you doing up here by yourself anyway?"

"Why, studying, of course," she says as she slides out of her chair and to the floor to help gather each book and bring them back to their place atop the desk.

"It seems like you're always doing that…" I point out. "What do you do for fun?"

"Hm? Fun?" Her eyes went wide and round like two big circles and she seemed almost at a loss for words. We both stand up and she sits back down into her chair. "Study...I guess." She shrugs. "I mean, I do quite enjoy studying, however it does become rather difficult at times," she admits. "Oh, but I do enjoy visiting my village when I have time. When I visit home, I like carving and decorating flutes with my siblings."

"Oh, you have siblings?" I ask, genuinely curious.

"Yes. I have an older brother, and two younger sisters. We're all incredibly close."

"That's nice. I always wanted an older brother. Someone to give me advice or beat up the bullies, you know?"

Autumn smiles at me for a moment, but then she shrinks back into herself, I suppose remembering her shyness again. After another moment of awkward silence, she asks:

"So, what did you come here for? To practice magic?"

"No, actually," I answer. "I was looking for a certain history book. Maybe you could help me find it."

"Oh." She stands up again and agrees to help. I explain to her that I was searching for the books on my S.E. and perhaps something on the Elemental War I believe Rose called it. As if it were automatic, Autumn spins around and heads straight to a particular shelf across the room and picks out three (very large) text books on the matter I mentioned. I had taken them and she returned to her studying, explaining that it was important she prepared for an upcoming exam to test her knowledge and skill on wandless magic. Which I do recall she was struggling with. But I leave her to it and go find a corner to settle down in and I read...For hours.

"Ethan! Are you in here?"

I'm startled as I open my eyes, almost unsure of where I was. I'd fallen asleep, and I notice a thick knitted blanket draped over me. I look around for Autumn, but she had gone. I pull it off and see Rose and Carson coming over. Carson's head was on a swivel as he followed behind Rose, in awe of the new room he entered.

"Hey," Rose says as she caught sight of me as I rose to my feet. "We were looking for you everywhere. We happened to run into Autumn before she went off to bed and she said you were here."

"Why didn't she just wake me?" I rub my eye, feeling a bit crabby after sleeping sitting up on the floor.

"Dunno," Rose answered with a shrug. "Maybe she didn't want to startle you." She smirks a little and motions for me to follow her. "We ought to get to bed anyway. We have a big day ahead of us! I think Carson's finally got the basics under his belt as well."

"Yeah," he huffs as we now followed her out of the study and down the hall, "after I almost broke an ankle trying to keep up with her circle dances. *AND* after hours of being forced to memorize *every possible* answer to any question or interaction I might have so I don't raise any alarms."

"Good," I say simply to hide my amusement. "Then your mouth won't get you into any trouble."

Carson rolls his eyes in return as we follow Rose out of the room and into the hall. At this point we said our goodnights and went to our respective areas. Rose had a spare bedroom all to herself just like Carson which was quite nice.

I go to bed, and thankfully morning came without any surprises. I was happy to be able to sleep in. Breakfast and lunch was quiet and River had gone to Lamia the evening before; Victoria had gone off to Julieth's Quarter for something, Jem disappeared apparently, and Autumn was living in her text books. Things didn't become chaotic until early evening rolled around and Rose was running back and forth like a mad man.

"CARSON!" she screams into the cracked door of the bathroom, steam billowing out, "YOU'VE BEEN IN THE BATHROOM FOR NEARLY AN HOUR!!"

"BEAUTY TAKE'S TIME, ROSE!" he retorts over the sound of the shower. "YOU'LL HAVE TO COME IN YOURSELF IF YOU WANT ME TO GET OUT ANY FASTER!"

I was sure he was just teasing as always. But Rose was rolling up her sleeves and raking her fingers through her loose hair and tying it behind her with her huge black scrunchie. I watch her storm into the bathroom, a toothbrush in my hand. The door slams behind her and in a second I hear a loud high-pitched scream, some wrestling, water splashing, floor squeaking, and things tumbling in there. Then in no time the door swings open again, Rose has Carson by the ear and she's yanking him out of the bathroom. He was clutching onto a single towel as best as he could while he was bent over to the side to accommodate Rose's height as she tossed him in the direction of his bedroom.

"Ow ow ow ow ow ow ow!" Carson was whining until she released him and he went stumbling to the door.

"Now *hurry up!* Else we'll be late!" Rose growls menacingly, causing Carson to run into his room and do as she asks. Her head whips around now as she faces me, her eyes glowing purple, her fangs bared and threatening pain. My own eyes widen and I scurry into the bathroom to finish washing up before she has to tell me to. Unlike Carson, I was done in no time, having finished brushing my teeth and showering in record time. Too scared to find out what would happen if I didn't. I surely didn't want her walking in on me like she did Carson. I left the bathroom for my room but as I was hurrying past Carson's I noticed his door cracked open, and quiet bickering coming from inside.

"*Stop it! It's not meant to be worn that way!*" I hear Rose hiss along with a ton of fumbling.

"But it'd be cooler if I wear it like this!" Carson whines in return. I hear a yelp, some slapping sounds, and I could only imagine Rose beating him down to get him into his clothes properly. Haha, sounds just like his mother.

I continue to my room and I hurry to wear my clothes. I was glad that when I jumped from hearing the door open, I was already fully clothed and fumbling with my hair in the mirror. Rose steps in and gently closes the door behind her. She looks over at me with an awkward expression and approaches me.

"Are you okay?" I ask her. She nods in response and offers a small smile.

"That friend of yours is terribly difficult to wrangle," she admits.

"Yeah, that's for sure," I chuckle. I watch her stop in front of me, pull a comb from her pocket and reach up to work it through the mess on my head. "Just needs a firm hand is all…"

"I learn quickly. I'm only glad I can trust you to do what you're supposed to."

"Sure. Why are you so stressed out, by the way?" I ask as I let her fix my hair for me.

"Tonight isn't that serious, is it?"

She's silent for a moment as I assume she's contemplating her answer. She then shakes her head and lets out a deep sigh.

"It's not like that," she says. "I mean, it isn't serious. But I guess I simply want everything to go right. It's your first time in eight years that you'll attend the ball. Although under different conditions, but it's more or less the same. And then of course we must be certain that Carson doesn't reveal the fact that he isn't Obscurian to all of Lamia. That would certainly complicate things, wouldn't it?"

"…It would…" I agree quietly.

"I think he will be alright," she says. "I would force him to stay if I didn't. It took a lot of encouraging, but he listened well yesterday to my instructions. I'm at least thankful for that."

I smile at her and she seemed a little surprised by it at first, but then she laughs. After combing my hair to the back and out of my face, and making it stay with some holding gel, she finishes and steps back to see her work.

"Perfect," she says with a bright smile. A huge contrast from earlier. She gestures for me to look for myself. I turn back toward the mirror and take a look at my reflection. Not bad.

"When did you become a hair stylist?" I tease with a small smirk.

"Just say you like it and thank me." She doesn't wait for an actual response though and she turns to leave. "We should get going. I shouldn't be late or my family will be looking for me."

I nod and follow her out of the room. We meet up with Carson down stairs who was wearing a grey tail coat, matching tie, pants, cummerbund belt, and albert chain all with gold accents.

"What d'ya think, what d'ya think?" he questions with his arms out stretched to showcase his look of the evening.

"You look fine, Carson," Rose shakes her head at him and walks him by.

"I know I look *fine*!" he calls back to her. "I mean with this really nice suit! How much was it by the way? I can keep it right? The girlies'll love this back home."

· No one answers him. I only clap my hand down onto his shoulder as I too walk by him. Eventually he follows after us as Rose and I were already going out the door and began our march to the nearest stage coach stop.

Upon arriving to the bustling little area where coaches and buggies came and left, Rose stops suddenly and is looking around to find something. I watch her for a bit and before I could ask she points to farther down the road where a white coach was waiting, with a fancy looking man in a feathered top hat at the reigns. She starts sprinting—I mean, *walking* towards the coach and I almost couldn't believe that we'd be taking such a nice one.

"Wow," Carson says as if taking the words right out of my mouth, "what's the occasion?"

"Occasion?" Rose looks at him for a moment as the driver hops down and approaches Rose, reaches out for her hand and does a bow.

"My lady," he greets, "I think you'll find everything is in order."

Rose smiles and does a small curtsy before he released her hand and he turned to bow in mine and Carson's direction. He then opens the door to let us in. We step up behind Rose who enters first, and I hear her greeting someone. It wasn't until she got out of the way did I see a very large man in Lamia's guard uniforms. I felt my heart jump from surprise, and somewhat fearful that he'd be taken aback by my presence. But I suppose I underestimated Rose as we all settled down into the car and the driver shut the door and began ushering the horses into the road. Rose sits up straight and lays the bag she carried on her lap. She looks beside her to the mysterious guard and then across the coach at Carson and me.

"This is my escort for the evening," she introduces. "Normally I don't like to have them but my family insists."

The man wears a gentle smile and *something* about him seemed familiar.

"Your safety is very important, Princess," the man said.

His voice as well. I had heard it before. But where?

"I can take care of myself," Rose pouts and crosses her arms in response. Yeah, that sounded like a teenager response alright. The man then turns to face me. I study his face hard and it seemed he noticed this. His brown eyes twinkled and he rubbed at his full black beard. For a good moment it was very quiet and the air was still save for the sound of the tires rolling over the gravel and the horses. And then the guard leans back and laughs a bit.

"Ethan Moon…" he calls, "your mother would be incredibly proud of you."

I pause as my heart skipped a concerning number of beats.

"W-what?" I question, feeling as though I could have just heard him wrong.

"My name is Esad Karim."

Thank you Esad.

I could hear my mother's voice clearly and just then it hit me. I remembered long ago after the accident Mr. Karim visiting my mother on behalf of the castle to inform her of Lamia and Artemis's wish to be rid of me. I stare longer at the man, taking in his aged face from a decade ago.

"Are you okay, Ethan?" Rose asks now as I was taking too long to make a comprehensible reply. I nod at her finally and lean back into the bench.

"I know it's been a very long time, Ethan," Esad continues. "I also know what's happened to you and your family. My condolences. Only understand that if you ever need my help, particularly within Lamia District, please do not hesitate to ask. My district has done some unspeakable things in the last ten years. I simply wish to somehow stop it."

"What sort of unspeakable things?" I ask now, suddenly able to find my voice again. "I mean aside from murdering my mother and attempting to assassinate me."

Esad clears his throat awkwardly and he's twisting the long staff between his fingers.

"Sierra," he says. "They've almost completely taken it over. There are still a select few rebelling, but only few. They've separated families according to their status. Caused famine. And an atrocious amount of poverty. Some are even being executed due to their rank. That part has been kept under wraps. But I believe more people should know. They're going to begin doing the same everywhere else. Your district is next, Ethan."

"Why are they doing that?" I ask. It definitely was upsetting to hear, and I couldn't believe they were getting away with it.

"It's the princess. Annika. She never approved of the king's way of ruling. And some speculate she is spiteful for not being crowned queen after his disappearance. Perhaps trying to prove she isn't weak. We all know her no good son does next to nothing but fool around and does as she says. If only King Xxavier could be found, or if Prince Aero would take his rightful place—"

Rose clears her throat and stares off with a complicated expression. Esad looks over at her and seems to feel sorry.

"I apologize, Princess. I've said too much."

She shakes her head in return and then her gaze finds mine.

"I know it isn't good…"

"Good?" I cut her off. "Of course, it isn't good. Why isn't anyone doing anything about it? I mean who is in charge of this place? Like, who keeps this sort of thing in check?"

Rose and the guard share a look before the girl answers first.

"Typically, each leader of every district oversees our realm," she says. "So, I suppose it's a good question, what happens when one leader steps out of line?"

"War," Esad answers with a grim expression.

"But no one wants a war. Not even Artemis and they're notorious for war. That is probably why no one has truly done anything yet. Sierra is very weak and their leaders I'm sure are easily persuaded. They probably needed nothing more than money to allow Lamia soldiers and as many Oddity Hunters into the district as they pleased. Greenwood is run by the H.D.O and as they are Druids they will try to find the most non-violent way to solve things as possible. Which clearly won't lead them anywhere."

"And Artemis?" I ask.

"Well, like I've mentioned before, Artemis and Lamia have similar ideas and will use each other for what they want for as long as possible until one betrays the other. So, Artemis is not looking for war, but they will not shy away from attacking or defending themselves when the time comes."

"So, what could anyone do if they wanted to stop it?" I ask this time.

"I imagine foiling the princess's plans should do it," Esad replied. "Though, no one knows what exactly her plans are in their entirety. Or even the true reason behind them. It's only presumed that what she wants is power over all the districts. But is that *it*? *You* could stop her, Ethan. You could find out her plans and end them. You have the powers to do just that and that's exactly why she feared you."

I frown a little and look down at my hands.

"But I don't know how to use my powers," I murmur. Esad shakes his head in response and offers a kind smile.

"You will. *That's* what matters. And I told you. If you need anything. I will help."

I see now. There's much more to this than I previously thought. I'm here not just to regain my memory or to find what I've lost. Not just to remember my friends and my family and my home. I was gotten rid of for a reason much bigger than what I couldn't have even begun to understand at such a young age. This plan of this Annika woman has been something at least ten years in the making. Perhaps longer. And getting rid of me was a part of it. I *needed* to help the people of Obscura. It seemed regardless of if I liked it or not.

Not much else was said after this. I was just learning more about all of whom I had in my corner, and those on the opposing side. We arrived in Lamia soon after and was quickly able to pass through the boarder. There were crowds of people and carriages and coaches that stretched on for miles the closer we came to the castle. It was brilliant, magnificent even up close. The gothic dark-stoned structure towered far above our heads and the warm glow of burning embers of each window, doorway, and corridor seemed oddly welcoming in contrast to the cold. There were men dressed in their best attire, women in huge frilly ball gowns of all shapes and sizes. Each person wore very unique handcrafted masquerade masks. Some modeled after animals, others were intricate and captivating designs.

Our carriage comes to a halt and immediately my body filled with nerves. I had no idea what I was doing. At least Carson got a whole lesson from Rose and I got absolutely nothing.

"Hey, where's your getup, Rose? You're going dressed like that?" Carson asks.

"What? Oh no," she answers. But for some reason she doesn't say anything else. Both Carson and I give her a confused look and then in the next moment our door is swinging open. The driver bows his head as he helps Rose out first. Esad follows after her and Carson and I are last to exit. Rose leads the way toward the busy entrance of the castle. People were lined up being let in carefully by guards protecting the entrance. And then Rose comes to a stop. Carson and I run into each other after realizing slightly too late that she wasn't moving anymore.

"I nearly forgot," she says and turns around. She opens up her bag and digs around for a moment before pulling out two different masks. She hands a very simple one to Carson that would only conceal his face around the eyes. It was painted silver and gold with rhinestones glued onto it. Then she hands me mine that was shaped like a bunny made from black wire and silver glitter. It had tall ears that would extend over my head. I raise an eyebrow at it, although it was kind of cute. "What?" Rose asks as she observes my expression. "You don't like it?"

I laugh a little at her and go to put it on.

"It's fine," I say. "I just wonder why you chose it." I look over at Carson and he gives a thumbs up.

She shrugs a little in response.

"No reason," she says coolly and continues to the building.

"Okay, but what about you, Rose?" Carson asks as we're now chasing after her to keep up.

"I'll meet you in the ballroom," she said.

"Wait what? You're not coming with us?" I question. I mean, how could she just leave us by ourselves?

"Yes, you'll be fine," she insists. "Just follow everyone else and don't make fools of yourselves. I must get dressed. I shall meet you inside." She looks back at me for a moment and then she offers a gentle smile. "Don't worry, Ethan. I won't be long."

She says this and then she steps into the crowd, slipping by the guards to enter her home.

My arm is grabbed and I jump a little until I realized it was Esad.

"Don't forget what I told you, Ethan. And keep it to yourself," he murmured close to my ear before he hurried by to catch up with Rose. I look to my side to find Carson and we pushed ourselves into the crowded line. It felt very strange to think that you were completely surrounded by vampires. I think even if I had my memory, it would still be strange.

When Carson and I reached the front of the line, we were stopped by two guards who one held out his hand expectantly. Both of us staired at him confused until he said: "Invitations"

My head spins around toward Carson and I just knew we wouldn't be allowed in. If only Rose hadn't left us behind. Carson stares back at me for a moment and then he begins feeling around his suit coat and trousers as if an invitation would magically appear. But then, to my disbelief, he pulls out two folded golden papers. And with a sigh of relief, he hands it over to the guard. They look it over for a moment before waving us through.

"Woo. That was close," Carson sighs as we enter the castle. I glare at him, but I don't say anything. I'm only then distracted by the interior of the castle. Very goth. Very smart. We were following a crowd of people down a very long corridor that arched with black intricate moldings. The walls were lined with stone busts of every passed monarch. The hall was illuminated by lanterns and antique ceiling fixtures.

We could hear the sound of music coming from the ballroom where we were headed. The farther we went into the castle, the more my surroundings felt familiar.

Come on, Rose! We're gonna miss the ball if we're late!
Wait, Ethan! Our parents told us to wait!

I could hear our small voices loud and clear. And for a moment I could see us pushing through guests and weaving through their legs to get to the ballroom as fast as possible.

Finally, we approach the grand double doors of which the masquerade ball was held. We file in after other guests and we're greeted by loud string music, huge chandeliers hanging over a vast dancefloor with a red runner carpet draped down the middle, leading up to a grand staircase that led up to a balcony. This balcony had five people sitting comfortably as they staired down at their arriving guests. There was a woman with a young face. Her hair was braided elaborately, half up and half down. She wore a golden dress with a high collar and a matching diamond studded crown on her head. Her eyes were almost as large as Rose's but they looked somewhat displeased or contempt over something. Beside her to her left was a man with slicked back dirty blonde hair. He wore a suit that corresponded with the woman beside him with a sash crossing over the front. To the left of this man was a young woman that looked like she could be mine and Carson's age. Perhaps a little older. Her hair was very long with loose curls that waved behind her back. It may have been bleached platinum and her eyes were strikingly red, even through the mask that covered her face. She looked disinterested with everything but the way her black manicure looked. On the other side were two other people. One was a younger man that looked as old as or maybe older than the girl with platinum hair. His eyes were also very red, and he wore a sash and a crown over his short curly hair. And beside him was an older woman with greying hair twisted into dreadlocks. The thick ropes were pulled up and twisted into a very unique bun that encased a shiny silver crown on her head.

This clearly was the royal family.

Rose's family.

"Oh my god. Look at that!"

My attention is pulled away from them to where Carson was pointing to. After finally being able to pull away from the crowd of guests and finding our own empty corner to stand in and grab our bearings, Carson takes notice of one whole side of the room with a long row of tables piled to the max with all sorts of meals, hors d'oeuvres, fruits and veggies, desserts, and a huge glass fountain of something very thick and red. I'd like to call it punch, but that just might not be the case.

"Let's go there!" Carson says eagerly and has already taken steps in that direction. But I grab his sleeve and pull him back.

"Not yet," I tell him. "Let's wait for Rose first before doing anything."

"Boo," he pouts but thankfully doesn't argue. "Well, this is fancy, huh? So, you've just been going to balls like this without me?"

I cock my head to the side but I had to remind myself he was almost entirely joking.

"I don't even remember it that well," I tell him plainly.

"But you do a little bit?"

I think about this, and actually, I did. Just like when we were entering the castle, I remembered Rose and I running through the corridor in order to not be late. And although many things still felt unfamiliar, there was something just out of reach, begging for me to take hold of it and remember. I shrug a little at Carson and I take another look at the room.

"Maybe a little bit," I answer finally. "But it just won't…come to me."

I think he noticed the strained look I wore. And in response he tried to get my attention again. He snaps his fingers in my face and then he waved me over.

"Let's go try some of the food," he encourages. Or maybe it was just a ploy to get his hands on it when I specifically told him to wait. But I follow him anyway and he leads me over to a section of the very long table draped in a fancy black lace cloth. He stops in front of a large silver pan piled high with something that looked like caviar and…cream(?)—cream cheese perhaps(?) in mini tart crusts. Carson narrows his eyes real small and then glared at me as if I've offended him or something. "Have you ever tried caviar?" he asks all of a sudden, as if it were an important test question. I shake my head in response and look back down at the stuff.

"I mean I've had it on sushi. Isn't it the same thing?"

He shrugs at this and picks up one.

"We'll just have to try it and see. Today we eat like royalty my friend." As he raises the tart up to his mouth, someone just beside him grabs his shoulder and almost shrieks.

"Just a minute, child!" the woman calls out to stop him. Carson's eyes are as big as golf balls as he turns to look at the woman with his mouth still hanging open. "Don't act so recklessly! You should have your blood first! 'Less you're looking to be ill the rest of the evening." Her frown peaks out from underneath her mask and she shakes her head with disapproval. "Have your blood child. Go on!"

Carson turns his head again to look at me, maybe to intervene. But I wasn't sure what to do. Both of our eyes trail over to the fountain of what has now been confirmed to be blood. I felt like my face was flushing with dread as I began to question where all of that blood came from? People? Animals? As the woman is now swatting at Carson to behave and do as she says, he finally stumbled over to the fountain.

"Okay okay, I'm sorry," Carson whines as he goes to pick up a small glass cup. He fills it up with the thick red liquid and then turns around again. And to his dismay the woman was still there, watching him expectantly.

"Go on and have it, child. I wouldn't know what I'd do if I knew you made yourself ill. Who are your parents? You both are quite big, aren't you? Are you related to Lord Channing by chance? I know he's got two boys."

Carson opens his mouth for a second, running through every possible thing he could say. But with great luck there were many gasps erupting from the crowds of people. Everyone turns toward the balcony and whispers began soon after. Even the woman all worked up over Carson's health for some reason became interested in it. Looking over the crowd to the balcony I could just see someone wearing silver entering through an archway up top.

"*It's the princess,*" some people are whispering.

"*Wow she looks amazing,*" another says.

"*It's simply a shame about her father disgracing our district,*" someone else murmurs.

It's Rose, gracefully stepping out onto the balcony and she turns to greet her family. She hugs the older woman on the far end to which now I assume is her grandmother. They smile warmly to each other, share a few words and then she begins her way down the stairs. As she came closer, I could see her dress was a huge ball gown with draping off the shoulder sleeves. Every inch of her dress was silver and sparkly. Her hair was tied up high on her head with a glittery tiara sitting delicately in her soft curls. She wore an elegant mask fashioned in the likeness of a bear with black wire and silver glitter.

She reaches the bottom of the stairs and is now passing through the crowd. Most people parted to make way for her, and others asked to shake her hand, bow or curtsy with her, and share a few words. Then finally she is approaching Carson and me. And just as she was about a foot away, she stops and curtsies to me, bowing her head low. I turned around stupidly, feeling as though she couldn't possibly be doing that to me. But when I realized that she was, something told me to bow back, and so I did. As I did, I could hear some people gasping and whispering, but I couldn't make out what they were saying at all.

Rose smiles at me brightly. She looked happier than I've ever seen her so far. She steps forward and on instinct I offer my hand that of which she takes. She picks up one side of her dress with her other hand and suddenly lively music began and then we're off.

"Well, I'll just be here then!" I hear Carson call as my feet have carried me off toward the middle of the room where others have also found their partners and joined in on the dance. The room was designed in a way that any and all instruments could be heard as clearly and fully no matter where you stood with the dome shaped ceiling painted with murals of vampire people. There were strings, piano, the organ, and even some guy with an accordion being played by masked musicians playing many variations of the waltz.

I'm looking down at my feet, feeling surprised at them for dancing without letting my brain know first. It wasn't until I could feel Rose's eyes on me as she held onto my arm had I looked up again.

"What's the matter?" she whispers as loudly as possibly over the sound of the music.

I shake my head as I spin the both of us around, take a step forward, take a step over, then back. I'm doing the waltz. And I was afraid to admit that it was kind of fun.

"I just don't know what I'm doing," I tell her with a light frown.

She shakes her head at me this time as we circle around the dance floor.

"Oh, lighten up," she sighed. "You're doing a fantastic job. Just trust yourself…and have fun."

We stare at each other seriously for what felt like a whole minute until I felt the tension in my body release after accepting what she had to say. By now, the current song ended and a new one began. Everything slowed down for a moment as the small orchestra started with light pizzicato, and everyone began to move outside of the dancefloor. The lights dimmed a little and, on the balcony, I could see all standing but Rose's grandmother. Rose pulls me over with everyone else as I stare up at the woman in gold whose eyes were seemingly looking back at mine as she whispered something over to the blonde man next to her. Something about that didn't sit well with me and I felt it would be better to look away in case she somehow suspected something out of the ordinary.

As the music continued, the young man and woman had joined each other hand in hand as they stepped down the stairs and into the dance floor and began their dance first.

"That's my cousin Ryland, and my cousin Fey," Rose whispers over to me. Now I understood, that man was the current so called "king" whose mother controlled him. Which then confirmed what I suspected about the woman in gold who was now taking her turn stepping down hand in hand with the blonde-haired man who joined in and began to dance to the slow music that was gradually beginning to pick up. "And that is my aunt Annika and uncle Zakirai. Ryland and Fey's parents," Rose continued. I watch them dance in slow circles. Do short lifts and continue. And then suddenly I'm pulled forward. My eyes widen for a moment wanting to panic as I'm thrown into the middle of the dance floor. The third to do this choreographed dance. I could only thank my lucky stars that my feet seemed to remember everything that my brain did not. Somehow. But I wasn't complaining. We dance in circles, her skirt sweeping the floor until my hands move to her waist and I hoist her up and back down again. And soon all of the guests hurry to join in as the music now picks up completely. We dance this dance, hoisting up our partners and spin around. I couldn't help but laugh as my nerves went away. I knew this dance. Rose smiles and laughs too as we spin and spin. And then the music slows once more. We all move slowly with our partners, arm in arm until the music stops. It stops momentarily, and then begins again in a different tune. Rose and I and all the others do the next routine, waltzing in three-fourths. I hear laughter from others, and although I wasn't quite sure what was so funny, I too laughed with Rose who tried keeping up well with the music. And then she gasps and points up to the ceiling.

"Look at that!" she almost shouts. I look all the way up at the ceiling where a hidden compartment was opening, and a very flexible woman in yellow and black tights and a flamboyant masquerade mask was being lowered down with black aerial silk wrapped around her body. She twists and turns to the staccato rhythm and flips about in the air with the black silk. And then the music is at full forte again, back to its original song. The dancing starts again as we spin around the dance floor, lift our partners, and lose ourselves in the music. As the song ended, Rose is dipped backward into the finale, and is pulled back up in a very breathless finish. We had danced so well that many others had stopped just to watch. Rose stares up at me for a moment as we tried to catch our breath and then she's suddenly pulling out of my grip and straightening out her gown. The music switches and the accordion begins again into a very spooky sounding waltz song.

"That was magnificent, Ethan," Rose says now with a smile. I look at her and return the smile.

"I didn't know I could do that," I say, out of breath. She laughs some and gives my arm a squeeze.

"I told you. You were always very talented. Especially when it came to the Lamia traditional waltz."

I open my mouth to respond but a group of people have surrounded the both of us, all speaking at once.

"My, how splendid!" one shouts.

"Yes yes! Princess, who is your partner? We must have a dance with him!" a woman asks.

"What is your name, sir? We must know what family you're from," another man inquires.

I'm almost overwhelmed with all the questions and the chattering. But Rose grabs my arm and smiles warmly to them.

"I'm sorry but we mustn't reveal our identities. That wouldn't be in the masquerade spirit, now, would it? Now would you please, we must go for refreshments." She excuses us and the small crowd of people bow and curtsy to us both as we move past them and head back to the area with food. And the area we knew to find Carson in. He was standing with a glass in hand talking to three women in very luxurious gowns and feathered masks. They all seemed to be engaged in whatever story Carson was probably making up, but I give him props for keeping their attention while hopefully keeping his identity concealed.

"Ethan," Rose calls as she reached for a slice of white cake, "would you please fetch me a drink?" she asks.

"Sure," I say as I look at her tired face. I turn toward the large fountain that I assumed is what she had in mind. I go and grab her a glass and fill it with the red stuff, and I grab a small water for myself before going to join her again. She was now standing by Carson's side, wearing a confused expression that was common for most who stood by him.

"Yes, I'm very close with the princess. But anyways, ladies, would you excuse me? My good friend has returned. And should I see you again perhaps I'll give you his contact information," Carson is saying as I hand Rose her glass. She mouths me a thank you as the three women giggle and walk away.

"What was that all about?" I grumble. "And what was with that weird accent you were doing?"

"Uh-hum, that was my noble voice. In case you haven't realized, we're around a bunch of rich noble families. We should play the part, right? I did good, didn't I, Rose?"

"I suppose," she scoffs and takes a sip of her drink. "Actually, I'm glad that you were able to behave, granted in your own way but you behaved. I thank you for that."

"Sure." He shrugs and takes a bite of cake that Rose seemed to have brought over for him. My eyes, however, move over to the glass of red stuff (maybe still in his hand from earlier?).

"I hope you haven't been drinking that…" I voice to him with sight concern. He looks down at it too and then he laughs.

"Of course not! But it really sells that I'm one of them if I pretend like I am!"

Rose laughs this time and pats him on the back.

"Impressive," she admits. "Way to really play your role."

The music has picked up again and people had begun to gasp and cheer as their attention was pulled back up to the ceiling. The woman entangled in aerial silk had begun doing a flying dance routine and she's pulled out a stick from her shirt.

"Oh! Let's go watch her," Rose voices excitedly as she hiked up her skirt to scurry closer to get a better look. Carson and I share a look and then follow her over. It was very impressive, and just as we thought it couldn't get any more interesting, she is suddenly swishing something around in her mouth. She's twisting each silk curtain as tight as possible above her and then hanging off of them, she begins spinning and blows out fire that captivates us all.

"Whoa!" Carson awes and starts clapping and cheering like everyone else. Rose clasps her hands together as she watches excitedly as the woman was now playing with fire. It was exciting, and I could now admit that I was glad I came.

I'm clapping and cheering the woman on until I feel someone grab my shoulder.

"*Psst. Hey kid,*" someone whispers into my ear. I flinch a little and I turn around, but I didn't readily see the owner of the voice. I was just about to write it off as hearing things until I caught sight of those unmistakable fiery eyes just a little ways away. Staring me down through a very dark mask and wearing a awfully cunning smirk. After being sure I caught sight of him he turns around and walks out of the room. I look froward again and beside me to my friends who had their attention on the dancing ceiling lady. Without saying anything, I slip away backward into the crowd, and quickly I move to catch up with the man I had completely forgotten about until now.

I step through the double doors and then I look left and right down the nearly empty corridor. Then I look ahead of me where I see the man peaking from around a corner. I move toward him and finally as I turn the corner, he smiles and waves me over to a dark quiet space.

"I thought you'd never quit your performance out there," Julian starts and pulls off his mask. "I can't breathe through this damn thing. I don't see the appeal of this sort of party." I frown at him as he goes on about trivial things. And when he takes note of this he chuckles and leans against the wall behind him. "I know what you must be thinking," he says. "'Why doesn't he just get to the point?' Sure, I could do that, but that wouldn't be fun now would it? Hey. Relax. I already told'ya I'm not gonna hurt you." He pats his hand down onto my shoulder and after it lingered for too long, I move away.

"What do you want, Julian," I glare and he only smiles in return.

"My, you have quite the temper. That's not how people remember little Ethan," the man chuckles. "But since you want to get straight to the point, follow me." He kicks off of the wall and begins walking down the corridor, farther away from the ball. I follow him timidly but I remind myself that he'd give me something in return if I helped him. The farther we walked, the quieter the music from the ball became. I was starting to feel sorry for not telling

Rose and Carson where I had gone. I look around my surroundings that was dimly lit by torches on the wall. There were many portraits here full of images of the royal family. Even Rose was in some of them.

"Do you know where we're going?" Julian speaks up, spooking me for a moment as I had become too focused on the fascinating interior décor.

"Should I?" I question in return. I hear him chuckle and I was growing to find it irksome.

"You should. It almost serves as your third home."

"Third?"

"Well…fourth, should you count the most recent one in Whitechapel. Or should that one be fourth? Hmm." My brow furrows and he leads me around a corner and finally to a round wooden door, unguarded and far from the lively part of the building. The man steps to the side and adjusts the grey suit coat he wore. "After you," he says and pretends to bow.

I wasn't sure what to make of it, but I decided if something happened maybe *someone* had to hear it. I pull the latch on the door and push it open. I am then greeted by a very large room with a high ceiling. There were file cabinets that nearly touched those ceilings and almost all of them were full to the brim. I felt that a room like this should have definitely been guarded, but because of the party maybe there was an acceptation of some kind. I step inside wondering what we could have been doing in what must have been the records room Rose had been telling me about and then I look back down at Julian who was closing the door behind him.

"Why would they need a room like this?" I ask him. "I mean it looks like it holds far more than records simply on Lamia alone."

"Oh, so you know this is where all of the records are kept."

"Sure. But why are *we* here?"

Julian clasps his hands behind his back and moves further into the room, eyeing one of the isles of cabinets.

"This district does a lot of digging and recording things that have nothing to do with them. Especially on things that have to do with magic. Because aside form super human strength or speed or some even have the flight ability, magic as a whole is out of their territory. And two of the four districts have abilities that they do not." I tilt my head as I listen to the man wondering where exactly he was going with this. He scratches his head for a moment after coming to a stop and then when he sees what he must have been looking for, he strides over to it. "Come here, I'll show you." I follow after him down a specific isle and he's eyeing every row carefully. "This here is most of their records on magical artifacts. They have something very similar and far more detailed in the H.D.O, but there's far too many guards and too many defenses set up to restrict just anyone from getting into sensitive material. But here," he laughs, "*they're so stupid*. If you have good reason to be in the castle, it's much too easy for people like *us* to get through anything. Especially on nights like this where we don't even have to try."

I look over at him again, now curious to know what he was looking for. He takes a step back and his eyes begin to glow as he's scanning the shelves.

"So, what do you want?" I ask. "Something that'll help find your daughter?"

"Smart boy," he praises. "But it's not just something. It's forbidden. But it's the only thing that will make it possible to see my Layla again."

"What happened to her?" I ask this time. I was definitely curious. If she's lost and needs to be found why couldn't any sort of detective do that for him. Or for that matter, if this artifact can find a lost person, why don't Lamia use it to find their lost king? I notice Julian hesitate at my question and I wasn't sure what I expected. He turns his head to look at me properly and he frowns.

"Someone took her," he states. "Very bad people. All I want is to get her back. I am a man of my word, Ethan. If you help me, I will help you."

"Okay…" I look down at the floor for a moment and then I look back toward the rows of cabinets. "So, what do you need me to do? Why did I need to come here with you?"

"There's more than one reason," he explains. "The first, is I need your help to find the file I'm looking for. I can't seem to scan for it which means the Elemalax must have put at least one spell in this room. You have the ability to work past it."

"How? If you can't do anything about it, how can I?"

He shakes his head almost irritably and then he holds out his hand. A small spinning sphere of fire sits in his palm and he seems to be offering it to me.

"Take this."

"What? I'm supposed to *touch* that?"

The man sighs lightly. He offers his hand closer and I decide to just trust him. I reach out and I feel that the flame is radiating cold before I could even touch it. As my fingers are just about to graze this sphere, Julian is suddenly pulling his hand far back. His eyes turn into flames themselves and then he throws his hand forward. A huge wave of fire comes shooting out of his palm aiming directly at me; very real and very hot. I yelp before my body could actually react, and although I only meant to jump out of the way, I flinch instead and everything becomes green. As my hands raise to shield myself from the sudden attack a force of electric green light launches from them. And as if everything was in slow motion I watched as this force visibly evaporates the dangerous fire inches away from touching me, and continues to wrap itself around the aggressor, shock him viciously and sent him flying backward. He yells in pain as he's thrown and lands with a heavy thud some yards away. I peek my eyes fully open and I stand up straight to look at my hands. Did that come from me? It all happened so fast that I wasn't so sure at first. Julian is groaning and rolling around on the floor, and now that I had time to register what just happened, my hands ball into fists and my eyes glow bright as an uncontrollable anger builds up inside of me.

"What the hell do you think you're doing!" I yell, storming over to him as my fists are emitting a green smoke. The man sits up with his hand on his chest, trying to figure out if he was breathing properly after having the wind knocked out of him. I raise a fist ready to do something again. Although I wasn't sure what, I knew I had the capability.

"Hey hey hey," the man is now waving his hand at me and then he moves to push himself up to his feet, "calm down would'ya?"

"We had a deal!" I growl. "You said you wouldn't hurt me if I helped you!"

"I know what I said, kid." Julian smiles that wide creepy smile and then he slides his hands into his pockets. "I didn't hurt you, right? Actually, it was quite the opposite." He frowns and looks off to the side. "I mean you did a number on my back…"

"But you attacked me!" I snap but I begin to lower my fists.

"No no no, you've got it all wrong. I didn't attack you. I helped you. Did you see what you just did? Bet you didn't realize you're able to protect yourself with magic, did you?" He scoffs a little and I begin to feel almost used or tricked. "You wouldn't have known if I hadn't of helped you. You probably would have just been running around with that silly knife on your hip." My eyes widen a little as I look down at my pants, wondering if the dagger I put under my coat was visible. "How did I know? I'm not stupid, Ethan," he laughs this time. "Anyway, now that you remember you can use defensive magic—*excessively*—perhaps now you will remind yourself that you have the ability to actually see enchantments and disarm them. I'm going to go ahead and guess that there is a sort of deflecting charm and or an enchantment that will notify someone if we touch any of the files without authorization." There was an awkward pause and Julian double takes at me after realizing I was just standing there. Honestly, I thought he was going to explain more of what I had to do. He scowls at me and gestures for me to hurry up. "Well go on then, kid," he snaps. "Use those crazy eyes of yours."

I make a face to myself and then turn back to the rows of file cabinets. I didn't know what I was looking for exactly, but I assumed when he said I could "see" the magic it must have been the same as seeing auras. So, I just go for it. I shut my eyes for a moment to try and focus, and after a moment I've opened them. I'm almost immediately unsettled as I see more than auras. Out of the corner of my eye I could see the small figure that seemed attached to Julian. Although I make a point not to turn to see it completely as I remembered how he reacted before at that clothing store. But there were other things. Ghosts or souls of a few, floating around, gliding across the room. They seemed unbothered and uninterested in anything going on over here so I thought it best to ignore them. My eyes focus in front of me and there I could see a pulsating golden light that in fact wrapped itself around every cabinet in the room. I could see the spells placed on them just as Julian said. "Well?" the man questions expectantly. "Do you see them or what?"

"Yeah," I respond. "So, what should I do?"

"Break it," he said simply in return. "You don't have to do the whole room, just this cabinet here."

"Break it…" I repeat. Then I frown and look over at him. "Like, literally break it?"

"Yes, you imbecile!" he snaps impatiently. I flinch a little but I move without thinking, reaching forward and closing my hands around the golden strings of magic. I wasn't expecting to actually feel anything, or that my hands would actually be holding on to anything, but they were. And it stung. Not so much that I couldn't endure it, but it was definitely unpleasant. I hear a sizzling sound as I'm now tugging the spell apart. It stretches in my hands like a taught rubber band. And with a little more strength it snaps apart and the two broken pieces crumble to the ground like broken chains. "Finally," Julian says as he's making his next moves immediately. His amber eyes glow again and he swipes his hand up and through the air.

"*Invenire*," the man utters boldly.

The cabinets begin to spin, shift, and rearrange themselves. A specific cabinet stacked nearly at the top moves forward from all the rest and then replaces itself to a lower position at a proper level for Julian to reach. One of its drawers opens and an aged folder comes flying out, lowering itself into Julian's grasp. He's laughing a very unsettling laugh and begins to open it.

"You did it," he says happily. "Ethan, I need to take this with me and find out where the artifact is located. I will contact you soon with what I need next."

"You mean that's not all?" I frown and stuff my hands into my pockets.

"Huh?" He looks over at me and then closes the folder. "Of course not. Your job isn't done until I get the artifact in my hands. Only then will I leave you be. In the meantime, I have something for you in return for what you've done here today." I tilt my head as he begins walking off. He rounds a corner and enters a different aisle. He stops in front of another stack of cabinets and he waves his hand around half-heartedly. "Break the spell here," he said half-heartedly.

I make another face at his command but I go ahead and do it anyway. I shift my vision and upon seeing the spell placed on the cabinet, I reach out and pull it apart. As soon as I do so, Julian says his spell again and the cabinets rearrange themselves until a folder presents itself. He reads it to make sure it was the right one and then he looks over at me. "Here," he says and hands it to me. I take it and watch him curiously. "I think you'll find this helpful. But don't read it here. Take it home with you."

My eyes narrow a little at him as I hold the folder skeptically. Something seemed very odd about it. Outside of how utterly creepy he was, of course.

"Why are you helping me?" I question now, but he scoffs in return and turns his back to me to make his way back to the door.

"I told you, Ethan," he began, sliding his hands into his pockets, "I only care about one thing. It does me no good if you get yourself killed before I get what I want."

I guess that was fair enough. Although his "helping" methods seemed unorthodox, at least I could trust him to not lead me to my death. I follow the man back to the door and he pushes it open. He peaks his head through and looks left and right first before stepping out completely. We walk back down the empty corridor and turn the corner. Then soon we're approaching the ball room as the music gradually became audible. He stops at the last corner of the path leading to the ballroom, and he looks over his shoulder at me.

"It would be smart not to let anyone see you with that," Julian points out before conjuring up the mask he was wearing earlier. He slides it onto his face, and with a very out of place grin, he strides away. After he was out of sight I look once more down at the file in my hand. On the front it was stamped "*CLASSIFIED*" with big black letters. And the files name was titled "*Invictus Project*". My head tilts a little at this as the word had been familiar. But there wasn't much time to stand here and study it. I needed to get back to my friends. I hold the file inside of my jacket and I step back into the ballroom. I scan the busy room of people standing and chatting and others dancing and laughing. But before I could spot either Carson or Rose, I felt my arm gripped tight and I'm nearly being knocked over. I stumble but catch my footing and turning my head I see Rose with a distressed expression.

"Ethan!" she yells over the music and pulls away from me. "Where have you been?! We've been looking everywhere for you! Carson got smacked by a lady because he mistook her for you!"

I look over at Carson who was rubbing his cheek and pouting at me.

"How could you have mistaken a woman for me?" I turn my nose up at him and he throws his other hand up in defense.

"She was wearing a fancy pants suit!" he whines.

"Where did you go?" Rose questions now. "You really shouldn't have snuck off like that! Anything could've happened!"

"I know, I know, I'm sorry. I'll explain it all in a minute but let's get out of here first." I pull out the file just a little so that Rose could see. And upon getting a glimpse her eyes are blown wide.

"Where did you get that?" she whispers harshly and moving to hurry and conceal it again.

"Let's go," I answer instead, and all together the three of us are hurrying out of the ball. We hurry down the corridor and scurry past the guards at the front door. Rose has her skirt hiked up in her fists and she seems almost angry, or worried, or both(?).

"How could you have snuck off without us?" Rose began in a huff. I didn't even have to see her face to know she was fuming.

"Where are we going?" Carson whines from behind as we're trekking down a steep grassy hill.

"My father's cottage!" the girl answers without missing a beat. I think for a moment on whether or not I should tell the truth of where I had been and who I was with. I wasn't quite sure how she might react, but I thought that maybe she ought to know. There's a pause where only the sound of stiff grass rustling and people talking in the distance could be heard, and then I look over at Rose again.

"I saw Julian," I finally admit to her. And almost automatically the girl halts to a stop and spins around, her heals digging into the dirt as she gazed over at me with wide glowing eyes.

"What?!" she yells. "You SAW him?! There at the ball, you mean?"

"Yes…" I answer and try to continue, but she cuts me off.

"Why didn't you say anything? Surely, he wasn't invited. And you went alone with him somewhere? Why?"

Carson has now caught up to the both of us as I'm standing there like a child being scolded by their mother.

"Is Julian that creepy guy who tried to kill us at the Halloween party?" he asks with a little tired puff. But nobody answers him.

"He asked for my help," I tell Rose. "He told me if I helped him with something he would help me. I'm not completely sure why, Rose, but he gave me this." I pull out the file again to show her and she seems almost at a loss for words. Both confused and still actively upset. She takes a moment and draws in a deep breath to calm down. Her eyes close and then open again and they've stopped glowing. She looks left and then right, and then she's looking between Carson and me.

"Let's talk about it when we get to my father's cottage. If there's any wandering ears we could be faced with a great deal of trouble." She hikes up her skirt again and begins toward her father's home once more. Carson and I share a look but he doesn't say anything, and neither do I. Not until we would arrive safely to the next place.

15

Prince Aero's Wish

Although you could see Rose's father's home from the castle, it was definitely a much longer walk than anticipated. We trudged down multiple hills and we were passing by a nearby field of wheat. Just looking at it made me feel butterflies in my stomach. Except I didn't know what I was nervous about exactly. Perhaps a reaction to the realization that I was truly home after a very long time. I saw that vision of Rose and I running through that very field, playing tag for the umpteenth time. The memory was becoming clear; much less choppy and obscure from over a week ago. My eyes had trailed over to Rose as I wondered what else I could pull from that shuttered part of my brain, but I still found it all too difficult.

We're stepping onto an actual path now. The path led right up to the front of the small home. A very sweet-looking English cottage that sat at the very edge of the castle grounds with an aging wooden porch and dangling windchimes blowing gently through the late autumn breeze. As Rose and Carson stepped up to the door and Rose was knocking, I was left behind, still standing there awing at the familiar home. My vision was shifting and I could no longer see Rose and Carson standing there on the porch, but instead everything was much brighter. The house seemed younger and livelier. The door was opening and an old woman was stepping out with a tray and a table, and two young children came running out passed her. They sat down cross-legged on the porch and the old woman bends down and sets up the small table and begins to place a tea kettle and two tea cups down, along with a small plate of cakes she must have baked.

I blink wildly, unsure of why I was seeing this all of a sudden, and wondering why I couldn't blink it away. I notice my grandmother smiling brightly, her hair loose around her shoulders and a colorful apron around her waist as she helps young Rose and I set up a tea party. Rose has a little brown teddy bear sitting up at the end of the little table and she's asking Gramma where the third cup was. But before she could react my mother and Rose's father is exiting the home. My mother pulls a small cup from behind her back, surprising Rose and setting it down in front of her bear with a laugh. Everything was inaudible, but I felt like I was right there with them. I feel my eyes welling up, and I thought I might cry until I heard my name.

"Ethan!"

I blink hard and the image is gone. My mother, my grandmother, young Rose and young me. No more tea party, no more happy home. I open my eyes and the house seemed dull and sad in comparison. Carson and Rose were still on the porch, looking back over their shoulder at me. And there with the door being held open was an older man wearing a long burgundy coat and a black vest underneath. His hair unlike in my vision was no longer cut short, and he was certainly not as young as I remembered him. His hair was long and dreaded, pulled back into a makeshift bun that rested behind his back. His face was stressed and tired, but his eyes lit up in amazement as he looked passed my friends at me.

"Ethan," I hear him call, almost unsure of his own voice as he gazed at me. I blink another few times and then wipe my eyes. "Ethan, come here." Immediately my feet carried me up to the house and up the porch. The man is holding his arms out and without question I go to hug him. "My god. It's been far too long," he says. I hear the tremor in his voice. He places his hands on my shoulders and holds me at arm's length. "Let me have a look at you." He's shaking his head and his hands cup my cheeks, scanning my face as if he'd find some foreign object. He sighs heavily and finally releases me. "Come in. Please, please you three, it's much too cold to stand here. Come in." He quickly steps to the side and ushers the three of us in. It was very warm and homely inside.

And to my surprise, I could remember it. I could remember being here a thousand times before and it looked exactly how it used to. I look over at Rose who was watching me with a concerned expression, and then I look back at Rose's father, Prince Aero who was shutting and locking the door and moving quickly to the kitchen where he was pouring three mugs of tea. He returns and hands us all some. "Please," he says and gestures over to the sitting area, "sit." He looks at us all and the three of us share a look before moving over to the couches and having a seat. It was heated by a hearty fire that almost felt like the den at the guild, but a much smaller space. Despite this, it felt very relaxing and very secure. I take a sip of what was apparently valerian root tea and I watch the prince move a book he must have been reading from his chair, sits it on the side table and has a seat. He's quiet for a moment, staring down longingly at the floor, until he looks up again and gazes at us all. He watches his daughter for a moment, and then he watches me. And then as if he just remembered, his gaze switches to the other, sitting with his hands wrapped around his mug and staring down tiredly into the steaming liquid. The man clears his throat in a delicate manner and lightly gestures over at the boy. "Who's this?" he asks carefully, almost seemingly trying to avoid offending anyone. Carson looks up from his tea between Rose and I before looking over at Prince Aero.

"Oh…" the blonde starts awkwardly. "I'm Carson. Ethan's friend… Uhm…who are you?"

Rose shoots him an annoyed look.

"*Don't you pay attention*," she snaps under her breath at him but refrains from saying or doing anything else. Her gaze lowers, I imagine in order to avoid being scolded by her father. Carson shrugs his shoulders at her and the man chuckles a bit and kindly responds.

"My name is Aero Ncuti. Or some may still refer to me as Prince Aero of Lamia. I'm sure you understand that I am Rose's father." Carson mouths an "oh" and sits back against the couch, clutching his mug a little tighter to get warm. Then Prince Aero looks at Rose and me. "Is this boy a nohabi?" he asks pragmatically. Both mine and Rose's eyes widen in surprise. Carson barely said anything and he already figured it out.

"Well, yes, Father, but—" she began, ready to defend him or his reason for being here illegally, but the prince simply waves his hand in dismissal.

"I simply guessed that Ethan would have no other friends but from the mundane world. I am not too worried about it; only I hope that the three of you are being careful. Now, Ethan. Please tell me where is your grandmother at this time?"

I frown a bit at the thought. I still couldn't believe that she was so stubborn not to return with us, even though this place is her real home. Even though she had the luxury to remember it when I didn't. I shake my head a little and my gaze falls back down to my tea.

"She didn't come," I answer. "She wouldn't come back to Obscura."

The prince's eyes widen for a moment and then he sits back against his seat. He looks to be carefully choosing the right thing to say or maybe mulling over a solution. He lets out a sigh and his eyes train on me once more.

"I was hoping to speak with her, you see," he begins to explain. "We haven't spoken in almost a decade. She must understand that there are a cumbersome number of devilish plans my sister will soon begin. Some have already begun. We could all use your grandmother's help." He pauses for a moment and then he cocks his head to the side upon remembering something. "How are you?" he asks all of a sudden. "Your memory, has it returned?"

I shake my head.

"No. Not really. Although I know who you are, it's only that I can't remember much but bits and pieces."

"That's unfortunate. And I'm sure incredibly difficult for you. But it is strange. River said that it would wear off by now."

"But she was always uncertain," Rose chimes in with a light frown. "Remember, Father, that she told us that there would be a possibility he may never have his memory entirely restored. They didn't have much time to test the potion."

"That's right, she did say something like that." The prince nods as he remembers.

"We did, however, get the chance to meet the H.D.O in Greenwood," Rose tells him. "The archdruid told us that the effects of the potion had in fact worn off a rather long time ago."

"Really," the prince began and looks over at me, "then how is it—"

"He informed us that the reason he is struggling with remembering is due to the trauma he suffered that night… Er…the night he fled to the port town, that is."

I look up from my mug after noticing the extended amount of silence that filled the room. I look between the prince and the princess and I am unsure of what either of them are thinking. It wasn't until the prince turned again to look at me properly did anyone say anything else.

"Do you remember that night, Ethan?" he asks.

Immediately my brain began running memories as far back as I could remember. It seemed my farthest memory as of now was Rose and I having tea parties as children. Rose and I playing tag often and sneaking about this very house. My memory skips a few times, very obviously being large chunks of time missing and yet to be recovered. It skips to the memory of my mother at the door with Esad discussing the very bad thing I had done and so on and so forth. But that night—the night of my mother's death—I could see nothing but flames. I could hear nothing but cries. And I could feel nothing but absolute dread.

Actually, at simply the thought of it I had gone queasy and I almost felt like panicking. So much so that I had dropped the hot mug in my hands and only the thud of the ceramic hitting the floor and the hot liquid splashing around my ankles brought me out of my own mind which I was beginning to find very scary.

All of us jump, and I'm wincing from the sting of the tea on my skin. I bend down to pick it up but my hands were shaking from being spooked.

"I'm so sorry…" I tell them, but the prince had already gotten up and picks up the mug before I do.

"Don't worry," he assures me and gently presses at my shoulder to make me sit back down. "My question was a little insensitive. Forgive me." He gives me a sincere look and then he goes to the kitchen. Rose stands up and follows after him, going to retrieve a towel to sop up the spilled tea. I look over at Carson and he's watching me with an expression I had never seen before. It made my stomach churn and for some reason guilt began to creep up on me. After a good minute of unsettling staring, he sets his mug down on the side table and then begins to study his nails as if they were interesting.

"Is something wrong?" I decide to ask after having enough of the anticipation. Carson's eyes meet mine again, and as Rose was on the floor cleaning up the mess I made, she also looks up over at the blonde. He shakes his head but it was clear in his expression he had something to say. And after no time he speaks up.

"I was just thinkin' again about it all," he starts, his brow pushing together. "Like how you can't remember how our friendship started. Or how it properly sits in a timeline for that matter." Rose sits up slowly and her head turns over to look at me. She wore a remorseful expression and I knew that Carson at some point would question how all of this was. I watch my friend carefully and he looks to still be pondering something. "I know I can be slow sometimes, but I seriously just don't understand. How could you have been here but in Whitechapel the whole time? I don't get it."

"Because he wasn't in Whitechapel the whole time," Prince Aero answers before any of us do. He's walking in again with a fresh mug of tea and hands it to me. And in the other hand was a steeped kettle which he used to pour fresh tea into the other mugs.

"Sorry?" Carson asks and looks up at the man. The prince sets down the kettle on the coffee table and he takes his seat once more.

"Your friend is an Obsurian. Born and—well, somewhat raised here in this realm. He was never in that port town until the day he was taken there ten years ago."

"But I remember—"

"You remember wrong," Prince Aero cuts him off and Carson looks more bothered than before. "Your memory has been tampered with. Fabricated. Made up. I'm sorry to tell you if your friends haven't already. You did not know Ethan Moon until ten years ago at whatever hospital he was brought to by that Valhera fellow. There was a spell cast upon the entire town in order to assist Ethan and his grandmother in settling down there undetected. It created memories for all of the citizens to believe they knew of Ethan and Catherine beforehand, so that he and Catherine could have a normal life. And to also protect Ethan's memory until the potion wore off."

"What was she supposed to do when it did?" I ask now. Although I was changing the subject from my friend being told what he thought he knew all this time was a lie, it seemed like information I needed to know. Prince Aero pulls at his sleeve a little as he thought about the answer.

"She was meant to bring you back," he replies. "Catherine, River, and your doctor originally had a plan to smuggle you back into the realm once your memory returned. And after that, you were to be taken to the H.D.O where they would test the control over your magic before allowing you to take the Lamia ministry to trial with the OLA."

"What is an '*olah*,'" I question with a frown.

"The Obscura Leaders Association," Rose answers from her seat she found a while ago.

"There are way too many acronyms," Carson grumbles and props his head up with his elbow.

"Regardless, things are far different now than they were ten years ago. And with what my sister has managed to accomplish, there is no sort of trial that will happen to allow you back your freedom. And I imagine that this is part of the reason why your grandmother did not bring you back as planned. There are too many uncertainties. I think you are very lucky, Ethan to have not run into any real trouble yet. Only I am sure your luck will begin to wear out. Especially as word of your return continues to spread."

"Yeah, I've heard that before…" I grumble.

"Uhm, hello?" Carson speaks up again wearing an irritable expression now. "So, what about me? I mean, did you know all that stuff about our childhood all this time? When did you find out and why didn't you tell me?"

I look up at him and I knew he was working himself up. But I wasn't quite sure what was the best thing to say to make it better. Should I have told him the moment I found out?

"I was just—" I began, but he's standing up now, shaking his head in dismissal.

"You were just keeping something from me," he finished instead. "Something that might have been a little important. I mean literally what I thought I knew was a lie. I mean if it wasn't for *magic* apparently, we probably wouldn't have even been friends!" Carson storms across the room and I begin to stand to stop him, but prince Aero holds up his hand at me.

"Let him go," he says softly.

I watch my friend leave the home, the door shutting hard as he'd gone off to who knows where. I look over at the prince as that guilt was starting to eat painfully at me.

"He can't go out there by himself," I say urgently. "What if something happens to him?"

"He will be fine, Ethan," the prince shushes me and leans back against his chair. "I sense he won't go too far. He only needs some time to cool off. Just imagine if you were in his shoes. How would you feel?" I lean back this time and think about it. My nose winkles up and I accept that keeping the truth from him was wrong.

"I guess I'd feel used…or kind of violated," I admit. "I should have told him."

"What's important is that he will forgive you. If you were truly friends all this time, that means something more than how the friendship came to be."

"I guess you're right."

The prince takes a few sips of his tea and Rose shifts awkwardly. She was eyeing my jacket and chewing thoughtfully at her bottom lip.

"I'm sorry," she exhales after a moment. "But, could we talk about where you had gone during the ball? And particularly that…" she nods her head forward at my jacket.

My brow raises and I move to pull out the concealed folder. The prince lowers his mug after seeing it and he looks up at me with surprise.

"Where did you get that?" he asks without hesitation. He sets his mug down and reaches out for me to hand it to him.

"The records room," I explain slowly and reach out to let him have it.

"Only he didn't go there by himself," Rose says matter-of-factly. "What were you doing with Julian, Ethan?"

"Julian?" prince Aero repeats. "Julian Hickman?"

I nod my head before answering.

"That morning when we went to that shop to get our clothes for the ball, he was there. I mean, he came out of nowhere. Just all of a sudden when I went to find you and Carson after purchasing my suit, he appeared and stopped me."

"Did he hurt you?" the prince asks seriously. His face grim and suspicious.

"No. No, he didn't hurt me. Actually, he told me that he wouldn't hurt me at all if I did something for him."

"So, he threatened you then," Rose concludes with a deep frown.

"Well, no, not exactly," I continue to explain. "He said he'd help me in return if I helped him. He said he was looking for some artifact that would help him find his daughter. Apparently, she was taken by some people, but he didn't say who or why."

"I didn't know he had any children…" Prince Aero says slowly. But he gestures for me to continue as he rubs the hairs on his chin.

"He doesn't seem to be lying," I say. "Although he's really creepy. But so far, he's kept his word—I think. He asked me to meet him at the ball and at the ball he took me to the records room. That's when I disappeared, Rose. I'm sorry. I should have told you where I was going. He took me to that room and he explained that Lamia had a file on some forbidden artifact, but he needed my help to get to it because of the—"

"Spells put on it by the Elemalax," Rose finishes for me.

"The Spirit S.E. can see and break complicated spells," the prince puts together. "So then, do you have all of your powers back, Ethan?"

"No," I shake my head. "No, I barely know how to do anything. But somehow, he 'coached' me to do what he wanted. I mean, one of the things he promised was to help me get my memory back, including using my powers. I'm not sure how he could do any of that but I *was* able to break the spells on the first try. So, after I got the file, he was looking for, he gave me that one in return."

The prince reads the file name and he's opened it up to look inside. Rose and I watch on with anticipation, and upon seeing the prince's stunned expression, we knew it was something probably worthwhile.

"What is it, Father?" Rose asks, leaning forward to try to see the contents inside.

"*He* gave this to you, Ethan? Julian Hickman did?" Prince Aero asks with disbelief.

"Yes," I confirm. The prince draws in a deep breath and looks up at Rose and me.

"These are my sister's plans for taking over the districts," Prince Aero explains. He moves some papers around, and his lips press together after lifting up a specific stack of papers held together by a paperclip. "And these…seem to be backup plans for you, Ethan."

My brow knits together and the prince leans forward to hand it to me.

"Backup plans…" I inquire as I take them to see what he was talking about. I look down and there was a photo attached of me, in black and white. It was the same as my passport photo as it turned left, right, and then an *embarrassing* pose at the end of me doing double bunny ears to myself, grinning like an idiot. I snort at the young image of me but I go on to read:

Regarding Ethan Moon
In the event that the Tier 1 Oddity, Ethan J. Moon, is found alive, the following measures *must* be followed.

As of June 27, 2009, Ethan Moon was officially banished from Obscura and if seen shall be captured and executed.
(*there is suspicion that he was never done away with on the day of Jiah Grey's execution)

Personal Information:
Citizen Code: ☼-🕮-2199
Occult: Witch (Spirit) | Unknown*
*Unknown occults have been proven to be exceptionally dangerous

Ethan Moon poses a threat to the Invictus Project. He is capable of stopping Oddity hunts, causing revolts like that of his father, Yohan Moon, and is more than capable of taking down an entire district if lead or encouraged to do so. Ethan has powers too dangerous for battle or long-term capture, therefor death be the only solution.

Plan ZE-Ultimate2 (Update):
The LEU is to study high ranking Oddities before sentencing them to termination. If Ethan Moon is found alive, proceed with caution and capture him. Bring him nowhere else *Alive* to the Lamia dungeons.

The study of extracting the abilities from Oddities will continue and should ultimately be used on Ethan Moon. Report to Prince Zakirai for questions, concerns, or knowledge of Ethan Moon's whereabouts.

Tip: Sunstone may have weakening effects to Ethan Moon as it has proven to weaken the father, Yohan Moon. Proceed with caution.

There was more. Multiple other pages of describing what they believe all of my abilities were and what sort of creature I am. Defenses, what to look out for specifically, and methods of capture. I frown deeply and look over at Rose who had crossed over to sit beside me and read the papers as well.

"I suppose it's important to know this information, Ethan," Rose began after noticing my gaze. "Look at this page here." She flips the pages twice to the third page where it focused on methods of capture. "We could be much more prepared when things get worse for you. Should someone be pursuing you we'd at least know what to expect."

"That's right, Ethan," the prince chimes in. "I don't know what Hickman truly has in mind, but I think we can agree that he's been helpful giving you that."

"Look at this…" Rose flips a page again and reads aloud:

"—CLASSIFIED—During Yohan Moon's imprisonment, the LEU has conducted several experiments and tests on the inmate in order to understand more about him. The LEU has agreed that the inmate is some sort of elemental unlike any from Greenwood, but something entirely different. Apart of the category of light and dark. Yohan Moon is some sort of elemental of darkness. Moon and son Ethan Moon, possess devastating abilities unlike anyone else in Obscura. Their powers are made up of pure Chaos magic. Which includes abilities noted by the LEU as controlling others against their will, devastation attacks stronger than any other magic, entering another person's head and distorting the mind (unlike that of Vampire Hypnotism), and many other abilities yet to be fully understood. Periodically the inmate demonstrates dissociation similar to that of someone possessed. In this state the inmate loses control of himself (particularly when angered/aggravated) and becomes irrationally violent and destructive. It is not yet understood what causes this…"

Rose stops reading and stares blankly down at the papers in my hand. She closes her mouth and then looks over at her father. Perhaps expecting a proper explanation of what had been read, but he looked as lost as Rose and I did. I swallow thickly as I read over the supposed abilities my father and I have, and I shake my head incredulous to the idea that I could be anything like what was described.

"I'm not like that," I say, in protest against what was clearly a fact. I push the file into Rose's hands, ready to dismiss it all as if it had never been said. "I couldn't be like that. There's no way. I've been angry loads of times, I've never lost control of myself, and I certainly could never attack someone!"

"Except you have."

I look over at Aero who was leaning back comfortably in his chair now, sipping on his tea as if he hadn't said anything at all. I was beginning to understand that Aero was a very matter-of-fact, no sugar-coating kind of person. Admirable, and certainly needed when in denial, but it was harsh, no matter how kind his demeanor was.

"You have never been struck for any magical outbursts that came from your Spirit magic," the prince begins to explain. "Although you've come close, the druids made a point to protect you do to the fact that you had no one like you to help you control those powers. But for that other part of you, the druids aren't able to do anything about it. Especially since the last thing you did before being taken to the port-town was murder someone with those same powers your father used to attack people." The prince presses his lips together for a moment as he rethinks his way of explaining the matter to me. And then he continues. "That night was not your fault. I understand that you had worked yourself up to feel so much pain that you completely lost control. You were just a boy. But you were a boy who carried more power than he knew what to do with."

My muscles untense as I take in what the prince had to say. Although I wasn't too sure what to do with the information yet, I knew that it was important to understand how I got in this situation in the first place.

"Who did I kill?" I ask after a moment of thought. Whether or not that information was important, I felt I needed to know.

"Her name was Viola Blackclaw," the prince answers. She was a werewolf from Artemis district who, granted, had no business being so far on castle grounds. But she was shifted and she was hunting. It was an exceptionally dangerous situation the both of you had been in. And really you saved yours and Rose's lives. But at the cost of another. And unfortunately for you, Viola was the daughter of a remarkably powerful man. That is a well-known family of great nobility in Artemis. And although you may have lived to tell the tale, that family will never give up seeing you dead. Viola's father, Theodore, is a man who very well can hold a grudge. Even if it was an accident. That reason—that incident is the reason why you *need* to learn about these powers and *control* them. We all know you don't want to hurt anyone on purpose, or by accident. That's why I encourage you to seek out your father. Even if he might have used his powers for the opposite reason, *you* are not obligated to. Even if they are as devastating as described, you can learn to use them differently than Yohan Moon did."

"You *want* me to find my father? But everyone else explicitly told me not to," I say with a small frown. The prince is dusting away lint from his jacket as if what he was saying wasn't that big of a deal. But it took only a second for

379

him to look at me with eyes large and round like Rose's filled with urgency and seriousness.

"They're only saying that because they're afraid of your father and don't want to give him a reason to do something rash. Like breaking out of prison for example. This fear, however, is very much flawed. How on earth do they expect you to learn to control and master your powers, thereby having less accidents, and more probability of controlling the situation you're in? The druids want to lock you away and study you. Everyone else wants to lock you away and see you rot. But there are others like me who know you can turn this realm around. As of right now we are headed in the worst direction possible, and I fear there is no one else to stop it but you. ...If you're up to the challenge, that is."

I look down at my hands now that the prince had finished speaking. It all felt so overwhelming. I was basically thrown into a situation I clearly had no control over. And none of it sounded like it was going to be easy. I needed to understand my situation and fast. And as of right now I was still lacking the number one most important thing—my memory. I knew it was only up to me to recover the missing pieces and no silly spell or potion brewed up by River would fix it. If I had my memory in its entirety, I'd be better equipped to navigate this world and have an easier time to do what had to be done. And it was sounding like it is all up to me put a stop to Lamia's plan to rid Obscura of oddities like me and ultimately screw up the realm.

"Rose found out that my father has been imprisoned somewhere in the Sierra district," I say as I suddenly remember this fact. Yes, it was already my plan to find my father regardless of what anyone else said, and I was certainly relieved to hear that someone was on the same page with me. It only made sense to find the only person like me to help me with something no one else could. And perhaps he could explain those terrifying incidents involving scary black shadow things and monstrous voices of course, can't forget *that*. "Perhaps you know where it is exactly." I watch the prince as he pauses to think for a moment. And then his face lights up as he rises to his feet and scramble around for something to write on.

"Ah!" he exclaims, "I'm not sure exactly, however I do believe that your father is most likely in Chukushmi Sierra. I can draw you a sort of map, although

I can't say how accurate as I have not been to Sierra in quite a while. Just a moment." Prince Aero has gathered some loose parchment and a fountain pen and he's quickly scribbling some lines and what I imagine are names of certain landmarks to configure a makeshift map. After he finished inking the page, he comes over and hands it to me. "It certainly isn't perfect, but I think it's the best way to get there. I'm sure on your way you can find a better map or someone who more accurately knows the way. I say that it's best to cross the border from Greenwood than Lamia, particularly for you, Ethan."

"Are you saying I can go as well, Father?" Rose asks to clarify if she had his permission to venture off with me. The man snorted a little bit at his daughter's question and then he crosses his arms over his chest.

"I imagine I shall allow it. I'm sure you'd go against my word either way, little one. Besides, Ethan will need someone who can navigate Obscura better than he can. Only I expect you to be the utmost diligent. Especially for your nohab friend."

Rose looks at me, excitement momentarily crossing her expression before she caught herself and levels. But then it occurred to me what should happen when the guild questions where we've gone. Certainly, it wouldn't be a day trip.

"What if River and the others look for us?" I inquire to him. "I guess we'll be in a world of trouble when they find out. I've also learned my aunt is kinda scary, and if anything, River might send her and my uncle our way."

The prince chuckles this time and shakes his head at me.

"Ethan, even if they do find out, they cannot stop you unless you let them. Remember that if they do try to stop you, they are only shielding and delaying you from the inevitable. That's the way I see it, and I'm certain deep down they can agree. This, of course, is the same reason why your poor grandmother has not come home yet. Perhaps no one can bear the thought of losing you for real this time. But I believe you will prevail. You're strong, you always have been. I can only encourage you to do what you feel is right. Not what anyone else says. Trust yourself above any other. …And…if push comes to shove, I'll vouch for you."

Prince Aero smiles and I couldn't help but to smile in return. Somehow, he made everything feel more attainable—more possible. We knew what had to be done, the only matter was doing it. I had to. I might not have been too sure why just yet, but my gut feeling was enough to fuel my motivation.

After the conversation seemed to have ended and we had somehow moved to menial topics such as new favorite foods, books, and life in the mundane world, Rose had given a big yawn and stretched her arms out wide.

"I suppose I'd like to get out of this itchy dress now," the girl said tiredly as her father smiled fondly over at her.

"Then we all should prepare for bed. Ethan, I'll set you and your friend up with some extra blankets and pillows. I apologize, but my home is far smaller than what you may be used to at the guild."

I shake my head at this to say that it was nothing to me and he went off to retrieve the extra bedding. Rose had gotten up to go to her room. Carson hadn't come back yet, and actually I was beginning to worry. Did something happen to him? Has he gotten lost? I frown a bit to myself, and just before I decided to get up to go check for myself, the door was swinging open. Carson was stepping inside until he stopped after reluctantly catching my wide-eyed stare. His face was dark and unhappy, but he very clearly seemed like he had done a tremendous amount of thinking. His shoulders drop heavily as he finally shuts and locks the door, and then steps fully into the room. He passes where I was awkwardly positioned in a half sit half stand pose and he plops down on the couch across from me. I blink a few times, bewildered that he hasn't opened his mouth yet, and I slowly lower back down into the couch.

Prince Aero is entering the room again, carrying two thick blankets and some pillows. His head swivels as he realizes my friend had returned and his gaze seemed to be looking between us both as he analyzed the mood. He sets the bedding down on the coffee table and then stands up straight again, stretching his back a little bit after having to bend over.

"Well…I don't know if you boys want to lay on the floor or the couches but it's entirely up to you. So, I'll just leave this here and you figure it out amongst yourselves. The washroom is just down the hall to your left. The door on the *left* side. Please do not barge into my daughter's room. Thank you. If you need anything you can find me down the hall to the right. Or you can ask

Rose if she's up. See you boys in the morning." He gives a kind of wave and proceeds to his bedroom, leaving Carson and I to ourselves.

After I was sure the prince was gone, my head slowly swivels around to see the upset friend. He was bent over, quietly unlacing his converse and pulling them off, and his eyes only raised to meet mine after he was finished. We sat there, the situation feeling like a stern principal ready to reprimand a student. Carson is the first to say anything.

"I thought about it," he began with a deep inhale. "I thought about it and I'm still mad about it."

"I'm sorry," I say first. "I know keeping it from you was a bad move. But I didn't know about it for as long as you might think." Carson eyes me, his blue orbs reflecting the light of the fireplace and searching for any trace of a lie.

"Even still," he said, "you should've told me the moment you found out. I'm mad about it…but, not that much anymore. I just think it's wild that anyone could do that to someone. I mean I was manipulated—as a kid. My mom too! It doesn't sit well." He shakes his head from side to side, his hair flying until he settles back against the couch and relaxes. His stern expression slowly melts away and I hesitated to speak again for fear of agitating him further. "It's kind of put things in perspective for me…" he continued quietly. "All of this is so strange…and so *sudden*. Like I'm basically a pawn in your crazy life! Except…I know it's not your fault. It's just weird to see it from that perspective…"

I frown deeply at him. How could he say that he was a pawn in my life, that wasn't true at all. It upset me to know that that's what he's chalked it all up to.

"You're wrong," I told him. "You've been only one thing for the entire time I've known you. And that's a friend. It *is* pretty wild how it all started but at the end of the day, Carson, you have been nothing but a good friend to me. I'm sorry that you were used in a plot to fix up my own…very…strange problems, but I am at least happy that we were introduced because of it. So…don't be mad."

He turns his head away but he's side eyeing me as he thinks about whether or not to release his reservations about the whole thing. He cracks a smirk but tries to hide it. I snort at him and rise up to my feet.

"Hey, come on," I urge, "don't be mad. You're still my...*BFF*," I say in Carson fashion, although it pained me to have to utter such an atrocity. He smiles at this and stifles a laugh.

"Your BFF?" he says in a quieted valley girl accent. "More than the vampire?" He scoots closer to the edge of the couch as if he were going to stand up. And as he rid himself of his sour feelings, he raised his closed fits up like he was preparing to celebrate. My shoulders drop. I didn't have Rose's feelings in mind (especially not her super hearing) as mine and Rose's relationship was still quite the blur. I nod my head wildly up and down to demonstrate my enthusiasm to the blonde who was growing his familiar smile from ear to ear.

"More than the vampire," I confirm to humor him.

"Uhm, wow."

I jump a little and Carson whips his head around in surprise as Rose stood there in an old-style white night gown and a small cup in her right hand. Although she was wearing the regal expression she normally wore to manage the emotion in her face, her lips couldn't help but oust her by forming a small pout. She traipses over and around the couch to join the both us. She sets down her cup on the coffee table and then picks up one of the blankets, unfolds it, and drapes it over the floor. She sits down and pulls her legs close to her body and stares into the fire of the fireplace.

"I'm glad you two made up," she says slowly, and although at first, I thought it was supposed to be a dig at one of us, I realized she was sincere, just solemn in the way she spoke. "I was thinking while I prepared for bed that we are going to need some help—*real* help." She turns her head and looks at the both of us. "Sierra District is very dangerous, specifically for the likes of you, Ethan. That place—it's crawling with Oddity hunters. Hunters make tons of money out of Sierra alone."

"What do Oddity hunters do exactly?" Carson asks. His smile had disappeared and actually he looked deadpan serious. "I mean, what's in it for them aside from money. What do they do with the oddities?"

"Well," Rose began, "Oddity hunters have always had the job of seeking out and capturing oddity citizen who have done a crime or used an ability that makes them 'odd' by mistake—or on purpose—that has hurt someone or something. They catch them and put them away. Or a more annoying procedure they began to do for some time now is carding. If the oddity citizen isn't carrying their registration card or have tampered with it to change their rank and tier or how many strikes they have, they will put them away for it. But ever since they threw Ethan's father in jail after his run-in with some Lamia soldiers, they've been hunting by tier and rank, whether the individual has done anything wrong or hasn't and taking them away. Only I have no idea where and what they do with them, it's just something that I have heard that's been going on. Another thing is that hunters can be paid off for bounty. If someone has something against a certain odd citizen…well unfortunately they've been getting away with hunting them down and getting rid of them for pay. It's gotten far out of hand, *especially* in Sierra. That's why I think we need to tell someone other than my father that we're going there." She turns and looks at me. "Maybe your aunt and uncle could—"

"No," I cut her off. "I don't think they would like to hear that I'm going against their word to find my father. They would probably stop us if anything."

"Well, we need *someone*, Ethan."

I think for a moment, the three of us eyeing each other until one of us came up with something. I could agree that we needed another Obscurian who we could trust to know where we were headed, to keep a secret, and come help us if we really needed it. But the only other person I knew that hasn't already condemned me for looking for the man who made me was……I really didn't want to say it…

"What about Victoria?" I suggest with a sour taste in my mouth.

"No," Rose protests this time and swivels her whole body around to face Carson and me. She props herself up on her knees and she shakes her head wildly.

"But Rose—"

"Absolutely not! If she ends up tagging along, I will have to physically remove my own *fangs* and shove them into my eardrums so I'll be deaf to her incessant blathering about inappropriate things!"

"…What sort of inappropriate things…" Carson mutters and side-eyes the girl. Well, he was clearly feeling better… (please hear the eyeroll in my voice). Both of us ignore him after a sneer from Rose.

"Look, sure Victoria is…conceited, and a little annoying but whatever you and her have against each other, I think it should be set aside just this once. I mean I'm sure she will understand the situation and be willing to help if we just tell her."

"She might want something for it though," Carson points out. He snickers a little as Rose and I look over at him. "I mean she seems like the kind of person to make people buy her silence."

"Well…" I say, "whatever it is, I'm sure it'll be reasonable. And besides, Rose, we don't have to just let her know, we can tell Autumn too. Maybe her magic doesn't seem to be the best…she at least seems very knowledgeable, so…that's all we really know, isn't it?" I watch Rose hesitate as she considers what I've said, and then she reluctantly nods her head in agreement.

"I suppose you're right," she says. "But if she comes along and says two words about my occult, I swear I will throw her into the clouds! I mean it."

"Oooh, I'd love to see that wrestling match," Carson chimes with a goofy look on his face.

"Shut it," Rose snaps at him in return and he raises his hands innocently.

"Okay…noted," I mumble. Telling Victoria would be the best option, I was sure of it, because if push came to shove and we were faced with real trouble, she could let the others know to help us. It was done. We would head over there tomorrow, give Victoria and Autumn the news, pack up any necessities and journey off to Sierra. I will meet my father…for the first time…tomorrow.

I frown to myself and the others pick up on it before I did.

"What's the matter?" Rose asks first. "All of a sudden you look so sad…"

"Oh…" I began. Actually, I wasn't entirely sure what I was feeling, but I certainly didn't feel good. I take my seat again on the couch and my gaze shifts over to the fire place. I watch the flames jump and dance around each other, and I shake my head as I found the words I wanted to say. "It's just strange to meet a parent you never knew before, I guess. And the amnesia doesn't count. I never knew him. And even still all I've heard are terrible things about him. Was he really *that* bad? It's a little scary to think that I could be like him…particularly when my memory comes back."

"But you're not like him, and you won't ever be like him," Rose says and rises to her feet. She comes over and sits close beside me. Unexpectedly she wraps her arms around me and squeezes me into a hug. It felt a little weird but I reminded myself that Rose has all the memories of caring about me that I didn't, so I knew that it shouldn't have been out of the ordinary for me. She rests her head against my shoulder and sighs deeply. "Perhaps that's your fear and like your trauma it could be stopping you from remembering everything. You're scared of misusing your powers and hurting others. Accidents happen, Ethan, but you are nothing like your father. You will do good things in this world; I know it."

Accidents happen. Those words stuck in my head more than all of the others. I look at her suddenly with a confounded expression and she leans backward to see me properly.

"Rose…" I began with a start, "tell me what happened!" I demand. "I mean what happened to *you*? Everyone, even you keep leaving that part out of the story."

The girl presses her lips together and retracts her arms and places them into her lap. It was clear in her face that she was racking her brain to come up with the right thing to say, perhaps and excuse or a diversion to the story. I catch her hand moving, rubbing at her arm in a sheepish manner, and then she lets out a slow breath.

"I was hurt that night," she begins to admit. Her voice was quiet and measured, and she looked nowhere else but her lap. "We were straying too far from home, and I struggled to keep up with you. You were chasing after a rabbit to see where it would go, but as I was calling after you to come back home… that's when we ran into…into—" She shuts hers eyes as if to rid herself of the memory. She swallows hard and took in another deep breath. "Viola killed it. That rabbit. It was gruesome—entirely awful, and you became so livid, so red hot over it that you didn't even realize that she was preparing to attack us next." Rose turns her head and finally her glassy eyes meet mine and she places her hand on my arm, giving a small squeeze. "You really did save our lives that night. But you lost control of yourself in the process. And you weren't using spirit magic…it was something else. It was frightening. She was nothing but fur and bone after it all. I didn't know what to do because you were still radiating with this…raw power, and you were still so angry even after you'd gotten rid of her. I needed to stop you, or to calm you down. I called your name so many times but nothing was getting through to you… So, I tried to take your hand… But that power—what you did wasn't your fault. It wasn't purposeful."

"What did I do?" I encourage her quietly.

"I don't know." She shakes her head and she's holding back tears. "It was like a shock, almost like I was struck with lightening. It burned so bad like acid and…well…" I watch her sigh as she collects her emotions and settles them. She shakes her head once more and then pushes up to her feet. "I'm sorry, Ethan, but I really don't want to talk about it anymore. Please don't make me." She looks over at me and I nod at her to acknowledge that it was still a difficult topic. But at least I knew the incident in better detail than before.

"I didn't mean to push you," I say and rise to my feet as well. I offer a smile and I place my hand on her shoulder. "Forgive me, Rose." She looks at me over her shoulder and she offers a faint smile in return.

"Let's go to bed. It's awfully late and we'll need our energy for tomorrow. We can plan our strategy in the morning."

Carson and I nod our heads and the blonde stood up as well. He smiles at the both of us and places his hand out like an awkward sports team break. When Rose and I eye him and his hand cynically he laughs and gestures for us to join in.

"Now that there's no more secrets between us—I hope, we should work together as a stronger team. We should come up with a fancy name and everything."

"We'll just leave that job to you then, Carson," Rose chuckles.

"Fine, team Foxxy Crew it is then. One, two, three, break!" He was the only one to throw his hand up in the air as Rose and I cringed at the title he obviously already had prepared. He's spinning away and went to adjust his bedding before plopping down on the floor in front of the fire. "Someone go cut off the lights," he calls and waves his hand back and forth. Rose and I share a look, and I watch the girl chuckle to herself and shake her head as she walked around the room to turn off the lamps and the overhead lights that were on.

"Goodnight, the both of you," Rose bids before she leaves for her bedroom.

After she had gone and I finished rearranging my blankets on the couch, I laid down to go to sleep. But it was much harder than I was expecting for that night.

I find myself staring ahead at the fading flickering light of the fireplace and listening to Carson's snoring as I struggled to put my mind to rest. I couldn't help but dwell over thoughts of my father, and really getting to meet him soon. What would he be like? Would he accept me even though he and my mother separated? Would he help me? Or would he turn me away? Was he as bad as everyone says?

I close my eyes, begging sleep to have mercy on me this once. I couldn't block out the sound of the crackling fire, nor the sound of Carson's nose choir. I wished to hear something else, or better yet nothing at all. I even resorted to counting sheep like my grandmother would encourage sometimes when I was a kid.

One...two...three...

It's definitely not working.

...four...five...six...

I can't even clearly imagine a sheep I—

...seven........eight...

"Ethan..."

I turn my head, or at least I thought I had. It was only that I hadn't realized that I had fallen into a dream at first.

"Love is so important. It's a necessity of life, for no matter who you are or what..."

I nuzzle my young face closer to my mother who had wrapped me up in her warm embrace. She strokes the hair at the nape of my neck and she continues.

"The man called Balance was very sad, and often very lonely. He had only one friend he called Counselor. And Counselor worked very hard each day to teach Balance about the differences between Day and Night."

"Day and night?" I question with a scrunched-up nose. "Everyone knows day is when the sun is up and night is when the moon is up! Balance must have been really silly, eomma." My mother laughs in response and shakes her head from side to side.

She pushes me backward a little so that we could see each other's face clearly and she goes on to explain:

"That's not quite the Day and Night that I meant, Hyunnie." She smiles brightly but something in her eyes seemed distracted. She takes in a breath and says: "Day and Night can mean a lot of things. But simply understand that they are opposites. They are different from each other, but both work together in many ways. Counselor told Balance that Day and Night cannot exist without the other. They need each other to thrive and to create peace. Balance tried his very best to understand Counselor's teachings. He thought about them every day at every minute and every second. He tried absorbing this knowledge like a sponge, he tried calculations and piecing it together like an elaborate puzzle. But Balance was always missing one single piece."

"Love!" I shout as I listen closely to my mother's story.

"Yes! You're right! That missing piece was always love. Balance couldn't understand love because he never grew up with it. He was always alone except for Counselor. And he was so much more different than anyone else he met and tried to befriend. He had so much difficulty as he thought over what it meant to have peace like Day and Night did. So much so that he began to only focus on one and not the other. He focused on Night. It was always Night that bothered him so much, he began to distrust Counselor, even when Counselor had nothing but the best in mind for him. He tried to remind him that Night cannot exist without Day but Balance felt otherwise. He said that there was only Night in this world. And that Day was only seen by a small privileged group of people. Sadly, Counselor gave up on Balance as Balance began to lose his way."

"What happened?" I ask. "Why won't he just listen to Counselor?"

"Well, one day, Balance found that one missing piece."

I gasp and cover my mouth. "He did??"

"Yes. He found it. But only for a very short time. Balance stopped listening to Counselor, and he tried to make his own way. But one day he ran into a timid young lady named Pariah. Pariah learned a lot of lessons in the short time she lived. Lessons that included understanding that imperfections are actually perfect."

"Really?" I ask. "How can something not perfect be perfect?"

My mother smiles again at me and taps the tip of my nose.

"Something that is imperfect is only an opinion made by the observer," she explains. "But really, imperfections are meant to be. They can teach us lessons that grow the way that we see or think. So, in reality, imperfections are always imperfectly perfect. Pariah tried to help Balance understand this after he had fallen for her resilience and the way that she observed her surroundings. In the beginning she believed that it was working as Balance seemed to be much brighter, much happier, and more forgiving. But this only lasted a short while. Although they loved each other a great deal—Pariah having fallen for his love of knowledge and poetry, and how deep down he wanted nothing more than good for everyone and everything, things began to change. And Balance stopped focusing on the life he promised to build with Pariah. He began thinking about Night and Counselor tried again to convince him to see otherwise. But the more he ignored the ones who loved him and who cared about him, the more he became unwell."

"Did Balance become sick?" I ask this time. I watch my mother's eyes drop and she nods her head slowly in response.

"Yes," she confirms, "he became sick, and lonelier than ever. Poor Balance lost his way even while he was trying to do what he thought was right. And then eventually, no one heard from Balance again… Love…is very important, Ethan. Never forget that. Even through our darkest nights, the ones we hold dearest will always be there to help. Only, we need to be willing to embrace it."

"So, the one called Counselor—Balance didn't embrace his help…right?"

"Right. One day you may meet Counselor. And if you do, treat him with care. And always heed his warnings, no matter what. Don't be like that Balance fellow."

"I'm a good listener, eomma! You tell me all the time! I bet I will be one hundred times better than Balance because I'm Ethan the Great! Knight of good listening!" I'm giggling and my mother laughs and squeezes me tight in response.

"You sure are, my brave knight. But for now, it's Ethan the Great's bed time."

My mother is kissing me goodnight and she leans over and blows out the lantern near my bed. And then the image fades away, and I'm left with nothing but darkness and a sore feeling of emptiness.

Something was happening now. As I felt like I was floating in absolute nothingness for however long, I saw a flicker of light. Like the first go of a lighter. And then all at once I could see nothing but fire. I could hear those cries that I often felt haunted by in Whitechapel. Flashing on and off like a failing monitor I could see bits and pieces of a woman, and a scene I couldn't make light of just yet. I could see her dark hair; I could see her eyes squeezed shut. She was stuck to something.

Eommaaaa!

I could hear my own young voice and I knew that what I was seeing...... may have been better locked away in the recesses of my mind.

The image changes for the last time. I can see what may have been another woman. Her silver locks were drenched in water. Her feet were bare. I couldn't help but notice the faint buzzing sound and the flickering image of a rather intimidating mountain range.

I felt like I was pouring sweat, and suffocation may just be the end of me. It wasn't until I felt two cold hands shaking the bejesus out of my arm did I jolt awake, sitting up and gasping for air like a fish out of water. Through my sweaty bangs I could see a slightly concerned Rose squatting next to me and patiently waiting for me to get a grip. As my vision clears, I look the girl up and down. She scowls at me in return after I had begun squinting quizzically at her.

"What are you wearing?" I gurgle through my morning voice.

"What's it to you?" she shoots back defensively as she sat a mug of tea onto the coffee table while she stood to her feet. She wore some elaborate looking black blouse that seemed like modern Victorian with its high collar clasped together with a fancy pendant. The sleeves puffed a little at the ends and there was some rather nice embroidered lace. She wore all black with form-fitting pants and knee-high boots with enough metal to be considered a weapon.

"I was gonna say it was nice!" I snap back. Yes, I definitely woke up on the wrong side of the—couch.

"In a goth vampire kinda way," Carson decides to add as he is entering the room and towel drying his hair.

I hear a scoff and over in the kitchen was Aero who seemed to be trying to throw together a breakfast for everyone. Obviously, I was late to the party in the getting up early department.

"I found out why your friend is ignorable. Rose was just telling me earlier," Aero says from behind the counter in the kitchen.

"UHHMM, I'm pretty sure Rose said *adorable*. NOT ignorable; thank you, sir."

"If that's what you would have liked to have heard, son," the prince answers with a snort.

"Drink that, Ethan. It'll help you—um…" Rose doesn't quite finish as she is turning away preoccupying herself with braiding up the ends of her hair. "Go shower and get ready, by the way. We don't have much time."

"What time is it, anyway," I grumble and I swing my legs over the edge of the couch. I rub my eyes, turning my head this way and that as the three others were already up, awake, and moving. I then spot a clock hanging on the wall across from me. I examine its crazy moving needles and its weird symbols, and then I breathe a heavy sigh.

"God, it's literally just 6:30. Why do we need to go *right* now?"

Everyone stops. Even Carson stopped scrolling through a graphic novel he had downloaded on his phone. Rose stares at me with wide eyes for a moment, and then she whips around to check the clock for herself.

"Ethan…" she began dumbfounded, "did you just read the time?"

I blink, now feeling unsure of myself and what I did only just a moment ago.

"Did I just read the time?" I repeat in the same tone as Rose and look back over at the clock. Suddenly it was very clear. Like I had been reading this sort of clock for forever. The symbols were easy. Very clearly Eastern Arabic numerals. Probably anyone would have guessed the time regardless if it weren't for the planetary symbols in between them and the extra hands pointing and spinning in all directions. There was Theban script on it as well and so were other indications of the phase of the moon, the current season, the time of sunrise and sunset, and the time of moonrise and moonset. Yep, everything looked in order.

"Ethan!" Rose brings me out of my thoughts and she's suddenly lunging her body over to me and gripping my shirt in order to yank me around the couch and over to the clock. "Ethan, what does that say?!" she demands me to read eagerly as she points up to the top of the clock with words written with Theban.

"Uh," I shake my head from the jolting sensation of shock and excitement this early in the morning, "I-it just says O.S.T. Which obviously stands for Obscura Standard time."

"Mm. Yeah. Obviously," Carson chimes uncomfortably close to my ear after having joined us by my side.

"And what about that?" Rose asks, now pointing to the bottom of the clock's face.

"M.E.S.T.," I read fluidly. "But…what does that mean?"

"M.E.S.T!" Rose nearly shouts as if it would make more sense that way. "Mundane Eastern Standard Time. The time in where you were living before. In Whitechapel."

The prince is rounding the kitchen counter now and he's drying his hands with a drying towel as he joins the three of us at the clock.

"That's right," the prince began, "I set the second time to the one in Whitechapel. It was just to keep up with the time it was there for when I communicated with Catherine," he explained.

"You mean…you talked with my grandmother while she kept the biggest secret of my life too?" The prince eyes me as he measures the correct thing to respond with.

"Well, when you put it that way it sounds as if I'd been plotting against you. Only I was simply trying to keep her updated of the state of Lamia district in order to predict a safe time for yours and hers return. What your grandmother decided to do in the end is between you and her."

Understandable…moving on. Rose turns around to face me, and she scans my face for a moment before she took in a breath to speak.

"Can you remember anything else, Ethan?" she asks hopefully. Well, I must have made some kind of progress if I am suddenly able to read the craziest clock ever known to man. But the more I thought about it the more I doubted if it made much of a difference.

"I don't think so," I answer disappointedly. Aside from remembering a story told to me by my mother, I just didn't think it made a difference.

"That's a shame…" Rose shakes her head and turns away. Her father watches her for a second before he clasps his hands together.

"Well, let's have breakfast, shall we?"

"That sounds good to me!" Carson says a little too loudly as he goes directly to the kitchen.

It was there that we were able to sit around a small round table that seated four. The prince had threw together scrambled eggs, orange wedges, and warm bowls of sweet porridge. As all of us sat down, Aero had gone to the fridge and returned with two different bottles. He takes the time to fill mine and Carson's glasses up with orange juice, and then a small glass of blood. Carson and I both couldn't help but stare as Rose thanked her father and he was turning away with a glass of his own in his hand, downing the stuff quick as he went to return the bottles in the fridge. I wanted to ask *so* bad what it was exactly and where it comes from. How does vampire blood drinking exactly work in real life. Should I be ready to invest in some neck shields in case someone gets a little…crazy… I swallow a bit as I watch Rose take a sip of that stuff, and then like knives impaling my eyeballs, Rose's eyes flick up and she glares at me as if I had been rude or said something offensive.

"Please explain!" Carson blurts out before I or anyone else could say anything. I inhale my entire soul and recoil with embarrassment as I fight the urge to Friday Night Smackdown the inconsiderate blonde. Carson shrugs as he sees me glaring at him and Rose let's out a sigh.

"I suppose there's nothing wrong with asking," she says and sets down her glass. "I'll make it long story short as I am sure you are not asking for an entire Vampire history lesson. As you are aware, Vampires need blood to live. Just like you need water to live. Except vampires need water too, it's no good to be dehydrated." She wrinkles her nose to herself and then continues, "It's common sense that hunting innocents and taking their blood without consent is barbaric and unlawful, and harming animals for their blood if they're not being used to feed the hungry is wrong. Many years ago, an alternative was created by a past group of Elemalex witches who famously created what vampires live on today. It's said to replicate the exact properties and nutrients of blood that vampires need without containing any substances taken from humans or animals. It's brilliant, and I am proud to know that I live in a time where this proper substitute exists."

"That's cool," Carson nods his head in approval but of course he couldn't just stop there. "So why do you look so ashamed every time we see you drink it?" Rose scoffs and shakes her head at the question.

395

"We'll see how you feel drinking blood in front of others who would inwardly be uncomfortable with even the thought of it. It's what I have to do but It's not my goal to make people watch!"

"Okay, fair," Carson admits. "But I just wanna know one thing."

"Please…" I beg quietly, knowing whatever it was would be more embarrassing than the last question.

"What? It'd be good to know. What if we have to keep an eye out for it?"

"An eye out for what?" I question.

"Are there ever times that vampires, like, lose control or whatever? Like, if they get really hungry and they can't help it or something!?"

The prince is returning from whatever he was doing over by the sink. He sits in the open seat making all of us close our mouths as if we were talking inappropriately. He chuckles a little to himself after seeing our hesitant faces all the while slurping up the last of his porridge.

"You know what," he began after he had cleared his mouth, "your friend asks really good questions, Ethan." My eyes widen at this. Although Carson had his times here and there, I wouldn't jump to any conclusions so fast. "On the rare occasion that a vampire is starving, there is in fact the need for concern of an involuntary attack. Vampires cannot drink the blood of other vampires as that would lead to horrid poisoning. So yes, I would not stick around a vampire who hasn't any access to blood. You'd find yourself drained in an instant. There is also a very small select few of vampires who—well let's just say they choose to not follow the law. If you aren't lingering around the very south side of Lamia Common, then I wouldn't worry about running into them. They typically confine themselves in that area and don't normally stray too far from it. This is good information to know for you boys. Do not make the mistake of trusting any vampire you see. That goes for anyone, really, not just vampires."

The three of us nod our heads in response to acknowledge that we all had been listening to the prince. And really no one said anything after that. Rose, Carson, and I focused on finishing breakfast as we needed to leave soon and head back to Greenwood with enough morning time to spare.

After breakfast and helping the prince clean up the kitchen and where Carson and I had slept to show our gratitude for his kindness in letting us stay (with a hot meal free of charge!), the three of us were now gathering our things and preparing to depart. Rose had strapped on a scary looking utility belt, filling a pouch with vials of something, storing a dagger in its holster and a few other tools that I didn't catch before she bundled herself up in a thick black cloak, complete with a big furry hood. She also had a bag that she filled with necessities, like extra packages of blood, snacks (thank goodness), and other stuff I didn't see. I watch her throw her hood up over her head and she is the first to step out of the house with Carson following after her.

I am the last to leave as I was collecting the file that that Julian fellow had me retrieve, and fumbling with my suit jacket. I sure couldn't wait to change out of it. Finally, I head toward the door and I step outside onto the porch. I was greeted by very chilly gusts of wind that made me wish I had a real coat on, and the chimes that clanked together suspending from the porch roof. Just as I was stepping down the porch steps, Prince Aero came out of the house and approached me. He placed his hand on my shoulder to get my attention, and then he gestures for me to follow him. The prince and I step down off of the porch and we round the house toward the back. Carson and Rose were standing afar, watching and wondering where I was going. But I gestured for them to wait a moment while I saw what the prince wanted.

I follow the man all the way to the back of the cottage and halfway up the hill where Lamia Castle could be seen clearly in the distance. The clouds hung low today. They were gray and melancholy; giving the castle a gloomy mood. The prince stands beside me, staring ahead at the structure with his hands deep in his maroon coat jacket. His expression was unreadable. Clearly a trait mastered by royalty to limit how much someone could read about them. But his eyes hinted at the fact that he was longing for something. Holding his breath until he got what he was looking for. I hear him draw in a deep breath and his gaze is unchanging.

"What do you think, Ethan?" he asks, seemingly out of nowhere. My brow furrows a little bit at this question as I draw my eyes away from the castle to glance over at him.

"Sorry?" I question. It wasn't a difficult thing that he asked. Only it took me by surprise. No one this entire time has asked me at all what I thought about anything.

"I imagine this is very tough for you," the prince adds. "Your poor memory is gone, and you've been thrown into an unfamiliar world entirely different from what you were used to. Not only that, but you find that this world has a number of issues left up to you to handle and work out. I'm sure it isn't easy."

"...I think you explained everything perfectly, sir," I respond quietly. At least it seemed *one* person understood if no one else did. "I have no idea what I'm doing..."

"I think we all feel that way in our lives," he offers. "Sometimes we are faced with difficult situations and tough decisions. And the scariest part is not knowing if we are making the right decision or not." I look over at the man who then spared another glance at me, offering a faint smile that faded as fast as he looked away again. "I regret a decision I once made," he suddenly admits. "A long time ago I saw the malevolence growing in secret within those walls. My father, King Xxavier, overlooked it, believing that there were only a spoiled few. Believing innocently that things would work out in the end. But he was wrong. And ultimately it was up to me to stop it before it erupted into what it is now. I saw what was wrong in the castle, and I chose to not be a part of it. I thought that by sacrificing the throne, it would demonstrate that my pointing out the ill-will of others would be taken seriously. But I was wrong. I regret that decision. Because I often think that maybe...just maybe if I had taken my father's place, I could have controlled the situation myself. And maybe none of this would have ever happened. Especially what has happened to you, Ethan. And for that, I am sorry." The prince finally faces me and he places his hand on my shoulder again as he gives me a sincere look. "Don't make the same mistake I did, son. Always do the right thing, even if it's hard. And if you find you've made a mistake, right your wrongs. That way you do not have to live a sad life of regret. 'Only you can be the change that you want to see'. Your mother used to say that." I watch him as he looks like he's just remembered something. He puts his hand back into his pocket and he began to pull something out. "Speaking of your mother..." he started, "this used to belong to her." He is handing me a small book. I take it in my hands and see the cover that read "Adventures of Minhyun Lee". "You enjoyed to read it a lot on your own," he explains. "But it meant a great deal to your mother."

"…Thank you," I say sincerely. "Truly."

The prince nods his head and then he turns back to the castle. He has his hands clasped behind his back now and I was sure the conversation had ended. But before I could even pick up a foot or bid a farewell, the man drew in another breath.

"Do you know why it's called Lamia Castle?" he asked.

"No…" I answer, unsure of where he was going with this.

"My ancestors long before me built this place," he begins to explain. "They wanted to create a place filled with warmth and light. They hoped that our piece of the realm could be somewhere everyone could count on to be safe, fair, and happy. So, they named it Lamia. They thought by giving a name that meant light would fill its surroundings with light." He pauses for a moment as he gazed upon the castle in the distance, but then he snorts to himself. "Lamia also refers to a monster with the head of a woman and the body of a snake who feeds on the blood of children, so take that as you will. I think what I'm trying to say is that if you ever feel pressure on yourself from the expectations of others, or even conflict within from your own expectations, remember that everything and everyone can be seen one way and then seen another by someone or something else. Right now…Lamia is a monster, but I hope that one day she can return to being a beacon of light." Prince Aero turns to me one last time and his expression was serious. "Let's not waste any more time, Ethan. You must go, and you need to get to Sierra and find your father. There's only a matter of time before my sister's plans have affected everywhere else, and you are truly the only one who can set things right. But in order to do that, you *need* to recover your memory. Or at the very least, to understand your powers enough to use them to your advantage. It has to be you. You hold the power to change our very existence if you chose. Believe in yourself, Ethan. And if you don't…believe in your friends and family. I wish for peace. I wish for peace for Obscura…and for you, you poor boy."

I frown a little at his words. There was the reminder that somehow the fate of Obscura was stored upon *my* shoulders. Did it really only have to do with the amount of power I had? Even while I still didn't know how to use it? But at the same time, I didn't want to let anybody down. The prince senses my apprehension and he places his hand on top of my head and ruffles my hair around.

"Don't fret. Now go on. I've wasted enough of your time already."

I nod at him as he pushes me along to walk back down the hill so that I could join my friends again. In no time they were turning their heads from whatever conversation they were having and wearing painfully curious expressions to where I had gone and what I may have been discussing with the prince.

"Where'd you go?" Carson was the first to ask once I was in earshot.

The prince starts waving at us three the moment I had joined them where they stood.

"Goodbye!" he calls as he began toward the porch again. "Take care of yourselves! And don't forget what I said, Ethan!"

The three of us wave to the man as we begin our way to the trail that would lead to the boarder. Rose taking the lead, of course.

"Bye!" Carson says in return to the man. "Thanks for breakfast!"

"Farewell, Father!" Rose bids with a smile.

I watch them both and then turn to see the prince watching with a now complicated expression. I blinked once and my eyes had shifted. I could physically see his looming worry and guilt in the shade of grays and browns. And beside him were two figures that weren't clear enough for me to make out. One of which had a comforting hand on his shoulder and lips that turned down with concern for the man. While the other stood with their hands clasped together in front of them. I couldn't make out any other features except for pupils that glowed an unearthly green. As I was walking backwards with Carson and Rose, I could not tear my eyes away until I felt Rose tug at my sleeve. I turn automatically to see her looking up at me also with a concerned expression. Clearly taking notice of the eye color change. When she didn't readily say anything, I turn my head back again to see those figures standing on either side of the prince. But they had gone, and my vision went back to normal.

It hadn't been a long time at all before we reached the Lamia boarder to Greenwood. We were able to cross through with no problems aside from unpleasant eyeballing and mean-mugging from guards. But after some encouraging from the princess to stop holding up our time as the guards were trying to figure out if my passport was real and if it was truly the fabled Ethan-Jae Moon we were able to flag down a carriage to cut down the arrival time back to Willow Way. Once we arrived and hiked down the path back to the guild, we were greeted outside by a perpetually grumpy looking Jem who happened to be chopping up some wood in front of the cottage.

"Good morning, Mr. Magno," Rose greets first to make sure he noted who we were approaching. After Jem swings an axe skillfully into one last block of wood, he stands up straight and stretches his back before his eyes rolled over to the three of us. He snorts a little, and I was sure he wasn't actually going to say anything at all, but then he points to the door of the cottage.

"You've got mail, kid," he grunts out. "River's been looking for you."

Carson, Rose and I share a look between each other and after I thanked him, we go to enter the home. I was the first to step inside and immediately my head was on a swivel looking for the old woman, but I didn't readily see her. Passing by the kitchen I caught glimpse of Autumn sitting at the kitchen table, her head propped up by her elbow over the largest book I've ever seen. But by her fuzzy pink slippers, her messy hair, and crooked glasses—and not to mention her nodding off and nearly face planting into the book, I knew she probably didn't get any rest during the night. I skirt around and come in to the kitchen to wake her.

"Autumn!" I call, basically scaring her as her hand slipped from her head, her forehead smacking the book before she pushed herself back in the chair against the wall behind her.

"DWAH!" she shouts before pressing her hand over her heart. She blinks her eyes open and then readjusts her glasses on her face before she noticed who I was. "Gosh, Ethan!" she whines and pouts at me. "I could have suffered a heart attack."

"You're too young," I say with an amused snort. "Autumn, is River home? Jem said she'd been looking for me."

"Oh…" She scratched her head for a second and then finds her fingers caught in a knot. After yanking her fingers free from the messy strands, she says: "She isn't home. She had a meeting over in Julieth's Quarter. I don't know when she'll be back." She gives a great yawn and then rubs her eyes underneath her glasses.

"Okay…" I say, "Jem also said I had mail?"

Autumn takes a moment to register what I said and then she points over to the counter near the sink. I turn and go to retrieve it after spotting it. Just as I took hold of the letter, Carson came bounding in the room directly headed toward the fridge like it was his house, only pausing once he took note of Autumn all disheveled at the kitchen table.

"Ew, haven't you slept?" He squints over at the girl from where he stood at the fridge, already pulling it open. Autumn scrunches up her face at him in offense as she begins to wipe the crust from her eyes.

"I did," she defends herself. "I took a 45-minute nap, exactly!"

"I didn't mean a *nap*, girl, I said *sleep*."

As they went back and forth over whether or not she's slept or even showered I focused on the letter addressed to me. I open the envelope and pull out a piece of parchment. The handwriting was big and elaborate, written with a sort of fountain pen or even a quill. It read:

> *Kid,*
>
> *I found a location where the artifact might be hidden. I know you will be in Sierra, looking for that father of yours, so when you get the chance, meet me at the south side of the Fichik Mountains. I could surely use your help. Don't forget our deal. If you come, I just might have something you will be greatly interested in. If you don't, I'd watch my back.*
>
> *Tata!*
> *~Firebird*

I frown a little at the letter. It must have been from Julian. I didn't know when I'd even get the chance to go to…where ever the Fichik Mountains were. But I guess after finding and settling things with my father perhaps I could head in that direction. I close the letter and shove it into my pocket, and as I turn to head out of the kitchen I am jumping out of my skin by meeting face to face with Rose.

"WAH!" I yelp involuntarily as she stands there with her arms crossed eyeing me. "God, Rose! Maybe you need a bell!"

"What was that?" Rose says instead, ignoring that fact that she startled me out of my boots.

"What was what?"

"*That*! That letter you had. What did it say? Who was it from?"

"…Oh." I reach back into my pocket and pull it out again to hand it to her. "It's from Julian…" I say quieter as to not bring the attention of Autumn this way. "He's asking for my help again."

She opens it and reads it over before shaking her head.

"I don't like this," she said with a deep frown. "Ethan, he's threatening you to do things for him!" I shush her and push her backward out of the kitchen and towards the den.

"I know. But there's something in it for me—which sounds terrible but that's not what I meant. I mean he will help me as long as I help him. And so far, it doesn't seem to be a bad thing."

"Famous last words," Rose sneers and turns away. "If you get hurt because of him there's nothing I can do. Because you made the decision on your own."

"Fine," I answer. "I will take that responsibility. Don't worry."

"Fine." She looks back at me over her shoulder and then she gestures toward the stairs. "Go get changed and packed. And hurry up, we don't have any more time to waste. It's better to take advantage of as much sunlight as possible."

"'Kay…" I take the letter back from her and then head toward the stairs.

"And Ethan," Rose stops me before I had gotten too far, "wear something normal today, will you? The less you draw attention the better."

I pout a little at her before I continue my way upstairs. So "normal" meant no hoodie, no sweatpants. Fine. But I'm still wearing my Air Max 97's.

16

Pressure

Princess Annika's POV

I don't know who I saw. There was no way to possibly tell. Ethan Moon is dead, and that's the whole of it. If I hear one more person tell me another roomer, made up, untrue—

"Princess," I turn my head to see my lady-in-waiting bowing her head to me by the door of my bedroom, "the head border patrol officer has requested to speak with you. Shall I let him know you'll be down?" Will it be the third time someone tells me they spotted that boy at the boarder? Certainly not. It's the busiest time of the season, there could be any number of reasons. "Princess?" she calls again after I hadn't answered.

"Yes, Nava. Tell him I'll be down," I tell the girl.

"Yes, Princess." She gives a curtsy and she begins to step out when I stop her again.

"Nava," I call, "come back and help me tie up my hair, won't you?"

"Yes, Princess," the girl says again with another curtsy. She leaves and I am again, sitting in my bed and stuck fretting the start of the day.

Nava had returned momentarily to help me into one of my favorite gowns with purple draping sheer fabrics that swept across the floor. She helped me knot my braids atop of my head to frame the tiara I wore. Then she was leading me out of the confines of my room and to the downstairs meeting chambers.

I step into the room where the head border patrol officer and two other border patrol guards were already seated. The three of them stood as I entered, and not far behind me had been my son, Ryland, who entered the chamber as well. I wasn't sure what to expect, but then again, deep down I did.

"Good morning, Princess Annika," the head officer, Esra, begins to greet. "King Ryland, thank you for seeing us today."

I take my seat first and my son sits beside.

"Yes, good morning," I greet first. "As this meeting was not scheduled, I will ask why we were summoned here today. Is there anything out of the ordinary?"

I watch the three men look between each other before one of the guards pulls out a sheet of paper. As it was handed over to me, I couldn't help the dryness in my throat upon seeing the printed image. There he was. My nightmare. My biggest headache to date. It was a snapshot of that retched Ethan Moon's passport. Updated, and unmistakable. He was no longer a small boy easily disposable. No, he was much older now, to my dismay. There was no telling what he could possibly be capable of now. And out for revenge for that matter.

"Ethan Moon was seen passing through the Lamia border into the Greenwood district," Officer Esra explains. "These are the guards there at the time earlier this morning. They snapped an image of his passport so that you could see, princess, that these are truly not rumors. Ethan Moon is alive. And he was seen with the young princess Rose. Along with some other Greenwood child. On each occasion that he has crossed the border, he has been seen with princess Rose and that other young man."

My teeth set together as I listen carefully to Esra. Was it safe to say that my suspicions were correct? Little Rose knew no other young men. None she would willingly participate in the ball with. That girl had the nerve to bring an *outlaw* into this castle and prance around the dance floor with him right under my nose. I am disgusted.

"Does anyone know where he's been all this time?" my son suddenly says. I turn to look at him, unimpressed by his involvement in all of this, as with anything. "Surely, he's been held up somewhere. Someone has taken him in until now. It could be anyone. Like our pitiful uncle Aero," he smirks, "or how about that guild he comes from? This should be investigated."

The officers look at their king with uncertainty and then their eyes turn to mine for assurance.

"What's more important is bringing him here," I tell them. "Until we know how we want to move forward with the matter his capture is pertinent to the continuation of our plans. That is to keep him from interfering. As for the guild, leave them be for now. Only keep a distant eye on their activity. I want it reported to me at the end of every week."

"But Mother, shouldn't we take a more 'hands-on-approach'? We know they've been holding Moon. So why not take them in for harboring a criminal?"

I glare at my son. What an idiot. I just can't understand his short-sighted thinking.

"We mustn't let the water Elemalex, River Dallas, know that we are putting new measures in place," I say through my teeth. "She is the most powerful witch we have working for us, and if she finds out we know about her involvement with Moon, there will be no telling what chaos would ensue next. Watch the guild, but find the boy and bring him here."

"What about Rosie, Mother? She must be in trouble too." Ryland grins and I only just hold off rolling my eyes. Childish.

"I will deal with Rose," I say. "Esra, you have your orders. As of right now Ethan Moon is a wanted individual. Find the boy. Use any means necessary. Let oddity hunters know, and be sure he is alive and…comfortable. We don't want any mishaps."

"Yes, Princess…"

Ethan's POV

"Ethan! What is taking you so long? Do you want the morning to end before we get anything done?" Rose is screaming at me from the bottom of the stairs as I am tugging awkwardly at my billowy sleeves.

"I'm coming! No need to shout," I grumble as I hop down the steps. "What do you think, Rose? I feel…weird."

"You look fine," she sighs.

"You don't look bad at all," Autumn is saying from the couch. Carson had finally convinced her to close her books and actually take a rest from her nonstop agonizing over her studies. "You even match well…aside from your…unique shoes. You look like a right real Greenwoodian."

"You think so?" I felt entirely out of place, but at least I could look the part.

"Are we ready or what?" Carson is saying as he's zipping his backpack closed. I throw on my cloak and bundle myself tight to be warm from the pre-winter air. And then I swing my packed bag over my chest, and stow my training wand in the holster on my thigh.

"As ready as we'll ever be I guess," I answer.

"I'm sorry, will you tell me one more time what you all are doing?" Autumn interjects nervously.

"Well, we were wondering where Victoria was," I answer. "But you should know too, and remember, don't tell River. She'll probably have a fit. Where is Victoria by the way? I've been expecting her to pop out of nowhere by now."

"She had gone to visit her family yesterday," Autumn explains. "She should have been back by now, however. I'm not sure what's holding her…"

"Well regardless…we're headed to Sierra to find my father."

"You're what?" Autumn's eyes blew wide and honestly her reaction was a lot more dramatic than I was expecting. She covers her mouth and sits up right on the couch.

"Don't tell anyone, Autumn, seriously. I just have to meet him. He's behind bars anyway so I don't see why everyone is so against it. I need help understanding the other half of my powers. It's that simple."

"What's that about powers?"

We all turn around to see Victoria stepping into the den, holding a duffle bag across her chest and looking a little lost. She eyes the three of us in the room who'd all gone silent and then she makes an annoyed face.

"What are you all up to? And why is fangs here again?" she asks suspiciously. "Don't make me ask twice."

Rose frowns and crosses her arms across her chest while I prepare to face her.

"We're going to Sierra," I say.

"For what?"

"So, I can meet my father. I'm going no matter what anyone else says, Victoria, but I thought that maybe we could trust you with that information…in case things go south. I didn't tell River…and I don't plan to. I'm telling you, because I trust you to keep a secret…and to maybe help us if or when we need it."

There was silence. It was so loud that I felt like I had just finished screaming my head off at someone. Victoria was frowning, but she also seemed to be thinking carefully about what I said.

"…What's in it for me?" she asks to my surprise. I blink stupidly at her and then she raises her brow expectantly.

"Well…what do you want?" I ask.

"Hmm…I don't know." She starts stepping slowly around the room, eyeing me in an uncomfortable manner. "I'll have to think about it a bit more carefully and let you know. I mean, this is a big ask, Ethan. To keep something from River? Ha. Yeah, you're going to owe me."

"Fine, whatever. You'll keep the secret, right?"

"Sure," she grins. "I won't tell River as long as I don't have to. But I can't go with you to Sierra. I have some place I need to be tomorrow. How long do you expect to be gone anyway?"

I didn't think about that. I look over at Rose for help but she just stares at me in return. I look over at Victoria again and shrug.

"I'm not sure. But depending how far away the prison is from here, I don't expect it will take more than a day or two. H…how do we contact you if something happens?" I ask. I suddenly thought about how no one had a cellphone. I was looking around at the three girls and I had caught glimpse of Carson at Jem's little table sniggering to himself. I then saw Autumn covering her mouth to hide her giggles and I couldn't help but feel embarrassed like I asked something silly.

"There's a couple ways to contact her, Ethan," Rose answers finally after she saw the pink creeping up my ears. "It would be hard to find a proper telephone in Sierra, and I don't think you understand wand calling yet, do you?"

"Didn't even know it was a thing," I frown.

"You can try that easy, Ethan. Just hold your wand like a telephone and think of who you want to call. It's an easy sort of spell. But if that's too difficult you can always use Thatch. That'll be good for long distance."

"What…is a Thatch?" I question with an uneasy feeling. Victoria rolls her eyes at me and in the next second she's whistling a specific rhythm. I tilt my head curiously as I watched her.

"Thatch isn't a what, he's a who," Victoria replied as she placed her hand on her hip. Then, a moment later, something small and black comes zipping into the room, making a loop here and a loop there as it finally lands on Victoria's shoulder. At first, I thought it was a whole bat! And before I could make a dramatic whaling sound from dreading the thought of an icky, scary bat, I realized the creature sitting on her should was a very small dragon, that could fit in the palms of your hands. It had a yellow stripe from the tip of its nose all the way down its back and to the tip of its long-jagged tail. It made a small… reptilian…sound and then snuggled close to the girl's neck. "This is Thatch," she says. He's an Elfin Stripeback dragon. They're known for being rather docile and of course their small size. People often use them for sending letters over large distances. So, I'll let you take him. He can go off by himself, but he'll need to be nearby to hear you call."

"Oooh my god." Carson is cooing as he had come over to see the small creature up close. "A real dragon! He's so cute!" He was slowly moving his finger close to it to pet its head or something, but instead the creature uttered an unhappy trill and then blew a tiny puff of fire at him. "Ow!" Carson yelps and retracts away.

"Don't do that," Victoria told him with an almost blank expression. "Take him with you, Ethan, but don't let anything happen to my baby." She pouts at me and I scratch my head, now being trusted to take care of a live creature. She scooped him up from her shoulder and then placed him on mine.

"Well, if that's all sorted," Rose says as she remembers that we were in a hurry, "we really must be going."

"Right," I nod and then look around me to make sure I had everything. "Victoria, it won't take long, as long as nothing goes wrong. If River asks, just say we went to someplace with Rose—I dunno. Wherever kids go our age."

Carson snorts and passes me, heading right for the front door.

"Let's go, genius," he chuckled. Rose follows after him and then I do as well; although, feeling a little reluctant. Somehow a part of me didn't want to go at all. I was afraid of what the outcome might be after meeting that man. And…maybe the repercussions to follow from miss River.

"Be careful, Ethan…" I hear Autumn's small voice call. I turn to look back at her and Victoria, and they're both waving.

"Yeah. Don't get your face messed up, pretty boy," Victoria says. I roll my eyes at her but wave goodbye and then I follow my friends outside, where our journey would truly begin.

· · ·

Rose, Carson, and I traveled through Greenwood pretty easily. Jem was no longer out front when we had left the cottage, so there was no need to explain where we were going to him. We had caught a carriage and headed north all the way to the border leading to Sierra District. The closer we got to the border, the more we noticed more and more unsettled and agitated groups of citizens. The moment we reached the border, which had a much shorter amount of people trying to get in and out compared to Lamia, there was a group of citizens who seemed frustrated and or anxious. The boarder was a huge magnificent limestone wall, much bigger and grander than what I had been expecting. Guards were stationed under and within the ginormous archway that was the entrance to and from Sierra from Greenwood. Rose was staring hard out of the window of the carriage and her expression was clearly concerned as we could hear people shouting who were on foot, and others fussing through the windows of their own carriages.

"Can we—can we roll this thing down?" I question urgently, wanting to hear what they were all saying. I was fumbling with the window when Carson leaned over and began turning the crank for me and rolled the window down enough to hear what was going on.

"What's the hold up?!' someone was shouting.

"Please, sir, I need to get back home!" some other person pleads.

The guards for this boarder were all dressed in green uniforms but were nowhere near as padded and weapon loaded like those in Lamia. Actually, they didn't have any weapons or armor at all. Perhaps because these people could use magic so it probably wasn't as necessary.

"It's because Ethan Moon is back!" a chubby older woman was shouting over all the others. "The Lamia Princess confirmed it this morning! The boy is alive!"

"Then what are you doing there, you lot!?" a man yells through the window of his carriage this time. "We need that boy! To save us from those wicked devils in Lamia! Why are you doing their bidding?!"

I swallow thickly at all of this, turning my head to look at my friends who were also looking at me worriedly. This wasn't good. Not at all.

"Settle down! All of you!" One older guard was now trying to gain control of the unruly crowd. He was standing up a little higher up on a platform built into the structure so that he could get everyone's attention. "This is only an extra measure that we have to follow. We have no interest in hurting the boy. Lamia Castle has only order to meet with him so we are only trying to find him and relay the message. We apologize for the slowed operations, but we just need to be sure of who we are letting through the boarder through this sensitive time! Bear with me!"

The crowd seemed to have listened…for a second, and then the shouting match resumed as some were arguing why they shouldn't get involved with Lamia district, and others arguing for my capture to end the oncoming madness.

"We need to go," Rose urges quietly as she looks between Carson and I. "Now." She was already opening the door of the carriage and while the driver was looking back and asking what she was doing, Carson and I came scrambling out after her. She goes around the front and pays the driver, thanking him and letting him know we didn't need his services anymore. Then she motions for us to follow her as she skirts to the right of the crowd and further down the border. "She knows," Rose says suddenly as Carson and I were struggling to keep up with her.

"What?" I ask.

"She knows, my aunt knows," she clarifies. "I mean," she stops and turns around to look at me once we were far enough away from other people, "she was bound to find out, of course, and we knew it was a risk to go to the ball last night, so we already knew what we were getting ourselves into. But, now that it's really happening…Ethan, there's no going back now."

"What do you mean?" I tilt my head, watching her usual composed expression melt away into panic. She almost seemed like she was going to cry.

"People are going to be looking for you. You already know this," she says. "I don't know what we can do to stop it. I just know that you need to get your memory back. Particularly the use of your powers part."

"Sure…" I nod. "Calm down…I understand that this was inevitable. But that's not going to stop us. Let's keep going, and get done what we need to get done. That's our focus, Rose. Rose!" I put my hands on her shoulders as I notice her heavy breathing to calm her. "It's okay. Don't freak out so early. I'm sure we're not even in the thick of it yet." I smile a little down at her as she nods and relaxes herself. After we let her take a minute to calm down, she wipes her face with her hands and draws in a deep breath.

"I'm sorry…" she began sheepishly. "I think I'm just really afraid of…"

She never finishes, but I knew what she was going to say. She was afraid to lose me again. I could feel it. I could feel the emotion of losing a dear friend as if I'd felt it myself…

"What are we going to do about getting through the border, Rose?" I ask her gently. She seemed unsure, but Carson came forward and threw his arms around both of our shoulders. Wearing a rather creepy smile might I add.

"Now, I might know a thing er two about bein' places I'm not supposed to…."

Ugh…don't remind me.

"I definitely know a thing er ten about gettin' over walls like this," he continued. I squint at him.

"Where on earth have you seen any wall like this?" I question.

"That doesn't matter." He clears his throat and then walks a little further down the wall. He looks left, then right, and then he looks way up to the very top of the structure. "We'll have to go over it. There's no way around it, obviously. And we can't go through. We gotta climb. *Or*, we'll need to use some magic stuff." He looks over at Rose now, and Rose stares at him for a moment before she shakes her head wildly.

"I don't have any magic; I'm a *vampire* remember?" she tells him.

"Can't you fly? Or levitate?"

"Well…sometimes. But I certainly can't fly that high. Neither could I with the both of you that high."

"Wait, you can actually fly?" I gawk in surprise at her. I *had* to see that. "What else can you do?!"

"Not now, Ethan," she retorts.

"Then you'll have to do somethin' buddy," Carson says now and turns to me. "Dig down deep in that magical brain of yours and remember something that'll do the trick."

I frown. How could I do anything like fly over a one-hundred-foot wall like that? Even if I could manage to get my feet off the grown. I surely didn't have any broom or something like what you'd think a witch would use to fly. But then I had an idea. I turn my head sideways and examine the wall a little more closely.

"What if we don't go over the wall…" I say slowly as I step up close enough to touch it. "What if we went through it?"

"Well, yeah, no duh, that's what we wanted to do but we kinda have a guard problem," Carson drivels.

"No, I mean, what if we actually go *through* the wall?"

"How?" Rose asks this time. She steps up beside me and watches as I reach out and touch the cold smooth stone of the wall.

"I don't know…" I answer under my breath. My brain was rattling. If it was mechanical, you'd see smoke from my ears. There was a small glimmer of a thought—a memory of a way to go from one place to another. I had to remember. Or we wouldn't be able to get to the district. But what was it?

Don't tense up

I shake my head.

Relax your body. Close your eyes if you're scared

I had a headache. No…it's been too long, I thought it was done and over with. My head was aching all of a sudden. A light pang here, a light pang there. And then a pang hard enough to make me wince.

"What's the matter?" Rose is asking me now as she grabs my arm.

Repeat after me…

That voice…I knew that voice…

Mevenlocum.

I had whispered the word without even realizing, and as Carson and Rose watched me with concern, my eyes had gone green and a bright white light came radiating out of my hand. It swirls around and the very wall began to swirl and distort like a filtered image until we were able to see passed it at the land belonging to Sierra district. I hear both Rose and Carson gasp, and even I was shocked at what I think I had done. But there was no time to marvel at it. We needed to move.

"Hey!" a frantic voice was shouting from afar. We all turned our heads to the left down where the true entrance to the district was, and a guard was running full speed in our direction. "Stop right there!" he screams and is gesturing for other guards to help him. But we didn't want to find out what they'd do if they caught up to us.

"Run!" Carson yells to break up our dazed stupor. He pushes both me and Rose through the apparent portal I had somehow created and we all find ourselves running full speed through grass that turned to dirt that turned to sand. It was so *hot* all of a sudden, like we had transported ourselves to an entirely different region. Like Arizona or Nevada. My head was spinning around like crazy as I looked this way and that to figure out if I actually had sent us somewhere by mistake. But this was Sierra District.

I didn't have much time to take in the scenery as the three of us ran for our lives as far away as possible from the border. We could here whistles blowing and loud deep tolls of huge bells variously placed within the walls of the boarder. Looking over my shoulder I could already see five or six men in matching uniform different from the ones Greenwood guards were wearing running full speed in our direction. They were holding weapons such as long curved swords, and something that looked like a lasso rope. We didn't have a second to lose to stay ahead of them. Our feet moved from hard sandy ground to a dusty bricked road that began the closest town in the district. We were now running past people who were alarmed by us being chased by shouting guards. We turned corners around old looking buildings and I had bumped into a woman holding a basket of fruits and vegetables. They had all scattered everywhere and I had only heard her scream, but I didn't stop.

We ran quite a great distance until Rose pointed out a place to slip into. There was an open door leading into a dark busy bar. We had rounded enough buildings where those guards had lost sight of us and we were able to slip inside and hide until they could completely lose out trail.

"Woo," Carson sighs out loud when we were finally able to take a breath. "I've been chased by some angry security before, but that was *nuts*," he says.

"Yes. We should try to avoid *that* as much as possible," Rose adds as she catches her breath.

I press my back against the wall of the building and then peak out through the open door to see if any guards were still around. At first, I didn't see any body. But then there were two of them who were looking this way and that before running right passed the bar until they were out of sight.

"Okay, I think we have a chance to keep going," I tell the other two. I pull out the map drawn by the prince from my bag and quickly try to examine where we need to go from here. There was a small city crudely drawn in the corner that seemed to represent where we must have ended up. Then there was a far stretch of desert that passed two other towns before a small stretch of land near some mountains that seemed to be where the prison was. We just needed to keep North. "Come on," I tell the others and stow away the map.

"So how do we get there?" Carson is asking as we step out of the bar and back into the street. We walk cautiously through the town as we enter what seemed to be a market place.

"We need to head north," I explain. "I guess all the way until we get to some sort of mountain range. But by the looks of it, it all seems to be desert. How are we gonna get all the way there on foot?"

The three of us look between each other until I notice Carson's eyes stray elsewhere and a grubby little smile etched across his face. I turn to see where he was looking, and there just ahead were two ATV-looking vehicles parked against a wall.

"…Well, that's convenient," I said.

This was the first thing I had a full handle on in this entire world. Of course, I would have never thought I'd see any sort of motor bike in Obscura but I wasn't complaining. Carson and I zipped as fast as we could through the rest of the market place and out of the town before whoever owned these things noticed. Rose sat on the back of mine, gripping a bit too tight at my sides as she went ridged from fear.

"Please don't crash!" I could hear her pleading to me as I jumped over sand dunes and slid down sand every so often. Carson and I used to go ATV riding a lot when we were a bit younger. Oh yeah, this was fun.

After some time, we passed another village called Luak Hina, and then a second one called Na Pakanli just like the map had said. Prince Aero was worried about the accuracy, but it was pretty good so far. Tall dark mountains came into view after a while. They seemed to scrape the sky, even some had snow at their peaks. They were jagged, and looked dangerous. Like not something anyone would want to go climb. And as we were approaching the mountain's base, we could see the stretch of land with a heavily guarded area. But something didn't seem right.

"Carson, wait!" I call after him after skidding my bike to a stop. Carson slows down and eventually he stops beside me. He looks ahead as do I to the scene below.

"What is it?" Rose asks after leveling her fear of crashing or falling off. She peers around my shoulder and I hear her gasp.

It was chaos down there. Guards were everywhere. What looked to be Oddity Hunters were gathering and dispersing in every which direction. We could hear frantic yelling and shouting. And in the next second the blaring of an alarm began. Something was terribly wrong. And for a moment I thought that somehow, we had caused all of this. But as the scene continued to unfold in front of us, I knew that it was something entirely different.

"Can anyone tell what they're saying down there?" Carson asks from his bike.

"An inmate has escaped," Rose answers in a solemn tone.

We look between each other as we think about what to make of this. Was it just coincidence?

"Men, I've got some very interesting characters in sight!"

…None of us said anything. We turn our heads to see where the random voice had come from, and only meters away was a man in accommodating clothing for the heat, and packed with all sorts of weapons and vials. And just behind him was a group of others who looked just as…unfriendly. As I made eye contact with him and nearly jumped out of my skin, his expression changed to shock and almost disbelief.

"It's the Moon kid!" he exclaims. Which was code for: It's time to get the hell out of here!

Carson and I were revving up the bikes again, and we wasted no time turning around and speeding away as best as we could.

The men were shouting amongst themselves before they had agreed to run after us, even on foot. I thought that it wouldn't be too bad since we were on bikes and they weren't. But only moments of now having to dodge things being thrown our way—knives, ropes, even arrows, something was thrown and attached itself to my bike. There was beeping noises, and then the next second BOOM!

Rose and I go flying off of the ATV and I land hard into sand that I wish was as soft as it looked. After getting a mouth, nose, and eye full of sand and tumbling a few times before I could sit up, I see Rose flipping over, and she had already jumped up to her feet and pulled out her dagger—taking a defensive stance. Carson came circling around and he was reaching his hand out for mine to help me up onto his bike.

"What about Rose?" I ask after swinging up behind him. Carson didn't answer, maybe because he didn't have one yet as he circles around again. "Rose, come on!" I shouted at her. Why was she trying to fight them all by herself? Her eyes were angry and they were glowing that scary purple color. We needed to help her.

I jump back down off of Carson's bike and he's shouting at me to come back, but I couldn't let anything happen to Rose. We had to get away from here. We didn't have any leverage out in the middle of nowhere. The men came closer and they were intrigued by the short vampire girl ready to fight back, but as I approached again their attention was back on me.

"So, it is true what Lamia said. The kid is alive. No wonder his freak father had the nerve to escape. He probably buys into the useless savior talk. But there is no saving freaks like him or you. Or whatever your friend is. Seems like a vampire got mixed up in something else," this man begins to speculate about Rose who had her hood pulled up to obscure her face. "But let's not waste any time boys, get them all! I'm sure they'll be a fair price for each of 'em." The man lunges toward Rose who swiped her dagger to ward him away. Three others come bounding toward me while the one other man is firing arrows at Carson who was still circling his bike, and waiting for Rose and I to join him again.

"We need to go!" I tell her. "We can't fight them all. Let's go!" The three men were just feet away. I had pulled out my wand, hoping that whatever I did would work more accurately if I used it. My eyes went green and I point the thing at them. And surprisingly to my luck I was able to send them all flying backwards with seemingly just a thought. But I didn't have time to marvel at it. The man in front of Rose was lunging at her again and they began tussling it out, with Rose doing some (rather impressive) martial arts. She had jumped up into the air and kicked the man twice in the head while still floating there. Aha…she could fly. When the man was disoriented and Rose was lowering herself back to the ground, I had gripped her by the arm and yanked her over to Carson who was circling around again. When she got the message that leaving now was the priority, we jumped up onto Carson's bike together and he sped away. But they were still pursuing us.

We had gotten pretty far. So much so that we were approaching the nearest town. We were *almost* there until one of the men had caught Carson's bike with some sort of explosive arrow. And BOOM!

We were flying off of the ATV again, but we had no choice but to scramble up to our feet and continue on foot. Running for our lives for some sort of cover from these hunters. We just made it into the town that was slightly different but nonetheless the same with the first one we were in. We rounded a corner just as one of the hunters had pulled some sort of gun from the holster on his back and shot a hot blue light that just missed my head and burned a hole into the wall it landed on. We were out of sight from the men for only a second and we knew at any moment they would catch up. We didn't know how to get out of this situation. Would we get captured?

Then in that moment I felt something firm grab at my collar and yanked me backward. I screamed out loud, knowing that this was it. I had been captured.

I heard Rose and Carson yelp as they were also yanked by their collars and then I hear a door slam.

"Wha—who are you?" I heard Carson questioning first.

"Hush!" A deep burly voice snaps at him.

I open my eyes after I realized I had been squeezing them shut that whole time, and there I saw a ginormous, burly man(?) that matched the burly voice holding the door shut with his massive fists. I couldn't help my mouth dropping at the sight of…whatever he was.

After another moment and hearing hunters hauling passed and out of sight, the man stands up straight and grips his belt with one fist and pulls out a toothpick from his teeth with the other. He looks at the three of us and says:

"The name's Homa."

17

Homa the Orc

"What were you kids thinkin'?"

Rose, Carson, and I were staring up at this massive man, in awe of his appearance. He was easily seven or eight feet tall. His body was massive, (and not just because of his jolly middle) but just by the size of his arms and legs. He could do some serious damage just with a pat on the back, I was sure. His skin was greyish or greenish in color. He had two small tusks erupting from the bottom of his mouth. His nose was pierced with a golden septum ring; his hair was glossy black that rested in soft curls around his very large head. He had one braid decorated with small turquoise and white beads, and a brown and white feather tied into it. His feet stomp over from the door and he walks farther into what was his home. Quite small for his stature as he often bent his head down as to not hit any fixtures attached to the ceiling. He's stepping into an area that served as a kitchen and he takes a seat at a table where laid a makeshift gun fashioned together with miscellaneous pieces of scrap metal and parts. In the corner of the room was a very old-fashioned stereo that was quietly playing blues music.

"Why did you save us?" Rose is asking as she hesitantly steps in his direction.

"Y'all were fixin' to get caught," he answers with a scoff. "And then what were y'all gonna do? Y'all ain't had not nary a plan and no way to help y'allself if thangs went south. What were you thinking?" I was surprised. Or at least I wasn't expecting that sort of response. I walk into the kitchen alongside Rose and Carson was following behind me as I watched the man stick his toothpick back into his mouth. Then he picks up a wrench and starts working on the makeshift gun. "Where were y'all headed to anyhow?" he asks.

"We weren't quite sure…" Rose admits to him. "We were just trying to escape those hunters."

"Picked the worst time to come down here," he said in response. "Your father escaped the prison this mornin'." He looks over at me and I tilt my head.

"You know who I am?" I ask.

"Do I know who you—'course I know who you are!" he nearly shouts with his booming voice. "An' it's 'bout time you showed up, anyway! People was startin' to lose faith in you. I'm su'prised you didn't come 'round sooner."

"For what?" I question. "I mean all I was trying to do was find my father?"

The man stops and turns completely to look at me. His face was both shocked and concerned.

"What would you want to go and do that for?" he asks. "There's a whole community o' people lookin' for *your* help! That Yohan Moon feller is opposed to any of that!"

"Why?" I say and step closer. "Who wants my help? And why would my father be against it?"

The man shakes his head and sets down his wrench. He dusts his hands off on his corduroy pants and gives me his full attention.

"Ethan," he began and looked me directly in my eye, "there is a not-so-secret secret group called the Odd Eye Syndicate. The syndicate's purpose is to stop the injustices happenin' to oddity citizens every day. It's only gotten worse over time. So much so that we fear we will need to fight somethin' awful to stop what the Lamia district is doin' to people like us."

"You're an oddity too?" Carson asks without hesitation.

Homa stops and his eyes turn before the rest of his body to look at him who seemingly regrets asking.

"Look at me, ya numbskull!" he barks. "Do I look right to you?"

Carson swallows hard but he doesn't answer. Instead, he shuffles backwards a bit behind me. But I felt curious this time. I mean…*look* at him. Except he really didn't look like anything else but some kind of ogre or something.

"So, what are you?" I ask him bravely. "Matter of fact, who did you say you were again?"

"I told you. My name is Homa. Ma' dad's an orc, ma' mama's a fairy—if you *must* know. My family both come from the forests of Greenwood. But I was born here. Any more questions?"

"Um, yeah...how does that wo—" I elbow Carson in the rib to shut him up. You don't just ask someone how their parents......*made them*. Although I honestly would love to know *cough*.

"No more questions," I tell him. "Just tell me more about this syndicate."

"Odd Eye is meant to fight off injustices toward oddities," he reiterates. "But our people have been goin' missin' left an' right. It's become too dangerous to even protest or ask civilly for any reforming of Obscura law. So, these days Odd Eye mostly serves as a sort of refugee house. Folks have been separated from their families, orphaned, or gone broke and lost their homes. These people have lost so much hope that they feel like the only way to stop any o' this is if you do the very thing most folk fear. They want you to overturn the government. But mostly the Lamia/Artemis side. Some of us might have magic, but Lamia has been building for years a different sort of power. Too much for any of us to overcome. Since you're the most powerful oddity of all, we all believe that you can right these injustices and restore peace in our land."

I sigh heavily. Mostly from being perturbed by what's going on around here. The more I learn about it, the more I hate it. But also, I was very unsure if everyone's belief in me was rooted in any true reality. Could I really be able to stop something like this single handedly? I couldn't believe that just yet.

"So how is it here, living in Sierra?" I ask him. "Are those hunters always around like this?"

"Well today, o' course, is a special day, as like I said your daddy broke out o' prison. But in its entirety, yes. Hunters are everywhere here, more than any other district. You're carded every day no matter where your goin' or what your doin'. They come up with all sort of reasons to turn someone in or... worse. I've lived here majority of my life, but I have seen things change over the years. Lamia wants to purge the whole realm of anyone and anything that threatens their rise to power. That includes anything as unpredictable as us oddities. I've nearly been captured and turned in a number of times. If it weren't for my…handsomely amazing skills and probably good looks, I'd be gone by now." My eyebrows raise. I didn't know what…the correlation of good looks was but…if it worked for him then… "I try to take care of the syndicate as best I can. If I'm captured, they'll lose a pretty good chunk of their protection."

"Where is the syndicate?" I ask. "I mean, we should go there. You should show it to us. If you all really think I can do something about this, I want to help."

"It's underground," he says. "I can show you where when you're ready to go. There are many ways to get to it too, 'cause of the tunnels that run underneath the whole realm."

"Sorry? There are tunnels underneath Obscura? The whole of it?" Rose is asking in disbelief. She knew quite a lot but she seemed to be learning something new.

"Sure is, lil' lady," he replies. "You can get passed each boarder without n'one knowin' too."

"That's preposterous. Certainly, the leaders of each district would know about it," she protests. "How could it be there and not sealed off at the least?"

"Don't you pay attention in history class?" Homa is rolling his big yellow eyes at her. "They were built durin' the Great District War. Folks wanted to travel between their home and their families in secret even while the borders were shut down. The syndicate has been utilizing them for the last forty years," he explains. "You know what, Ethan. Your father started the syndicate himself." I tilt my head in response.

"Really?" I ask. "But you said that he didn't want me to help the syndicate. Why wouldn't he then, and why isn't he still apart of it?"

"I'm not entirely sure the answer to that, kid," he says. "Your father's sick. He started Odd Eye with good intentions, and he was doin' really good things with it. But he started becomin' violent. And he was doin' things we're opposed to. I mean it's what landed him in prison in the first place. So, his close friend that helped him run it in the past has taken over it now. His name is Yew. I'm sure you'll like 'em. But in terms of your father, Ethan, that man has become something monstrous. Evil even. He ain't like how he was in the beginnin' at all. Not one bit. It's almost like he was possessed by some evil spirit. Before he went to prison, he ran away to the top of Fichik mountain. That mountain you see outside. They say he lived in some nasty cave up there. And he was killin' folks here and there or possessin' them with some sort of dark magic to do his biddin'. I'm tellin' you, kid. Yer daddy ain't right no more. That's why you shouldn't try messin' with him."

Well…that was unsettling information. I didn't know what to make of it quite yet, but I knew it couldn't deter me from talking with him. I had to for the sake of understanding my powers. At least that's what I've convinced myself anyway.

"So, what do we do now?" Carson asks as he crosses the room and takes a seat. Homa watched him with an expression that read he didn't invite him to get so comfortable but he didn't say anything. "Surely, we can't keep goin' after your dad, Ethan. We don't even know where he is now."

"You're right," I answer. "I think we'll have to put that on hold for now. I want to meet the syndicate," I tell Homa. "I know I can't do much right now in terms of my powers but if there is something else I can do to help, and stop those people from suffering, I will do it."

"Wait, wait. Whaduya mean in terms of your powers?" Homa questions, his face animated and ready to say he heard me wrong. "You *can* use your powers, can't you?"

My lips press together. I guess the people who have supposedly been waiting for my return expect me to know about my magic and know how to use it. But I didn't. And that was a bit embarrassing to have to admit.

"Ethan's memory hasn't quite returned," Rose speaks up for me. "We're hoping that…*when* it does, he'll be able to get a hold over it in a timely fashion."

"Ain't that 'bout nothin'," Homa frowns. "Your powers are kinda the whole point, kid. You're the savior of the oddities—some like to say." He clears his throat awkwardly. "I dunno if I'd give ya that big of a title, but hey, I look up to you too, kid." The man stands up, and he seemed like he was going to continue speaking, but he stops as something comes darting through a slightly open window and lands clumsily…on my head.

"OW!" I cry out and swat at the sharp-clawed creature. It clammers down and then finally settles on the table. It was the little black dragon Victoria had sent me with. I had quite literally forgotten all about him, and couldn't recall when he had flown off. I rub my head and scrunch up my face at the thing. "Did you have to stop on my head?" I fuss at him. The dragon shakes its head in a way that seemed dismissive rather than a response. He drops a rolled-up piece of parchment onto the table, makes a soft screeching sound and then blows a puff of smoke. Clearly, he felt nettled over something. Was it something I said?

I reach down for the parchment, untied the string and pulled it open.

"Who's it from?" Rose asks first as she comes over to look over my shoulder.

Time's running out, kid.
I don't like to be kept waiting.
~Firebird

I frown at the small note. I didn't have time for Julian either. I look up at the three in the room and my shoulders drop.

"The syndicate will have to wait," I tell them. "There's something I need to do."

"Why does that sound like you're gonna go off by yourself?" Carson asks skeptically.

I fold up the letter and shove it hastily into my pocket.

"Because I am. Stay here; I don't expect it to last too long."

"Ethan, you can't possibly go out right now by yourself! Those hunters know that you're here, they'll be looking for you," Rose is protesting. I shake my head at her though and I pull up the hood on my cloak.

"I can't let you come," I say. "I don't know what I'll do if any of you got hurt from this. I won't be long, Rose. Please stay here."

"It's Julian, isn't it?" She was becoming increasingly frantic as she reached out to grab my arm and convince me to stay. "You can't go! You can't trust him, Ethan! I just have a terrible feeling, please just stay!"

I stop and I grab her by her shoulders to still her.

"I have to go," I tell her calmly. "And I will be back. I promise. The faster I get this out of the way, the faster we can focus on what's important. Stay here, Rose." She watches me with eyes full of something just short of betrayal mixed with fear and frustration. I knew she was just worried that something would happen to me, but I would not let that happen. I could deal with Julian.

My eyes trailed over to meet Carson who didn't say anything and only gave a silent complicated look. And then Homa drew in a breath. He seemed unsure of what was going on and how exactly to ask, but he moved to usher me to the door. As we got there, Homa stops me and leans against the door with a hand on his belt. He bore into my eyes with his yellow ones and he took a moment to assess the situation.

"Listen," he starts in a sotto manner, "you sound like you've got a lot on your case. Although you didn't *ask* me," he rolls his eyes, "I'll watch your friends for ya. I don't know exactly what's goin' on, and I'm not gonna ask, but you should know that I am a friend. An ally. I want to help you, kid. At any time, you need ol' Homa, I'll be there, alright?"

I nod my head to him and offer a slight smile.

"Thanks," I tell him sincerely. "That really means a lot."

He offers a wide pointy grin, revealing one large golden tooth. He gives a charming wink and then he opens the door. He pokes his head out first, looking left, then right, and when he thought everything looked clear he opened the door wider and gestured for me to go.

"Don't be long er I'mma be lookin' for ya," he tells me finally before he closes the door.

I sigh as I took my first steps outside. The sun was lowering in the sky and I knew I needed to get a move on. Being out after dark didn't sound like it would be pleasant. As I began walking in the direction of the mountain in the distance, I began to wonder if I could get there any faster. Obviously, those ATVs were out of the question (sorry strangers we stole from), but I did remember the spell I used to get through the boarder. Why wouldn't it work again?

I stop for a moment and I take out my wand, hoping that will ensure its success. And as I envision the base of the mountain and repeat the words: **Mevenlocum,** I felt a rush of energy, and I was expecting to see a sort of portal open. But instead, out of the tip of my wand came very explosive shots rushing straight into the air and popping rapidly like fire crackers or something. I jump backward in total surprise and I stow my wand away as quicky as possible.

Let's not try that again.

On foot it is.

It took a good chunk of time to get *all* the way back to the mountain. Every so often I had to hide from guards or people that looked like hunters. I couldn't afford to get caught. I kept my hood up on my head and my face out of view as best as I could. And thankfully, it worked.

As soon as I approached the base of the mountain, I heard a loud whooshing sound behind me. Just as I turned around, I saw black smoke and then a man standing there with his hands in his coat pocket. That man was Julian Hickman. A wide, off-putting smile creeped onto his face as he took his first few steps slowly in my direction. His eyes were flickering an amber color and he was laughing for some reason.

"Ethan!" he calls out and opens up his arms as if to be offering a hug. "Finally, you decided to show up. I almost began to doubt you."

"Well, here I am," I grumble. "Now, what d'you want? Let's get it over with already."

"Oh," he sings, "you're eager? I like that. Then let's waste no time. You're gonna enjoy this one."

That didn't sound good. He comes over and suddenly he's wrapping his arms around mine to hold me still. And before I could properly struggle, he's shouting: "Up we go!"

I'm surrounded in black smoke that was extremely suffocating. And before I knew it, my feet were off of the ground and I was shooting upward into the sky. I couldn't even bring myself to scream, only chokes and frantic gasps left my mouth. And then soon after my feet were on rock. Julian was beside me now and I had stumbled forward, gasping for a proper breath. The man was shaking his head at me and he chuckles.

"Poor kid can't even go for a flitting ride. What a shame."

"Don't do that again!" I snap through my labored breath. "At least warn me first!"

"Well, what would be the fun in that?" He rolls his eyes and then gestures for me to follow him. "Come on, this way."

We were at the top of the mountain. Not the very top, but high enough where it was cold and shadowy. It did not feel very welcoming up here at all. I looked around me to see the sharp jagged edges of the mountain that seemed like one slip and you'd fall to your death. And of course, I looked down at that point. Oh yeah, it was a long way down. I had to turn away so I wouldn't throw up in terror.

I jogged over to catch up with Julian who had gone quite far into the plateau. We were walking for quite some time, climbing up and over wall blocks, and avoiding sharp rock that jutted up out of the mountain. I slipped a few times where Julian had to catch me. But we carried on to where ever he was leading me.

"So, I was analyzing the file we got from the castle in Lamia," he begins to debrief, "and it led me to a book that could be found in the library section in the H.D.O. Center. The book was on a collection of recordings of abnormal oddity phenomenon from 1838 to 1856. One of the recordings involved the artifact you're helping me look for."

"And what is that exactly?" I ask. "Is it like a…magical…GPS or what?"

He shot me an irritable look, but he didn't speak on whatever his thoughts might have been.

"The artifact is actually not quite an artifact," he says. "It's instead a sort of elixir, said to be bottled up in an enchanted vial and hidden in an unknown location. 'The Elixir of Everlasting Knowledge is where there is no end, guarded by a serpent of flames and death'. I heard that after doing further digging around." He smirks back at me but I had no reaction. I just knew I didn't like what I was hearing, neither did I want to deal with what sounded like a big scary reptile on fire. "Ah, there it is," I hear Julian say brightly. "The elixir is where there is no end. That has to be The Cliffs of Never Ending Echoes, obviously. I'm sure it is—I think."

We walk over to a very long stretch of land that extended far from the mountain itself. We approached the very edge of what was a very steep cliff, and somehow looking down I couldn't see the ground at all. Not like before. It was foggy and grey down there. I gulp and Julian is picking up a loose rock. He lights it on fire with his magic and he hurls it over the edge and watches as it plumets down…down…down. Through the fog we could no longer see the rock but only the glow of the fire. Until you couldn't see that any more. There was no sound of it ever hitting the bottom. I stand up right and look over in disbelief at the man.

"I know we're not going down there," I told him. But he laughs wickedly in response.

"Of course, we're not going down there!" he says. "But *you* are!"

"No way!" I protest and back up from the edge. "There is no way I'm doing that. What would even be the reason? How could I even survive that?"

"Look kid, you've survived much worse," he tells me. "You just need to jump down there—your magic will kick in, just trust me. You'll avoid whatever beast is down there, swipe up the elixir and come back up. No. big. deal."

"What makes you so sure it's that simple? What if my powers don't kick in? I'm not doing this, Julian."

The man is shaking his head at me and something in his eyes seemed to be flickering. Like emotions having a tussle between anger and compassion. He takes in a deep breath and breathes it out before stepping closer to me.

"Listen. I know it sounds outlandish and all, but I wouldn't ask for some kids help if I didn't think you were capable of succeeding. I'd just do it myself. I get that you're all weak for now, but your magic is still waiting around to be used by you. I'm under the impression that should you be in a position where you absolutely need to use it, it flips on like a switch. Am I wrong?"

He pauses to wait for me to protest, but as I thought about it, he wasn't wrong…I guess. He looks over the edge of the cliff for a moment and then he glances back at me.

"I don't want to threaten you, Ethan," he says through grit teeth. "All I want is your help. If I can get this elixir, then I'd be able to track down my daughter. That's all I want. So don't make this complicated, alright?"

I press my lips together. Yes, he was unpredictable, but his ultimate goal was consistent. I sigh heavily now knowing that I was going to hate every second of this, but I step up to the edge of the cliff once more and I start pulling off my cloak and rolling up my sleeves.

"Okay," I say finally, "tell me what I have to do."

18

The Fire Serpent

Julian is grinning ear to ear at me as I was hyping myself up to do the craziest stunt ever in my entire existence. I must have been out of my mind or drunk on some kind of Obscura fumes to even rationalize that jumping off a so called "never ending" cliff made even an ounce of sense. But there I was with my sleeves pulled up and my sneakers at the very edge of the stretch of land.

"Now, all you need to do is use your spirit sight to locate whatever beast is down there potentially protecting the elixir. If you find a sort of small island of rock on your way down, it's most likely on it. Use your magic to control the speed of your fall. Or else you will plummet to your death," Julian explains.

"Great," I comment sarcastically as I stare down over the cliff and into the dark ominous fog. What have I gotten myself into? "What if I don't find the elixir?"

"Then we'll have to start at square one." He sounded impatient now, but I still wasn't that sure of the rate of my survival.

"But how do I get back up? I can't fly!"

"You'll figure it out, kid," he groans and in the next second I felt his hand on my back. "Just get *down* there!"

He pushes me hard over the edge and my arms go up and flail around for anything to grab on to. God if I knew magic well, he'd be in so much trouble for this. As the cold air hits my face and terrified screams rip from my throat, my body is picking up incredible speed as I plunge further and further down.

Well one thing was for sure, the cliff was not close to any land one bit. Although I could barely see through the thick fog and the water in my eyes, after falling for like a minute now I had time to wrap my head around the situation.

One. I am falling. Good, that's out of the way. Two, I needed to use spirit vision to see a beast or something. Okay, but I hoped that didn't mean I had to go *toe to toe* with one. I blink my eyes hard and soon they had shifted green. (I was getting pretty good at that.) I scan my surroundings as best as I could while falling a good eighty miles per hour or so. But I didn't see anything but fog and wind. The farther and faster I fell, the more I was sure I was going to die. I was beginning to doubt Julian's motives. Could this all have been a trick? A ploy to bring me up here unwittingly and dispose of me the way Lamia wants? God, I had no idea, and I began to regret going alone after Rose demanded I didn't. How could I have been so stupid? So gullible? I was going to die.

"That's enough!"

Something deep-voiced and sinister barks out at me and I'm startled by where it had come from. I look around, this way and that, but I don't see a thing.

"Stop whining," it tells me, "It's time you grow up!"

What in the world was going on? I try to flip my body upright (though I'm not sure what a good of job I did), and I take another look around as best as I could. There was a smell. Something was burning.

I look up now, and there above my head I could see thick black shadows rolling in. And I was horrified. I recognized them right away from the first night I spent in the guild and the other night when I had been paralyzed by that monster. I did *not* have the mental capacity to see him again while I was currently falling to my doom.

I'm flailing around again as I try swimming my way through the air away from the shadows that were floating closer and closer to my head. I'd rather find the ground than have them touch me.

I was now head first, paddling my arms and legs as hard as I could until I could see a pale orange glow through the fog. The closer I got the brighter and clearer it became.

In seconds I could see the silhouette of something large and long-bodied. Spikes stuck out of its back all the way down to its tail. Its head was large and bulbous and I noticed it was glowing all over. Not just the light its soul gave off. I needed to slow down because I knew I was going to hit something, whether it was the creature or the ground.

I ball my fists up tight, and without thinking I pull them in to my chest and then push one hand out and the other behind me. I felt my momentum begin to slow while I could see the beast coming into proper view. The fog was fading away and I could see a sort of island like that Julian mentioned, and the body of the beast coiled up like an oversized snake. It was red and scaley. Its eyes were fiery yellow and it had an unfriendly set of long pointy teeth.

Soon, my feet reached the ground—a little faster than anticipated. I went tumbling forward after landing and had to roll over back onto my feet. Here on the ground, I could see my surroundings perfectly. Aside from looking up to see a thick blanket of fog, I could see the island of land was small and could be crossed in a matter of steps. I could hear water rushing. While looking down over the edges of the slab of land there were waterfalls shooting out of the rock walls that surrounded the area—falling for who knows how far.

I push myself upright and my eyes go straight over to the creature who had begun to move. Its head wobbled this way and that before it slithered down to the ground. Its eyes were searching for what had made a disturbance. While it hadn't caught sight of me, I tried my best to see where the elixir could have been. There were no clear places it could be stashed, and I wasn't sure if it could have been buried within the thick rocky soil. I hated to think that the only place it could be if it existed at all was within the coils of the creature's body.

I gulp, hearing it make a low threatening growl. Its head continued to slide from left to right across the ground as it seemed to be sniffing out an intruder. Me. There was not a single place to hide, and certainly nowhere to run. I thought that if I skirted the circumference of the area while the creature uncoiled its long body, I'd get a shot at securing the artifact and getting out of here before things took a turn. Of course, that would be the ideal scenario. In a second the creature turns its large head and catches sight of me. As soon as its eyes met mine its entire body ignited into a hot inferno. Fire spewing in every which direction. It opened its mouth wide, bearing its slimy sharp teeth and it let out a hiss-like roar before it came chugging in my direction. Its entire body uncoiled and slithered around the small stretch of land, and I went darting to the center, hoping to find if anything had been hiding there. The only thing I could do was avoid the creatures head, but it moved a lot faster than expected, and its body was unbearably hot.

Jumping over a stretch of the creature's tail, I ran as quickly as I could to where it had been resting. But there was nothing but dirt and rock. I looked left, and right, but I didn't see any sign of an elixir or any other such artifact.

I hear roaring again and as I turn around there is a cloud of flames shooting from the serpent's mouth as it had made its way back around to attack me. It was dangerously close as it moved way faster than it seemed like it would. The flames were just inches away from scalding my face, and ducking out of the way was not going to save me. In less than a second, I whipped out my wand, hoping that it would somehow save me. I covered my face with both arms while pointing the wand in the serpent's direction.

"Please work!" I shout aloud and squeeze my eyes shut. To my luck, a transparent shield had appeared in front of me in the nick of time, blocking the hot flames from touching me and giving me enough time to scurry away from the monster that had its jaws wide open, ready to make me its evening snack. As I moved to the opposite side of the piece of land, the tip of my shoe caught on the serpent's tail, and I went stumbling forward and back onto the ground. It was already at my heels again as it climbed over its own body to reach me. I had no time to fumble, and zero time to strategize. I knew what I needed to do, but I just didn't know how to do it. I raise my wand again at the blazing creature as I scramble backward to keep as much distance between me and it as possible, and I search every crevice of my brain for some sort of spell or something that would make sense in this situation. But then something catches my eyes.

I look up above me to the sky. And through the fog cut a black shadow. And another. And another. They were still coming. The thick black wobbly masses floated their way down closer and closer to where I was, and I wasn't having it. I pointed my wand away from the serpent and instead at the sky. And with no thoughts other than "get rid of them," I started shouting and doing magic without direction.

"GO AWAY!" I screamed at them as they seemed to be multiplying and filling the sky until it got dark. My wand sent shots of green light up into the air, making some disperse, but they only came together again.

As I was now distracted by the ghostly shadows that I have come to feel threatened by, I'd almost completely forgotten about the train sized snake chugging in my direction until it had rammed its entire body into mine. I went flying up into the air—oh, and it didn't stop there. The serpent was now speeding upward into my direction, propelling itself forward into the air with me until it collided with me once more, bringing me higher until it was ramming me into the rocky wall of the cliffs. I felt the air leave my body and my skin burned at the hot touch of the serpent. When I opened my eyes, I saw that I was quite a few stories up as the island the serpent had been resting on looked ten times smaller in comparison. And as I was looking down at what a fall that might be should the serpent unpin me from the wall, my wand slipped from my grasp and demonstrated the descent for me.

I cursed under my breath and the monster began moving again. It drew backward enough for me to start slipping down, and then it came forward once more, using its nose to volley me back into the air. I went spiraling until I was dropping back down. This thing was throwing me around like a rag doll. I needed to get out of here and fast. The serpent's mouth was wide open, showing off its slimy teeth. I did not want to end up in there, so I did what I had done before to slow my momentum while falling the first time. I pulled my arms in and out, and in a panic, I was slowing down but very much unbalanced as my body twisted and turned uncontrollably. I was able to push myself forward to miss the creatures salivating mouth and instead I landed with a hard thud at the top of its head. Then down I went, slipping down its neck like a playground slide (or more accurately that crazy slide in Belle-isle). I slid down the length of its body until the creature twisted around and blew another cloud of fire at me. I jumped off to dodge it, but the serpent had flicked its tail, colliding into my abdomen like a truck. It flung me right back into the air and I was free falling once more.

I was screaming. Terrified that this was not going to end well. I tried balling my fists up to try my hand at attacking the serpent even without my wand that's supposed to help with accuracy. I pushed my hands out with all my might and a similar force like what I used to attack Julian came shooting from my palms and into the face of the serpent. Aside from causing it to stop and shake its head, it kept coming. Barely fazed by what I had done. I was getting tired, and feeling weak from the amount of magic I'd done in a short amount of time. It wasn't looking good.

My eyes are back on the sky as it had become almost black now. Those shadows were swirling together like menacing storm clouds. I was starting to hear buzzing, and I was feeling slightly light-headed. The serpent is spitting fire at me again as I'm plummeting back down toward it. And as I am about to try moving away, I feel a ripping pain shoot through my skull. It caused me to waver backward, and I am struggling to bring myself back upright to defend myself against the raging monster. It was coming at me still without fail, and a second time I felt my skull splitting and pounding. Everything seemed to be slowing down. The serpent, moving in slow motion. I began feeling more like I was floating rather than falling. The ache in my head worsened in a matter of seconds, but I knew I couldn't stop. I raised my hands at the serpent and with everything I had I sent another wave of green light at it, hoping that this time it'll slow it down and give me some time to figure out how to flee. As the force released from my palms, I felt another big toll on my body, and the image in front of me began to dim.

I could see the shadows coming closer. They were just feet away now. The pain I felt in my head moved to another level, causing me to struggle to keep my eyes open.

Ethan!

I could hear that sinister voice once more.

Wake up!

"Keep your eyes open!"

I look around me. The voice was so close, there was no way it was just in my head. But I was struggling to stay alert. The serpent was stopped for a moment just like before, but it continues speeding up—defying gravity, to get to me.

But then I see it stop a second time, stunned by something I didn't catch. It was stunned for so long that it began plunging out of the sky as much as I was. We were both rapidly plummeting until we were nearing land once more. Something came zipping through the sky, and as the serpent came to and began blowing fire, a wave of oceanic water came hurling into the creature and it crashed into the land below it.

"Ethan!" I hear someone call.

I look over my shoulder to see someone riding barefoot on a huge wave of water. Surfing along as she zipped down to the serpent who began to rise again, and threw whips made of water at it. She cracked the creature multiple times until it let out a shriek and backs off. And then in one fail swoop, the woman snatched me out of the air and began surfing upward away from the dangerous monster.

I blinked my eyes a few times, but everything became too dark, and I felt my whole body go numb. As my vision dimmed, the last thing I could see was my grandmother before everything went black.

They say she fought the fire serpent off. Using her water magic to counter the creature's fire. She had weakened him, nearly drowned him in an oversized bubble. She worked him around so much that the beast had gone disoriented and went slithering right off the edge of the island, plummeting to its end.

As for me, I wasn't out for long. I had been taken back up to the very top of the cliff, laid down on my back until I came to. I could hear voices, all of which were familiar to me.

"Will he be alright?"

"He looks pretty bad…"

"Ethan. Ethan, wake up."

My eyes were opening, and as my vision cleared, I could see hovering above me three figures. Carson. Rose. And Gramma. I sit up too quickly and wince at the soreness in my ribs, but I look around me frantically. First looking for the man that caused all this.

"Where is he?" I inquire quickly. "Where's Julian?!"

"He's gone," Rose answers first and gestures for me to settle down. "He wasn't here when we arrived."

I relax, although I wasn't entirely sure how I felt about that fact. He abandoned me. While I was doing something *for* him. But I didn't want to think of that now. Instead, my eyes trail up to the tired woman whose wet silver hair blew loosely in the wind. She stared down at me with a complicated look. The corners of her lips turned down with worry. It almost seemed like she wasn't real. But there she was, finally, after so long.

"Forgive me…" she says quietly to me. Her eyes bore into mine and she seemed close to tears. "I didn't mean for—" She stops suddenly. All of them did. Everyone's expression twisted into something like shock or uncertainty. I watched all three of them, confused as to what they were reacting to, until my vision blurred and went purple. I blinked a few times, feeling as though it would make it go away, but it didn't. Something was happening to me.

The ache in my head crept up again and I felt a sense of looming dread as I looked passed my grandmother to the edge of the cliff where shadows were slithering up and over. Buzzing rang through my ears, and it intensified in a matter of seconds as I felt my entire body vibrate.

"What's wrong?" I hear my grandmother ask. "Ethan, what's wrong?"

I squeeze my eyes shut and I'm pulling my arms into myself. As my grandmother shook my shoulders lightly to get me to look at her again, their voices began to fade away. I felt like I was slipping out of my own body, but I knew I needed to fight it. I had to open my eyes. Slowly, my eyes open, and I wasn't met with the familiar faces of my family and friends. Instead, everything was black, and dark, and cold.

I turn my head around, searching my surroundings. But there was nothing but darkness. Nothing. As I turned my head once more to face forward, there in front of me were bright red eyes.

"Finally," it said.

19

Counselor

It came into view, the monster in front of me. It revealed itself. A shadow of smoke and blackness. It had no body or form aside for its arms that were outstretched—long like a skeleton. Its fingers were sharp and inched close toward my face, but it never touched me. Its eyes were the only thing of color. Two red small dots. Somehow through the mass of shadows and smoke, I could see the jagged curvature of a grin that reached from one ear to the other. It loomed over me, hovering just a few inches off the ground. Its very presence was hard to comprehend, and its being electrified the air. Perhaps it was where the buzzing was coming from.

"Can you hear me?" it asks me in a voice the same as the cold dark waves deep within an arctic tempest.

I nod my head slowly, my mouth slightly open as I gawked at the being in front of me.

"Can you see me?" it asks this time.

I nod once more before gulping the pool of saliva in my mouth.

"What…are you?" I ask quizzically. The being glides backwards some. Its body flickered like it was coming in and out of existence, and then it came forward again.

"I am you," it answers, "I am…a part of you. I have been with you since the beginning."

I didn't understand. My brow furrows as I find the strength to stand in its presence. One foot after the other I pushed myself to my feet, standing before the chilling entity.

"*Who* are you?" I question next. "Are you…a person? A ghost?"

The being makes a rumbling sound before it morphed into discernable words again.

"I am neither," it states. "I have never walked the Earth. I am not alive, nor dead. I am no man nor woman. I just am. I only exist. I am what some may describe, an elemental."

"What do you want with me?" I ask now. "I've seen you before. What have you been doing to me?!" I couldn't describe the emotion I felt, but after the few times I suffered after having encountered this so-called elemental, I wanted to know what it was about. And put an end to it. I already had enough on my plate.

"I want nothing from you, Ethan," it says lowly. "Only, I have come to tell you the truth. Finally, you can stand to see me. I am no threat to you." The being begins circling around me, moving ever so slightly as it makes its way around me. I stood still, afraid that if I made any sudden movements that it would truly turn out to be a threat despite what it said. I was in no position to defend myself against it. "You are a part of me, Ethan. My energy lives inside of you. This is the long-awaited answer to your question. What. Are. You. The answer is, you are me. Your father Yohan is me. He is my shadow. And so are you." It stops in front of me, its being fading in and out again before hovering a little lower to the ground. "Yohan is not entirely human. I created him from a piece of me as I longed for a pupil. Someone to learn from me, and see this world my way. A child. I've tried before. To create a child, but all have sorely failed. Their forms were unstable; they could not live outside of the shadows. They could not fit into society. They could not head my warnings. I made Yohan, and he had been my most successful child. Until he was consumed by hatred. And unfortunately, could not handle the power within him. He is…haunted. But I cannot bring myself to end his life. He is simply…lost. Since Yohan, I have created another. She thrives. She is what I longed to have. She understands the importance…of balance. Ethan. Yohan is the only being I have created who has survived long enough to bear a child. That child is you. I am a part of you, Ethan. I am who they call DARKNESS. My powers are far greater than this realm, and far bigger than any human. I did not create you, therefore you have missed my guidance. And I…have failed you."

Darkness's eyes bore into mine with much intensity. I felt almost sorry to hear its story. Something about it sounded familiar, somehow.

"You've failed me, how?" I inquire with a quieted tone.

"I have failed you," it repeats. "I allowed FEAR to influence my actions. I am no god. But I am responsible for my own doings." Its voice shifts into something like a monstrous growl, before morphing back into clear words. "Because of me, you have suffered. I...am sorry. I am the cause for your lost memories. I have withheld them from you as a way to deter the unleashing of my power. Because I have not been there to guide you. It is my responsibility to teach you about what lives within you. But...because of your displacement from this realm...I was unable to reach you. You could not hear nor see me. You forgot who you were. I feared that once you remembered and once you could return here...the piece of me inside you could not be controlled. And I believe that this could still be true. But...I...could no longer see you suffer. You...are weak. You are unable to defend yourself. You are brainless in this realm. It is my fault. From this moment, Ethan, I shall return your memories to you. And once I do, you shall have full access to your power. Both yours, and mine. But I must warn you. And I urge you to listen unlike your father. I have told this to all of my children. You, although only half, are my shadow. Darkness lives within you, but that does not mean you are bad. In this world there can be no light without the dark. Balance is key to peace. And that applies to everything, Ethan. Darkness can feel like chaos. It can intrude and take over you if you are unfocused on who YOU are. But darkness can feel just as equally comforting and consoling. The only difference is how you control it." Darkness rises and it seems to grow in size as it inches closer to my face. The air feels entirely charged, like it could catch fire at any second. Those shadows were coming into view again through the dark surroundings, inching and floating this way and that, but the only thing I could pay attention to was the elemental in front of me. "I'm warning you, that if you lose your sense of balance, you will become lost, and you will unleash chaos upon this world. You hold something no other shadow of mine has ever possessed. And that is the power of Spirit. The complete opposite of what I am made up of. Balance will be your toughest challenge. Your volatile emotion can and WILL be your downfall. Be wary of your powerful emotions, Ethan. But do not worry. You will not be completely alone. As long as you accept me, I shall be there as counsel. I owe it to you as one of my own."

Counsel. That's what it was. It had been on the tip of my tongue the whole time. He is the one in my mother's story called "Counselor". It was a story about my father, the one she called "Balance". It all made sense now. She warned me that day that someday I may meet him. Someday, I would meet Darkness. The being that had a part in my creation. Which now made me question if I was human at all. Well, I suppose I had to be at least half…No, that was something I surely couldn't begin to think about. My eyes drop from the elemental's and I shift my thinking to its warnings. Balance was key to peace. And that may be the key to control myself. It's what everybody feared in the first place. If I couldn't control myself, all hell might break loose.

"I will return your memories," Darkness says. He's reaching a long boney finger out until it has pressed against my forehead. I couldn't even think to say anything, what was there to even say? But I knew that it wouldn't be the last I'd see of him. The second his finger grazed the skin of my forehead I was blinded by a stark white light, and the air completely left my lungs. I felt like someone had grabbed a hold of my skull and was violently shaking it around, and I knew that I had completely lost consciousness. Only until I began to see…everything. All at once, imagery after imagery, I could see every one of the memories that had been withheld from me this whole time. Memories of my life in Obscura. Memories of my mother. Memories of my family, of River, of Jem. Sweet memories of Gramma smiling and reading me stories. Memories of my dearest friend, Rose and her father. All the times we played together and spied on her family in the castle. All the times we took etiquette classes together or were bullied by her cousins. I could remember my home, and I could remember how much I studied and how much I…suffered.

My heart thumped hard in my chest, like it was going to burst or give out entirely. I felt dizzy and sick like I might vomit. My hands began to shake, and I could suddenly feel my eyes welling up with tears until I felt myself crying. No…not just crying. I was sobbing. Wailing like a fool. But it wasn't for no reason. I could remember it. I could remember what happened, though still not entirely.

I had a few incidents of losing control of myself. I was very young, too young to really remember. But the only thing I knew was that I had destroyed a chunk of the forest in Lamia. Not only that, but every bit of life had died. This happened a few times. But the one that destroyed my family was the night we ran too far from the cottage, Rose and I. All I wanted at the time was to see where the small rabbit would go. How far would it run? Could I keep up with it? It was only when it had been scooped up by that snarling beast—the one they called Viola Blackclaw, who had ripped it apart in front of us. I didn't see her as human. She was a monster, and she wanted to attack us next. I couldn't help the amount of anger that boiled up inside of me so quick. It was pure rage as I had been distraught over the loss of innocent life. I killed her, after unleashing all of my powers on her. She had been torn into pieces, and those pieces were obliterated. But I didn't quite know that at the time. But I could see the imagery. I saw what the aftermath was. And I remember hearing Rose, screaming at me, until her screams turned into cries. I'd hurt her by mistake. And after that…after falling ill for weeks from the whole ordeal, my mother was died trying to protect me. I remember being there, the night I was to be taken to Whitechapel. I heard that something was going to happen to me and I went looking for my mother, running as fast as I could through the courtyards of Lamia. And there she was arguing with vampires. Vampires everywhere on their way to capture me and have me put to death for my crimes. Chaos breaks out as others try to stop them. People fighting and screaming at one another. A fire had broken out on the yard. But I am still trying to reach my mother until someone has grabbed me. Even through the blur I can remember the Earh siblings, Ryland and Fey, were the last people I could see clearly, as they watched on with their evil gazes as I had been injected with the potion that would wipe my memory. And within the excitement of the crowd, someone who was reckless and violent tried to have a taste of my blood with the jagged dagger in his grasp. My mother was there, trying to help pull me away. And with the blade meant for me, it is plunged into her side. The dagger ripping and twisting unforgivably. I couldn't do anything but scream and cry as I had watched my mother die that night. Until I could see no more.

I was falling to my knees, and as my hands touched the cold hard ground, I was suddenly able to see clearly again. The buzzing stopped, and the air had returned to a heavy breeze. I was gasping, fighting the urge to retch and heave. I was being shaken, Rose's hands on my shoulder as my grandmother was pushing my hair out of my face.

"Ethan, please!" I hear Rose begging and sobbing. I finally raise my head to see them. After I had the strength to push myself back into a kneeling position, I looked at the three before me. But something still wasn't right. Something was churning deep within me. It felt like too much. I fall back over onto my hands, and I'm holding my breath as if the moment I breathe again something terrible might happen. But whatever it was, was already in the works. I feel light headed one moment, and then the next I feel *everything*.

My entire body explodes with raw energy. My body is shooting high up into the sky, and out of my eyes, mouth, hands, and feet blares green light that twisted and swirled around like smoke, and a purple light that zapped around like lightning. I couldn't hear or see anything. I could only feel the unimaginable power that had been dormant until now. I felt free, like a part of me had been locked in a cage for ten years. It felt good at first, but then in the next moment, I felt overwhelmed and sensitive. There was something coming and I was painfully aware.

"Ethan! Come back down!" I heard my grandmother call. There were other distressing noises, but one caught my attention more than anything else. My body relaxes and the light goes away except for a bright green glow that surrounded me. I was able to see again. My eyes zero in on the fire serpent my grandmother believed she had gotten rid of. It releases a loud roar as its long red body shot up from the pit it had fallen into, ready to attack me with a vengeance. But instinctively, I knew what to do. The power coursing through my very being ached to be properly released. And I was ready. I didn't have to think. I saw my target, and everything else followed naturally.

I zipped through the air. My hands were outstretched as I collected as much energy as I could. A large ball of purple electricity grew withing my hands and without hesitation I shot it directly into the creature's wide-open mouth. My hands glow green now as I use my powers to manipulate the serpent to shut its own mouth and to hold it closed. I drop myself below the creature so that I'm right beneath its belly, and there I used my powers and shot the electric energy into it. The serpent struggles for a moment before it implodes. Purple lightning bolts shoots all over from withing, tearing it apart and ultimately destroying it.

As soon as it was dead, I felt the high of my magic die down almost immediately, and before I knew it, I was falling right back out of the sky. My body had gone limp, and my mind could no longer focus on anything. In the next second I black out, and anything that followed after was a complete mystery to me.

20

Catherine's Return

I found that I had been sleeping for over 24 hours. I didn't know how or when I had returned home. I didn't know where Rose, or Carson, or my grandmother had gone. And I didn't know that I had been laid peacefully in my bedroom in Greenwood. Everything felt like a dream. But I can say for sure that it definitely was not that. I didn't dream of anything while I was out, though I saw visions of happier times. When I was young and in the arms of my mother who's love and selflessness I will never allow myself to forget again. I was happy to say the least that finally my mind was whole again. And my body was healing from (not just getting my butt kicked by a giant snake), but from the sickness caused by my ten-year dormant powers. I didn't know it, but I had been ill that entire time. It's no wonder why I felt like crap for so long and was continuously in and out of the hospital. But I hated that it took this long to find out why.

I open my eyes and I stare at the ceiling for a while. I felt different. Like I had been factory reset like some computer. I look down at myself, realizing I was covered in bandages. My entire left arm had been wrapped up from the wrist to the shoulder. I pulled back the blankets from myself and saw that I was wrapped up tight around the ribcage. I was scraped up and bruised. I thought about how the whole situation started, and I could easily blame it all on Julian. Although I didn't know where he had gone, I did know that I was done with him. He was dangerous and unpredictable just like Rose warned.

I soon hear my bedroom door slowly creaking open, and tiptoeing through was Autumn, holding a tray of tea and porridge. She didn't notice my eyes on her at first as she must have thought I was still sleeping, creeping across the room as quietly as she could while eyeing the tray hard to make sure nothing rattled around. Then I took it upon myself to clear my throat so she'd get the hint. She flinches in response, the tray clinking until she steadied herself again. She looks up at me with a sneer and then casually walks over.

"I didn't know you were awake…" she says quietly before sitting on the side of my bed. "How are you feeling?"

I blink and look down at myself again.

"Like trash," I grumble in response. I drew in a breath and began pushing myself to sit up, and that was when I really felt the horrible pain in my ribcage, causing me to grunt and groan.

"Be careful," Autumn said. She set the tray down on the bedside table and moved to assist me in sitting up right. "You've broken a few ribs…" she tells me gently after I got situated.

"A few?" I ask in surprise, my eyes wide.

"Um……three, actually…" she says now. She wore an awkward expression before reaching up to fix her ponytail. "They said you took quite the beating. Doctor Valherra came in overnight to examine you. He told us that you had broken your ribs, fractured your wrist, and he had to mend quite the gash running down the length of your arm…"

"So, I got stitches?" I ask for clarity, but she gave me a confused face in return.

"I don't know what stitches are…" she replies slowly, "but if you're talking about how he mended your arm, there are salves for that. Anyway, Ethan, you need to eat. Your grandmother said that she will be up here soon to speak with you. Actually, I'm quite excited, I always wanted to meet her and I finally did. Now hopefully she can teach me all that she knows!" She was grinning as she retrieved the bowl of porridge from the tray, and then without warning shoved a heaping spoonful into my mouth. "That is of course after everything settles down. I mean she just returned, so I shouldn't ask her now." She starts rambling and I'm almost choking on the food that came suddenly. I frown at her as I swallow to protest.

"I think I can feed myself Au—"

"Nonsense," she cuts me off and shoves another spoonful into my mouth as she continued on about how she hoped to be as successful as my grandmother had been and to use her powers to help those in need some day.

I hear the door opening again, and the both of us look over to see Rose walking in with Carson following close after her. They both seemed to be in poor spirits, wearing expressions you might see after getting told a pet died. Carson goes straight to the corner of the room, his arms folded against his chest and his eyes on the floor. Rose walks over to the front of the bed and leans back against my dresser.

"What's wrong?" I ask the moment my mouth was clear. I waved Autumn's spoon away before she could accost me with it again. Rose drew in a breath as she looked everywhere but at me, but she proceeded to answer me first.

"There's a few things you are not going to like to hear…" she sighs.

"What is it?" I watch her expectantly as she chews at her lip. She turned her head to look at Carson who only shook his head back at her before she turned around once more.

"Lady Catherine will tell you. You should just be prepared for it. Carson and I…overheard her speaking with miss River, and we think—"

"You think what, Rose?"

All heads turn toward the door as my grandmother glided into the room. Her long grey dress dragged across the floor behind her. Her hair was pulled back into a low ponytail and her face reflected her exhaustion. The room fell silent as she stopped just a few steps away from the bed. River stepped in next, closing the door behind her while wearing a look of worry. She was chewing at her thumb nail as she leaned against the wall, pretending as if she wasn't there at all.

"What is going on?" I ask her. I try to straighten up some more but the sharp pain in my ribs stopped me.

My grandmother stairs down at me, it almost seemed like pity in her eyes, but there was some other emotion entirely.

"How are you feeling?" the woman asks to my surprise. I gave her a confused look, but I answer.

"I've definitely been better," I grumble. "What about you? The last time I saw you, you were—"

"I'm fine," she cuts me off in a straight forward tone. "But…I'm in hiding. I've broken the number one law in all of Obscura ten years ago. You should know that I can't be seen. All of you need to know that, and understand it. Make sure you watch what you say in public." Her eyes seem to land on Rose at the last part. The young girl's eyes fall to her feet.

I squint a little in my grandmother's direction. Something about this whole situation reminded me of a conversation she once had with the prince of Lamia.

"There's some things that we all need to agree on, because everything is too unpredictable at the moment," the woman continues. "That includes the state of Ethan's powers…"

"Does this have something to do with the research you've done?" I ask her, reminded of her and Aero's conversation. "You learned something ten years ago. Something that suggested that my powers are conflicting with each other."

Her eyes widen at this and she shoots me a complex look.

"How do you know about that?" she questions. "Did River say something?"

"No," I answer matter-of-factly. "I heard it that night. That night you and prince Aero were talking. Rose and I both did. You said that I could be ripped apart and put everyone in danger with me."

The room is silent again once I've stopped talking. Everyone is looking between each other with a sense of uncertainty. Like every one is checking with each other to see who exactly said what to me. Gramma turns her head and she looks over her shoulder at River who stared back at her worriedly. And then something snaps where she's shaking her head and her hands around frantically, beads and bracelets jangling as she stepped further into the room.

"I don't know anything about it, Cathy," she protests as if she'd been accused. "Accept I've seen the study, at work, of course. I never told him myself, however!"

Gramma holds up her hand to silence her. River stopped almost immediately and her hand went to fiddle with a strand of her white hair. My grandmother's eyes left River's and did a slow swipe across the floor and around the room until she settled them on me once more. Her brow had furrowed together, and she seemed to be silently putting together something in her head.

"Ethan…" she began quietly, "what do you remember?"

I felt everyone's eyes fall on me and it only struck me in that moment that I was the only one who knew that my memory was restored. I hadn't told a single person. Of course, when would I have done that given the fact that I had only came to from the incident not so long ago. I look at everyone, and for some reason I wanted to smile. Though I forced myself not to. It was only at the realization that my mind was fully intact—that I could say confidently who I was and what my life has been like up to this point made me feel incredibly…relieved.

I am Ethan-Jaehyun Moon, Tier 1 oddity Spirit element witch of Holly's Grove, Greenwood District. And I have, without question, been entirely screwed over by the idiots running Lamia District.

I meet the eye of my grandmother now as she watches carefully for my response. And without hesitation, I say:

"I remember everything."

I see my grandmother and River share a long powerful look and my grandmother is breathing out an unsteady breath.

"It was inevitable, Cathy," River says in a careful tone to her. "I feared it may never…I don't know what's changed but, Ethan, I'm so happy for you." She offers a smile in my direction, but she seems to be tip toeing around my grandmother's feelings for some reason. My attention only turned from them once I heard another emotionally stricken sigh. I looked over at Rose who seemed to be quietly rejoicing to herself. Her hands covered her face and she bounced slightly on her heels. Once she finished and her eyes caught my gaze she only grinned and came over to sit on the bed beside Autumn. But she refrained from saying anything as there seemed to still be something left unsaid from my grandmother.

"You…" Gramma begins in a measured tone, "remember everything? All of it?" she asks.

I nod my head in response.

"Yes, I do. All of it." I couldn't help but glance at Rose once more. There were certainly things that now needed to be addressed between us. Particularly about the incident that happened ten years ago.

"And your powers, Ethan?" the woman questions. "What about those?"

I look down at my hands and study my fingers. Small green sparks sparkle from my finger tips until I close my fist and sigh.

"They're all here," I confirm. "…all of them." I think back to Darkness and what he told me. I felt uncertain about all of it, but I understood that controlling it—my shadow powers, would keep me from going corrupt like my father did. But it didn't sound like it was going to be easy.

My grandmother is stepping closer now. Her eyes are trained on me the whole way until she's sat down in front of me on the bed, causing Rose and Autumn to scoot back out of her way. She grabs my arm and squeezes it some, eliciting a small wince from the bruises there

"Then it's settled," she says. "There's no going back now."

"…What's going to happen to me?" I ask. But she shakes her head and her hand moves up to cup my cheek.

"Oh, my grandson. I spent all this time *anguishing* over this day. I never wanted it to come. It is why…I was so hard on you. When we there in that port town, it was like our lives were put on pause. It was as if…the longer we could stay, the more we could forget about this. I'm so sorry for what I've put you through, Ethan. You may never truly know how sorry I am. But just know that everything that I had done was because I wanted nothing more than to protect you. You're my only grandchild after all. What could I have done had I failed?" Her eyes are welling up, but she fights off her tears. She was frowning, looking as though she was angry with herself. "Our relationship has suffered because of it…hasn't it?"

My shoulder's drop at these words. It was certainly nothing I ever thought I'd hear that woman ever say or admit. But I'd be lying if I said that I didn't think she was truly aware of the damage caused. I was at a point where I resented her. I felt like she would never be honest with me even while I was clearly suffering from it. I know why she did it. But it hurt nonetheless.

"Ethan," she began, "I need you to listen to me carefully. Because now that your memory is back, your troubles have only just truly begun. While I was in the Lamia Elemalex Unit, I was tasked with studying the way that your magic may work with the mixture of powers. This meant that I needed to work to find out what your father is, and what he is capable of. Still, no one is entirely sure of that, however we had come to the conclusion that your father's magic comes from another unusual element. And although we are unsure of which one, we are sure that the way that this element works is entirely opposite of that of the Spirit element. The spirit element works through light and life. It is the very essence of what gives any and everything life. The magic your father possesses seems to manipulate and distort a living being into chaos. It conflicts with your Spirit magic, and depending on which powers you use, there is always a chance that it will backfire and cause destruction. You are unstable to say the least. The Elemalex has found that your instability has dire consequences. And that goes for you *and* the people around you. We have come to the understanding that it was able to be avoided as long as your powers had been shut off. Which is one of the reasons why we came to the decision to wipe your memory before bringing you to Whitechapel. With your memory wiped, your powers were dormant. We have calculated that you have only so long from the moment your memory has been restored that you will lose control and your powers will clash, causing you to basically blow up in plain terms. You will go off like a bomb full of negative energy, and that magic will reach as far as other surrounding districts from wherever you are and essentially kill or wound millions."

"What?!" I look at her as if she were crazy or at the very least over exaggerating. "Are you telling me I'm going to die and kill millions of people at the same time?!" I choke out. The quick rising of my chest sent shooting pains through my ribs.

"You will die," she confirms, "*if* you don't find a balance between your fathers magic and your spirit magic."

Oh, who's told me that before? Looks like the Darkness creature already beat her to it, but if failed to mention that I could *die* AND *kill* others in the process.

"There's got to be another way," Rose speaks up now, her expression frantic and unaccepting of the severity of the situation. "He's already used his magic a few times now, not to mention what happened last night, and nothing has yet to go wrong. Certainly, the odds aren't so out of his favor."

"But that's just it, Rose," my grandmother answers, "nothing has *yet* to go wrong. His powers will grow fast now that he has access to them again and is of a mature age. As his powers grow, the more likely there will be conflict and mistakes out of his control. If Ethan cannot find a way to get a handle on the power that he possesses…well, I'm afraid that we're all in danger."

"How much time does he have, exactly?" River asks quietly.

My grandmother looks over at her for a moment before looking down at her hands in her lap.

"I can't say for certain," she admits. "If you calculate how much time is needed for his magic to catch up, we're looking at anywhere between…a hundred and…two hundred days."

So essentially, not that long.

I felt my heart race as the severity settled onto my shoulders. I look between my friends and the others in the room who all seemed at a loss for words and the inability to react.

One thing was for certain if nothing else.

My troubles have only just begun.